BELLRINGER

BELLRINGER

J. ROBERT JANES

A MYSTERIOUSPRESS.COM BOOK

OPEN ROAD

INTEGRATED MEDIA

NEW YORK

This is for Gracia so that calm will remain in house, since I am happiest when working.

It is in the shadow of dreams that we park reality, forgetting for the moment that life goes on.

Author's Note

Bellringer is a work of fiction in which actual places and times are used but altered as appropriate. As with the other St-Cyr/Kohler novels, the names of real persons appear for historical authenticity, though all are deceased and the story makes of them what it demands. I do not condone what happened during these times; I abhor it. But during the Occupation of France the everyday common crimes of murder, arson, and the like continued to be committed, and I merely ask by whom and how they were solved.

1

To Vittel's Parc Thermal there was but irony. Landscaped vistas of field, forest, and distant hillslope stretched to and beyond band shell, pavilion, and storybook chalet through the gathering ground fog of evening, offering nothing but a constant reminder of freedom denied. Shrouded in barbed wire, the two luxury hotels near its entrance—one of five storeys, the other of four—rose in a multitude of makeshift rusty stovepipes protruding this way and that from every window and trailing woodsmoke into the frost-hazed air.

It was 1522 hours Berlin Time, 20 February, 1943, a Saturday, and things were far from good, St-Cyr felt. The Kommandant who had summoned them from Paris with such urgency hadn't bothered to stick around or leave a note or word of advice, his replacement being most notable for his own absence. True, they had been expected six days ago—another derailment by the Résistance, who were still learning their lessons and fortunately hadn't put the whole train off the rails—but they were starting out here with virtually no information.

'*Gott im Himmel*, Louis, what the hell have we been saddled with this time?' said Kohler. 'Something no one wants, eh? A nothing town in a nothing place!'

That could not go unchallenged. 'An international resort. A spa, Hermann. The former playground of kings, queens, and tsars, the *bourgeoisie aisée*, especially.'

Almost due south of Nancy, due west of Colmar, and tucked away in a forgotten corner of southernmost Lorraine, the Parc Thermal faced the rounded summits of the Vosges to the east, and was well out of sight and mind for most.

'*Ein Internierungslager, Dummkopf,*' retorted Kohler. 'Der Führer, who is always right, must have thought it a marvelous joke.'

An internment camp for foreign nationals . . . 'Whose population, unless I am very mistaken, Hermann, is presently crowding those very windows to watch every move we make.'

The hotels in question were perhaps three hundred metres from them, across a Siberia of hard-trampled snow to which the day's thin sheath of ice had come.

'Nine hundred and ninety-one Americans, Louis, who failed to leave when the Führer thought to declare war on America on 11 December, 1941, yet neglected to lock them up until September of '42.'

'In the Hôtel Vittel-Palace, the four-storeyed one to the right and a little more distant from us,' said St-Cyr.

'And sixteen hundred and seventy-eight British in the Grand and locked up since September of 1940. Two Louis XIII, Renaissance-style henhouses side by side and packed solidly with women, most of whom have been starved for male company for years. They'll tear us apart and you know it. What are we supposed to do, question each of them?'

Vittel's population alone was less than 3,500, but Hermann often tended to jump to conclusions.

'Or let them watch us work, Inspector?' suggested St-Cyr.

And take note of their reactions . . . Kohler knew this was what his partner had implied. 'You or me?' he asked, turning his back on the hotels.

'Me, I think,' came the usual reply. Louis was always better at it. After nearly two and a half years of working together, one simply knew.

The signboard, in place since the day the camp had been established, gave notice in heavy black type: ACHTUNG: BETRETEN VERBOTEN. DÉFENCE D'ENTRER. ENTRY FORBIDDEN!

Built in 1923, the stable, Le Chalet des Ânes, had once held the half-dozen donkeys that the children of the wealthy would have ridden, but since the Defeat and Occupation of June 1940, the building had been empty. Suitably Alsatian and near enough to that new border of the Reich, its darkly timbered, white-plastered walls and solid oaken door made it look like a little place in a little forest of its own. There were even windowboxes with hearts cut into them.

'A bit of *Hansel and Gretel,* Louis.'

'Freud, or was it Krafft-Ebing, maintained that fable had deep sexual undertones.'

'Jung . . . I'm sure it was him. Girls with girls, eh? But hard to gain access without being seen. Those trees might help, but the circular track beneath that snow and ice makes the view far too clear from far too many angles. Two thousand, six hundred and sixty-nine pairs of eyes out having a stroll just to catch a bit of fresh air and have a peek at what was happening.'

'Or find a bit of kindling, Hermann.'

Kohler jabbed a forefinger at the padlock, a curiosity in itself. 'How many of them saw this thing being opened, not picked, not out here in full view?'

It was a good question. 'But was the stable then entered by one, or by two, and if the latter, was the former expecting that person?'

'Or surprised by her or by someone else?'

The victim was fully clothed and lying flat on her back in the middle of the three stalls to their left. Light entering the diamond-shaped panes of the windows behind them gave a languidness to the settling dust. Long-dried dung and mouldy straw were strewn about. A froth of blood and oedematous fluid had erupted from the mouth. The eyes, perhaps a girl's most treasured feature, were hazel but were staring unfeelingly up at a painted ceiling where swans, fairies, and wood nymphs frolicked.

Still in rigor mortis, one hand clutched at a wounded chest, though this had not been a last impulse. 'First she slumped to her knees, Hermann, her back still being against that far wall.'

'And only then was she tidied, that hand being placed where it now is?'

'Be so good as to examine the weapon.'

'*Ach,* I'm really all right.'

'Of course, but I believe our killer wiped it clean. At least five of those tines must have . . . '

'The lungs, the heart . . . '

'The diaphragm, too, but especially the pericardium.' The sac around the heart would rapidly have filled with blood as that thing had been yanked from her. 'Anger, then, Louis. Hatred, jealousy, rage in any case.'

'Impulse, Inspector? Let's not forget that, since the chalet has been locked and placed out of bounds.'

'And the killer couldn't have known of the pitchfork. Silenced, then, Louis. Told to shut up or else.'

'Perhaps, but then, *Ah, merde alors, mon vieux,* is it not too early to say?'

Of hardened steel, the tines, each five centimetres apart and a good thirty long, were curved in a gentle arc whose maximum depth was the same as the spacing and ended in exceedingly sharp points.

There were six of these and, as Louis had noted, each had been tidily wiped clean before the hayfork had been leaned upright against the wall behind the victim. Fingerprints would be out of the question. In this weather, gloves or mittens were mandatory—even spare socks in lieu of either—but did it really matter? There was never time to dust for fingerprints. Always it was blitzkrieg, blitzkrieg.

The handle, long and of oak, had been polished smooth by years of use, but irony of ironies, 'The metal's been stamped "Made in Austria," Louis. Exported to America well before that other war, then brought back but branded "US First Army" on the handle.'

General Pershing and the 1914–18 war. An American, then, killed with an American-owned Austrian hayfork. Kept busy, Hermann seemed to have conquered his little problem. 'There's something else, *mon ami.* Our victim has at least three dozen of the Host in this coat pocket. God has been most generous and has given her a snack.'

And hadn't that telephone call to Kommandant von Gross-Paris to urgently summon them here mentioned a ringer of bells? But that had been six days ago, of course, and by the look of this one . . . *Ah, bon,* Hermann had finally realized. 'She hasn't been dead that long, has she, Chief?' said Kohler lamely. 'Even if we allow for the degrees of frost to defer and lengthen rigor while retarding putrefaction.'

'Relax. You're learning. Being with me has been good for you, but I'm going to have to take her temperature. Let's concentrate.'

'Before we find out who the original victim was and where that one's being kept?'

'Patience, Inspector. Patience. Sometimes it's necessary.'

The grey, silk-lined woollen overcoat was stylish, having a broad, sensible collar and two prewar pockets with generous flaps, all unheard of attributes if made these days since they, and a lot of other such things, had become illegal. The style was not American, though, but British.

'From Barclay's at 18–20 Avenue de l'Opéra, Hermann, but in '39 or before.'

And since then, the shop's Paris signboard would have been torn down and replaced with something more suitable. 'The scarf is Hermès.' Louis had left that for him to find, but accidentally fingers had touched cold, soft, opaque, and waxy skin . . .

'L'Heure Bleue, Hermann,' came the urgent interruption. 'This little box is from Guerlain—the silver sprays of an Art-Deco fountain as its logo, *n'est-ce pas?* The bottle's from Baccarat and long empty, since it was made as a presentation for the close of the 1925 Exposition.'

'But she can't be any more than twenty, can she?'

'Are you really all right? I ask simply because . . . '

'*Jésus, merde alors,* I'm fine. It's just that the young ones . . . '

Hermann swiftly turned away to do the unforgivable for a fifty-five-year-old former captain in the artillery and a Detektivinspektor der Kriminalpolizei. Once, twice, three times he emptied himself of what one could only guess, for they'd eaten so little since leaving Paris, the memory of a last meal was still with them. Well, with one half of the partnership.

'*Ach,* I thought I was over it.'

A hand went out to steady him. 'You *are*! It was only a momentary lapse. You do that pocket. Let's see what we can find, since her papers seem to be missing.'

Relieved to be busy, Kohler slid a hand quickly in, only to yank it out with a '*Verdammte* nettles! The dried leaves, stems, and roots, tied with twine of the same.'

'*Urtica dioica.* It's curious, isn't it?'

'Since she couldn't have gathered them at this time of year in a place like this.'

Very quickly, though, two Hershey's Milk Chocolate bars were found and then a small, white cardboard box of Cracker Jack Nut Candy Popcorn and a packet of Wrigley's Spearmint chewing gum—six sticks in all and still tightly wrapped.

'Beechnut oil,' said St-Cyr, of a little amber-coloured bar of soap. 'Definitely not the National.'

Which was of grey slaked lime, ground horse chestnuts, sand, and wood ashes, and cast into cubes heavier than a brick but no bigger than a die, and one for every month of the year, not that a lot of the French bothered too much with bathing, but a bar of Lifebuoy Soap was retrieved from the pocket the *sûreté* was avidly mining, and then a rain of shiny, yellowish-brown seeds.

'Alfalfa,' said Kohler, glad to be of help.

There was a sigh. 'Sprouts if sown indoors, Hermann. A much needed source of vitamins and minerals, but also a hopeful abortifacient.'

Scheisse, must Louis mention it at a time like this?

Hermann's stomach rumbled but a paisley sewing pouch was quickly found. He set it aside with everything else in a tidy row beside a tidy victim. They were working now as they should, thought St-Cyr. Two detectives, one from each side of this lousy war and Occupation, the first, it must be admitted, a chief inspector of the Sûreté Nationale; the second of a lower rank but from the Gestapo, since all such had been placed under that roof whether they liked it or not, and of course the Germans always had to be the overseers since the French had to be kept out of trouble and working hard for them, but then, too, this one just happened to have had the good sense to have learned a proper language as a prisoner of war in that other war—the one the Germans had lost.

Kohler found an oval seashell, maybe three centimetres long by two in width—a porcellaneous, creamy white-to-yellow thing with a row of coarse teeth on each side of its top-to-bottom aperture: something the victim had found or been given and had probably kept for the memories it would have brought.

A sachet of herbs smelled of lavender. A small cough syrup bottle held honey, but when one of those yellow cloth stars with a *J* on it was retrieved, he knew he couldn't help but swallow hard. 'Louis . . . '

It dangled from capable fingers, bringing its own memories of Hermann's Oona, the woman he had rescued from just such things and still lived with when in Paris. Well, one of the women. There were two of them.

'It's been removed from someone's overcoat. The needle holes . . . '

'Are clear enough, but why keep it, Louis?'

Since doing so could but bring its terrible punishment. 'Are there Jewish citizens in this camp?' said St-Cyr.

'*Ach*, why ask me? Ask yourself. Though the Wehrmacht run the camp, Vichy suggested its being set up here and gave their OK, didn't they?'

The government of Maréchal Pétain, in the town of Vichy and another international spa, one they'd left not so very long ago, that investigation settled.

'But was that star crammed into her pocket in haste?' Or carefully hidden?

'Crammed.'

'Then perhaps she was given it during an argument, or after death.'

And this murder was now looking more and more challenging.

'There was also this,' said St-Cyr. A thin, white pasteboard card held its little message in a script of blue-black ink whose many flourishes held no pauses. 'It's in English, Hermann, a language I unfortunately have little knowledge of.'

'And what memories I have of it,' said Kohler, 'are just about as rusty as those stovepipes.'

In the mid-1930s, Hermann had been sent to London on a police course and had earnestly worked at the language so as to enjoy himself and make the best of it instead of spying for the Reich.

Bit by bit it came out: 'You have been chosen and are cordially invited to attend. Please bring what you have.'

'That Shield of David?' asked St-Cyr.

'Then tell me why the party-throwers would want it?'

'Assuming that the invitation was to such a gathering.'

As always, there were no easy answers. Seed packets gave carrots, peas, lettuces, and even pumpkins, each with an artist's rendition of the same. 'And all sent from home in Red Cross parcels, Hermann, but was she intending to sell them?'

A much-worn packet of Craven A cigarettes held a logo: a faded black cat on a red background. Tobacco being in such short supply, Kohler thought they'd best try one. 'It'll help us think,' he said, but when he had one of the hand-rolled fags between his lips, he had to spit it out. 'Thorn apple!'

'Angel's trumpet. *Datura stramonium.*'

'Was she accustomed to getting high on it only to be thrown into an agony, eh, whose sole memory would be just that?'

'The dried leaves are sometimes smoked to treat asthma . . . '

'If so, then she's one dead herbal.'

'Who couldn't have become one without a little help,' muttered St-Cyr.

'Our bell ringer? There was also this.'

Hermann was very good at finding such things. Having carefully felt the underside of the coat collar, he'd come up with a hidden pocket. The note, written in a far different hand, was in French first and then in German: 'Please tell the Kommandant that was no accident. I saw it happen and know who did it. Miss Caroline Lacy, Room 3–38 Vittel-Palace.'

But by signing it, had she then signed her own death warrant?

'At least now we know who she was,' said St-Cyr.

'And have a motive. She must have been about to meet one of

the guards. Two chocolate bars, the chewing gum if necessary, then the bar of Lifebuoy Soap as a last resort. Such a big payoff implies considerable risk.'

'Only someone got to her.'

'And left that star.'

'Perhaps, but then . . . '

A fist was clenched. '*Verdammt,* that's how it happened. Don't keep hedging!'

'Take the easy route, Hermann?'

'It might help—have you ever thought of that?'

'And have you, Inspector, paused to even consider why that note was written in *two* languages?'

Ah sacré nom de nom! 'The *français* can't have been for one of the guards, can it? Do they have French doctors in the camp?'

'Or *Tirailleurs sénégalais,* Hermann? The ones we caught a glimpse of. Former skirmishers from a defeated army who are now here as prisoners of war doing the bidding of their masters, namely the heavy work.'

Again Kohler asked what they were dealing with.

'The usual. Now go and find our acting Kommandant but please don't enlighten him about that note and the invitation. Let him find out when necessary.'

'And our first victim?' To whom the note must have referred.

'We'll get to her soon enough.'

'Enjoy yourself then. I'll see if I can find us a place to stay.'

'In town. It's very provincial and hardworking but insular, Hermann. As with Les Francs-Comtois in the province just to the south, they tend to keep to themselves, especially at times of defeat like this, as in the Franco-Prussian War. So you may need to use your Gestapo clout. We'd never get any sleep in either of those hotels knowing what we do now.'

But where, please, were her papers? wondered St-Cyr. And why, really, had she been tidied? She was of a little more than medium height and slender, and her legs had been placed side by side as if for burial, her right arm bent and lain precisely across the chest. All down the length of her there wasn't a thing out of place. The saddle shoes—very American—were scuffed and worn, but here, too, the thought was that a moment had been taken to clean them of their straw and dried dung; and yes, the soles were all but gone. After two and a half years of shortages in France, neither leather nor rubber could be found except perhaps by the privileged few.

'Were you a ballet dancer or still a student?' he asked her and himself. 'You have the build, the look—all such things. A real stage presence, *n'est-ce pas?'*

Her French would have been perfect. Her ash-blond hair, beneath its knitted, soft grey toque, was in a tightly pinned chignon, but here, too, things had been tidied. Some strands, having come loose over the brow, had been smoothed back into place.

'Please, I must,' he said and, turning her onto her side, hiked up coat, skirt, and slip to pull the underpants down and gently ease the thermometer into her. 'Hermann can't stand me doing this, but it's necessary if we are to have some idea of when this happened. Given the frost, the night, the shelter here, and the fact that you were fully dressed and wearing your overcoat and must have been terrified—all such things—perhaps a fall of one-and-a-quarter degrees Celsius per hour. If outside, it would have been more—two degrees per hour. One has always to wait when taking such readings, and Hermann has neither the patience nor the stomach for it.

'*Ah, bon,* 7.2 degrees Celsius, with a drop of 30 degrees, giving us somewhere in the neighbourhood of 1600 hours yesterday. Were many of you still out and about?'

She would have been terribly embarrassed by what he had just done and would need to be distracted. Tidying her, he removed one of the woollen mittens. 'Since none of the Host wafers have been eaten, we can assume that you must have met our bell ringer, if that one really is a priest, at quite close to the time of death. *Bien sûr,* I realize such people can murder just like any other, but was he your herbalist?'

The wafers, in themselves, didn't mean a sacrilege, for in better days, churches, monasteries, and nunneries had often sold the scraps and even half-kilos of the whole, and these had only been of the latter.

'Mademoiselle, your skin was very dry, but did he prepare this lotion for you? Chamomile with lavender, but rose and neroli also, on a base of honey and almond oil. I'm sure of it.'

There were dried, finely chopped lavender flowers in the sachet, but also dried chamomile flowers and orris root, to which droplets of oil of lavender had been added. 'Has this Occupation of ours put us all back into the Middle Ages?' he asked. 'The smells in that hotel, the stench at times? Were they so bad you and the others had taken to carrying these little sachets for their moments of hurried relief?'

She had done her lips with what appeared to be a lipstick of beeswax, henna, and almond oil. Far softer and gentler on the skin than what was usually available these days, it had produced the necessary effect. 'Chamomile,' he went on. 'You've applied it as a rinse to lighten your hair. You took your time in getting yourself ready for this meeting. More and more you are telling me that my partner and I had best talk to this bell ringer.'

The face was thin but finely boned, the forehead high and smooth, the nose sharply defined. The eye shadow would perhaps have been made of kaolin clay, talc, cornstarch, and, for darkening, iron oxide. Mascara had firmed the eyelashes. Again the hand cream had been used on the face as a base, but a blush of henna had been added to brighten an otherwise winter pallor.

She had been caught unawares, had been forced back against that wall, the pitchfork having been snatched up by the killer. 'Did you plead you wouldn't tell a soul? Was pressure then released, your thinking it a reprieve?'

The star was not something to be carried or taken lightly. 'Did you snatch it from your pocket and thrust it towards your assailant? Did the two of you argue vehemently? There are no frozen tears, but were these wiped away and the makeup smoothed over their traces by your tidier, or was the star not hers at all but yours?'

To have remained hidden among so many would have been a terrible ordeal.

'Were you still alive when that fork was withdrawn? Did you see the look in your killer's eyes? Did that person then angrily stuff the star back into your pocket, and if so, why?'

Already there were no easy answers. 'You were then carefully laid out. We do know you had come to meet someone who was either French-speaking or German, but as so few of the latter speak our language, I have to wonder about the former. Had this person agreed beforehand to the meeting place? You couldn't have been the one to have arranged it, otherwise you'd have known what language that person spoke.

'But did you unwittingly ask your killer to speak to him on your behalf, and what, please, was the invitation to, and what, of course, were you to have brought? This Shield of David?'

A careful survey of the stall found only an overturned water pail; a small, sharply cut-off sprig from a beech tree; and three curls from the inner bark of the same. These last items had probably been dropped either by the assailant or the victim and were halfway inside the stall.

A sadness came, and he couldn't help it. 'Spring,' he said. 'Were you thinking of it as you felt each tiny, spear-shaped bud or merely planning to chew them and the bark for a little nourishment, as did the Iroquois and other North American tribes?'

From every window Kohler knew he was being watched. They would be whispering to each other, asking, What did they find? Is that why he's trying to hurry on that ice? Was she naked? Was she cold? Did they realize Caroline wasn't the only one who had died?

The camp offices were in the casino, and as he turned away, he knew how disappointed they would be at losing sight of him. Attached to the southwest corner of the Hôtel Grand, the casino would, he knew, have direct access, but here the main entrance was, of course, close to the camp's gate and directly across from the Gothic spire of a church-cum-chapel in its own little forest. Prayers, then, in the old days before entry or upon leaving if bankrupt or in clover, but now . . . why, now, if one had gained the necessary pass and safe-conduct to leave for something better like one's flat or house, that was OK, but if being sent on to somewhere else, well, definitely not.

Even here the threat of deportation to a concentration camp would always be present. Four staff cars lined the road out front, any of which would do nicely for Louis and himself. All had been requisitioned from the Occupied and painted with the regulation Wehrmacht camouflage so as to let folks know who was behind the wheel. Two large white-domed, circular rooms anchored what would once have been the Salle des Fêtes, the reception hall, but before he got there, steps led up to a broad terrace and then an Art Deco door, with an etched glass fountain just like the one Louis had been on about. Yet another female watcher opened the door, but this one was a BDM, one of the Federation of German Milch Cows, the Bund Deutscher Mädel, the League of the same. Earnest girls from home doing their duty in uniforms so grey the French had taken to calling them *les souris grises*—the grey mice.

A lisle-stockinged, tight-skirted leg was lifted as a black brogue was stamped and the regulation salute and Heil Hitler given. Even a smile wouldn't work, though he'd try.

Ach, thought Dorett Lühr, no return salute had been received from this one, and the faded blue eyes that might at times be full of mirth seemed only to be mocking her. Shrapnel scars from that other war were there, but so too was that of a more recent slash from the left eye to chin. A duelling scar? she wondered, trembling at the thought, for he was still handsome, if in a rough and incredibly virile way. '*Bitte,* Herr Detektivinspektor, you are to follow me.'

'Actually, Herr Hauptmann *und* Detektiv Aufsichtsbeamter would be better if you want to use my rank from that war we lost, or simply Herr Detektivinspektor der Kriminalpolizei—i.e., der Kripo, *ja?* Der Geheime Staatspolizei.'

The Gestapo . . . That did it. She shuddered nicely, thought Kohler, and would no longer give trouble. There wasn't a sign of a roulette wheel, baccarat table, or any other such temptation. So puritan was the casino, the Salle des Fêtes, of gymnasium size, was barren of everything but a huge swastika, *ein Hakenkreuz,* that was draped above the regulation portrait of the Führer.

Here the internees on arrival would have had to line up in front of the one suitcase each had been allowed to bring, this being laid open and the contents spread out for inspection under all eyes, especially those of their fellow inmates. And wasn't it a marvel how utterly thoughtless the Wehrmacht could be?

Right behind the Salle des Fêtes, there was the Grand Hall, and here Red Cross parcels were being counted, ticked off, and piled to the ceiling: American to the left, British to the right. At desks nearby, NCOs busied themselves lest they experience life on the Russian Front. BDMs hustled files or typed as though their lives depended on it. Always it was papers, papers with Berlin, and always he had to ask himself: With a war on, who the hell had the time to read them?

A corridor, totally barren but for its hurrying BDMs, led first to the censor's offices—letters and postcards being pored over in there and blacked out, of course—and then to one of the former smoking rooms where leather club chairs would once have offered solid comfort, brandy, and cigars but now held the Spartan desk and armless chairs of the local Himmler, the camp's acting Kommandant, Col. Löthar Jundt of Mannheim, Baden-Württemburg.

Not a moment was lost in pleasantries.

'Kohler, it's about time! They are terrified another of them will be killed. *Ach,* they don't express it in so many words, but one can sense it. They duck back into their rooms in the Vittel-Palace, exchange rapidly downcast glances when passing one another in the corridors or on the staircases, and when I encounter a babbling group in one of their rooms, they all shut up well before I am even seen. *Verdammte Amerikanische Kaninchen, die Schlampen* have lookouts posted. I'm certain of it!'

Damned American rabbits, the sluts. And trust the Wehrmacht brass to overlook the simple fact that the sound of jackboots on marble floors might have been overheard. 'And when they're all together, Colonel?'

A fist was clenched. 'They're never all together. They refuse to eat in their dining room. "It's too cold. It's pathetic," they yell at me. I ask you, Kohler, what is the matter with those people? Declaring war on us, their friends? I've a second cousin in New Jersey, an aunt in Dayton, Ohio, who is married to a banker, a sister to an *offi-*

cer in that *Navy* of theirs? Have the Jews got at them and destroyed a once fine nation?'

Uh-oh. 'And the British internees, Colonel?'

'A world of difference. They come out of their rooms to speak to me in a language I cannot understand, of course, but one can tell.'

The side of a nose that must be accustomed to it was tapped with a stiffened forefinger that was now being wagged for emphasis.

'They gather in their dining room for meals, and the noise, it is unbelievable. Such joy, such laughter.'

'Until you enter that room?'

Kohler . . . What was it he had been told about him? Insubordination? A former member of a *Himmelfahrtskommando* that had dealt with unexploded bombs and shells in that other war, one of the trip-to-heaven boys, the assignment earned through having absented himself from duty. A girl . . . An affair of the heart. Over just such a thing had he disobeyed his orders, young though he must have been at the time. A swollen testicle, was it, the girl playing nursemaid to him, a fever as well and fear of Army surgeons? But there had been other infractions since, far too many of them, especially that 'duelling' scar an SS rawhide whip had given him for he and that partner of his having pointed the finger of truth.

'The British, Colonel?' came the reminder.

'Naturally they, too, are worried, but so far the deaths haven't been one of theirs. I want this matter settled. Berlin . . . Need I say more?'

A cigarette had been left to waste its life in the ashtray. 'Colonel, your predecessor mentioned a bell ringer . . . '

The head was tossed.

'A nothing monk, a stroller about town in cloth. He comes and goes, and my predecessor let him, since he apparently has a calming effect on them. They love him, those women, if I can use that word with such as him. They are happiest in his presence, and he, I must say, adores them. *Lieber Gott*, he's like a fat little dog! His is but to serve and lick, and theirs but to receive. I'm sure he knows them all by name. Both the Americans, who seem to favour him most with presents, and the British who worship him.'

This was getting deeper and deeper. 'An herbalist?'

J. ROBERT JANES

Kohler had yet to sit down, so *gut, ja gut*. Kept on his feet would
be best.

'You might call him that. If not making the order's Host then it's
the soap those people sell on the *schwarzer Markt*—I know they do!'

The *marché noir*, the black market . . .

'And if not those, his herbs, potions, and honey. The hands, the
feet, the face, the skin. Frankly, I have no use for him or for the
French. They still encourage such people. When the Führer has
time, I am certain even that matter will be settled.'

And uh-oh again. 'A warm brother, Colonel?'

'That is putting it politely. *Ein Arschficker,* Kohler. I'm certain of it.'

The thought to ask, 'How certain?' was there but had best be left.
'And he comes and goes?'

This time a hand was tossed. 'His kind are apparently harmless,
though we shall see.'

'But are there others who come and go?'

The eyes were lowered to the cigarette, then took their time
in lifting. 'This latest death was not of an outside origin, Kohler.
Women, cooped up together month by month and year by year, can
be every bit as aggressive as men, if not more violent. My predecessor, if you can believe it, *allowed* them to discipline themselves and
look where it has led. They are accustomed to being locked into
their hotels each night, but are free to stay up and move about for
as long as they wish, though only if the blackout drapes are tightly
drawn.'

So as not to send a signal to the RAF, who might be passing overhead on their way to a bombing run in the Reich. 'Those stovepipes,
Colonel . . . '

'Certainly they have had their little fires, or so I have been told,
but someone always smells the smoke or sees the flames.'

'And are they allowed to visit from hotel to hotel?'

Had Kohler come upon something already? 'Only during the
day unless permission has been granted, as on last Christmas night,
when the British entertained the Americans.'

'And no nighttime sleepovers?'

'*Liebe Zeit!* If they should choose to stay to pursue such filthy practices, that is currently their concern, though we shall soon be putting a stop to it and they have little time to spare for such activities during the day.'

'Chores keep them busy?'

'There is no daily *Appell* as yet, though that is going to change.' No lining up at dawn and counting of heads.

'They have to queue up for bread, soup, their parcels and mail, Kohler. Hauling water or firewood, doing their laundry—all such things keep them occupied, but the question you must ask and answer quickly for me, is will there be another murder or suicide?'

And uh-oh yet again. 'Not if my partner and I can help it.'

The cigarette's little life was abruptly ended.

'Not if *you* can help it, *mein Lieber*. I've arranged for you to stay in the hospital. Four of the doctors there are French, as are the nursing sisters, but the one who is in charge of those is English, and there is another doctor—a Scotsman best left alone. I can't make apologies for their presence. That is how I found things. The patients go to them, in any case. Dr. Schlieffen oversees and looks after us, but has his surgery and rooms in one of the other villas.'

'We'd prefer to live in town, Colonel. A bed-sitter.'

And defiance already? 'That is not possible. Transport simply isn't available. You are on call at all times and will take your meals with us in the canteen, and you will not discuss the war with the internees or with those damned doctors and nurses. To all such enquiries—and there will be many—you will simply say, *Verboten*. For them, they are here to enjoy the safety and goodwill the Führer provides and that is all there is to it.'

Day to day, hour by hour, and with no news of when their little stay might end.

'As soon as you have settled the two who have died, they will be buried side by side but not in this park, am I understood?'

'Definitely.' And wasn't this one just their luck? A real *Mitläufer*, a fellow traveller of the Nazis, if not a dyed-in-the-wool *Eingefleischter*, the hypnotized. 'My partner and I will do what we can, Colonel.'

'Correction. *You* will do as you've been ordered. Now, I really must get on with things. Supper is at 1830 hours—no later, no earlier—and it will not be dragged out as the French invariably do with their meals.'

Louis definitely wasn't going to like that, either. 'And the first victim, Colonel? Where might we find her?'

'At the bottom of one of the elevator shafts in that hotel of theirs. Don't ask me how she got there or why that *verdammte* gate was open. That is for you to find out.'

It fluttered down, and as they looked up from the foyer of the Hôtel Vittel-Palace, the brassiere, the tiniest thing possible, floated lazily in some up-draught, only to trail one strap as it finally took the plunge.

The railing, three storeys above, was now completely clear of laundry, as were the staircase railings on either side of it. Trapped, the makeshift garment lay on the Art-Deco mosaic of the marble floor at their feet, where Neptune, in all his glory, was being enticed by golden-haired mermaids to take the waters.

'Hermann, allow me.'

Two lace-trimmed handkerchiefs had been refashioned. Repeated gentle washing, with water of stewed ivy leaves and then that of pine needles, had given it a scent both halfway between and all its own. The straps, however, were of cotton scavenged from a shirt-blouse. Instead of the usual clasp, a safety pin would have been used but such a valuable item had absented itself either through need or safekeeping.

There wasn't a sound, and how was it that nine hundred and whatever people could make themselves so scarce that not a one of them could be seen or heard? Had they climbed to attic garrets, gone into the cellars, or both? And if so, who had such a power over them that one's orders were completely obeyed?

Carefully folding the garment in half, Louis started out, their overboots left just inside the door as a sign of trust, perhaps, and a gamble at that.

Room 3–38 was no different from the others they had been able to glance into as they'd passed by open doors. It, too, was devoid of occupants but otherwise crowded.

'Hermann, a moment.'

Ach, the cinematographer!

'You start from the left, I from the right," said St-Cyr. 'Give the room the careful once-over.'

Commit the 'film' of it to memory, then make the traverse in reverse. Photos, cutouts, maps, and such covered whatever wall space had been free. There was a lacrosse stick, two tennis rackets, an American football, quite worn and obviously used by male hands and boots, but . . . *'Mein Gott,* the room's tidy. What more do we need?'

That, too, could not be allowed to pass. 'What did the years in Munich and Berlin teach you? To concentrate only on the obvious and ignore the significant?'

'Temper, temper. Don't let all those missing girls unsettle you.'

'Ah, mon Dieu, is it not evident I want us to use the opportunity they have unwittingly provided? It's curious, isn't it, that only one of the occupants was sitting on her bed just prior to their leaving?'

The beds were ex–French Army portable iron cots with straw mattresses, and there was a dent in the one Louis had noted. A game of solitaire had been in progress there, the cards laid out with a precision that defied reason.

'An evident reason, Hermann, for this one couldn't have been watching at any of the windows in use, could she?'

Since the windows here wouldn't overlook those sections of the park they'd had to cross. 'These ones face north and northeast.'

'Ah, bon, Inspector. You've already learned something significant.'

'And since she once played lacrosse, no one, and I mean no one, has dared to cut away any of that stick's leather webbing no matter the need, or to borrow the hard rubber ball that is nestled in its crotch.'

Two of the beds, one on either side of the door, were against that innermost wall. End to end, sets of two others occupied opposing walls, the area immediately in front of the floor-to-ceiling French windows being left as a sort of common space, replete with three fold-up, portable wooden-slatted café chairs and an upturned half-barrel as a table and reminder of what they'd once been allowed to partake of with pleasure.

French and German magazines and newspapers were there—
collaborationist and Nazi and obviously weeks and weeks old and
cartoon-decorated in ridicule; an ashtray, too, but no cigarette butts.

Storage was under the beds and in armoires that had been scavenged and to which shelving had been added. A pantry, a little
kitchen . . .

'That stove to the right of the window is French, Louis, a Godin.
Asbestos paper has been stuffed around its pipe to seal it in and
keep out the wind, but at night the blackout drapes would have to
be helped when drawn.'

'But of what date is the stove?'

Ach, must he! 'Eighteen-ninety, I think.'

'Try 1916 to 1919.'

'And that other war?'

'You're learning. Didn't I say you would? Vittel's Parc Thermal
and its hotels became a giant hospital camp for *les Américains* when
the French cases were moved out in 1917, myself among them. Perhaps this indicates the origin of that football you noticed.'

The things one didn't know. Louis had been wounded twice in
that other war but had never said where he'd been sent for treatment.

A chipped, enamelled metal stew pot, something kept from the
Reich's inevitable scrap drives and left over from those doughboys,
no doubt, sat atop a small, electric ring whose cord, by the look, was
dangerously frayed. 'Are they able to call in an electrician now and
then, do you think?'

'Perhaps but then . . . The meal, Inspector?'

Steam was rising from the pot. Kohler started forward only to be
held back. 'There is no need. The aroma,' said St-Cyr.

Louis would have separated that one smell from all the others
that had been coming at them like those of tennis shoes no amount
of washing could cure, given the sachets of lavender that had been
tucked into them. 'A rabbit stew, I think.'

'*Un garenne, mais bouilli à l'anglaise,* and without its stuffing of
veal, egg, lard, or fat and bread.'

Boiled wild rabbit, in the English way.

'The flesh is firmer and has a better flavour, Hermann, than the domesticated. Perhaps that is why there are two string snares now washed and ready to be used again and waiting under one of the beds I was preparing to thoroughly scan.'

With the cameras of his mind, and the nearest of the two against one side wall, the same as had the game of solitaire, the dent, and the lacrosse stick. 'A loner, is she? Those pelts have been cleaned and stretched.'

'And there are two rabbits in that pot. Are moccasins in the offing?'

Since a pair of the same were already neatly side by side next to the latest Red Cross parcel whose string had been carefully coiled for use in other snares and such like . . .

'That curtain line next to the ceiling on your side, Hermann? Were the two who slept there accustomed to shutting themselves off from the others?'

And trust Louis to have noticed it first! 'That vase of silk chrysanthemums, the arrangement of them, that portrait of Pétain . . . A Tricolour pinned to the wall above a map of France which shows absolutely *nothing* to signify the country's defeat and partition into a *zone occupée*, eh, and a *zone non occupée*?'

'And the catches on the suitcase beneath that bed, Hermann? It's from Goyard Aîné at 1233 rue Saint-Honoré.'

'And the catches are considerably different in style than on those of the others.'

'*Ah, bon, mon vieux*, you really are learning.'

European-style catches: a French occupant, then, and the Americans.

A pair of pink satin ballet slippers hung from a corner of the armoire between those two beds. 'And right above our second victim's,' said Kohler. 'And if I check the Red Cross parcel will I find chocolate bars and chewing gum absent but present in all the others?'

'Or is it that the occupants of Room 3–38 pool such resources for the common good?'

That pantry and *merde* again! 'Did they not always get along, the French one here and the Americans?'

'Of those two beds, Hermann, is the one closest to the window that of our victim's guardian?'

'Was Caroline Lacy her ward?'

'Was the girl the daughter of the woman's benefactor, Hermann?'

Everyone knew that before this lousy war a lot of the French had been damned poor due to a constantly devalued franc until opportunity had come along from across the sea.

Whereas there were photographs of ballerinas and ballets of note that had been cut from magazines and pasted up on that wall, and one of a villa in Provence and a few of family members, above the other beds there were the brightly coloured, large-lettered pennants college students would madly wave at football matches: 'Marquette University in Milwaukee, Wisconsin, Louis. Michigan Tech at Houghton, Michigan, the U of Wisconsin at Madison, and . . . '

'St. Olaf College, in Northfield, Minnesota.'

A map of America had pins to locate both college and home. There were photos, too, of pet dogs, of fishing expeditions with father, grandfather, and brothers; of a fiancé, too, in uniform; a sister, an aunt and uncle. Candy floss and candy apples at a fair.

'Louis, why the hell did they have to stick around and get caught up in this lousy Occupation?'

'Perhaps they'll tell us, but since each went to a university that was reasonably close to those of the others, is it that they met here quite by accident and sorted themselves out that way?'

A common bond. 'Except for Madame Whatever-Her-Name-Is and our victim, Caroline Lacy.'

'Who might, quite possibly, have been foisted upon them.'

'They didn't get along—is this what you're saying?'

'Madame's sympathies are obviously not those of the others.'

That photo of Maréchal Pétain. Loyalty, then, even now when increasingly the country was turning against the Victor of Verdun; Pierre Laval, the premier, being in charge anyway.

'Each has a little library, Louis. Detective novels, romances, historical fiction . . . and most probably borrowed from the camp's or hotel's communal library.'

'But textbooks in mineralogy, geology, biology, and zoology? Our moccasin maker values them.'

'Houghton . . . is there a school of mines at Michigan Tech?'

'Or one of trapping.'

'I still say it's a tidy room,' muttered Hermann.

'And are there not degrees of tidiness? This is a utilitarian tidiness given of necessity. It is not that of our killer, who, unless I am very mistaken, is compulsive.'

The Americans were down in the cellars and there were a lot of them, Louis having stayed upstairs. Under the dim light from parsimoniously spaced forty-watt bulbs, the corridor was standing-room only and must have run the full length of the hotel. Others strained to look over or past still others, and not a one of them moved or made a sound.

Kohler was transfixed by the hush, the stillness, the watchfulness of the middle-aged, the young, the old, the tall, the short, the faces round, thin, angular, the hair straight, curled, waved, cut short, worn long, with and without colourful ribbons, some even in abandoned masses of curls like Shirley Temple in *Curly Top*. Others like Garbo in *Grand Hotel,* and wasn't that a coincidence; others still, like Mae West in *Klondike Annie* or Ginger Rogers in *A Fine Romance*; and still others in the many, many hairstyles of America's Sweetheart, Mary Pickford.

Curiosity was everywhere, interest evident, anxiety rampant, the fear that there was a killer among them, but also the hope that there wasn't.

'*Inspektor, mein Name ist* Mrs. Eleanor Parker, and I have been chosen to speak with you. If you like, I am house mother to them, though such a title was never sought nor has it ever been abused. From time to time a spokesperson is required to take matters to the Kommandant.'

They hadn't chosen the oldest or the youngest, nor the most attractive or sophisticated. Instead, they had picked a real ramrod fluent in *Deutsch* and complete with heavy black horn-rimmed specs and a look that would defy the Führer himself.

'And now?' asked Kohler.

That was better, thought Eleanor. 'I think you will find that some ground rules had best be established. This unfortunate incident . . . '

'There were two of them.'

Ach, a Bavarian, and wasn't it typical of them! 'Please have the courtesy not to interrupt me. This unfortunate incident has made everyone nervous. That, in itself, is understandable, but clearly there is no cause in house for such alarm. The girl in question . . . '

The flat of a firm right hand was held up to stop further interruption.

'As I was saying, Inspector, the girl in question suffered from a terrible delusion and had few, if any, friends here. Certainly others amongst us have delusions but that guardian of hers, that governess . . . The poor child dreamt of becoming a prima donna. She would dance with Serge Lifar? Boris Kniaseff was to feature her in his *Triomphe de Neptune*? I urged patience on the part of the others, caution, understanding—after all, she was very young and her career had been nipped in the bud. I told them all that ridicule was something that would not help the collective psyche, shunning not being any way to treat another no matter how difficult.'

'But it did no good?'

'She simply sought out others who encouraged her, and it is amongst those that I am certain you will find her killer.'

The British of the Hôtel Grand. 'Shunning . . . ?'

'When two or more are talking and another comes along, the first keep on as if that person doesn't even exist, or immediately cease all conversation.'

'And break up with but a knowing glance or nod to each other?'

'Inspector, if you persist in interrupting me, your investigation won't even get off the ground!'

'*Ach, du liebe Zeit,* forgive me.'

'Certainly, but only if you will listen. A week ago there was a terrible accident. One of our girls fell, and her body has still not been removed, but ever since then our ballerina has claimed it was no accident and that she, herself, was the intended victim. Given her habit of persistently badgering any who would listen about her career, is it any wonder none would?'

'Yet someone must have, and that someone, in turn, felt threatened.'

'Precisely! Now, if you have any further questions you will bring them first to myself, who will then be present at all times when you interview any of the others. Is that understood?'

Mein Gott, had she Prussian ancestors? 'Perfectly, Frau . . .'

'Mrs. Parker, if you please! It's tragic enough that you people have chosen to crowd us all into such a hovel behind barbed wire. What on earth were you thinking? These girls, these women . . . of what danger to the Reich or to anyone else could they possibly have been?'

'And yet . . .'

'That is *not* what I meant. Hers is a special case. No doubt, when the current state of emotional devastation has passed, Madame de Vernon will vehemently accuse those who were forced to share Room 3–38 with her and her ward and will then, at random, target others amongst us, myself especially.'

'French, is this guardian?'

'She claims a lineage to the Sun King, but if you ask me, her family was nothing more than of *les hobereaux*.'

The country squires, and the ultimate put-down—the lesser aristocracy, the little hawks the Paris Establishment had always derided. And hadn't there been a well-thumbed photo of a villa on that one's bit of wall space? 'Another dreamer was she?'

Had she broken through at last? wondered Eleanor. Detectives could be so difficult. 'The more we speak, the more I come to see that we understand each other. Now, may I tell the others they can return to their rooms and their tasks?'

'Parker . . . I seem to have heard that name before.'

'The fountain pens. My father . . . The family . . .'

She was actually blushing over the recognition! 'Single out the other occupants of Room 3–38. Keep Madame de Vernon here and three of the others, but send the one from Michigan Tech up to talk to my partner, Louis. The others can stay here as well until I'm satisfied.'

Had she not succeeded with him at all? 'Madame de Vernon is in the hospital under sedation.'

'Good. Simply hold back the three and send on the other.'

'Then I shall have to go with her.'

'Unless you want to stay down here with me.'

To be singled out and sent upstairs alone was not good. Nora knew she had done everything she could to have stopped it from happening. In alarm, she had made eye contact with Mrs. Parker, who, knowing full well the implications of being singled out, had simply shrugged, having had to make a decision of her own.

Surely though, even a Nazi detective would know how difficult life could then become for that person? Had this Kohler and his French partner *wanted* this to happen, and if so, why? Had they realized that she had *wanted* to remain alone in the room while the others had rushed away to crowd the windows and watch them?

The urge to scan her bed for the reason was resisted, she remaining in the doorway and unseen as yet, for the one called "Louis," having gone through everything he could easily search, had taken to fingering things in Madame de Vernon's suitcase. Letters, money—jewellery—were they so blatantly dishonest they would rob defenceless women who had little enough?

Quickly he emptied a thin envelope of its photos and, holding one up next to that of Madame's former villa in Provence, muttered to himself, 'The year 1910, madame. It's curious, *n'est-ce pas*? Firstly, because there is no more recent photo and, secondly, why keep a dog-eared photo from the past pasted to the wall beside your pillow when you have similar and far better ones tucked away? Was it so that each night before sleep you would be reminded not just of the house but of something else?'

While saying her prayers, Inspector, thought Nora. While begging God to forgive and release her from this place, but do you always speak to an empty room as if the person were right there beside you?

He still hadn't sensed her presence, was not nearly as tall as the Bavarian, was of medium height but as broad across the shoulders and with the hands, the fists, and lightness on his feet of a former *boxeur*.

He moved easily, fluidly, thoroughly and carefully. Fifty . . . fifty-two . . . Was he three years younger than that 'partner' of his?

There was a wedding ring, though the shabby overcoat showed no sign of such a one's attention. It being open, buttons hung by their threads or bits of string, and the right pocket, crammed with the things he'd already found and taken, was torn.

One strap of Caroline's spare brassiere dangled from that very pocket. The grey fedora he wore was pushed well back of what must be a broad forehead. Had he a mustache? He looked the type—would smoke a pipe, too, when he could get fuel for that little furnace.

Quickly he replaced the photos. Now he felt along the back edge of the suitcase and when he had what he wanted, drew that little cedar box out and held it up by its tie of braided parcel string.

But instead of opening it, he set it down and, turning his attention to Caroline's shelf, ran a forefinger quickly over the little bottles with their labels. 'Borage,' he said *en français*. 'Marshmallow, thyme, and the ground, dried leaves and stems of the *Datura stramonium*, the thorn apple, though being *une Américaine*, Mademoiselle Lacy wouldn't have known it by that name, would she?'

Ah, merde! 'She suffered terribly from asthma, Inspector. Night after night she'd be up, wheezing, trying to catch a breath while Madame patted her on the back, as if *that* would have done her any good! "Steam," I would hiss at them. "Boil a little water."'

'And?'

He had taken the datura bottle from that shelf and pocketed it. 'Brother Étienne reluctantly prescribed the jimsonweed. We call it that because the settlers who first found it in America lived near Jamestown, Virginia. The name then became a contraction of that. It can, of course, cause terrible highs. Everyone knows of this and has been warned of it by him.'

He reached for the little white porcelain mortar and pestle Madame had also kept in her suitcase, and brought it up to a nose that was full and robust, his dark brown ox-eyes never once leaving her. He *did* have a mustache, full and thick and dark brown, but didn't look so frightening after all, which could only cause her to worry all the more.

'Madame,' said Nora, 'would grind a few of the seeds and then add them to the shredded, dried leaves and stems to make a batch of Caroline's cigarettes. Maybe five at a time. This place . . . the ever-present . . . '

'Dampness. The walls have mould on them, the windows their hoar frost. Nothing ever really dries, does it? Not with so many of you indoors most of the time. Did smoking those cigarettes help her?'

'A lot. Brother Étienne said that for centuries the Nubians had been using the dried leaves like that to treat asthma. It opens the bronchioles.'

This herbalist, this bell ringer, was getting more interesting by the moment. 'And the nettles?'

'The alfalfa seeds, as well. Both are sources of vitamins and minerals, particularly Vitamin A.'

'Did Caroline Lacy also suffer from night blindness?'

That lack of Vitamin A. 'It often took her ten minutes to get back her sight when going from a lighted room into darkness.'

'But here the corridor lights, though infrequent and of low wattage, are left on all night?'

He was on to things already. 'Unless the Boche turn them off as a punishment or simply to show us who *les gros légumes* really are.'

The big vegetables, the big bosses, the *Oberbonzen,* and of course the *Bonzen.* 'Your name, mademoiselle?'

'Nora Arnarson. Well, actually it's Arnora Arnarsonsdottír, but my grandparents simplified the matter.'

'Icelandic?'

Few would have known this. 'On my father's side. Mom's French Canadian—a Métis.'

'Half-and-half French Canadian and native North American Indian, but you're American?'

'As are my parents and grandparents on my father's side. You can go back three generations in his family, if you like. Gimli, Manitoba, in Canada first, and then Houghton, Michigan.'

She had a fierce way of saying it, as if to say, Don't you damn well challenge me or I'll take my lacrosse stick to you. Her hair was light auburn with streaks of still lighter blond. It was cut short, worn well off the shoulders in a style reminiscent of the '20s, parted high on the left and feathered back to curl behind the ears, framing a sharpness whose nose and slightly parted lips matched the instant alertness of dark blue eyes. Hermann would have said, Don't be so hard on her. Even in a heavy turtleneck and cords, she's a catch.

'I'll be twenty-six years old next Wednesday, Inspector. I'm not married and don't even have a fiancé anymore. My life is in suspension, and I have no money, since our government, unlike the British, doesn't send us any and I've none myself, and I happen to think you people who collaborate with the Boche are just as bad as them and a lousy bunch of sons of bitches. You're both going to lose this war and when you do, we're going to beat the shit out of you.'

'*Ah, bon,* we understand each other. It's always best. Now, please, this cedar box of Madame's. All the while we've been talking, you've been giving it hesitant glances.'

Shit! 'Brother Étienne told Madame to keep it safely locked away, which means of course, Inspector, that you have somehow unlocked her suitcase.'

Her chin was sharp, the throat tight, and again that defiant fierceness had leapt into her eyes.

'Would you be good enough, then, to open the box for me?' he asked, and she knew that she couldn't refuse, that to do so would be to confess.

'Listen, you. We all knew of it.'

'But that is not what I asked.'

Salaud! her look seemed to say. Crossing the room, she undid the string and opened the lid but caught a breath. 'There . . . there were three of the dried seed capsules lying side by side. They all but filled the box.'

Wincing at having instantly betrayed herself, she glanced sickeningly from him to the remaining two capsules whose prickly brown casings had opened to expose the flattened, oval- to kidney-shaped seeds that were black to dark brown and each from two to three millimetres in size. Then she looked at him more steadily. 'Madame . . . ' she began.

'Kept a key to this suitcase on her at all times, but its spare hidden in the room in case the other was lost or stolen. Did you find it as I did?'

'No! I'd . . . I'd never think of . . . '

'Mademoiselle Arnarson, please, let's not waste time. The seeds . . . '

'And the fruit are the most poisonous parts of the plant and contain from zero point two to zero point four percent hyoscine and hyoscyamine, which means atropine and scopolamine also. Brother Étienne didn't want to give those capsules to Madame. There were far too many seeds, maybe six hundred in total, maybe as much as twelve hundred, but Madame . . . '

'Can be very forceful?'

He was standing so close to her now she could feel the presence of him. 'Caroline's family are stateside—in America, in Bethlehem, Pennsylvania. We'll win this war because of people like them, not just our boys.'

'Iron and steel.'

'And money, Inspector. Caroline's family is loaded.'

'Yet their daughter was left behind to end up here.'

'Their youngest daughter, but perhaps you'd best ask Madame why that happened.'

Even though one of the enemy to her, and tarred with that and the Gestapo's brush, Hermann would somehow have gotten through her armour. He'd have smiled at her, encouraged those little nuances of male-female jockeying, would have asked of her home, her family, her state of well-being—anything so as to show that he really did empathize and would eventually have broken down that barrier of hatred and caution, but time and patience sometimes didn't allow for such things, and Hermann was a sucker for any female and could easily become putty in the hands of such a one as this.

'Tell me about the first victim, mademoiselle. Tell me if you think she, too, was murdered.'

He was pocketing the little box of datura, wasn't going to leave it in Madame's suitcase, but had he sensed that she, herself, had been involved in that first tragedy? If so, how could she make him understand? 'In the beginning, like everyone else but Caroline, I thought it an accident, but now . . . '

'Since the death of Mademoiselle Lacy.'

'*Oui*. Inspect—"

It was Hermann.

'Louis, you'd best leave that and come with me.'

Wielding brooms, canes, billiard cues, knives, boards—anything they could have laid hand to—they were crammed into the foyer and crowding the corridor that led to the steps to the cellars, and in a rage. Having rushed the doors en masse, they shrieked, yelled, jeered, and bellowed at the Americans in French and in English. '*ESPÈCES DE SALOPE! ROULEUSES! VIPÈRES!*' Fucking bitches, sluts, serpents . . . 'COME UP AND TAKE WHAT WE'RE GOING TO GIVE YOU!'

As one, wearing hats, scarves, overcoats of every description, the colours faded by the years of use, the 'delegation' ceased its racket at a shout from its leader, and collectively turned to look up.

A ripple of what must be happening ran down into the cellars to silence the Americans.

'Who the hell are you, luv?' called the woman in English, the throaty yell of it echoing.

'I think she means you, Louis.'

'You're mistaken, Hermann.'

'But you're the chief inspector, aren't you?'

'*Sacré nom de nom*, Hermann, *elle est la plus formidable*! Madame,' St-Cyr called down *en français*. 'What seems to be the trouble?'

In French she answered, 'Those bitches are trying to put the blame on us. If they want to kill each other, that's their business, but we had nothing to do with it!'

Foolishly Louis held up a hand to intercede. One could have heard a pin drop were it not for the sounds of collective breathing and the smell that arose from the assembled.

'THEY'LL NEVER GROW A GODDAMNED THING IN THEIR GARDENS THIS SUMMER, MISTER!' shrieked someone in English.

'WE'LL TEAR TH' FUCKING THINGS UP!' shouted another.

'WE'LL MAKE THEM EAT THE SHIT THEY'LL SECRETLY SPREAD IN HOPES OF GETTING BIGGER SQUASH AND TATERS THAN OURS!'

'*Taters? Ah, merde,* what on earth are they?'

'Potatoes, Louis. Last autumn the Americans raided the British vegetable gardens in retaliation for the way they'd been treated. When they first got here, they were billeted with them.'

A sigh would have to be given. 'Things didn't work out to everyone's satisfaction.'

'Food had to be shared and they had none to contribute since they hadn't Red Cross parcels of their own. A lot of them also had to double up and sleep on the floors between the beds of their hosts. The drains packed it in because of the traffic. The bathtubs and washbasins were never cleaned. Hand soap was stolen from the Americans, what there was of it. Cigarettes, perfume, costume jewellery, lipsticks too, and cash . . . '

'The two hotels, being side by side, they are Allies elsewhere but enemies here—is that how it is?'

'Don't get huffy. The new Kommandant did indicate the British had invited the Americans to a party they'd put on last Christmas.'

'To make amends?'

'Perhaps. Now, deal with it, will you? Mrs. Parker and that one faced off on the stairs and guess who won?'

'That why you're looking so rattled?'

'They've got my gun.'

'*Ah, bon,* a difficult assignment. If I don't get it back, I'll be blamed.'

'And if you do, they'll be eating out of our hands.'

2

The fist that clasped the broom handle was beet-red, the fingers painfully chapped and thick, but on the third, fourth, and fifth digits there were rings, the look of which no soap or margarine would ever free. Bolt cutters would possibly be needed, thought St-Cyr. It was that or determination.

The little finger wore a ring whose faceted rectangles were of clear-white diamond and dark-green emerald, the design from the early '20s and Art Deco: Van Cleef & Arpels, no doubt. Then came a canary-yellow diamond of at least sixteen carats, the faceted *navette* surrounded by brilliants in the style of Boucheron and probably dating from 1915.

The last was a sapphire cabochon of thirty carats and exquisite colour, with brilliants all around—Cartier, he was certain—the three rings a tidy fortune for such a one as this, to say nothing of the fact that she was in an internment camp where such items were invariably taken from one and an oft-worthless receipt given.

'FERME-LA, MES AMIES!' the woman shouted to shut up the racket. 'GIVE US ROOM WHILE I DEAL WITH THIS TURD AND PULL HIS LITTLE CHAIN!'

The laughter and other disturbances died off as if struck. Shabby, thin, tall, gaunt, dumpy, or not, to a woman they wore hats. Some of these were tiny, like this one's, which was perched atop hennaed hair whose roots were fiercely black. Uncompromising, the hair was thick, long, and wiry and pulled back into a bush that was tied with a Union Jack. Others, though, wore hats that were large and floppy; others still, tiny pillboxes with bits of forgotten veil, but all used hatpins that were obviously daggers in their own right.

Surrounded, collectively the looks were contained but in ribald expectation of the fistfight to come.

Ah, merde, thought St-Cyr, chancing a glance back and upward to Hermann who had remained standing at the third-storey's railing with Nora Arnarson. Perhaps the girl had gripped the railing out of fear of heights, Hermann having laid a hand firmly on hers.

'Madame . . .'

'IT'S SIMPLE THEFT, *COUILLON!* A PHOTO, A POSTCARD, A LITTLE BIT OF GLASS, A PEBBLE, A ROCK CRYSTAL!'

Must she call him an asshole and let her voice fill the hotel? 'Madame, *un moment, s'il vous plaît.* Simple theft?'

'IT IS THEN THAT EVERYTHING BEGAN, FIVE MONTHS SINCE THOSE *CHATTES* ARRIVED HERE!'

Those cunts? *'Ah, bon, je comprends.* When the Americans arrived, the thefts began, and from petty theft things developed into an accident, and from there to murder—is that how it was?'

'Oui.'

The once navy-blue overcoat, still with all of its buttons after the years of internment, had a sable collar that would be pleasantly warm but definitely didn't belong with the original coat, and though the eyes were small and of a dark grey-blue, they were swift and hard behind octagonal gold-rimmed specs that must have belonged to someone else. 'Your name, madame? The face, the figure, the stature . . . Was it in Honfleur that we encountered each other? La rue du Dauphine, perhaps, or was it Le Havre and along le quai Videcoq?'

The docks, in any case.

The grin was huge, the teeth tobacco- and tea-stained, and broken or absent; the woman as tall and big across the shoulders as Hermann, who was probably congratulating himself on the little problem he had managed to dump on his partner.

'This Occupation, madame,' said St-Cyr. 'This war. People come into contact in the strangest places only to lose contact while others come back unexpectedly.'

I had better drop the voice, she thought. 'Listen my cow that moos, I've never seen you before.'

And gangster slang for police, but one must be cheerful and sing out, 'Ah, the dialect, that's it. One hears so many in my line of work, one automatically tries to place them. Les Halles, madame? The rue des Lombardes? The house at number twenty-seven. I'll have the date in a moment.'

The belly of Paris, the central market, and an unlicenced house. '*Couillon, ferme-la!*'

'Of course, but one good turn deserves another.'

And wouldn't you know it! '*Qu' est-ce vous désirez, Monsieur l'inspecteur?* The love of the chase, the hunt, the young and beautiful or the more mature?'

'Our overboots and my partner's gun, and not without every last one of its cartridges, which I will have already counted.'

He was definitely a shitty bastard. 'Marguerite, hand over the gun, Hortense, give back the overboots. There'll be another time.'

Was Hermann pleased? wondered St-Cyr. He didn't smile, still stood with that hand of his clamped over that of Nora Arnarson of Room 3–38. They were talking. The girl looked as though trapped . . .

'You're afraid of them,' confided Kohler to the girl.

Nora winced. 'Please let me go, Inspector.'

'Not until you tell me. That woman down there mentioned stealing little things of no earthly value and you immediately began to tremble. I'd like to know why.'

'You don't understand, do you? You can't. But you're letting them all see me with you. They'll think I've told you things and ratted on them. They'll wait. They'll find a moment when I'm not watching out for just such a thing.'

'And then?'

'They'll shove me.'

Louis had the gun and the boots and was quietly asking the woman down there something . . .

'Your name, madame,' said St-Cyr, 'so as to clear up that little problem and remove the necessity of my asking one of the others.'

The shit! 'Léa Monnier.'

'I knew it! Your husband was at Verdun, a corporal and terribly wounded, but one of the lucky.'

Ah, mon Dieu, what was this, sympathy from a *sûreté?* 'He never came back. I had to leave his medals at home when the cows rounded me up and gave me a lift in the salad shaker.'

The Black Maria, but one had best shrug and gesture at the help-lessness of turning fate aside. 'So many didn't survive, did they, but I seem to recall that neither shell nor bullet, bayonet, poisoned gas, or illness got him, yet he left you with a bronze.'

The medal for five children that was pinned high on the left breast of her coat! 'The youngest turned seventeen in November, so the green beans, having decided that they'd better, had to let her go home, since she wasn't eighteen.'

The Wehrmacht wore grey-green, thus earning that epithet, but con-cern had best be shown. 'Home, and without the benefit of a mother's guidance? The *salauds!* It makes no sense, does it, when you could have made a fortune with all those boys on leave and wanting company?'

'Don't try to pound the bread dough too much, Inspector. Tell me what else you want and I'll see to it.'

She would never back off, not this one. 'Peace for now and the right to talk to those among you who might be able, if you were to persuade them, of course, to shed a little light on the investigation. A couple of cigarettes, too, if you can spare them so that all present will see that we have parted on the best of terms.'

The Lucky Strikes were not from a British Red Cross parcel, and were taken not from a packet, but from the silver, diamond-and-emerald-encrusted case Van Cleef & Arpels had crafted in the '20s to go along with the diamond-and-emerald bracelet that went with the first of those rings.

'*Ah, bon, merci.* My partner will be certain to return the favour with interest as soon as possible.'

Hermann's Walther P38 had all eight Parabellum cartridges in its box magazine and one up the spout.

'We don't steal things, Inspector.'

How watchful she was. 'Only the Americans do that?'

'They've plenty now, yet they still torment us.'

'And you've ways and means of finding out who the thief is?'

'A magpie, that's all we know for sure. Things are stolen for their colour or the temptation of it, the thrill, *n'est-ce pas, le grand frisson.*'

L'orgasme, the great shudder. 'And not for their use or need? A kleptomaniac?'

'Call the slut what you will, but it's still stealing. If you find her, remind her that Madame Chevreul keeps asking, and that soon Cérès will give us the answer even if you don't.'

Hermann was still standing up there with Nora Arnarson, who was confiding something to him. Just what that was, one couldn't tell, but it must have been given with a certain desperation, for they faced each other and the girl had at last managed to free her hand.

'Léa Monnier isn't the ringleader of the British, Herr Kohler. She's just head flunky.'

As he came down the stairs and into the foyer, the others having left, Hermann was in high spirits. 'Limehouse, Louis. The docks along the Thames in London couldn't hold our Léa, and she came over here in 1914 as a truck driver in that other war but found love drove her. Married a Claude Monnier in the autumn of 1917 while he was on extended leave. Learned the language, had five kids, collected his medals and his pension—Verdun as usual.'

Such naiveté always needed clarification. 'While working her way up to becoming madame of the *clandestin* at 27 rue des Lombardes, *mon vieux,* to support Monnier in the style to which he had become accustomed. Sénégalais porters, coal sellers from the Auvergne, farmers from the Vendée, Orléans, Nantes, and other places. All as customers bearing ducklings, fresh-picked asparagus, young spring leeks, Charolais beef, sausage from Lyon and oysters from Concarneau. Good country people with a little time on their hands after the onion soup.'

Les Halles after that war to end all wars, and with overblown memories of what it must have been like before this Occupation! There was a sigh.

'But she had kept her passport,' said Kohler. 'How many of those British women did you know?'

'None, but working with you has been good for me. Ah, your Walther P38, Inspector. Please see that better care is taken of it.'

'Still got that Lebel six-shooter I made sure the Geheime Staatspolizei were good enough to let you carry?'

'The Modèle d'ordonnance 1873?'

'The one with the eleven-millimitre low-pressure, black-powder cartridges no one wants when things get tight because they've been stored for such a long time and might be damp.'

'It's where it ought to be. Silent until needed.'

'Maybe you'd better let me have it and I'll get the Kommandant to lock up the firepower.'

'Don't be crazy, not with Madame Monnier and her hatpins. Now, please be so good as to carry your own overboots. You might need them.'

The first victim wasn't easy to get at, for the elevator, in the farthest wing from the entrance of the Vittel-Palace, had been decommissioned like all the others in September of 1939, its cage left in the cellars at the bottom of the shaft.

'Someone opened the gate on the third floor, Louis. The corridor lights were blinking on and off—another electrical problem for which the electrician from town was later brought in. Caroline Lacy had had a rough night and was out along the corridor trying to get her breath and light one of her cigarettes. Mary-Lynn Allan, from Sweet Briar, Virginia, was coming toward her and Caroline thought the girl might need a little help, but then there was a scream.'

'Why help? I thought Caroline Lacy was the one who needed it?'

'Mary-Lynn was unsteady on her feet. Drunk perhaps, on home brew.'

'And Nora Arnarson, who divulged this information, where was she?'

'On the stairs. She swears it.'

'And also drunk?'

'A little.'

'Date?'

'Saturday to Sunday, the thirteenth and fourteenth.'

'Time?'

'About 0100 hours on the Sunday and the reason for that urgent call to summon us.'

'And why was Nora on the stairs, Hermann, since she obviously hadn't gone to help Caroline Lacy?'

'She and Mary-Lynn had been to a séance in the Hôtel Grand.'

'Madame Chevreul?'

'How the hell did you know that?'

'The Ouija board I found under Nora's bed and the words of Madame Monnier, but for now it would take too long to discuss it. Find us a flashlight. This candle stub of mine won't last.'

'*Ach,* I'll have to go out to the gate. No one here is allowed one.'

'And when the lights go out, it's pitch-dark. *Ah, merde,* Hermann, what have we got ourselves into?'

'A problem, especially since the Kommandant who asked for us but has now been replaced must have given the two permission to be out late that night, as well as letting them keep such personal items as watches, rings, and bracelets.'

With the cellars at close to freezing, only now were there touches of yellowish-green to copper-red discolouration, but the veins in the neck and on the backs of the hands, where marbling was present, were a dark purplish blue.

St-Cyr looked up the shaft of the elevator's well. Mary-Lynn Allan had fallen the four floors from that third storey, had instinctively grabbed at cables that were shamefully frayed, considering it had been a deluxe hotel when built in 1899 and partially renovated in 1931. The palms of both hands had been badly torn, the left cheek as well.

She had then turned over and had plunged to land facedown

with arms flung out atop the elevator between its two cables, the rest of her bent over the iron bars to which those same cables were bolted.

Blood had drained. Within about twelve hours, postmortem hypostases had coalesced and made the face, ears, and neck livid in their lowermost parts. The eyes bulged, the mouth, teeth, forehead, and nose were broken, as were the arms, legs, ribs, and shoulders. Having emptied herself instantly, the rats had got at her.

'Ah, *mon Dieu,* Mademoiselle Allan, Hermann had best not see you. Death has haunted him since his days in the Great War from which a prisoner-of-war camp saved him but allowed time to dwell on the matter. Outwardly he puts on a veritable show, but inwardly . . . It's not just that the big shots of the Gestapo and SS will use this against him, a detective of theirs who no longer has the stomach for it, but though he would never admit it, he's far too old for the Russian Front and has already lost his two young sons to that. Boys . . . They were only boys. Yet, still, it's really just Hermann himself. We've been through so much, have constantly been in each other's company and yet have survived while displeasing virtually everyone else. Those who stood to gain and those who hoped to, even those remotely connected who simply wished the status quo to continue.'

The thighs were bare, the foetus absent, the placenta wrapped around the remains of the umbilical cord.

As gently as he could, he covered her. 'Two months, three, mademoiselle? Had you told anyone, the father perhaps? Was he a guard, one of the doctors . . . the electrician who comes from town? The dentist, or one of the camp's officers?

'And why, please, was that gate deliberately opened when it should have remained closed and locked?'

The candle stub flickered in a down-draught that drew the little flame to one side, threatening darkness. Several photos lay about— snapshots from home she'd been carrying, and also a beautifully carved *cavalier,* a knight from a chess set, the wood light-red to reddish-brown.

'And hard, and moderately heavy, and very straight grained.' It had fortunately tumbled to the far left front corner of the elevator's roof, where it had remained clear of everything else.

'Mary-Lynn Allan was twenty-seven years old, Louis. Two brothers in the service, the girl the youngest. Father Ed . . . '

'Killed during that other war?'

'*Ah, mon Dieu,* how the hell did you . . . '

'The snapshots. An officer.'

'Killed during the Meuse-Argonne advance of . . . '

'Hermann, I'm aware of the date. Twenty-six September, 1918. Fog got them. Buried tank tracks and other shot-up armour threw their compass bearings off, they failing to realize this until it was too late.'

The poor bastards had been green and almost straight off the boat from home, but Louis, like most of the French, would still be thinking *les Américains sont toujours merveilleux.* 'They'd not had any food for at least four days and little if any sleep, *mon vieux.* You know how it was. End of story. First Army, Thirty-Fifth Division under Major-General Traub.'

'The east bank of the Aire River well to the northwest of here and of Verdun, Hermann.'

'She couldn't have known him, would only have been about two years old but wondering all her life.'

The photos had been of the deceased father, the *cavalier* having belonged to him. 'That why the séance with Madame Chevreul?' asked St-Cyr.

'For which she handed over a cheque for the princely sum of fifty dollars American.'

This investigation was getting deeper and deeper. 'Which bank?'

'The Morgan.'

'With headquarters in New York but a branch office in Paris, Hermann, the cheque negotiable after this war since Madame Chevreul could not possibly get there to cash it even though that bank is still open. *Ah, merde . . . '*

The candle had snuffed itself. 'Two of the guards are bringing an extension cord,' said Kohler. 'They'll lower a light to you.'

'Why don't they open the ground-floor gates?'

'*Ach*, I didn't think to tell them. The crowd, I guess.'

'Then be so good as to clear all corridors and find our trapper. Pick up where I left off by asking if any of that *datura* has gone missing before.'

'Missing . . . ?' Did Louis *want* to warn everyone of it? 'Was she drugged?'

Good for Hermann. 'At this point, it's simply an alternative to the effects of alcohol. She'd have lost focus, been very unsteady on her feet . . . '

'Hallucinogenic?'

They'd all be listening now, felt St-Cyr. 'It's just a thought.'

'But don't jump to conclusions, eh? And Madame Chevreul of the Hôtel Grand?'

'Leave her for now. Let others tell her of our interest. Chevreul was the nineteenth-century Frenchman who popularized the use of a pendulum to induce hypnosis. She may have borrowed the name, which would imply study of the process, or simply have married someone related or totally unrelated.'

The listeners would think about that too. 'In addition to getting in touch with her father, Louis, Mary-Lynn Allan wanted to know where he was buried since he was one of the hundreds of thousands who were never found. Blown to bits probably, or simply left in the cesspool of a shell crater to eventually be covered.'

A sigh would do no good. 'Hermann, please do as I've asked. Since you've already been talking to Nora Arnarson, continue your conversation with her, then find out whatever else you can here.'

'But leave the Hôtel Grand for later. A pendulum and two bodies.'

'The theft of little things of no consequence.'

They'd all know of that anyways. 'A trapper, Louis, a bell ringer, and a flunky.'

'And a chess piece, Hermann.'

'Oh, that. The wood's from a Kentucky Coffeetree. The father carved it when he was a teenager. The mother sent it over with the snapshots in a Red Cross parcel. That's why the ex-Kommandant who asked for us but left without leaving any information readily agreed to the late-night visitation and attended it himself as a firm believer.'

Ah, sacré nom de nom!

Room 3–38 was far from happy, thought Kohler. The blue-eyed blonde whose cot was under the St. Olaf College pennant tried to light a cigarette but was so nervous, match and fag fell to her lap, scorching the grey tweed of a slender skirt.

'Shit!' she cried in English. '*Don't,* Marni. I'm warning you.'

That one, whose cot was next to the innermost wall and under the Marquette U. pennant, and who had helped herself without the chef's permission to a cup of the rabbit broth, had been about to quench the fire.

'Should I have let you torch your beaver?' she yelled. 'The *préfet de police's* goatee, eh?'

The police chief's beard and prostitute talk, the insult not really meant but . . .

'That's it!' cried the blonde. 'I'm not living here a moment longer. I can't *stand* the stench of that!'

The rabbits, to which the trapper, Nora Arnarson, having flung a desperate look of censure at the green-eyed redhead with the mass of curls who'd helped herself to the broth, was now slicing peeled sow-thistle roots to be added to the pot.

She dumped the lot in and began to slice the hell out of an onion, though how she had come by such a rarity was anyone's guess unless on the black market.

'I don't know how you can kill things like that, Nora,' started up the blonde again. 'I really don't. They're God's creatures.'

'As was the pig from which the SPAM you eat must have come,' came the retort from Nora.

'*At least I was spared the agony of having to watch the poor thing being skinned and butchered!*'

Shrill . . . '*Jésus, merde alors,* ladies . . . *mesdames et mesdemoiselles,* a moment. My English, it's not enough. I'm not here to accuse any of you, why would I? My partner and I just need a little help.'

'If you're to stop another of us from being murdered—is that it, eh? Why don't you just say it?'

That had been Jill Faber, who slept end-to-end next to Becky Torrence, the blonde, and was sitting under the U. of Wisconsin pennant.

'Are we all to be poisoned?' wept Becky. 'Those damned seeds, Inspector. If Nora's right, each one contains at least a tenth of a milligram of the datura poison atropine. Ten to thirty seeds will make you very sick and hallucinating in hell; a hundred can kill you.'

'And for all I know, they could already have been added to our supper,' said the chef, to which the redhead with the broth added, 'Nora, darling, you don't really mean that.'

'We all knew both of them, Inspector,' countered Nora, dribbling diced onion into the pot. 'I wasn't the only one who was near Mary-Lynn the night she died.'

Swiftly they made eye contact, but with it had they instantly come to a consensus on how best to deal with him? wondered Kohler.

'Darling, you weren't as drunk as she was,' said Jill, who was in her late thirties and maybe ten years older than Becky, the youngest of them. Jill had dark grey eyes that could set off the whole of her if she would but let them and if things had been better.

'I was drunker,' said Nora. '*Mon Dieu,* I could hardly get up those stairs and kept telling her to wait for me.'

'She was in a hurry, was she?' asked Kohler.

The others were now intently watching the trapper-cum-chef.

'She said she was going to be sick, Inspector, and needed the *vase de nuit.*'

The night vase, the chamber pot. 'The one in Room 3–54?'

He'd think the worst of her if he ever found out the truth, thought Nora, but something had best be said. 'And the room right next to that elevator shaft we both had to pass.'

'People come and go at all times of the night, Inspector,' quickly offered Jill, who flicked a glance past him to the redhead called Marni.

'It's the shit you Germans give us to eat,' said Marni. 'It gives us the trots.'

'Black bread that's more sour than green apples; sour cabbage, too, and potato soup that always seems to have lost its potatoes,' said Jill.

'But with the chance of a knuckle from a long-dead horse,' offered Marni.

'*Stop it! Stop it! Please!*' cried Becky.

The cigarette had fallen to the floor this time to roll under her cot.

'Stay where you are. I'll get it,' said Nora.

She brushed it off and held it out, fondly touched the blonde's cheek and said, 'Why not let me rub your back? You know it'll help because it always does, then I'll make you some chamomile. I'm sorry about the rabbits. I should have realized and waited until you'd gone out.'

They weren't just nervous, felt Kohler. They were worried about where each of them fitted into these killings, were tense as hell, and desperately tired of one another's company and of the room.

'It's the winter, Inspector. It's been getting to us,' offered Jill with an apologetic shrug. She had straight black hair, a nice wide grin, certainly dimpled cheeks, and did look like she could be a lot of fun, but they'd had one death a week ago just along the corridor and yesterday another, taken from this very room.

'First,' he said, pointing at Nora, 'tell me if any datura has gone missing before?'

She had better not look at the others, thought Nora, had better just gaze levelly at him and shake her head.

'OK, now you,' he said to Jill. 'Tell me about the girl who fell.'

Herr Kohler was a little frightening after the celibacy of the past five months, thought Jill. She knew her nervousness stemmed from that as well as from everything else, but had he noticed it already? Was that why the others could see what she was thinking? If so, he would be bound to exploit it and then where would she be? 'Sweet Briar's essentially a girl's college. You could say, I suppose, that Mary-Lynn had led a sheltered life, but then came Paris. Before it was closed and taken over when you people declared war on us in December of '41, she worked as an interpreter and sales clerk at Brentano's on the avenue de l'Opéra.'

The American bookstore.

'Her German was almost as good as her French and because of it, she thought she was safe,' said Marni, the redhead from Marquette U.

'She hoped to attend the New York School of Fine and Applied Arts, in Paris,' wept Becky, 'but . . . but you people came to put a stop to everything. Just everything!'

'Jill, for God's sake, tell him,' said Marni. 'If you don't, I will.'

'Perhaps you'd best then, darling, since you knew far more than any of us, even Nora.'

'Jill, how could you do that to me?'

'I just did. Now, tell him.'

The redhead lowered her gaze and fingered her cup. 'Six months before our boys landed in North Africa in November last and you people rushed to take over the *zone non occupée,* the *zone libre,* for God's sake, Mary-Lynn fought off all her prejudices and fell for a German, a Sturmbannführer, a Major Karl Something-or-Other.'

'She liked older men, Inspector. She felt more at ease with them,' said one of the others—which one, Kohler wasn't sure.

'Oh for God's sake, Nora, she wanted a father figure,' said Marni.

Springtime in Paris, thought Kohler, but one of the SS, which meant, of course, the avenue Foch and Karl Albrecht Oberg, the Höherer-SS und Polizeiführer of France, an acquaintance Louis and he wished they'd never had to meet. 'Couldn't the Sturmbannführer have lifted a finger to stop her from being sent here?'

'He refused,' said Jill flatly. 'There were plenty of *très chic Paris-iennes* to take her place.'

'Begged him to do something, did she?' asked Herr Kohler.

Again that rush of warmth came and though she wanted it to continue, Jill fought it down, yet he had the nicest of smiles. Soft and warm, kind and considerate—boyish, too.

'Well?' she heard him ask, and had to smile softly in return and say, 'That and other things like offering to marry him.'

A sigh would be best and then another smile, thought Kohler. 'But he was already married and had kept that little secret from her?'

Ah mon Dieu, that look of his! 'And now you know why she despised herself.'

The timing had been perfect, but had Jill caught him off guard? wondered Marni.

'That why the séance attempts to contact her father?' he asked.

Even with that terrible scar from the left eye to the chin, he was adorable, thought Marni. Shrapnel? she asked herself. A fencing sword? but that couldn't be possible with one such as this. He was far too down-to-earth and would be accustomed to bullets. 'The attempts, Inspector. There were more than one of them. Five actually.'

The others hadn't moved. 'At fifty American dollars a crack?'

He was making her flash a grin, thought Marni, knowing the others would be thinking the very same thing, especially Jill—that to be alone with Herr Kohler, to feel those hands of his, would be to live that dream. 'At two hundred and fifty, one-fifty, one hundred, and then fifty. Madame Chevreul offered to continue on an installment plan. Mary-Lynn blamed herself for the séance failures and had become convinced her dad must have known all about her affair with the Sturmbannführer.'

'Even the most intimate of details,' interjected Jill, watching for the effect of her words.

'And definitely not approved of,' said Marni, tensely watching him now, the tip of her tongue touching the crowns of her teeth.

'The dead looking down on the living—that it?' asked Herr Kohler.

'Love, yes, as I used to know it,' said Jill.

Louis should have heard her! 'And she was feeling sick the night she died?'

It couldn't be avoided, thought Jill, and certainly Herr Kohler would know all about such things anyway. 'I had found her being sick one morning about a month ago.'

'OK, so every young lady needs a bit of company now and then and the Sturmbannführer couldn't have done it by mail. Did he pay her an extended visit?'

It would be best to be harsh. 'We don't know who the father was,' said Jill, 'only that it definitely couldn't have been him. She wouldn't tell us.'

'She was afraid to,' said Nora. 'You knew she was, Jill, and so did I. Sure, she was looking for a father figure. That's why she was friendly with Colonel Kessler, the former Kommandant. She had never known her own dad, Inspector, and had always regretted this.'

'Brother Étienne said he would find something for her,' added Jill quickly.

'And did he?'

'We were never told,' said Jill.

'Holy bitter, Indian brandy, juniper or yew leaves . . . '

And Marni again, thought Kohler.

'But also aloes and canella bark,' she went on. 'Rhubarb and nitrous ether; an emmenagogue in the hope the uterus will contract and get rid of the problem.'

Becky was looking positively ill, but what the hell had they agreed to hide? wondered Kohler.

'*Ignis sancti Antonii* perhaps,' offered Jill, again intently gazing at him.

St. Anthony's Fire and an ecbolic if ever there was one. The deadly ergot fungus from rye flour or bread made from the same.

'Apiol, Inspector,' said Nora. '*Petrosilium crispum* or common parsley. Large doses of the leaves and stems, or the oil if distilled out, the apiol stimulating blood flow to the uterus, but apiol and the rest of the oil can cause polyneuritis and gastrointestinal haemorrhages if one's luck has run out. Brother Étienne told her not to worry, that "The Grace of God invariably was on the side of the grazer," and that if it didn't work, he'd increase the dose.'

They had put the run on him to see if they could take the heat off themselves, thought Kohler. It was either that or to cover up for one of them. 'Parsley?' he asked.

'*Oui.*'

Just what the hell was this trapper of theirs hiding? 'And did he bring her enough last Saturday?'

Uh-oh, Herr Kohler did have a way about him, and the others would already have noticed it, thought Nora, especially Jill who, like everyone else in the room, had known of the parsley.

'Well?' he asked.

'Late in the afternoon. He'd been delayed. A flat tire.'

'His *petrolette,* Inspector,' said Jill. 'Our former Kommandant allowed him a small weekly ration of gasoline.'

'So that he could make it from where to here and back?'

'Domjulien. It's about eight or ten kilometres if the road is OK.' said Jill. 'If not, he uses the cutter, a small, one-horse sleigh.'

'The former Kommandant OK'd that too,' offered Becky, having at last found her voice again. 'The one who had to leave right after Mary-Lynn fell.'

'The one who left us with that little Hitler who now runs the camp,' said Nora.

The blonde had dried her eyes, the cigarette and the back rub having helped to steady her nerves.

'And now another murder,' she managed under his scrutiny. 'What's happening to us, Inspector? We're the forgotten of this war, but has God also deserted us?'

'Becky, you were out in the corridor,' said Marni. 'You had gone after Caroline.'

'Me? Not likely. I'd have let her wheeze.'

'But you didn't let her,' said Nora gently. 'The corridor light was blinking on and off. She couldn't see a blessed thing at first because it was pitch-dark. You know that as well as the rest of us. She was trying to get at one of her cigarettes when that damned light came back on. You had grabbed her by the wrist to steady her hand.'

'Darkness . . . ' began Herr Kohler.

'Night blindness,' said Jill. 'Caroline had been having a terrible attack of asthma.'

'She was in tears, Jill,' said Becky, 'was very upset and madly searching for those damned cigarettes Madame had hidden on her and you then found. You did, Jill. Please don't deny it. I got out of bed and turned the room light on and tried to calm her.'

'Of course I found them, but then you went out into the corridor after her.'

'Jill, you don't know what you're saying,' said Becky with a wince. 'We were nowhere near Mary-Lynn and Nora. Sure, we heard the scream and then . . . '

'Then what?' asked Herr Kohler, reaching for her cigarette to take a few drags himself.

He was looking at her now, but what did he really see? wondered

Becky. The weakest link? 'I . . . I grabbed Caroline. She had started to run toward the elevator shaft when we . . . we heard Mary-Lynn hit the bottom. The *bottom*!'

She went all to pieces. Nora moved; Jill did too. Both sat at her side and tried to comfort her. The cot sagged.

'You held her, Becky,' said Nora gently. 'When I managed to get up the stairs, I saw the two of you. You saved Caroline. She would have died as well. I'm certain of it. She'd have chanced a look and, in her state and still trying to get her sight back, would have tried to get a breath and fallen.'

Yet hadn't.

'I lit one of her cigarettes,' managed Becky. 'I did get her to take a couple of drags. That's all she really needed. Right away there was a change for the better. She even gave me a weak smile, only to again burst into tears.'

'By then the rest of the floor were out in the corridor, Inspector,' said Jill, 'and others, too. Mrs. Parker soon came up and somehow got everyone calmed down, then closed the gate but couldn't put the lock back on where it should have been.'

'Caroline was upset, that it?' he asked Becky.

'We all were.'

'But before that, before Mary-Lynn Allan fell?'

'Yes. Then too.'

'And was anyone else on the staircase when you went up it at 0100 hours or thereabouts?' he asked Nora.

Herr Kohler wasn't one to fool with. 'Inspector, I was so dizzy, I really wouldn't have known. I was drunk and seeing things. Worms crawling all over me, bats tearing at my hair. I . . . I can't remember a thing.'

Yet had remembered enough. 'And during all of this, where was Madame de Vernon, your other roommate?'

Thank God, he had finally asked, thought Marni, but one ought to be careful, otherwise he would think she'd been pleased with the question. 'In bed, where else?'

'Yet Mademoiselle Caroline was having a severe attack?'

The poor man now looked so helpless, it would be best to tell him, but first her hands would be placed on her thighs and moved to her knees as if wanting him. 'Madame de Vernon claimed it was all in the girl's mind and that Caroline need never have the attacks if she would stop being so emotional and just stay calm and tell herself not to gasp for air.'

The redhead named Marni had lovely green eyes but the offer of the rest, though enjoyable no doubt, had best be ignored for now. 'Well-liked, was she, this Madame de Vernon?'

Had he seen right through her? wondered Marni, disappointed by the thought but glad he had finally asked. 'Hated, more likely. Nothing was ever right. The food, the lack of it, the room, the heat, the cold, the smell, the constant comings and goings in the corridor.'

'Yes, but was the curtain drawn in front of those two beds?'

'Every night.'

'Then she might or might not have been in bed—that it, eh?'

The others were all holding their breath and intently watching him. 'Yes. I . . . I guess so.'

There was even a collective sigh. 'OK, for now, enjoy your supper. I'd better find my partner.'

'Is he *un lèche-cul*?' asked Jill.

An arse-licker, a toady. 'Hardly, but I'll be sure to tell him to interview each of you, then you'll know for sure.'

As with the Chalet des Ânes, the padlock was distinctive and similar: a Harvard long-shackled six-lever, with a twenty-three-centimetre nickel-plated chain that had somehow absented itself by having fallen to the bottom of the elevator shaft.

'Nervous was she, our lock opener?' asked Kohler. No third-storey eyes were watching, but nearby ears behind closed doors would be straining.

'And opened with its key, Hermann?' whispered Louis. 'We would have had no problem picking this, but others might, given the closeness of the nearby rooms and the threat of traffic.'

'We'll have to ask them but is it yet another example of French frugality? Luxury hotels . . . '

'*Ah, mon Dieu*, why must I continually have to defend the *Troisième République*? This lock and the other one are American.'

And left over from the Great War. 'But if opened with its key, who the hell is supposed to be keeping an eye on those, and where are they being kept?'

'Perhaps the new Kommandant will be good enough to tell us.'

'Jundt won't want to ask, since the answer might reflect on Wehrmacht Command stupidity.'

That, too, was a problem, but Louis wasn't yet prepared to leave, even though suppertime had run out. Pacing off the distance to Room 3–38, he turned and followed Caroline Lacy's and Becky Torrence's steps, pausing as if for the one to catch up with the other, the forty-watt overhead blinking on and off, the hotel's wiring still heavily overloaded. 'Is it that Room 3–54's door was left open for Mary-Lynn Allan's return?' he asked.

Kohler shrugged. Louis tossed a disparaging hand at a question that should have been asked of the inmates had opportunity allowed, which it hadn't.

'*Ach,* you don't yet know what they're like,' confided Kohler. 'Just wait until they get *you* between them!'

From the top of the far stairs to the elevator's gate and shaft was but a step or two, but where had her killer been waiting?

The staircase to the attic? indicated Louis. It was just along the corridor and right at the far end of the wing. Step by step they went up it, silently cursing the single overhead light yet searching, too, for some sign. Anything.

'*Ah, bon,*' sighed the *sûreté,* having run a hand under the railing.

Chewing gum. 'Dried?' whispered Kohler. 'Don't forget the cold and the dampness.'

Which would have slowed the drying. 'Spearmint, and fresh enough, though a week old if left by the killer.'

With his pocketknife Hermann gently pried it off. 'Our killer was nervous,' he said. 'The gum was to calm herself. Becky Torrence was the most nervous. Really keyed up. Terrified I'd find out something.'

'Even though she stated she was out in the corridor with Caroline Lacy?'

'At first she denied it but then Nora said she'd seen the two of them together.'

'But only after that one had reached their floor.'

Time . . . Had there been time for Becky to have done something else? 'Becky did say she and Caroline heard the scream and then the bump.'

'But Caroline Lacy, our second victim, can't confirm this, can she?'

'And Madame de Vernon, her guardian, could well have left her bed earlier and none of them in that room would have known.'

They went on up the stairs to the attic only to find its door solidly locked and its rooms closed off for the duration. 'But here we would have had a problem, Hermann, for it's a pin tumbler that would, in a hurry, definitely need a key.'

'But did our murderess have one?'

'For the moment we'll disregard your concluding the sex, but was the killer waiting on this attic staircase for Nora Arnarson and Mary-Lynn Allan to return from that séance in the Hôtel Grand?'

And after the killing had the killer then departed in the confusion? Kohler knew this was what Louis was asking.

'And was Mary-Lynn really the intended victim, Hermann? That, too, must be asked.'

'Or Nora?'

'Or Caroline Lacy, who claimed she was and has since been taken care of?'

They went down the staircase to the ground floor and the cellars. Step-by-step, they patiently searched, but even the leavings of spent chewing gum were absent.

'Everyone must need it, Louis, to seal up holes in their shoes and boots. It works, but only for so long.'

And said like a former prisoner of war.

The barracks, the luxury thirty-suite Hôtel Continental that had been built in 1899, was just to the other side of the casino, with an entrance on the avenue Bouloumié and not hard to find, given the gates to the camp and the barbed wire.

Irritably having an after-dinner cigarette and fussing by the moment, Jundt sat stiffly alone at the head of an otherwise abandoned dining room. Towering pseudo–Gallo Roman columns, after the Emperor Caracalla, were behind him. The modernized update of Art Deco urns was incongruous, their two-metre Kentias looking downright thirsty.

'Kohler, did I not tell you eighteen thirty hours?'

Must everything be *auf nazitisch* with this one? 'Colonel, investigating murder doesn't run on meal times.'

'Cooks do, and from now on you will damn well obey me.'

Had he dreams of becoming another Caracalla? The roast pork was cold, the sauerkraut, too, and the boiled potatoes. The soup, though tepid, was thin until the rest of the meal had been hastily added to that *sûreté* bowl by Louis, along with the one allowed slice of bread.

'There is no wine?' he asked facetiously.

'Kohler, who the hell is that?'

It would be best not to say, The one who caused the delay . . . 'My partner. He's senior to me.'

'A Frenchman? Get him out of here. He can eat in the cellars with the blacks.'

'Colonel . . . '

'Hermann, *einen Moment, bitte*? It's a good idea, isn't it?' said St-Cyr.

'Two of them may still be in the kitchens, Kohler, where they're supposed to be doing up the pots and pans and cleaning the ovens. Those *verdammten* layabouts are probably smoking tobacco they've stolen. They'll be using that gibberish of theirs no one can understand.'

Discreetly gathering up his soup plate and spoon, Louis tucked the half-round remains of the bread under an arm and departed.

'*Ach,*' continued Jundt, flattening his big hands on the table, 'I can't stand the French. Little better than the eastern labourers, Kohler. The horsewhip and a damned good thrashing are what they need. Ten of the best and the boot! Now, what have you for me?'

Thank God, Louis hadn't heard him. 'Two possible murders, a terminated pregnancy, a kleptomaniac, a medium who overcharges, and one datura capsule that contains from two to four hundred seeds and has gone missing.'

'Datura . . . ?'

Instant suspicion had registered, but perhaps it would be wise not to tell him the whole truth. 'Some kind of herb, Colonel.'

'You'd better ask the monk. A kleptomaniac?'

Berlin was going to hear of this last—Jundt had that look about him. 'A compulsive thief, Colonel. Little things of no use or consequence.'

'Or reason for murder? *Das Motiv,* Kohler? Isn't that one of the first things an experienced detective looks for? You *are* experienced, aren't you?'

'We're working on it.'

'Are you indeed? I give you two days. If you don't come up with something solid, Untersturmführer Weber will be given the order he wants: others, Kohler; others from Berlin who will soon sort this matter out. Colonel Kessler was wrong to have asked the Kommandant von Gross-Paris for help. Paris-Central should have known better than to have sent you and that other one.'

'Afraid of what Weber and the boys from Berlin might do, was he, this Colonel Kessler?'

Kohler had earned that gash down his face from the SS during a murder investigation near Vouvray in December, and understood the whip better than most yet had still chosen to remain defiant of authority. 'The Untersturmführer is in charge of security. Colonel Kessler should by rights have left the entire matter in his capable hands.'

A second lieutenant in the SS and wouldn't you know it! 'Your predecessor, Colonel . . . We understand that he availed himself of Madame Chevreul's séances.'

'You want them stopped?'

Must this one be suspicious of everything? 'Not yet. Better to let them continue.'

Jundt tapped that Wehrmacht nose of his with a cautioning forefinger. 'But you think they're involved. I can tell.'

'We just need a little time to sort things out, that's all.'

Perhaps some reason for Kessler's having attended the séances should be given. 'Colonel Kessler's wife of thirty-seven years was killed during the bombing of last September. The house was unfortunately flattened.'

And houses these days were important, considering what the RAF were doing at night and the USAF during the day, but best not to mention that, either. 'Anything else?'

'The Kesslers' little maid, Kohler. A girl the couple had taken an interest in was also killed. I gather he was very close to both of them.'

And if that wasn't a hint, what was? 'Did the medium get through to them?'

Did they talk to each other from beyond the clouds? Such persistence could only mean Kohler thought he was on to something juicy. '*Ach*, I know nothing of such things. Colonel Kessler must have held this Chevreul woman of yours in high regard, for he specifically asked that if you thought it best, she be allowed to continue her valuable work. "It keeps them happy," he said.'

And so much for who was going to be held responsible for letting the séances and all the rest of it continue but . . . 'Untersturmführer Weber told you this, did he?'

'That is correct, since the outgoing Kommandant was no longer present to do so himself.'

'Séances night after night?'

'Sometimes two sessions if the sign of the Zodiac is in conjunction with atmospheric conditions, but no more than ten to fifteen in attendance at any one time. Otherwise, the spirits might become distracted.'

'And ten times fifty American dollars . . . '

'Profitable perhaps, but *ach*, there are others of them who do it. The circle, the holding of hands with the eyes closed and thoughts concentrated, the table that tilts when the fingertips are pressed to it as the questions are asked by the medium who strives to make contact with the deceased. The crystal ball, as well, and the Ouija board, the palm readings too, and tea leaves—they get tea in those parcels of theirs, Kohler. *Tea* when we have none!'

And so much for Jundt's not knowing a damn thing about the spiritualistic goings-on around the camp. 'But these other mediums aren't as good as Madame Chevreul?'

'I believe his very words were, "She is the only one who can do it."'

According to Unterstürmführer Weber. 'Had the Colonel tried others?'

'Several, I gather. Weber will know.'

'And the name of the Colonel's interpreter? Just for the record.'

Did Kohler already suspect there was a killer amongst those at that last Saturday evening's séance? 'Colonel Kessler spoke English, which he was perfecting, and perfect French. That was why he was chosen for this position.'

'Then tell me, why was he recalled?'

Certainly Weber had let Berlin know how things were, Jundt felt, but the recall had come with such short notice that one had to wonder. Perhaps it would be best, though, to offer some other reason so as to distance oneself further. 'The languages, *mein Lieber*. With so many Allied prisoners of war to be interrogated, the High Command have had to make choices. Now, is there anything else?'

The pork was even colder. 'Just one thing, Colonel. Why on earth was that poor unfortunate girl's body left at the bottom of that elevator shaft? Surely someone should have—'

'Removed her? Is this what you mean?'

'You know it is.'

'Kohler, Kohler,' he muttered, shaking his head in dismay at such insubordination. 'Colonel Kessler had ordered that she not be touched until the two detectives from Paris had examined her. Need I remind you that you were to have been here late last Sunday or on Monday? An eight-hour trip becomes a delay of six days? The Unterstürmführer had to have guards posted on every floor of that *verdammt* hotel to keep those bitches from trying to see her and destroying what might well have been valuable evidence. One can't see her, by the way. Not from above. I made certain of that. The elevator shaft is far too dark.'

'Did any of the doctors get to her?'

'The Scotsman was awakened by one of those women who wore

dark horn-rimmed glasses. A Sister Jane then asked that a priest be summoned and the last rites given.'

'And were they?'

Another cigarette would be best, the offer of one expected but withheld. 'The Untersturmführer, as was correct, told her that, like everyone else, God would have to wait for you. That third-storey gate should simply not have been open. When I first arrived here four days ago, the Untersturmführer and I made a thorough examination of every facet of the camp. I tell you Kohler, that padlock was on and secure last Saturday at seventeen hundred hours, as was its chain.'

Yet he'd not been here to see it himself. 'And its key, Colonel, where might that have been kept?'

'You think it was stolen, do you?'

'I'm just asking.'

'Then understand that it is and was exactly where it ought to have been—right with the others on the wall behind the Untersturmführer's desk. As head of security, is that not where such keys should be kept?'

'Only to then have another one borrowed, Colonel?'

'*Ach,* what is this?'

'The stable.'

'You and Weber had best go over things in the morning. Breakfast is at 0600 hours.'

Berlin time, which, in winter, included an hour of daylight saving.

They were coal-black and there were at least twenty of them in the cellar under a distant forty-watt bulb. Some were still eating, others already in bed, the bunks in tiers against the far wall, but what one most noticed, thought Kohler, was how trapped they looked yet grins flashed big white teeth and whites of eyes that quickly darted away from him to politely seek something else.

Les vaches—'the cops'—was written in every one of those grins, of course, but never mentioned. Instead, Louis sat as one in a circle of eight, and the feeling was that the centuries of colonial rule and two European wars these boys and their fathers had never wanted to join, had been set aside so as to return to their roots.

'Ah, bon, Hermann. *Salaam aleikum.* That's peace be with you.'

'Aleikum asalaam,' came the reply. And peace be with you, and then, wonder of wonders, Hermann shook hands with each of them, betraying a knowledge he'd not yet let his partner know of, and asked how things were with each, their answers being, Fine, and how are things with you?

A space was made on the carpeted floor of the circle. Rice, not seen anywhere in years, was in one tin bowl, nice and fluffy and piping hot; a paste in another, a sauce of what looked to be and smelled like mashed sardines, corned beef, potatoes, sow thistle, and kale with broken crackers, walnut pieces, chestnuts, and dried prunes they'd got from God knows where, the whole blended with the liquid remains of the Kommandant's soup as a reminder.

'And Libby's beans, Hermann. Two tins. It's curious, isn't it, since these boys are no longer receiving their Red Cross parcels.'

The rice was taken with the right of hands that had first been washed. It was then rolled into a tight little ball and the fingers of the right hand then transferred to the sauce, which was scooped out as it was added.

Then one sat back and ate slowly, enjoying the meal and the company. Kohler couldn't help but recall those early days of September and October 1940 with Louis guiding him along the muddy roads in the suburb of Saint-Denis to the north of Paris. A little field trip for this Kripo to get to know the city better. Filth, no sewers or running water, ramshackle huts, and kids—kids everywhere— smoke, too, from the ash and slag heaps as well as from the stove-pipes.

Asnières had been no better, nor Villejuif and Vitry-sur-Seine to the south of the city. Fully sixty percent of all common crime in the Département de la Seine had been laid at the feet of men like these, Louis had said, and had gone on to add, "Yet in the last half of 1917 who was it who showed the rest of us they still had the stamina and will to fight?"

And having all but come through a winter like no other but this one.

'Sergeant Senghor here holds the Croix de Guerre with two palms, Hermann, but doesn't wear its rosette.'

Since the guards and their officers would get upset, and he was needed by the others.

'He was just telling me how they came by the tinned beans and the rice.'

That one's grin grew even bigger, yet his gaze passed momentarily over this Kripo to settle on the meal.

'It's a slinging match of the good God, Boss,' said Senghor.

The patois was something else again, thought Kohler, but unlike the French of the middle and upper classes—somewhat easier for a foreigner like him to understand. 'A little barter and on the quiet, eh?'

Had this one really been a prisoner of war as the *sûreté* had said? wondered Senghor. If so, it could only mean trouble, but had it been said as a warning and bargaining chip?

'The guards do it,' said one of the others. Bamba Duclos, thought Senghor.

'Every man for himself, Boss,' said another. Blaise Guéye for sure. 'We defend our beefsteak.'

We're only standing up for our rights. 'And you have a system just like everyone else, eh?' asked Kohler.

'Are not all circumstances to be beaten, Boss, by those over which they form a lid?' replied Senghor.

And no fool. 'Did any of you agree to meet with Caroline Lacy at the Chalet des Ânes?'

'Hermann, go easy. The negotiations are at a delicate stage.'

Still there was that grin, the teeth really very white and big.

'No, Boss. None of us talked to that girl. *Les Américaines* . . . '

'They call us lazy niggers,' said one of the others, also with a grin.

'Even though you cut and haul the firewood and do all the other heavy chores?' continued Hermann, bent on unwittingly laying to waste all that had been gained.

'*Ah, oui, oui,* Boss,' said Senghor, 'but not all of those girls are like that. Only some. The mademoiselle Lacy was young and pretty, and for her sake as well as for our own, none of us would have spoken to her.'

'When others were nearby, eh?'

'Hermann . . . '

'Louis, leave it. Let him answer.'

And spoken like one of the Occupiers: 'For fear of reprisals, Boss. Herr Weber is a tough, hard person.'

'Who remembers well the occupation of the Rhineland, Hermann.'

In 1919, when the Allies moved into the area, France, thinking it best, had sent the *Tirailleurs sénégalais* and other coloureds as their contingent, thus spawning hatred from the occupied Rhinelanders then and retribution now.

'The usual distressful stories of rape, Hermann. Herr Weber had a sister who was found amongst some ruins. Her clothes had been torn, her neck broken.'

'Half our number are out in the forests, Boss, cutting and hauling firewood and logs for lumber,' said Senghor. 'Half are here, and every two weeks we change. Those that are left come home and those that sometimes don't must wait for spring until the ground becomes unfrozen.'

'Hermann, some of the Americans are fond of calling them "fresh." Herr Weber knows this and waits for it.'

'Even though some will wiggle their breasts and bottoms at us, Boss, and try to play us up in other ways, are we not men?' asked Senghor, still with that grin of his.

'And the British?' asked Hermann, wanting to air all the linen.

'What do you think, Boss?'

'That they're far more friendly.'

'Since many of them come from slums like us?'

'And like a bit of fun?'

This Gestapo wasn't going to be easy, thought Senghor, his collaborator of a partner no pushover either. 'They love to haggle, and always it is best that they think they're getting the better of us, so we let them.'

A man of truth, was it? 'And Madame Monnier?'

Hermann still wasn't going to leave it.

'The juju lady's lead henchwoman. With her we must be very careful, Boss, so if we can, we do as asked and get her whatever she wants.'

'Chocolate, Hermann. She has a sweet tooth.'

'The juju lady or Madame Monnier?'

'Both.'

'Extra firewood,' said someone, reaching for more sauce.

'Wallpaper,' offered another, thinking to help his sergeant.

'Paper, Corporal Rivette, to light their stoves and cooking fires.'

'*Ah, oui, oui, mon sergent.* For the fires.'

And for a little something else? wondered Kohler. And where, please, would they be getting it when the rest of the nation couldn't? 'Those golf balls,' he said, pointing to a string bag that held a good hundred and far too many for one game unless an absolutely lousy golfer.

One had best heave a sigh. 'The former Kommandant, Hermann. One or another would caddy for him.'

Was it safer ground, wondered Senghor, or was it more likely that one would never know with these two until it was too late? 'As many days as possible in summer and autumn, Boss. In the spring, too, once the rains had stopped and the ground had dried a little, but he wasn't like the new one. If he had a good day on the course, we were always given a little something.'

'Colonel Kessler tended to spend a lot of time in the rough, Hermann, so they always kept themselves prepared.'

And don't you dare ask where the golf balls came from!

Coffee, made from wild rose petals gathered in summer and dried before roasting, fortunately intervened and was passed round to be sweetened with Borden's condensed milk courtesy of a Canadian Red Cross parcel.

'The Americans distribute all parcels for the Western Allies, Hermann, except for those of the British.'

The things one had to learn. 'Are there Canadians here?'

'Australians, too, and others from the Dominions.'

'But only a few of them, Boss,' said Senghor. 'Mostly the British internees are British but married to Frenchmen, the Frenchwomen in the Grand married to Britishers or widowed, but then there are also the British-British, like the English girls.'

As chorus girls were known in France, since they had invariably come from Britain.

'There is also *bishap,* if you would prefer it, Inspector,' said Louis. 'A tisane of hibiscus leaves, a favourite from the homeland some of them left a good many years ago, but a local source.'

'Brother Étienne again?'

'But of course.'

Woodbines, Players, Chesterfields, Pall Malls, and Camels circulated. Having none to offer and having shared the meal, Hermann hauled out the partnership's bankroll and, peeling off not one but *two* one-thousand-franc bills, added a further five hundred!

'Louis would have left you a paltry fifty, if that,' said the banker.

To all things from the Reich come all things good, was that it? 'You're very free with our money, Inspector.'

'Consider it a down payment. The sergeant understands that we need their help but aren't about to run to Weber or the Kommandant about anything incidental we might discover, since none of these boys would have killed either of those girls. You can see it as well as I can, so it's best we ask for their help.'

'And is that an order, Herr Hauptmann und Detektiv Aufsichtsbeamter?'

'*Jawohl.* Now, let's pack up and get some sleep. We've an early morning ahead.'

3

Vittel and its environs were pitch-dark at 2122 hours, their voices overly loud, or so it seemed.

'How could you, Hermann? Am I to call you "Boss" from now on? When a chief inspector is conducting an interview, his subordinate does not, I repeat *not,* start in as if "fresh."'

'I think they heard you, Louis, even though I had them convinced I really was your boss. Now, tell me what I need to know. How many of those boys knew of you?'

From the old days, those of *sûreté* and *flic* raids that had smashed doors, windows, and walls to grab the running and apply the truncheon both before and after the bracelets.

'I seldom took part in such things. I was away from Paris a lot.'

Hence the loss of the first wife who had run off with a door-to-door salesman or truck driver to marry a railway worker from Orléans.

'I stood back and observed, Hermann. It's what a detective does best.'

And no mention yet of the *sénégalais* dockworkers in places like Marseille and Nice. 'Oh for sure, but did any of them remember you?'

'One, perhaps two. *Ah, mon Dieu,* the Santé and Fresnes prisons were second homes to them. The murder of a disobedient wife who was cleaning maid to the Marquise de Montreuil yet her secret lover; the robbery of the *Crédit industriel et commercial* at 66 rue de la Victoire that was so bungled, the manager, M. Olivet, who had opened the safe, was able to slam it shut and press the alarm button. If I hadn't put them away for threatening to shoot him to death and giving him a heart attack, someone else would have.'

'But are they apt to understand and forgive?'

'Of course not.'

'That sack of golf balls came from somewhere.'

'*Merde,* I was on the point of teasing that out of them!'

'Now, don't go on. Libby's beans, hibiscus leaves, chocolate . . . '

'And night after night the juju woman!'

They hit the main doors of the Hôtel Grand, crossed its massive, high-columned marble foyer and started up one of the twin staircases as the crowd poured from the dining room and surged to a stop.

A sea of female faces looked up at them: round, thin, dimpled, pasty, hollow-eyed, or not—lipstick and rouge on some, and all startled.

'You shouldn't be here,' came the soft-spoken voice of a tiny bit of a thing. 'Those doors are customarily locked at sundown. Men are not allowed in after dark.'

'Police officers are.'

'Hermann . . . '

'Louis, let me deal with this.'

'As you shall, Inspector, for I have long awaited your visit. Now, if you gentlemen would be kind enough to come down and follow me to the Pavillon de Cérès, we can discuss the matter of these tragedies there while enjoying the peace to which I am accustomed when working.'

'Cérès, Louis?'

'The Roman goddess of agriculture.'

'The mightiest of asteroids, Chief Inspector, as defined and discovered by the Italian astronomer, Giuseppe Piazzi, on New Year's Day of 1801. She lies between the orbits of the planets Mars and Jupiter and graciously guides us in our travels.'

A flower in a garden of oft-broken, dried, and crowded stems, a belle both firm and clear, she entered the Pavillon de Cérès but couldn't help but step to one side so as to catch and study their expressions.

The room, projecting from the ground floor of the Grand and overlooking the Parc Thermal, was solarium, sunroom, and more, especially in winter and in spite of its drawn blackout drapes. Art Deco pillars geometrically rose like great golden, honey-coloured lances at some medieval yet modern jousting match, the light automatically stepping the gaze and heart aloft to a central lamp.

'Is there a more godlike room, inspectors? Immediately one feels at peace and in communion.'

The doors had been quietly closed behind them. Three wooden-slatted café chairs had been positioned under that light, two side by side and the other facing them.

'Inspectors, be so good as to sit and close the eyes but for a moment in repose. Let the spirit cleanse itself as the problems of this world arrange themselves in trine, gracing harmony with utter unanimity. When at peace, I will answer truthfully every question you should choose to put to me.'

They did as asked, noted Élizabeth, the Bavarian so much taller and bigger than the Frenchman, but it was in the hands that one felt the difference between the two. The fingers of both were hard and worn, the Frenchman's no more sure, she felt, than those of the other, but in these last there was yet again a delicacy of touch that must surely have come from his having defused unexploded bombs and shells in the Great War. Recently he had suffered a terrible loss and then another. Two young sons in battle, and then a wife, a childhood sweetheart who, having a relative amongst the Nazi *Bonzen,* had been allowed a divorce in order to marry an indentured French farm labourer, a *paysan* from his partner's country.

And that one? she silently asked. That one has also suffered a terrible loss but bears the guilt of having received in the post the challenge of the Résistance, the little black pasteboard coffin reserved for collaborators that have been marked down for working with the Germans, and yet . . . and yet, being away from Paris on an investigation at the time, he had been unable to warn his new wife and little son of what those people and then the Paris Gestapo might well do and did. Leave the bomb the first had left.

'Are we at peace, my brothers?'

'*Jésus, merde alors,* Louis, what the hell is this?'

'Zen, Hermann. Don't blaspheme.'

'*Merci, mon cher* Chief Inspector. The gods are present, the planets observe, and between two of them Cérès flies.'

'Let's start with Mary-Lynn Allan,' said Louis.

'I never discuss the outcome of a séance. I leave that to the sitters.'

'Make an exception,' said Hermann.

'Really, Inspector Kohler, is it that you know so little of my work? I personally am not present except as in the physical sense. If the séance is to be successful, I must transcend the human state so as to be in clairaudience with the one who controls who I am to reach and what that person then has or has not to say, Cérès speaking through me to those whose hands have remained joined and whose eyes have remained closed.'

And if *that* wasn't a dressing down, what was? 'Not all séances are successful, Hermann.'

'*Ah, bon,* Chief Inspector, you *do* have some experience. I thought so!'

'Hermann, if not all the sitters have reached that state of peace . . .'

'In trine, Inspector.'

'The result can be either a total or partial failure.'

She would have to keep the pressure up, decided Élizabeth. 'All must be united, inspectors. Only then will they receive, measure for measure, what they have given.'

Madame Chevreul's accent was definitely of *les hautes* and well educated, too, thought Kohler, but was there not something a touch off? 'OK, so what about that late-night session of last Saturday, early Sunday?'

Herr Kohler was clearly not a believer, nor did he seem to have the self-control to transcend the practical. 'Once again I must stress, Inspector, that I have no knowledge of what went on, only that the séance was a great success. Colonel Kessler, our former Kommandant, was most appreciative, as was Mary-Lynn Allan, whose tears were those of joy. I did worry about the aura the girl exuded, for it was especially pronounced and vibrant. I did decide to warn her to take great care, and insisted on this more than once. As a result,

Colonel Kessler offered to escort her and Nora Arnarson home, as a gentleman should, and right to the door of their hotel.'

'And then?' asked Herr Kohler, still looking as though feeling definitely out of things.

'Sleep would not come. Usually when I retire from a séance, sleep overtakes me immediately—one is utterly exhausted—but on that terrible night, I tossed and turned.'

'And came back down to this room,' said Louis.

'Chief Inspector, I did! I tried to reach Cérès. I cried out to her. I begged her to watch over all, not just Mary-Lynn Allan, but Cérès can be difficult. She . . . she had gone behind the clouds.'

And lost herself amongst the planets! 'Conveniently, eh?' snorted Kohler. 'And the word was out, wasn't it, that Mary-Lynn was sure to run into trouble and did!'

With the consequent increase in reputation, thought St-Cyr, and so much for not being able to recall things, but . . . 'Hermann . . . '

'Louis, this is going to take all night, and unless I'm very wrong, we'll be none the wiser.'

It would be best to be firm. 'Inspectors, a datura seed capsule is missing, and you wonder, too, if Nora Arnarson and Mary-Lynn Allan were drunk on home brew or had taken a tisane of that herb Brother Étienne had prescribed for Caroline Lacy.'

They waited as they should for her to continue. *Bien sûr*, Herr Kohler was now telling himself that she must have connections everywhere, whereas St-Cyr was but quietly impressed. Though they couldn't yet know to whom her connections were: guards to guards, inmate to inmate or guard, or even to the Untersturmführer Weber, who considered himself to be the font of all knowledge. Nor did they yet quite know with what they were dealing, for to be able to reach the gods was to be uniquely gifted, and mere mortal men, being accustomed to dominating women, were reticent and oft-unwilling to accept such a challenge or even to recognize it.

'We always place a lovely cut-glass bowl of water in the centre of our circle, inspectors, and from this I fill my chalice before lifting it to the goddess. Those who wish may dip the fingers to brush the Sign of the Cross over the brow. The water of life is always that which flows from La Grande Source. We do not even use that of La Source Salée, and of course not those of the Marie or Demoiselles, which have all but ceased their issue.'

Vittel's spa waters, but what was it about her, wondered St-Cyr, beyond that deliberate yet carefully contrived evasiveness? 'The water is cold and flat, Hermann. Eleven and a half degrees Celsius and flows at a rate of just over 5,300 litres an hour.'

How good of him to have remembered, thought Élizabeth. 'And with .6039 grams per litre of calcium sulphite, inspectors, and .2393 of magnesium sulphite.'

And a healthy dose of the trots! She could see Herr Kohler thinking this, but his partner quickly covered for him by saying, 'Vittel's waters are odourless and colourless, Hermann, and all are very fresh-tasting.'

'You were here when wounded, Chief Inspector. Your memory is . . . '

'Matched only by my curiosity, madame. Your husband, please?'

He hadn't even questioned her about how she had known such a thing of him. 'Ah, the name Chevreul. Like so many, the war drew me to Paris as soon as the call went out. I had had little enough experience as a registered nurse compared to what I was soon forced to learn. The Marne, of course, and the horrible stalemate that followed its battle. Verdun later on, for the French needed me too, and I could speak the language. Later still, the Somme, of course, and then a ward I will remember for the rest of my life here on earth and will carry to those who have passed over. I paused on its threshold. I *knew*, inspectors; love is sometimes like that, is it not? André had lost his sight— that terrible gas—but he and I . . . how can I say it? He would touch my face and I would know we belonged to each other, but it was not to last, yet I think in no small part he held on for those brief two years of married bliss entirely due to the love we bore each other.'

And so much for financial security—was that it? wondered Kohler. Blond, blue-eyed, petite, and still quite handsome, she was a woman to be reckoned with.

'Chevreul . . . ' began Louis.

Suspicion would be paramount with these two, but no matter.

'It's an old family name. I was left with the Château de Mon Plaisir in the forested hills near Mortagne-au-Perche in Normandy. That is how the house and grounds were always known to my husband and me, and I lived quietly there tending his grave and those of his family until . . . well, until I was forced to remember that I still possessed my British passport. The Occupier, of course, wished the use of the house and stables, and the horses we bred, and of course I have been trying ever since to make them see sense and let me return, yet know I have found a calling here that transcends all others. Now, please, there are questions to which you need both direction and answer. Let me be but your guide and willing servant.'

'Things have been stolen,' said Louis.

'Caroline Lacy had an invitation in her pocket,' said Herr Kohler, snapping his fingers until his partner, digging deeply, retrieved it from a pocket though there was no need.

'The ballet dancer came often to my chambers, inspectors. She seemed sincere. If at first one doesn't succeed, does one not try again and again, and is that not a sign of artistic determination? Léa . . . Madame Monnier finally asked if I could fit the girl in and I, in turn, said to set a date and I would write and send that card you have, which I did. Was her death unpleasant—please, you must spare me the details. I can see the answer already in your expressions.'

'*Ah, bon,*' said Louis, 'you mentioned setting a date, but there is none on the card.'

Of the two, was he the stickler for details? If so, she had best keep it in mind. 'A date, you ask? None was necessary. It was to have been for tonight at 2200 hours sharp.'

'But death intervened,' grumbled Hermann, not believing a word of it.

'Precisely, Inspector, and I shall, in tonight's séance, be asking Cérès to contact that poor child so that she can speak through the goddess to me.'

'And reveal who her killer was or what she wanted to tell the new Kommandant?'

'Hermann . . . '

'No, please, Chief Inspector, let me answer. Caroline was convinced

Mary-Lynn Allan's death was not an accident. Things had been stolen . . . little things; seemingly worthless things. When women have so little, even the smallest, most insignificant item to male eyes could well be the most treasured: the essence of a cherished memory, the feel, the touch, the smell of an object, a bit of cloth, a seashell perhaps—all such things can have their intense value to a woman, no matter how coarse or common she might appear to you men.'

A seashell . . . 'Caroline was asked to bring what she had,' said Kohler. 'Be so good as to tell us what that was?'

Had she said too much, gone too far? wondered Élizabeth. 'Always, for every sitter, the invitation says the same thing: They are to bring something—anything—that will form a bridge to what they most desperately want to know. Cérès needs such items upon which to focus, but as a result of these continual thefts, a degree of bitterness and viciousness far beyond the measure of each loss has entered our community, our two houses, if you like.'

'And the thefts?' asked Louis.

'They happen in an instant. None are planned—I'm sure of this. The thefts are random and governed totally by impulse, and I am certain too, that whoever is doing this, that poor soul is in torment and unable to resist the impulse yet exceedingly clever at accomplishing it and hiding her identity.'

'And her hiding place?' asked St-Cyr.

'Though there are those who search, no one, insofar as I have been told, has ever found it.'

'Hence Madame Monnier's suggesting, Hermann, that if we were to discover who it was, we were to tell the thief that Madame Chevreul would keep on asking even if we didn't confide that information and that soon Cérès would give her the answer.'

'Léa has her uses, Chief Inspector.'

'But has Cérès been more forthcoming?' he asked.

'Chief Inspector, surely you are as aware as I that there are those who steal and those who attempt to.'

'And those who will accuse without sufficient evidence while demanding their anonymity.'

'Precisely! And how, please, am I to differentiate?'

Had she led them into admitting that the séances might well have their uses? wondered St-Cyr. 'If not by placing a suspect and her accuser before you and asking Cérès enough questions to settle the matter.'

'But Cérès only speaks with the voices of those who have passed over and I have no knowledge of what is said through me.'

'But Léa Monnier does?' he asked.

'As do others of my staff.'

'Are the sitters always different?'

'There are the regulars, there are those who have been summoned, those with special needs and requests, and those, as in the cases of Colonel Kessler and Mary-Lynn Allan, who were initiates passing through to becoming regulars. Each séance needs its core of believers. They give the whole process backbone, but even then, many sessions fail because of a doubter. Unfortunately I cannot always weed these out beforehand. Nora Arnarson had her doubts but came, and was allowed to sit, since her dear friend Mary-Lynn required her presence and was uneasy without it. Failure after failure until at last a breakthrough.'

And then a death. 'And the home brew, their state of inebriation?'

Must Herr Kohler continue to be such a doubter? 'I think, if I were you, Inspector, I would ask myself where Nora and Mary-Lynn went *after* Colonel Kessler left them at the door to that hotel of theirs. Mary-Lynn was happy. Tears of joy had filled her eyes. Answers, though I know them not, had been received, having flowed from Cérès through me to her.'

'And to the ears of the other sitters, Louis, not just to Colonel Kessler.'

'Who had grown ever more close to her, Inspector,' she continued.

'Too close?' he asked.

The pregnancy. 'That I wouldn't know.'

But probably did. 'Madame,' said St-Cyr, 'when precisely did the séance end?'

Grâce à Dieu, he had asked, but she would give things a moment, would wait, yes, until the urgency of knowing made Herr Kohler fidget. 'At 2330 hours.'

Had he given the sigh of the defeated?

'And one and a half hours *before* the first killing, Louis,' he said.

'Did Nora not inform you of this, inspectors?'

Ach, how sweet of this celestial dreamer! snorted Kohler inwardly. 'It must have slipped her mind.'

'Did she accompany Mary-Lynn on each of the previous séances that one had paid for?' asked Louis.

'No one pays me, Chief Inspector. The service I provide is absolutely free and freely given.'

'A *yes*, then, to the question,' said Kohler, 'but if one wishes to leave a little gift, one can. That it, eh?'

'Hermann, leave it for now.'

'Louis, this one's been raking it in.'

Herr Kohler would have to be given an answer. 'Nora accompanied Mary-Lynn to each séance that one attended and sat always on her right as instructed by me. Colonel Kessler sat on the girl's left. Beforehand, the couple would exchange pleasantries, the Colonel always asking after her well-being and that of her friends, and if there was anything they needed.'

'And was there?' asked St-Cyr.

Was he not the more dangerous of the two? 'Things like more firewood or even coal if possible for their stoves, or perhaps could he allow another visit from the maid of a roommate. There was a girl in Mary-Lynn's room whose maid had been left to look after that one's flat in Paris on the avenue Henri-Martin and but a few steps from the Bois de Boulogne and lovely, if I do say so myself. There were, I believe, several very valuable antiques and paintings this Jennifer Hamilton had purchased for wealthy clients in America but had been unable to ship due to the hostilities, so she was, understandably, concerned and had asked Mary-Lynn to speak to the Colonel on her behalf.'

Jennifer Hamilton of Room 3–54 the Vittel-Palace, and if this one wasn't well informed, who was? wondered Kohler.

'Her family in Boston have been dealing in European art and antiques for over forty years, inspectors. The girl is really quite shy and very nervous, or so I have been given to understand. Mary-

Lynn was simply trying to help her. Things can be so very confusing for the young when they're away from home only to then find themselves locked up in a place like this for years on end perhaps, who knows? Caroline Lacy and this Jennifer Hamilton had become good friends and would visit back and forth. Nothing untoward, I assure you, though girls of such a tender age as Caroline sometimes welcome the reinforcement of the physical contact and warmth of another who is a little older.'

And uh-oh, was that it, eh? thought Kohler, since up to now they'd been given to understand that Caroline had had to visit *this* building and its British to find someone to talk to, but the doors to the inner sanctum had been softly opened, the wraiths appearing.

'Ah! A little refreshment, inspectors. A choice of chamomile or a particularly delightful tisane of hibiscus leaves and rose hips, sweetened with a touch of honey.'

'Courtesy of Sergeant Senghor, Louis.'

'And Brother Étienne, Hermann.'

And no mention of the datura, thought Élizabeth, but a taste strong enough to mask it—was Herr Kohler not wondering this?

'I think I'll pass, Louis.'

'Sleep calls, Madame Chevreul.'

'It's understandable. You have had a long and what must have been tiring day but surely a cupful will not hurt?'

'There is just one thing,' said St-Cyr. 'Have you yourself lost anything to this kleptomaniac?'

'Me? Why . . . '

Instinctively she had touched the base of her throat and instinctively they had known the answer, which could not, unfortunately, remain totally hidden. 'Why, yes, I have, but it's of no consequence save only that it unites me more with those who have suffered such losses.'

'And the item, madame, just for the record?'

Must St-Cyr be so persistent? 'I have already forgotten it.'

But has Cérès? 'For now then, madame, *bonne nuit*. The morning will come soon enough.'

'But you've not partaken of your refreshment?'

'Another time,' said Louis. 'It'll save us from getting up during the rest of the night.'

The room was pleasant and totally unexpected. Tucked away in a far, third-floor corner of the camp hospital, the former villa of two doctors of thermal medicine, it had not only comfortable beds and a welcome fire in its grate, but warmed bricks tucked in under the covers at the foot of each bed and an unopened, unheard-of bottle of cognac, a Bisquit Napoléon.

'Pure gold, Louis.'

'And two unopened packets of Pall Malls. A wonderful welcome, *mon vieux.*' That is, *Is someone trying to buy us?*

'*Liebe Zeit,* let's enjoy a sip and light up.' *Or simply loosen our tongues?*

Hermann indicated silence. Both began to search, and when they found the microphone placed behind a framed print of a Vittel *demoiselle* taking the waters circa 1894, they left it exactly where it was.

'In the morning, Louis, I'd best fill Untersturmführer Weber in on things. We're going to need all the help he can give us.'

'But for now let's get some sleep. *Mon Dieu,* I don't know about you, but I'm exhausted.'

Pillows were thumped, a mattress sighed. A cork was pulled, glasses were clinked, a match struck, and an appreciative sigh given as Louis went over to the blackout drapes and, indicating that this partner of his should switch off the light, opened them and silently felt about until he had what he wanted.

Together, bundled against the night and with bottle, glasses, and cigarettes in hand, they slipped out onto the porch to softly close the doors behind them.

'There are fifteen of these villas, Hermann. All but a few were built in 1930 along the same chalet lines, though this one is larger and earlier, 1899 if I remember it clearly. Terraces, sunrooms, and porches forced the *curiste,* during his twenty-one-day course of treatment to take the infrequent sun.'

'When not busy chasing his mistress or downing that damned water with her?'

Cigarettes were enjoyed, the glasses given more than a splash while above them the stars were out, and were it not for the degrees of frost, the night would have been fine.

'You or me, Louis?'

'Me, I think.'

'Agreed.'

'An elevator gate that must have been closed in September 1939 and padlocked late in '42 when the Americans were moved in, is unlocked and left open and yet only Caroline Lacy claims it wasn't an accident? She insists that she saw what happened yet suffers from night blindness and a shortage of breath that has made her panic.'

'And claims that she was to have been the intended victim.'

'Only to be silenced a week later, Hermann. Surely all others in the Vittel-Palace must have known it was no accident?'

'Were they afraid to say it was murder, Louis? Mrs. Parker did come up to calm them. Even she stated it was an accident.'

'But did they agree to say that, and if so, was it out of fear of making life far more difficult for themselves?'

'Since Weber would have turned the place upside down and found someone to accuse, even if the wrong person.'

'Ah, bon, it's possible they all felt it was murder, Hermann, yet were afraid to state this, except for Caroline who might just have been obstinate.'

'But who then made an even bigger nuisance of herself only to become a corpse that was then tidied.'

'Which brings us to Madame Chevreul, who wishes us to concentrate our efforts on Jennifer Hamilton, roommate of Mary-Lynn Allan and close friend of Caroline Lacy.'

'While Mrs. Parker, patently forgetting about Jennifer, suggests we look elsewhere, namely the Grand, since Caroline had few if any friends in the Vittel-Palace and had been shunned.'

The cognac was infinitely smooth, the two of them leaning on the railing to look out over the darkened polo grounds and racetrack.

'The one lives the dream of being the mouthpiece of Cérès, Hermann.'

'And unless I'm mistaken, the other fancies herself as having come from the family that make the world's foremost fountain pens.'

'Caroline Lacy lived the dream of being a prima donna and badgered everyone about it who would listen.'

'While her governess, Louis, dreamt and still dreams of what?'

'A dog-eared photo from 1910 of a villa in Provence, better ones in her suitcase but none from beyond that date.'

There had also been a photo of Pétain on that wall above her bed and a map of France that hadn't even recognized the Defeat. 'A governess who thought that girl's asthma was nothing more than a state of mind,' said Hermann, who, as a former prisoner of war, instinctively cupped his cigarette in hand to hide even that tiny glow.

'Yet insisted Brother Étienne, the visiting monk, provide an overabundance of datura seeds, from which she dutifully ground a little powder to mix with the dried and shredded leaves and stems.'

'Before rolling them into the cigarettes that girl could not have done without. Roommate Becky Torrence claims Caroline was very upset and in tears when she came back to their room and began to search for her cigarettes, Louis. Becky turned on the light and tried to calm her while Jill Faber found them. Though she at first avoided admitting it, Becky followed Caroline out into the corridor to help her. Oh for sure, both heard Mary-Lynn fall, but was Becky really the friend in distress? And where, please, was Madame de Vernon while all of this was going on?'

'Two victims, Hermann, the one claiming she was the intended and that the first killing definitely wasn't an accident.'

'Even getting someone to arrange a meeting for her with one of the *sénégalais*. It has to have been one of those boys, Louis. A note in French and then in *Deutsch*.'

'But not translated by Mary-Lynn, who spoke German so fluently the former Kommandant had offered to help make her life a little easier, and perhaps that too of Jennifer Hamilton.'

Whose flat in Paris was full of client antiques and artwork, and whose maid was looking after things and visited her when allowed. 'But did the killer make a mistake, Louis, and compound it with the second killing?'

'Madame Chevreul having warned that first victim to take great care.'

'And having enhanced her reputation by that one's death, she then sends an invitation to the second, telling her to bring what she had but not telling us a damned thing more.'

Their glasses were refreshed. Another cigarette was found and shared. Louis would be longing for a little pipe tobacco. 'That juju woman has power well beyond her celestial orbit. Those skirmishers of yours were afraid of her and you know it.'

'Wallpaper, Hermann. Why use that to light a stove when collabo newsprint from Paris is clearly available?'

'And whatever Léa wants, Léa gets.'

'But not golf balls, which must have come from over there. Beyond the racetrack, there's a golf course and beside it, the Hôtel de l'Ermitage that was built in 1929 to offer luxury in excess even to that of the Grand, only to find the Great Depression on its doorstep and then, after but a few years, this war and Occupation.'

'Mothballed, is it?'

'Certainly it is well on the other side of the wire that encircles the landscaped parts of the Parc Thermal that are open to the inmates, and that has to mean it's out of bounds for them but not necessarily to our Senegalese, since Colonel Kessler must have gone there with one or two of them to get his golf balls.'

Again they paused, both warming their cognac by cupping the glass in hand, Hermann even blowing cigarette smoke into his.

'A truck driver from Limehouse, Louis.'

'Madame Léa Monnier wearing jewellery as if she was a safe deposit box.'

'She'd have spent time at Besançon.'

Where, on December sixth, 1940, the British females, almost four thousand of them who had been rounded up by the French police, had been housed in the old brick military barracks that had been vacated but a few days before by a division of the Army of the Armistice, who had mistakenly thought the Wehrmacht were to be moving in and had wrecked the place.*

No heat, no window glass, and no plumbing, to say nothing of the absence of food and water in the first few days. Latrine trenches, then . . . there had only been three of them, and in winter who could have dug others? And that, why, that had left the courtyard to be used even during the blizzards that would have hit the plateau.

'The old, the young, the very young, Hermann. It's a cross we all have to bear, not just me.'

'You weren't to blame, and neither was I. We didn't even know about it until later that month.'

'*Ah, oui, oui,* Inspector, but their graves are witness and I must go there someday to pay my respects.'

'Don't take it so hard. Our Léa's a survivor.'

'As is Madame Chevreul, who claims she came to France as a nurse, but when exactly, and from where? What family? What circumstance? There is something about that woman that isn't quite right, Hermann. Wealth, breeding, and a good education, yet she chooses as her henchwoman one with whom she can have absolutely *nothing* in common?'

'Did our truck driver become an ambulance driver in that other war?'

It had happened lots of times. 'Did they meet en route only to lose contact for all the intervening years and then find themselves together again in Besançon? Interred, the two of them, but whereas the one now wears a fortune, the other doesn't even wear her wedding ring yet speaks fondly of undying love and a departed husband who left her his family home and Percherons.'

'Six hundred francs, Louis. That's all they were allowed to keep on arrival.'

'Watches and jewellery . . . Shouldn't they have been handed over and put into safekeeping on receipt of the usual piece of paper?'

---

* The *armée de l'armistice* of 100,000 was disbanded on 21 November, 1942, after the Wehrmacht took over the *zone libre* on the eleventh of that month.

'Maybe Colonel Kessler felt he'd have a riot on his hands.'

'Both at Besançon and here, Hermann? Perhaps, but some items being handed over and others not?'

'Those last having been kept hidden.'

'That still doesn't explain the blatant display.'

'To which others were definitely silent, but afraid to mention it for fear of Léa beating them to a pulp?'

Ash was flicked, their glasses drained. 'Perhaps, Hermann. Perhaps.'

'Things have been stolen. Little things, not the big and the obvious.'

'Items so insignificant to male eyes we couldn't possibly realize that they could well have been the essence of cherished female memories no matter the coarseness of their former owners. Why make a point of saying such a thing?'

'And when asked, Louis, admit to having suffered such a loss herself but having forgotten entirely what it was.'

'Another splash, *mon vieux*. Just a touch to wet the throat.'

'Four splashes. Weber might decide to remove the bottle tomorrow.'

'*Ah, bon, merci*. Now, where were we? Madame Chevreul gets us to accept that for her to differentiate between a suspect and that one's anonymous accuser, she must place both among the sitters while asking Cérès to speak through her, thereby disclaiming all responsibility.'

It had to be asked. 'Have they been holding secret trials?'

'Indirectly she did ask us to understand that she had no other choice but to look into the matter.'

'Since she had lost a little something herself, Louis! Now tell me where Nora and Mary-Lynn went *after* that final séance and why our trapper didn't bother to enlighten us. An hour and a half. Drunk and hallucinating—that much Nora *did* tell me, Jill Faber claiming Mary-Lynn was the drunker, Nora insisting that she was and that she couldn't remember a thing, but obviously could.'

'And was very afraid, Hermann, and thinking she was the intended victim—is that it? She knew where that spare key to

Madame de Vernon's suitcase was kept and had looked into that little box well before I did, had known there had originally been three of the seed capsules.'

'But who needs one of those when there's a handy elevator shaft and a pitchfork that's been branded by the First American Army?'

It was a soldier's breakfast, if one who was under fire could ever be so lucky, and served piping hot at 0610 hours in the casino's canteen: Schmalzbrot und Stammgericht—black bread with lard spread on it—before salting, and the dish of the day, a viscous soup of potatoes, potato flour, lard, salt, and suggestions of questionable meat.

Weber was already having a cigarette; Louis had wisely stayed behind.

'Golf and the clay pigeons, Kohler? Attending séances? *Mein Gott,* what was I to have done? Colonel Kessler was all too familiar with the enemy. Berlin were not pleased.'

'The murder of Mary-Lynn Allan finished him off, did it? A girl in different circumstances?'

'*Ach,* you use the polite term for pregnant? That damned whore repeatedly opened her legs. She spoke our language. She knew books and Colonel Kessler loved to talk of them with her because she also gave him the opportunity to polish his English. A coffee, a glass of wine in his office; strolls, too, in the park, and visits to the dentist in town? I tell you, Kohler, when that one claimed he couldn't come here as required, Colonel Kessler took her in his *own* car, himself behind the wheel and *knowing* the prisoners were never allowed to leave the camp unless under orders from Berlin!'

There was more, and Kohler was waiting for it with bread and spoon poised as he should.

'That monk he favoured tried to help her, but is it that Colonel Kessler told him what to do, Kohler? Milk, cheese, eggs, soap, herbs, and honey—always that monk had a little something for that girl. Had he been *paid* to bring her things that the others couldn't afford? Things the child might need in the womb?'

And if that wasn't a hint, what was, the bread being sour, the soup bringing but memories of that other war and idiots like this. 'Your superior officer did say Brother Étienne was harmless.'

'A homosexual is harmless?'

Must he be so shrill? 'When Colonel Kessler telephoned the Kommandant von Gross-Paris, he mentioned a bell ringer.'

'*Ach,* I thought so. The brother rings the order's bell for vespers.'

Again the Kripo waited like a dog for its master to tell it to continue eating. 'He also oversees their dairy, Kohler. Endless vats of milk, cream, and whey. Butter and cheeses, the Port-du-Salut those people call it, and the Camembert.'

'Is he into soap as well?'

'And the black market, you ask?'

'I'm just filling in details.'

'Then keep in mind that we're going to get the monk on that charge if needed.'

And from three to five years of forced labour, if lucky. Weber was a dyed-in-the-wool Nazi who looked like a heavyset schoolmaster, boyish even at the age of thirty-two, the light brown hair cut in military style, the big hands folded on the table as at a high-level conference, the gaze not only steadfastly watchful but accusative, the world at large always being distrusted. The jaw was bony and prominent in defiance, the frown permanent, the look perpetually wounded, so one had best ask, 'Does the brother also bring things for the Senegalese?'

The shoulders were drawn back, the hands placed flatly on the table before him. 'He is friendly with all and makes no distinction whereas I do. My sister Sonja, the light of a small boy's life, was torn from me, Kohler. Ripped! Ended! A Friday, 23 December, 1921, at 1807 hours. Left behind the burned-out shell of the house on the Rheinstrasse where I used to play with my friends. She had been to the Liebfrauenkirche nearby to distribute soup to the destitute and had given, I tell you—*given*—a cup of it to one of those . . . those *Neger Untermenschen*. He was "cold," he said, when arrested and beaten senseless by the men of our district. *Cold,* Kohler!'

In 1921 and the Allied occupation of the Rhineland: the Americans having negotiated a separate treaty with the Germans on 2

July, which their Senate had then ratified on 18 October of that year; their troops had left, France's moving in to take care of things in Koblenz. A Negro subhuman.

'He followed her on her way home. It was getting dark. He hit her twice to silence her before . . . '

Even now Weber couldn't speak of it, tears moistening his dark blue eyes. The Nazi Party pin was touched as if a talisman—the badge, too, of a party cell leader and the one for a *Motorgruppe* in 1937 when he must have been a navigator in the rally car of a friend, or had helped out in the repair pit, and so much for who his sister's killer had really been.

'Let me tell you, Kohler, they are paying for it now and I'm making sure they do.'

Louis would advise backing off. 'But does Brother Étienne bring things for them?'

'The soutane has many hiding places, the clergy being the most insidious of liars, but things are going to change now that he no longer has the protection of our former Kommandant. The brother just hasn't realized it.'

And Weber would now have the backing of Jundt. 'Colonel Kessler allowed him a gasoline ration?'

'And complete freedom to come and go as he wished, often staying later, I tell you, Kohler, than the 1700-hour curfew for all visitors and non-camp personnel.'

'Did they often have a little chat on the way in or out?'

'Often. Things were handed over. I know this for a fact. A round of that cheese he makes, a kilo of butter—some of the order's *Schnapps*. This I have seen.'

'But did they talk about the camp and its inmates?'

Had this *Schweinebulle* the snout now to the ground? 'Brother Étienne was full of stories he then embellished for the colonel's ears.'

'An *éminence grise* or simply an informant?'

'Both, Kohler. Both, but his usefulness has been brought into question with the change in command.'

'You've other informants and don't need him.'

Would Kohler now understand how useful this head of security could be to him if approached properly? 'I have never had any need for his services. Cigarette currency, *ja*? As a former prisoner of war, you will know that tobacco paves the road with gold. Those bitches will answer anything just so long as I give them a smoke. Both the British *and* the Americans.'

And Kessler hadn't entirely trusted this one's informants and had used the brother's word on such things. '*Ach,* my partner and I enjoyed the cigarettes and cognac. That was kind of you.'

And no question yet, thought Weber, of where the directive was on the first killing, a document that Colonel Kessler would most certainly have left for them, especially since he had been using the whore. '*Gut.* It's that partner of yours I want to speak to you about, but come. A little tour of our operations here will, I think, be of some use.'

'Louis should be with us.'

'It's better we leave him behind. Then we can speak as country-man to countryman.'

Sister Jane, the British nun in charge of the other nursing sisters at the hospital had seen many wars, not just this one, and when she filled the doorway to the room Hermann and he had been allotted, St-Cyr knew it.

'Chief Inspector, Madame de Vernon isn't well. If you were to place in front of her those items you took from Caroline's pockets and have hastily gathered from your bed to keep from my eyes, she might . . . well, I hesitate to say.'

'At the first sign of trouble, I'll call you.'

Must this *sûreté* be so stubborn? 'Can you not understand there may well be no outward sign? Her state of illness isn't physical. It's mental. We have little enough sedative. Already we have had to use three ampoules. I really can't afford to use any more. She cries and no one gets any peace, not our other patients, nor ourselves or the doctors. Last night was but the exception.'

And this morning as well. 'She knew my partner and I were in-house and just along the corridor?'

'*Oui, c'est correct*. She's had a hard life. First the loss of her family's home. Her husband sold it without even telling her.'

'Then ran off to spend the money with his mistress who was not only beautiful but fifteen years younger?' It was really just a guess.

'That, too, is correct, but he also had a passion for casinos, as did the girl.'

'And the money was lost?'

'I believe so.'

'Yet still she uses her married name?'

'Why, I simply do not know. Perhaps the Great War intervened as it did for so many.'

Widows being the norm. 'How long had Caroline Lacy been in her care?'

'Three years. Four perhaps.'

From the age of fifteen. 'Sister, the girl's passport and papers were not with her.'

'And since the camp's administration require us all to look after our own, this being but an internment camp and not one for prisoners of war, you are wondering if they had been stolen?'

'It's possible.'

'Not with Madame. She insisted she carry Caroline's passport and papers at all times as well as her own.'

'Even in Paris?'

'Inspector, I think you will find that poor unfortunate girl never went anywhere without Madame.'

'Until Vittel.'

'Even here she was being constantly told to stay in their room unless instructed to fetch something, but always to come straight back.'

'The girl rebelled.'

'Can the young not be headstrong? She desperately wanted and needed friends. I myself, when taking the air in the Parc Thermal, occasionally spoke with her. Never have I seen a child so anxious for the kind attention of another human being, someone other than . . . May God forgive me . . . than that woman. The girl couldn't dress, bathe, eat, or sleep without Madame's scrutiny and tongue. Caroline was never right; always there was castigation. An aspiring ballet dancer? Does one not need self-confidence in measure and to build it repeatedly?'

'Was the girl afraid of her?'

It would be best to tell him. 'Afraid is perhaps not the word I would use. Terrified would be better.'

And the months, the years passing her by in a place like this. 'Why didn't Madame see that the girl was sent home before the bottom fell out of France?'

'Or before the Americans entered this war? To all requests from Caroline's family, I am sure there were . . . '

'Please continue.'

She crossed herself.

'It is only that to all requests from them, I am sure there were delays aided and abetted by the Occupier and the regulations that swamped everyone. The post wouldn't arrive or be lost en route, the telegram addressed incorrectly or not received, the telephone line disconnected. Perhaps Caroline was the daughter Madame never had. Perhaps she represented something Madame could never attain. One thing is certain and this you must understand. To Madame, Caroline Lacy was hers to control. Now that this duty is gone, Madame has found life bankrupt. Please be gentle. Try not to challenge her, lest we have another insane flood of tears and she does herself grave injury.'

A nod would suffice. The room was just along the corridor. Propped up in bed, Madame Irène de Vernon had steeled herself for the interview and had no doubt been defiantly waiting for hours. The rounded shoulders and prominent bosom were swathed in a crocheted shawl of many years, two knitted cardigans, and a white blouse. A strand of pearls, her mother's perhaps and saved from the ravages of time, war, and camp by her tongue and spirit of will was beneath the double chin, the neck powdered. The pudgy hands and thick wrists looked capable enough of using a pitchfork. Several modestly expensive but showy rings, on the fifth, fourth, and middle finger of the left hand gave her station in life and determination to resist bartering them off out of necessity—a wristwatch also—but of tears there were none, though the grey eyes behind the wire gold frames were red, the lids puffy.

The cheeks were pale, in spite of applied rouge saved also from those same ravages, the reddened lips thin and uncertain now that she took him in a little more.

'Police' was written in the look she gave. The short, curly dark auburn hair was hesitantly touched and then lightly primped.

'Madame, a few small questions. Nothing difficult.'

'*Questions? Difficultés*? Sister, am I to be subjected to an interrogation?'

Ah, merde, need she be so excitable?

The sister tried. '*Patience, ma chère Madame. Patience.* Please just listen to the Chief Inspector. He and his partner, Herr Kohler, must . . . '

'A German? A member of the Gestapo?'

'A detective, madame. He and the Chief Inspector need all the help we can give them.'

'He has questioned you already, has he?'

'*Oui,* a little.'

'And *what,* please, have you told him? That I controlled Caroline's life with an iron fist? That she was rebelling and was terrified of me? Ah, I can see that this is what you have done. Crucified me while in your care. Well, just you wait!'

'*Ah, bon,* madame,' interjected St-Cyr. 'It's essential I establish a few simple details.'

The look was swift. 'Simple? An innocent in my care is violently murdered? A dear, sweet life taken and you treat the matter as simple when I am left alone? *Alone,* I tell you!'

'Chief Inspector, please be gentle. Gentle, you understand?' Sister Jane implored.

'Certainly, Sister. Certainly. Madame, let's go back a week ago, to the night Mary-Lynn Allan fell.'

'Of her own accord, is that not correct?'

'Perhaps. It's still under consideration.'

'Is it? That girl and others in her room, and in ours, *encouraged* my Caroline and that . . . that Jennifer Hamilton of Room 3–54, the same as that first one's room. Holding hands in the corridors and on the staircases? Flirting? Kissing when they thought others were not watching?'

Sister Jane gestured in despair and said, 'Madame, you don't know that.'

'I do, I tell you! Brushing up against each other in the crowd for bread and soup. Making eyes? Writing notes? Wanting to attend one of that . . . that Chevreul woman's séances? Wanting to talk to the dead? What dead, Inspector?'

'You tell me.'

'Ah, Sainte Mère, Sainte Mère, why must I be put to the fire like Jeanne d'Arc? Those others in that room of ours, that Jill Faber. They *thought* Caroline's disobedience a cause for mirth and whispered asides, but wait until I tell you about them, then we will see who is laughing.

'That Faber girl and the Senegalese, Inspector, that Marni Huntington and the guards; Becky Torrence, too, I tell you. It wouldn't surprise me if they hadn't arranged a little liaison for my Caroline just to teach the girl what sex with a man was really like to them and that she had absolutely no reason to be afraid of it, that everything I had told her was wrong, Inspector. *Everything!*'

Was this one about to have a heart attack? 'Madame, let us hold the lightning and the thunder while we let the rain wash away the clouds.'

'Intransigent. Capable of deceit . . . '

'Yes, yes, but please don't start the typhoon up again. Mademoiselle Caroline had rebelled. She had finally, after many attempts, arranged to attend last night's séance with Madame Chevreul.'

'Only to have my Caroline not present. *Not present,* Inspector, because of her murder!'

'Yes, yes, but whom did she wish to contact and what was so important?'

Merde, had she let her tongue run away with her? 'I don't know, and now never will. *Never,* I tell you.'

But Jennifer Hamilton might—this was written clearly in Madame's moistening eyes and she now realized that this *sûreté* had seen it.

'De Vernon, madame? You were married to an American.'

It couldn't be avoided. 'A man who insisted I have an American passport so that he could take me to visit the mother who had all but disowned him. Now look what that passport has done: made me, who has always been a French citizen, a prisoner in my own country.'

'But what city or town was he from?'

The head was tossed as if struck, suspicion instantly registering. 'Why should that have any significance?'

'Please just answer.'

'Or you will have me arrested? A woman bereaved. *Une sainte* who did everything she could for that girl with little thanks, I tell you.'

'Now, now, madame, please calm yourself,' urged Sister Jane. 'Your heart. You know what the doctors have said. You know it will only do harm if you get upset again.'

'You said it, Sister. I did not!'

They waited as they should, Sister Jane with eyes downcast, the chief inspector silent. 'Barre, Vermont. His family had made a fortune in granite and tombstones but he . . . well, he was simply not cut out for it. He was wounded at Cierges-sous-Montfaucon on 29 September, 1918, and died in 1920 leaving me without a sou. Now I have only the pension, but it never comes.'

And so much for his first name, the years between 1910 and 1918, and for remaining married to him. 'Were his wounds treated here in Vittel?'

Did this *sûreté* actually *think* he was on to something? 'Surely, Inspector, you shouldn't need to ask, or is it that you spent the years of that war in Paris?'

He didn't answer, but felt for his pipe and tobacco pouch, and seeing that the latter was indeed empty, put it away but held the pipe for comfort.

'On the night of Saturday to Sunday, the thirteenth and fourteenth, madame, were you awakened by the screams and tears of the others? Mademoiselle Lacy must have been terribly upset.'

Ah, bon, how perfect of him. 'Awakened, yes. One of the others was with her.'

'Becky Torrence, the blonde?'

'*Oui.* They spoke rapidly. The Torrence girl said that Caroline must be mistaken, that no one would have pushed Mademoiselle Allan, but Caroline, she . . . she wouldn't listen and said she had seen someone push the girl. A shadow, she said, and that she herself had been grabbed by the wrist and had then been pulled back from the brink by Mademoiselle Torrence.'

This he readily swallowed as a *sûreté* should. 'Inspector, that girl of mine couldn't have seen a thing. The room light had been on. Caroline had been unable to find her cigarettes in the dark. The corridor light was off, then on, then off mostly and had been like that for days. When stepping from a lighted room into darkness it would take her a good ten minutes for the eyes to have adjusted enough for her to have seen anything. We were planning to grow more alfalfa shoots to give her the necessary Vitamin A.'

'And what about you? Where were you, exactly?'

And said like a compiler of notes but one who had written nothing down. 'I had been asleep, had I not? Jill Faber, the one who is friendly with the Senegalese, finally found the cigarettes for her where I had left them out on that . . . that thing they call a table. Caroline went into the corridor, the Torrence girl turning off the light and closing the door after following her out. Jill . . . that Jill girl is also friendly with the guards, Inspector. She and the others put things together and she takes them to trade, though that is forbidden. She also places barter notices on the board in the empty dining room so that all in the lineups will see them. Chocolate for a needed box of matches, chewing gum . . . '

'Spearmint?'

'*Oui.* They receive that in their parcels, but I don't care for it. Mostly when not trying to obtain paper from the guards for the toilets, extra firewood, or more and better vegetables—an onion perhaps—she tries to pry news from them, but the guards are very hesitant with that for it, too, is *verboten*.'

'She speaks German?'

Why should he be so anxious? 'A little. I really don't know how much.'

'Are extra favours then offered?'

How polite of him to shield the sister's ears. 'By some perhaps.'

'But not by Jill Faber?'

One must be firm with this one. 'That I didn't say, Inspector. That one did, however, speak of the Senegalese in terms that would burn the ears of a saint. She doesn't wonder what sexual intercourse with such would be like. She describes it in vivid detail for the others. Caroline and I, from behind our screen, would often hear them whispering and tittering at night, especially after someone down the corridor had cried out in ecstasy or begged for more. The things I have been forced to overhear and accidentally witness . . . '

'Yes, yes, so when Caroline took up with Jennifer Hamilton of Room 3–54 you were upset.'

'Wouldn't you have been had you the responsibility of keeping that child safe and pure? Wicked is what I think of such behaviour. Wicked, I tell you.'

'But you were asleep. The light was off.'

'At first, yes. Earlier the Faber girl had been flashing around in the nude with her towel, having just come from the bath. Mocking me. Warming her *cul* at the stove and then her *nénés* and her *chatte*. Telling the others that she was going to ask that . . . that Parker woman to request the Kommandant to have the swimming pool filled this coming summer. "Oh *là, là,*" she said, snapping the towel away. "No bathing suits, eh?" Their French is terrible, Inspector. Every day and night the ears are assaulted.'

'When they weren't speaking English?'

'*Oui.* I understand it too, just as well as they.'

'And they know this?'

Ah, bon, she had struck a nerve. 'They are still uncertain. Me, I never speak it to them, nor did Caroline. We were in France, therefore we spoke a civilized language. Jill was always leaving her laundry under that cot of hers for days, Inspector. Days. The smell.

'Farting . . . Enjoying the sound of it, knowing she would cause me to cringe and shout at her. Never enough food. Always taking more than allowed. Borrowing things without asking. I tell you, I have lived in hell. No privacy. Always someone watching. No peace, no quiet, no pause in the corridor traffic or exploration of the room, the overt, shameful promiscuity of girls with girls . . . '

'Yes, yes, the laundry. Mademoiselle Caroline's brassiere. Ah, I have it here.'

Merde! 'She . . . she had left it in Room 3–54, Inspector. I . . . I made her wash it.'

'Yes, but who returned it and when?'

'On Friday early. The . . . the Hamilton girl. Jennifer.'

'And how long had it been missing? Come, come, madame, it's necessary that you answer.'

It would have to be said. 'Since . . . since a week ago last night.'

'*Ah, bon,* so on the evening of Mary-Lynn Allan's death, Caroline Lacy was not in Room 3–38 but with Jennifer Hamilton in Room 3–54—is this what you are saying?'

Some things must choose their time and place. '*Oui.*'

'Until when, exactly?'

'That I don't know. I had gone to bed. At my age . . . '

'Madame, she had disobeyed you?'

'And had slammed the door of that room in my face, Inspector. My face!'

'You weren't asleep, were you?'

'I was, and that is the truth. I was emotionally exhausted.'

'Her heart, Inspector,' managed Sister Jane.

'Later I did hear Caroline struggling for breath but she had done it so often, I . . . All right, I let her search for the cigarettes and matches that I had left out for her.'

'But not in their usual place?'

'The room light was finally turned on.'

The screen would have been drawn, but in her panic, the girl might not have realized Madame's bed could well have been empty, and neither would any of the others. 'The datura, madame. The others have said that you insisted the girl's asthma was but a state of mind yet you demanded that Brother Étienne give you not only the dried leaves and stems, which are usually quite sufficient, but far more of the seeds than he felt prudent.'

The little box was found in a pocket and placed on the bed before her.

She would snap her fingers, thought Irène. She would demand what was necessary as was her right. 'The warrant, Inspector. Even here we are still under French law, and to have searched that suitcase of mine or that of Caroline, you must first consult the magistrate who reviews the evidence and only then decides if such a document is necessary.'

'Hermann gave me the OK.'

'The Gestapo?'

'That is correct. Now, please, the datura.'

'Perhaps it is that you had best ask the brother, since not only was he treating my Caroline but Jennifer Hamilton, though not for the same condition.'

Were the seeds to have then taken care of that one? he wondered. Not only had there been Caroline's outright disobedience, there must have been hatred and jealousy.

'And on the afternoon of Caroline's death, madame?'

'The touch of a cold. One has to be careful at my age. The girl wished to take the air and I . . . I foolishly agreed to let her and must blame myself.'

'Yes, but had she arranged to meet someone?'

'That Jennifer Hamilton, is this what you have discovered, that my Caroline had been going to meet her to end their affair?'

'Why would she have done that?'

'Because on the night the other one died, she and that . . . that Hamilton girl had been arguing. My Caroline had been very upset and in tears.'

'Yet she had slammed the door in your face?'

'That is correct.'

'Only to then come back to Room 3–38 in tears before the mademoiselle Mary-Lynn Allan fell?'

'*Oui.*'

'Jennifer and Caroline having had much more than a simple lover's tiff?'

'*Oui.* Both were . . . were in tears. I'm sure of it. Why else would she have killed my Caroline?'

'And before your ward left the room on Friday?'

'I asked, as was my duty. She said, "It's not what you think," and I . . . why, I left it at that.'

'But must have known her coat pockets were full of things to trade.'

'I needed aspirins. None had come in our latest parcels. My headaches . . . The neuralgia, the migraines . . . Caroline said she would see what she could do. A breath of her former kindness and love for me. I was encouraged. It is a memory that will stay with me.'

Yet Jill Faber was the room's trader. 'One of the Senegalese?'

'Inspector, she would not have gone to one of those, not after what that . . . that Faber woman had said of them. *"Une sacrée bonne baise."'*

A damned good fuck.

'"Une grosse bitte."'

A big cock.

'"Endless staying power that lasts until a woman is satisfied"? Is it any wonder I find it degrading to have to share a room with such people?'

'Forgive me, madame, but I've been given to understand that some of the Americans don't like the Senegalese and consider them "fresh."'

'The blacks, that's what they call them, but men are men and savages all the better, it would seem, for certain things.'

Like cutting firewood. 'And when, please, did Caroline leave the room to go outside?'

'Late. At about 1530 hours. She was withdrawn, had been upset and worried for days—terribly hurt, I think, ever since the night of that other one's having fallen, and when I asked what was wrong, she said I would know soon enough.'

But had the upset been because of what had happened with Jennifer or with Mary-Lynn or both? 'And did you find out?'

'Of course not!'

'Who else was in the room?'

'So as to be a witness? That Jill Faber and that Marni Huntington. Nora Arnarson was out somewhere by herself—she's a loner, that one.'

'And Becky Torrence?'

Ah, bon, the blonde. 'She left right behind my Caroline.'

'Dressed to go outside?'

How eager he was. 'That is correct.'

'Then for now, madame, we'll continue our little discussion at another time.'

She didn't even pause but said, 'Sister, I am well enough to return to that room to which I have been assigned. I must pack Caroline's things and see if they can be returned to her family. They'll be devastated. We must see that a proper letter is written. No details beyond a case of the flu. Night after night, my tireless attempts to save her. They must understand that I did everything I could to shield the little girl they had entrusted to me.'

Even lying about it. 'Sister, please see that one of the doctors checks Madame's blood pressure before she leaves,' said St-Cyr.

Give me time to go through Caroline Lacy's things.

Hermann . . . where the hell was Hermann?

The line was long and it stretched from the kitchens of the Vittel-Palace through the unused dining room to the foyer and even up the main staircase, to its left and right. Sleep-fogged, wearing winter coats, housecoats, cardigans, flannel shirts, and nightgowns or pajamas, the feet in heavy woollen socks, the hair still in paper twists on some or under nets that had been mended with parcel string, they coughed, muttered, dinged their canisters and pots, swore at would-be line jumpers and generally were miserable since Berlin Time definitely did not agree with them.

The room representatives of the 990 tenants, two perhaps chosen from each six or so, had been detailed for the day's firewood, soup, and bread. Some smoked cigarettes they'd managed to save, some kept stepping up and down, wanting to make a run for the toilets yet knowing they would lose their places.

'It is this way, Kohler,' said Weber with a grin. 'A shortcut.'

Barging through the lineup, he headed for a side door and went down a corridor toward the kitchens and the smell of boiled, ripe cabbage with suggestions of blood sausage.

Wehrmacht mobile canteen trolleys were in use, the cooks with ladles in hand, the officers in their greatcoats and ready to hand over the already-sawn slabs of black bread. Unabashedly some of the interred had unbuttoned their coats, et cetera, to give tantalizing glimpses in the hope of getting a little extra.

Others had secreted things to trade, but the cooks had to watch out for the officers and were wary.

'Let me show you how it's done,' confided Weber, all spit and polish in his grey greatcoat, the collar up, the shiny peak of his cap glistening, its white skull and crossbones clear enough. Black leather gloves, too.

First the soup canister was filled, then the measured slab of bread was thrust, by an officer, so hard into waiting hands that the girl, the woman, would gasp, bend forward, slosh the hot soup if still holding it and sometimes be forced to clean up the mess, the others having to step around or over her. But every now and then there would be a smile, a larger slab, a more gentle thrusting as soft brown eyes were lifted and lips that might once have driven some boy crazy, quivered.

At thirty years of age, a girl is reduced to this? thought Kohler. *Ach, du lieber Gott,* she had even brushed her pale cheeks with some of the brother's rouge and had touched up her lips. A comb had been hastily run through the fair, shoulder-length hair, which was worn parted high on the left and pinned back by a dark blue Bakelite butterfly that let a wisp fall over a furrowed brow as the head was ducked and wounded eyes were lowered. The nose was sharp and fine and turned up a little, and on the left of the dimpled chin there was a childhood scar, maybe two centimetres long, its stitch marks still evident.

'*Danke,* Herr Untersturmführer,' she said as the slab of bread was gently handed to her, the voice so soft it was but in the motion of those lips that it was really heard against the incredible din.

'Some we treat a little better than others,' confided Weber, intently watching her departure.

Awkwardly soup and bread were carried away, the girl concentrating on them so as not to spill or lose any.

Out in the foyer, Louis was going up the stairs two and three at a time.

4

The Vittel-Palace was chaos. Some were brushing their teeth or having an impromptu wash, others combing their hair or trying to sleep or hurriedly getting dressed, still others lighting the stoves or complaining about the smoke that filled the corridors at times for the pipes often ran along them.

Unheated, the hotels would normally have been closed at the end of the season on 15 September, but now, thought St-Cyr as he hurried, carelessness and inexperience, if nothing else, were threatening to burn this one down.

There were lineups for the toilets. Doors that should have been closed were wide open to air the smoke, space at an absolute premium, the shrieks, yells, and whistles shrill at the sight of a lone male hurrying down a corridor to Room 3–38.

'Inspecteur!'

'Ah, merde, pardonnez-moi, mesdemoiselles. St-Cyr, Sûreté.'

He didn't wait. Jill paused in pulling up her slacks; Marni had yet to put on a blouse; Nora had to step out of the way with the soup and bread; Becky was using the vase de nuit.

'Mademoiselle Arnarson, a moment.'

'I have to get the firewood, Inspector. If I don't run like the blazes, we won't get any!'

'Madame was supposed to have helped her,' said Marni. 'It was her turn.'

'Go, then, but hurry back.'

'She'll have to, won't she,' said Jill, 'since she has already lit the stove?'

That one was watching him closely now, as were the others. That one had yet to even find her brassiere.

Still he didn't hesitate, thought Jill, but went straight to Caroline's bed and, taking the suitcase from under it, found the case locked.

'*Sacré nom de nom*,' he swore, 'I should have realized Madame de Vernon would have locked it too. Where is the spare key to this?'

No one moved. All shrugged. Pocketknife in hand, he ruthlessly did the necessary and flung back the lid, going through everything with a speed that was impressive.

Not finding what he wanted, he ran a hand under the pillow, thumbed through the books on ballet and the scrapbook, too. The ballet shoes were checked, the remains of the latest Red Cross parcel, the clothes in the armoire, even the vase of silk chrysanthemums, but of course Caroline would never have hidden anything in that, not with Madame rearranging those flowers every day, but he couldn't have known of this.

The mattress was searched along its edges for a hidden seam that would have given away its little pocket. 'Something,' he said, finding the three of them staring at him. 'Madame Chevreul asked that girl to bring whatever she had to the séance. What was it and where is it?'

They glanced from one to another. Again they shrugged, then the older one with the straight black hair, dark grey eyes, and dimpled cheeks, the one called Jill, found her brassiere, and still dangling it from a hand, said, 'Perhaps she left it with Jennifer.'

'Room 3–54, Inspector,' said the green-eyed redhead named Marni Huntington, whose bed was under the Marquette University pennant. 'The same room as Mary-Lynn's.'

'Was Mary-Lynn Allan Jewish?' he asked, startling them. 'Come, come, an answer is demanded.'

Was he thinking of Caroline, too? wondered Jill.

'Those people are in the Hôtel de la Providence, Inspector,' said

Becky, having leapt to her feet and hiked up her pajama bottoms. 'There aren't many of them.'

'Most have Honduran passports and are waiting for permission to leave or hoping that they'll just be left alone,' said Jill, wondering what had caused him to ask such a thing. 'Though their hotel is out of bounds to us, they do walk in the park, but Caroline and Mary-Lynn . . . Neither would have had anything but casual contact with any of them. Those people tend to stick to themselves, Inspector. Most speak fluent German as well as their native Polish. Some speak French very well, but . . . but we seldom mix.'

There had been no mention of their speaking Spanish, which they should have if from Honduras. 'And you, Mademoiselle Faber, have you spoken to any of them?'

Shit! thought Jill. 'I've spoken to some. It helps, *n'est-ce pas?*'

'Everyone yearns for news here, Inspector,' Marni interjected quickly, but he wasn't to be distracted.

'And do those people worry about being deported to the concentration camps in the east?' he asked Jill.

Still she faced him; still she held her brassiere. '*Oui*, they're terrified of it, poor things.'

'What about Jennifer Hamilton?'

'Is she Jewish—is this what you're asking?'

'You know it is, Mademoiselle Faber. Please understand that neither my partner nor I would do anything to see her arrested for such a thing.'

That was a very dangerous thing for him to have said, thought Jill, but under his scrutiny she was now blushing—she knew it, felt it, couldn't understand it, and said weakly, 'She couldn't be a submarine, Inspector. Not living here. Things are far too close for anyone to hide something like that.'

The euphemism of a diver was also used by and for those who walked the streets but had gone into hiding with false papers or none at all. '*Ah, bon, merci*. Forget what I've asked, all of you. Just understand that if you want to help my partner and me, it would be best to keep it to yourselves. Now I must find this Jennifer Hamilton.'

'But Nora hasn't come back,' objected Becky, distressed by the thought.

It was the Faber woman who quickly said, 'It's this way, Inspector. I'll take you. It . . . it might help.'

'So that you can keep an eye on things?'

Jill swallowed hard and knew that he had noticed this. 'Not at all. She and Caroline were more than friends. If I'm there, Jennifer won't deny it, nor will the others try to protect her.'

'Otherwise they will, Inspector,' said Nora, her arms laden with wood. 'We all do. Each room, each little enclave shrinks unto itself as in even the smallest school of minnows where there is still the thought that safety lies in numbers.'

And detectives are predators? thought St-Cyr, for given the line-ups, she had returned far too quickly and had obviously bought the wood from one of the others and had been listening at the door.

'Perhaps you had best come with us.'

'Is it necessary?' She winced.

'You give me no choice.'

Room 3–54 was little different from Room 3–38, its frost-rimmed windows also facing away from the Parc Thermal. Film posters from home were on the walls to spice things up; photos, too, and maps and pennants: Duke University, North Carolina State, Ohio State, Rhodes College, Sweet Briar, and Massachusetts College of Art.

Clothing was still scattered, yet there was that same utilitarian tidiness if one allowed for the chaos of waking hours with but one exception.

Under the Sweet Briar pennant everything of Mary-Lynn Allan's, except for the items on the wall, had been packed and set precisely in order on top of the cot. To the far left, the blankets had been perfectly folded and lay under sheets and the pillow. Closed, the suitcase was next in line, then her coats, the summer, that is, and the rain, all neatly folded. Two pairs of shoes and one of rope-soled sandals and two hats came next, and then a gathered few items in a Red Cross box, its top closed and folded in perfectly.

'It isn't much, is it?' he said, for they had all stopped whatever they had been doing and were watching him closely. All five of them. Jill Faber and Nora Arnarson were still standing at his shoulders, one on either side.

'Who did it, Inspector? Surely you have some idea,' said the tall, thin brunette with the uncooperative hair who'd been fanning the firebox and silently cursing it. 'The wood's wet again,' she went on. 'We've no kerosene. At home my dad always added a splash. I'm Dotty . . . Dorothy Stevens, Ohio State. That one. That one there.'

The cot next to the door and on his left.

'*Et vous, mademoiselle?*'

Somehow the fair-haired one beside Dorothy found the will to smile. 'I'm the week's soup-and-bread carrier, Jennifer Hamilton. The Massachusetts College of Art. That one.'

The cot in the far left front corner.

'It's always cold on the feet being next to the window, but we drew lots and fair's fair.'

'And grief, mademoiselle?'

She didn't hesitate but looked steadily at him.

'Grief?' she said and there was music to her Parisian French. 'Grief is in all of us, Inspector, me especially, but we decided a brave front was what was needed.'

'Jennifer's right, Inspector,' said the little brunette who had been putting her hair into a ponytail. 'Tears only go so far. We've each day to overcome and, like you, need to know who did it and that you'll find this person quickly before another of us is killed. I'm Lisa. Lisa Banbridge. Duke University. That one.'

The bed that was end to end with Jennifer Hamilton's, the ages of these three varying from the thirty-six of the one who spoke of the fire as if still at home to the thirty perhaps of the buyer of antiques and paintings to the twenty-two of this last.

'It's impossible being locked up like this, Inspector,' said Lisa. 'We didn't do anything. *Zut,* we aren't killers. How could we be?'

'And I'm Candice, Inspector. Candice Peters, North Carolina State at Raleigh and a long, long way from home.'

And with frizzy brown hair still in paper twists, a toothbrush in hand whose disreputable state she suddenly realized and quickly tucked out of sight. Age pushing forty, grief held back admirably, a cool, firm handshake and a 'Welcome, Inspector. We're all grateful you and Herr Kohler finally got here. Jen was just telling us that she had encountered him downstairs with Herr Weber.'

'He's a lot taller than you,' said Jennifer. 'Did he get that scar from fencing? *Ah mon Dieu,* he looks the type. I . . . I was quite shy, I'm afraid. Herr Weber is overwhelming enough.'

'Inspector, I'm Barbara Caldwell, Rhodes College, Tennessee. I expect you'll want to know what we're all doing here. I think we'd like to know that too.'

This one's age was perhaps thirty-two or thirty-six, and her dark auburn hair fell naturally in waves to shoulders that were bravely squared under scrutiny, but in the dark olive-brown eyes there was doubt, hesitation, all manner of things. Had this Barbara Caldwell tidied Mary-Lynn's last effects?

'My bed's that one,' she said.

The one on the other side of the door.

'I'm the week's wood-getter. That's why my bed's not made yet.'

As if one needed to apologize for such a thing. *'Ah, bon,* mesdemoiselles, please go about whatever you were doing. Mademoiselle Hamilton, a few questions. Perhaps we could find a corner, the four of us.'

'Jill, why have you come?' urgently whispered Candice Peters in English.

'Nora, what's happened?' whispered another, also in English.

'I'm going to have to fess up if he asks, Barb. I can't avoid it.'

'Ah, merde, mesdemoiselles, have pity on a poor detective. Repeat to me *en français,* Mademoiselle Arnarson, exactly what was said.'

Did he think her guilty? wondered Nora. Desperately she looked at each of the others, even at Jill, then shrugged and said, 'It wasn't anything of consequence.'

'Yet you all knew, mademoiselle, that of the two of us, only Hermann speaks your language and not very well at that. Your bush telegraph . . . '

Nora knew she couldn't help but smile. 'It's pretty good, isn't it?'

'Please just do as I asked.'

Jill gave her a nod, a comforting hand on a shoulder. Repeating everything, Nora warned herself not to avoid eye contact even for a moment. As with the Boche, so with this *sûreté*. He was standing so close to her anyway it would have been doubly noticed had she lowered her eyes. She could smell the wet wool of his shabby over-coat, the lingering of stale pipe smoke too, and as with so many of the French, that of the anise confections they loved.

'When Mary-Lynn and I were at the séance, Inspector, only Jennifer and Caroline were here in this room. The others . . . '

'Were playing poker,' said Jill. 'Me as well, and Marni Huntington. Becky hadn't been feeling well. Her period again. Every Saturday night a gang of us get together in what used to be the hotel's two smoking rooms. They're on the ground floor, near to the main staircase and have a folding partition between them that can be opened to make one big room. We light a fire in the grate, each contributing what she can—snacks, too, if possible, and then . . . then we play. Twenty tables, twenty-five, whatever suits and Five-card Stud, High-Low, Shotgun, Spit in the Ocean, or Cincinnati. Dealer's choice.'

'Cigarettes are used instead of chips or money. Well, actually, they *are* the money,' said Dorothy Stevens, the brunette by the stove. 'Sometimes one of us will bankroll another. Becky gave me two packs of twenty up front. If I'd won, I would have covered her first and then split the rest fifty-fifty.'

Had the stove-lighter said it to distract him? wondered St-Cyr. 'Mademoiselle Arnarson, the firewood you went to get. Is it that you paid for it?'

He hadn't moved. She couldn't lie, thought Nora, but could she find the will to weakly smile at being caught out? 'I had to offer four packs and will be bankrupt for weeks and weeks.'

It was Jill Faber who quickly said, 'Nora really is afraid, Inspector. That's why she had to listen. What happened to Mary-Lynn Allan could well have been meant to happen to her, or to both of them.'

'But why, mademoiselle? What had either or both done to warrant being murdered?'

The others didn't stir. All looked at him as if searching for the answer until he was forced to say, '*Ah, bon,* let's get the times down.

This poker session on the night of thirteenth, fourteenth . . . when precisely did it break up?'

He'd find the truth, felt Jill. He had that look and wouldn't budge until he had. 'The time? At about two usually.'

But long before that, felt Kohler, Mary-Lynn had fallen and the echo of her scream would have caused them all to run to find out what had happened. 'Where were you when she fell?'

'Marni and me, we . . . *Merde,* I hate to use the term, Inspector, but we had lucked out at around twelve fifteen and were back in our own room by twelve thirty, I guess. Becky couldn't sleep. Caroline . . . Caroline had come back to the room but was having . . . '

'A moment, please. Caroline Lacy?'

This, too, couldn't be avoided, Jennifer told herself. There simply wasn't a way out. Jill and Nora had come with him to make sure she told him. 'Caroline was here with me, Inspector, until about midnight. Her chest was bothering her. The poor thing could hardly breathe. She went home to beg Madame de Vernon to forgive her and let her have one of her cigarettes. Madame could well have denied her. Caroline was terrified the woman might hide them or put them somewhere else other than usual just for spite. I said I'd come with her, but . . . but she said that would only make things worse.'

Even though gasping for air. 'So by then Jill, Marni, and Becky were also in Room 3–38, you alone here in 3–54. That leaves . . . '

He had turned to face her and Nora knew exactly what he was going to ask.

'That hour and a half, Mademoiselle Arnarson, from the time you left Madame Chevreul's séance in the Hôtel Grand until you and Mary-Lynn Allan started to climb the stairs in this wing of the Vittel-Palace at close on 0100 hours?'

How could she avoid telling him the truth without being absolutely sure each of the others would back her up? wondered Nora. 'The apricots we get in our parcels have a yeast on them. I . . . I've a still in the cellars which I use from time to time if the Senegalese will let me have enough wood and we share up. Everyone contributes, but I'm the one who looks after it. We had only a half a jug left, which I'd hidden at the back of the room, but I'd told everyone we were out until another batch was ready. I have to do that; otherwise the Senegalese will make their demands.'

'The blacks, Nora,' said one of the others, but which one he couldn't tell.

'And you and Mary-Lynn sampled it?' asked St-Cyr.

'She needed something. She *believed* Madame Chevreul had really made contact with her dad. Never have I seen a person so happy. I . . . I thought the *eau-de-vie* a little off, but its flavour was a bit strong anyway. Mary-Lynn said I was crazy, that it was perfect. "Let's get drunk," she said.'

'Then you really were drunk when you climbed those stairs.'

'*Oui.* That's . . . that's what made me dump the rest after what happened. This morning, actually. First thing before any of the others were up, not even the lousy cooks that boil that soup while their officers dole out the bread.'

'Caroline thought she was the intended victim, Inspector,' said Jennifer, still from across the room, for no one had yet moved.

It was Candice Peters of the frizzy brown hair who said, 'We all agreed that Jen and Caroline needed a little privacy. Girl with girl was OK by us. Life here is lonely enough. So what if they held each other? It did no harm and made them happy.'

'Caroline blossomed,' said Barbara Caldwell, the one who had graduated from Rhodes College. 'Living here has taught us all a lot, Inspector. We know it's illegal and that whatever church one goes to would consider it evil, but it *does* happen here. *Ah, mon Dieu,* at any time of the day or night you can come upon a couple or hear them. Jennifer and Caroline weren't alone in that. *Bien sûr,* Madame de Vernon hated the thought. She demanded that Caroline break it off with Jen, was fiercely jealous, and if you ask me, violently possessive. Some women *can* be like that, can't they?'

'We . . . we didn't think she'd do anything other than object,' said Jennifer, 'but . . . but now I'm not so sure, Inspector. Am I to be next?'

Merde, thought St-Cyr. The room was crowded enough, himself the lone male, they all watching his every move like a herd of wildebeest who would form a circle round the defenceless as the jackals prepare to rush in.

'Madame Chevreul . . . ' he began.

'*Ah, oui,*' said Jennifer, brushing her fair hair back off her brow. 'Caroline and I had been to see her time and again, trying to get permission to become sitters at one of her sessions. At . . . at last we had succeeded only to then . . . Forgive me, I can't say it. I'm sorry.'

Where, really, wondered St-Cyr, did this one sit in things since there had been no mention yet of Caroline Lacy's having been emotionally upset and in tears *before* she had returned to her own room on the night Mary-Lynn Allan had fallen? *Bien sûr* this buyer of antiques, Old Masters, and other paintings for her family's business in Boston seemed independent of mind, exuding strength and forthrightness in the face of grief, but she had been the lover of one of the victims and a roommate of the other, and was now suggesting that she, too, might be in danger. Had it all been a performance? 'And were you to have attended last evening's séance as well?'

Had he questioned her sincerity? wondered Jennifer. 'Léa Monnier made the rules. Although Caroline desperately wanted me to be present, I was told I would have to wait outside the Pavillon de Cérès, where a chair would be left for me.'

'And the fee that was to be paid?'

'Five hundred greenbacks—oh, sorry. US dollars, a cheque. Caroline didn't mind. She would have paid five thousand. Anything, I think.'

Had it been clever of her to have suggested this? 'For Madame to ask Cérès to talk to whom?'

'She never said.'

'Come, come, Mademoiselle Hamilton, we haven't time for this!'

To flash a grin wouldn't be wise, felt Jennifer. He wanted the answer and would have to be given it. 'Madame de Vernon's husband. Caroline had a photo she'd taken from Madame's suitcase but was terrified Madame would discover it was missing before she could put it back.'

'And the photo?'

'It was of the villa Madame had once owned in Provence. I . . .

well, I burned it in the stove after Caroline was killed. I didn't want Madame finding it here.'

'Because she would have blamed you for encouraging Caroline?'

'That is correct. Inspector, Madame de Vernon hated me for having freed Caroline from her grasp. *Merde alors,* all I'd done, and everyone will agree, was to let Caroline decide to have a life of her own for once.'

'Yet the two of you quarreled on the night Mary-Lynn Allan fell?'

Madame de Vernon must have told him this. 'It was nothing. A simple misunderstanding. We embraced and . . . and made up.'

'Then there was no thought of her breaking off the affair?'

'None whatsoever.'

And determined about it too. 'This photo, mademoiselle, was the husband in it?'

She would shake her head and watch him closely, felt Jennifer, the others all intent. 'He was the one who took the photos, for Caroline had said there were others. Madame didn't find the prints until after he had left her. Always, though, when in Paris or anywhere else with Caroline, she kept them in her purse, but when they got here to their room, she . . . she put one on the wall beside her pillow.'

And kept the others safely in her suitcase but had this one known the whereabouts of that spare key Madame had hidden to that very suitcase since Caroline Lacy must have? 'For now, mesdemoiselles, that is all. You've been most helpful. I must find my partner.'

'Inspector . . . '

It was Nora. '*Oui?*'

'Those missing datura seeds . . . '

'Ah, like you I wish I knew where they were, which brings us to a parting question: Have any or all of you had anything stolen? Some small, insignificant item, of little or no use beyond sentiment and the memories it might have brought?'

Quickly they glanced from one to another, then Jennifer Hamilton said, 'All of us have lost things, Inspector. Some of us more than once.'

'There hasn't just been a rash of these thefts, but a plague of them,' said Lisa, the little twenty-two-year-old brunette from Duke

University with the hazel eyes and ponytail. 'Whoever does it is really, really fast.'

'Like Houdini,' said Jennifer.

'Me, I've lost things too,' said Nora, 'but the best was the Indian Head penny my dad sent me for good luck. It was dated 1907 but he had found it on the day I was born. At least . . . well, at least that's what he always told me. The second luckiest day in his life.'

'And the first?'

'The day he met my mom.'

Each of the others wholly believed this pathos, their concern for her loss all too evident, but was there only one way to deal with this lot: divide and conquer? *'Ah, bon, mes amies, merci.* For now, let me leave you to get on with things. Mademoiselle Arnarson, be so good as to show me your still.'

He didn't wait until they were there, but once out of sight of the others and alone on the cellar stairs, he stopped her.

She had to face him. 'Mademoiselle, upstairs you said Mary-Lynn Allan had had more of the home brew than you.'

'She . . . she felt sick and had run on ahead.'

'Ah, oui, oui, but earlier, when interviewed by my partner, Jill Faber said you weren't as drunk as Mary-Lynn. But you, however, claimed you were the drunker and that you had been hallucinating.'

'That is correct.'

'Perhaps, but it doesn't add up, does it?'

'I . . . I really was feeling dizzy.'

'Bien sûr, but given everything, including the presence of *Datura stramonium,* a known hallucinogenic, you then deliberately destroy valuable evidence not after Mary-Lynn is killed but after Caroline Lacy, and with two investigating officers on your doorstep?'

Ah, damn it, did he forget nothing? 'All right. There wasn't any *eau-de-vie.* Mary-Lynn insisted we drop in to the poker game to tell them all the news, that Cérès had said her dad had at last made contact and had forgiven her for having had a love affair with a German and that she wasn't to worry anymore but simply to take great care, that it was really he who was worried about her. It was all a pack of lies, Inspector. Fog . . . the stench of mustard gas. Compasses whose bearings would make them lose their way? Machine-gun fire and grenades, her dad crying out to the daughter who had never known him but through Cérès from a battlefield to the north of here twenty-five years ago? The poor thing was so relieved, yet it was absolute rubbish and damned cruel of Madame Chevreul to have taken advantage of her. The cost alone was horrendous, given what most of us have to spare. She was all but broke. I'd loaned her that last fifty . . . '

'A cheque?'

'Yes, of course. Who has any cash?'

'And Madame Chevreul knew of your feelings?'

'That's just the rub. I think so, then I think not, then I think it again when not worrying over Caroline and Madame de Vernon and that damned datura.'

'With which you were never hallucinating, nor was Mary-Lynn.'

'Look, I'm sorry. I . . . I thought maybe I was doing the right thing by alerting you to the possibility of its having been used.'

And the others, letting her lie to a police officer about the *eau-de-vie* so as to cover for her. *Merde!* 'A believer and a disbeliever, a set of stairs, an argument, hurt feelings, the one not really sick but running up the stairs in tears ahead of the other.'

'A Kommandant who is a confirmed believer and is very close to her, Inspector. Too close maybe. We really don't know, because Mary-Lynn, though afraid herself, and a close friend of mine, would never tell any of us who the father was.'

'And a medium who charges whatever can be taken from the sitter even if exorbitant.'

'Mary-Lynn was pushed, Inspector, but was I the one who should have been?'

From what he'd seen so far, thought Kohler, the English camp was better organized than the American, but bedlam still. They ate in shifts, all 1,678 of them, the dining room of the Hôtel Grand deafening: constant gossip in two languages, recipes, makeovers, hairdos and don'ts, the hair up in curlers, pins, bandanas, or turbans—this last the latest Paris fashion—housecoats on some, overcoats on others, and fingerless gloves. In all, it was the rule of the vulgar and the loud, and God help those who were refined or timid or simply wanted a little privacy.

Lines of tables, placed end to end, ran parallel and between rows of those same Pavillon de Cérès honey-coloured marble columns that were nearly two storeys high. Cherubs with armorial shields were up there on the ceiling, a leftover from earlier days; chandeliers dripping crystal on Kentia palms in dark-blue Art Deco jardinières, the whole perhaps looking of the Otherworld or at least making the interned seem damned out of place.

To the soup and bread, lumps of what appeared to be boiled mutton had been doled out, each table, each group left to fight over the division. Inevitably squabbles had broken out and rose above the general discourse, rocketing into fiercely slapped faces, savagely yanked hair, shrieks, and swearing not only coarse but equally in French and English.

Bartering was everywhere. Since this was the only meal served by the Occupier, a daily ritual at 0700 hours Berlin Time, items from Red Cross parcels augmented the fare: luncheon meat and paste, milk powder, crackers, margarine, jam, marmalade . . .

'Inspector,' someone called out, 'are Saint-Nazaire and Lorient in ruins? My daughters . . . '

'Don't answer!' snapped Weber. 'The British bombed the hell out of those towns last night.'

Because of the U-boat pens that would have remained virtually unharmed, but how had that woman known to ask unless one of the guards had told her?

Weber knew the inmates who counted most for him as informants and would find out soon enough, but didn't speak to any. Instead, he insisted on walking the narrow aisles between the chairs, and as he passed each back-to-back pair, these were immediately shunted closer to their respective tables.

'It's like this, Kohler,' he said in *Deutsch*. 'I can point a finger at any one of them or tap a shoulder, and that one must immediately get to her feet and leave the dining room to wait for me outside my office in the casino.'

To illustrate, he began to pick and choose, sending at random fifteen, leaving soup to chill with opened tins or packets as the noise momentarily abated to muttered curses and warnings of 'Don't you dare steal my things.'

'*Meine Spitzel* are many,' he said of his informants, 'but none of the others know exactly who they are, since I always send out more than needed.'

And so much for his thinking none of those present would understand a word of *Deutsch*.

'Is there anyone in particular you'd like to question?' asked Weber.

'Léa Monnier.'

'An excellent choice. You must tell me what she reveals, then we'll compare notes.'

And if that wasn't an uh-oh, what was?

'There's little I don't know, Kohler, and well in advance.'

Even two murders?

'Inspector,' sang out someone nearby, 'you want to watch our Léa. She has it in for that partner of yours.'

'He can't be saying things about her past in France like that,' said her neighbour, mutton dribbling grease on pudgy fingers, tired brown hair in curlers and faded pink housecoat over cardigan-padded shoulders. 'She had to run from the coppers, did our Léa, when she left the Old Blighty for Paris.'

'The Old Bailey?'

'Blighty. London, for God's sake!' shouted the woman. 'The prison came first, same as for the one she serves, apart from herself.'

'The one who talks to the asteroid?' he asked, startled.

They'd teach Léa to lord it over everyone, thought Blanche Gilberte, formerly Blanche Whitehead from Surrey. 'I'd watch that one too, if I were you, Inspector.'

Cold corned beef was accidentally scattered as she gestured for emphasis. 'Madame Chevreul?' he yelled.

'She's not the one who led the mob,' said a tablemate, shaking her head.

'Which mob?' asked Kohler. 'The one my partner and I encountered yesterday or . . . '

'Another, Inspector? Another they'd best forget?' asked Blanche.

'No one crosses our Léa,' said the tablemate.

'Inspector . . . Inspector,' someone called out, only to have everyone get to their feet as the sound of 'God Save the King' started up in English from the other end of the room, defiantly growing louder and louder until Weber shrieked, *'Ruhe! Alles hinsetzen!'*

Silence. All sit. 'Their stupid, stupid patriotism is the only recourse they have, Kohler, but they know I'll cut off their hot water, their food, and even their parcels.'

Yet who but Léa Monnier had ordered them all to get up and sing to stop a few from having it in for her? The Old Bailey and a mob, she and Madame Chevreul then having to leave the Old Blighty for the Continent.

'Inspector . . . Inspector,' came the urgent call again, 'are they still serving *le canard pressé* at the Tour d'Argent?' The woman had even dressed up for the morning's dish-out.

'Nothing's changed,' said Kohler with a grin. 'It's all the same for those with the money and connections, even the pressed duck.'

'*Paris,*' she said with longing, the accent perfect and of *les hautes*.

'Have you people *Wunderwaffen*?' asked another.

The V-1s and V-2s, the Führer's miracle weapons.

Weber pointed at the woman and immediately she got to her feet in tears and left the room, knowing she would have to tell him which of the guards had said such a thing.

An urgent voice rose up from four tables away, the woman in her late sixties and standing now in despair. '*Monsieur le ministre de l'éducation nationale, un moment, s'il vous plaît.* Someone has stolen my stamp.'

Not my soup. Murmurs fled from chair to chair and table to table as Weber led the way from aisle to aisle.

'Postage?' asked Kohler, mystified by the illustrious title she'd given him.

Puzzled, the woman began to tremble with indignation. 'What is it you're saying, *Monsieur le ministre*?'

Would an understanding smile help? 'A stamp for that letter you've been writing?'

'It is not a letter. It is my date stamp, the one that I put at the top of every page in my exercise book. This is the ink pad for which Brother Étienne brings me the ink. Where is my rubber stamp?'

'Kohler, leave it. She must be crazy.'

'Isn't having that ink pad illegal?'

Weber went to snatch it away and it was passed from hand to hand until he backed off and shrieked, 'You see how slack our former Kommandant was? Letting them keep things like that from which the stamps for false papers could be inked?'

Devastated by the loss, the woman wept. 'All the girls are being noisy and bad this morning, *Monsieur le ministre*. The Reverend Mother is going to be very angry with us, but if I had been allowed to start my page, she would have seen that I've been busy doing my catechism and not making trouble for her. Now . . . oh now . . . '

'She must think she's in school, Kohler. School! Colonel Kessler had to be replaced. This is just one more incidence of his slackness.'

Another dreamer, felt Kohler. Well, two of them. 'Let her keep the ink pad and the stamp when she gets them back. We've trouble enough.'

'You lot,' he called out in English, 'return them now.'

A frizzy-haired ginger head was tossed. 'Or else you'll think it's one of us who's been stealing little things?'

'Things like a small, oval seashell with teeth, Inspector?' asked another.

Or a yellow cloth star? Did they know of it as well, and if so, how the hell had they found out?

'It's one of those American bitches,' said yet another, dangling a tinned sardine by its tail. 'They've murdered their own, haven't they? Girls with girls, eh? Oh *là, là*, Inspector, that Vittel-Palace is a hothouse.'

'*Lécheuses des chattes*,' roared another, to much laughter.

Cunt lickers. 'A lovers' tiff, was it, this latest killing?' shouted yet another. 'Both of those girls were upstairs here in the Grand time and again.'

'Both had plenty of chances to steal things, let me tell you,' said another with tinned custard on her chin.

'We don't do things like that. We'd never steal from her or anyone else,' said another, wiping a runny nose.

'But she stole from Madame Chevreul, is that it?' he tried.

'Warned . . . The first was warned to be careful but failed to watch out, the other . . . Well, what was she doing in the *Chalet des Ânes*? Isn't it *verboten*?'

'*Ja, ist verboten,*' said another, nodding furiously.

'And then there's Madame de Vernon,' said her neighbour. 'Possessive. Keeping that little piece of goods all to herself? Billing the parents in America a fortune for a career that never happened?'

'Our Léa had to fix a time and date but first Madame Chevreul had to interview the ballet student and her lover seven times, Inspector. *Seven!*'

'Kohler, I really must insist,' said Weber.

'*Ach, du lieber Gott,* not now, Untersturmführer.'

Again the singing started up with 'Praise the Lord and Pass the Ammunition.' Again Weber had to shriek, and then . . . then from a far corner, a lone woman standing, came a voice and 'All Things Bright and Beautiful.'

The entire dining room listened. They all stopped eating, some of them even cried, and only when the hymn had ended and the one with the golden voice had sat down did the ones nearby Kohler start up again.

'That Nora Arnarson, Inspector, she's going to have to watch herself. Speaking out like that against Madame Chevreul when so many of us believe and welcome what that amazing woman is capable of. Cérès is very angry, and when Cérès gets angry . . . Well, you're dealing with the gods.'

'She's a dark one, that Nora,' said a neighbour. 'Turns up in most unexpected places. Having a look about our hotel, asking a lot of questions like where that little ballet dancer and her lover have been.'

'Watching our Kensington's *Ten Golden Blonde Girls* while they practice their routines so as not to forget them. Caroline Lacy loved to do that too, and then talk for hours if she could get one of the girls to listen to her.'

'And what about Madame de Vernon, eh?' asked another. 'Insists on seeing Madame Chevreul five times herself. *Five,* I'm telling you, Inspector. Argues with Madame and our Léa. Doesn't want her ward to hear what Cérès has to say.'

'About what?'

Blimey, but that had got him going! 'Urgent business. I'm sure if you ask, our Léa will be only too glad to tell you for a price.'

Cold Kam was thumbed from a tin bearing that name, the meat pink and laced with fat. 'They didn't exactly get on, Inspector,' she said, wolfing the morsel.

'*Monsieur le Ministre,*' came the urgent but now distant cry in French. 'I have my date stamp and ink pad. I have!'

Distracted, Weber turned away.

'Wallpaper?' hissed Kohler at one. 'Why did your Léa ask the Senegalese to get her some and where the hell did they get it, if not from the Hôtel de l'Ermitage?'

Instantly heads were bowed, soup earnestly taken, crumbs sought, a sardine fished from its tin as oil dribbled down pudgy fingers that then had to be licked to avoid the waste.

'All right, damn it. What was stolen from Madame Chevreul?' he asked, leaning over the table to pluck the tin away as objecting fingers lunged for it in panic only to be hastily withdrawn.

The bulging throat rippled, the watery blue eyes found his at last. 'Her talisman.'

'*Ah, bon, merci.* Now, enjoy the rest of your breakfast.'

There was no sign of Léa Monnier who had obviously ordered up 'God Save the King' and done a bunk. Out in the foyer, some carried handbags that had never left them since they'd been taken into custody in December of 1940; others had sewn purses and tied these around their waists as in the Middle Ages. Most wore the signs of underfeeding, the lack of minerals and vitamins, the skin dried and cracked, the joints sore. All were cold and often yawning or coughing up their lungs, and halitosis, with or without their fags, depending entirely on fortune.

That seashell, that yellow star, that date stamp . . . Kohler knew he couldn't leave it. 'Has anyone escaped?' he asked.

Weber was taken aback. 'From here? Where would they go?'

'I'm just asking.'

Had Kohler found out something he shouldn't? 'No one has escaped. I would be the first to know and put my pistol to the back of her neck. Those hills and forests are frozen. Without adequate clothing, she'd be but food for the elements or the wolves. Ask any of the Senegalese. They'll tell you. We often seem to lose one or two from the wood-gathering details.'

'I thought so. I just felt I'd best ask since that partner of mine will. He's a damned nuisance at times. Always the obscure, the less than obvious, but he's French so one has to make allowances.'

Ach, and speeches now? 'Kohler, when you find Frau Monnier and are done with her, send her to me.'

'But what about the rest of the camp? Aren't we going to see it?'

'The Hôtel de la Providence—is this what you're after? Those people don't matter. They'll all be gone as soon as the *Sonderkommando* comes from Berlin to check their passports and papers more thoroughly than they'd like. Colonel Kessler overlooked far too much, but now it's all to be taken care of.'

Don't interfere. A special commando from the SS, the boys who ran the concentration camps and were the worst of the worst.

Blacked-out, the Vittel-Palace waited in the early morning with a hush so deep St-Cyr knew he couldn't help but feel its collective anticipation. In spite of the lack of daylight, every window facing the Parc Thermal had been crowded at the first cry from one of the lookouts who had heard the distant sound of sleigh bells. Gathered in the freezing cold, they also stood out on the balconies, but would Brother Étienne be allowed in? they whispered. Would the change in Kommandant not stop forever the visits they desperately needed even though it was a Sunday and he'd only just been here on Friday and really wasn't due back again until next Wednesday?

'He'll know how worried and afraid we are,' said one. 'He'll reach out to us and pull us to him. Oh, I'm so glad he told us he'd come back today. I do hope he's brought the poultice for my knee. Every night's been an agony. I don't sleep. I can't. The pain is terrible.'

'He'll dry my tears and pat me on the back. He'll tell me everything is going to be all right, that now with two detectives from Paris here, we needn't be so terrified. He'll see to my hands. More cracks have opened. This morning they were bleeding but he'll have an answer. I know he will.'

'My gums . . . '

'My period . . . '

'You should have listened to me, Yvonne.'

'I didn't do anything like that! Brother Étienne said I should wait, that it's probably just the lack of food, of vitamins and minerals, and that he would be bringing me one of his tonics.'

Ah, merde, this crowd, thought St-Cyr, the sleigh bells sounding, a collective sigh rising as it would also from the Hôtel Grand. *'Mesdames et mesdemoiselles,* permit me to see Brother Étienne.'

'Let the Inspector through, girls. Let him see the one who gives us hope and belief in ourselves.'

Perfume, sweat, soup, farts, canned fish, lavender, orris root, and woodsmoke—all such smells assailed St-Cyr as he pushed through to the railing.

'Don't touch the iron, Inspector,' warned someone. 'Your skin is warm and will stick to it.'

There were no lights on the cutter whose bells now jangled with increasing loudness, the softly falling snow making visibility clear enough, but one could have heard a pin drop when those little bells ceased their ringing. Snow-covered, a heavy fur rug was thrown back and a hooded head bared. *'Mes chères,'* came the basso profundo from below, the arms thrown wide, the sadness and concern immediately evident. 'Another violent death, I'm told. Our precious little ballet dancer. Who would have done such a thing? Had her suffering not been enough? You will all be brokenhearted. When I left our cloister this morning, and the brother abbot informed me of this latest tragedy, I told myself that somehow I must find a way to ease your pain. Angèle did that for me, wise as she is. She stopped on the road as we came down from the hills and there . . .

there in the distance was a doe and her fawn. A sign, I tell you, *mes chères amies*. A sign. Spring is coming. The little one was at the teat and could hardly stand, and the mother had to wait as your Étienne walked gently towards her until, finally, the teat was left and the two delicately picked their way into the forest, and do you know what? Angèle, she came towards me without my whistling. Two miracles in as many moments. May the great blessings of the Father who watches over all be with you.'

Two of what appeared to be bulging burlap sacks were offloaded to be later carried toward the hotel.

'He comes here first this time, Inspector,' whispered someone. 'The British camp will be jealous, but on his next visit he'll go there before he comes here. Oh, he sends shivers right through me. He's the gentlest of beings. Intently he listens to every word that is said and intuitively knows and understands exactly what is needed.'

'A massage. My ankles. My feet. Some of his cream,' said another.

'His very touch is like a balm, Inspector. Pure magic.'

'Pure love, if you ask me. He cares. He really does.'

'And always there is that smile of his, now warm, now gentle, now bright.'

'He has the most sensitive eyes, Inspector. They never look through you, only with you. Empathy is what he has. Concern.'

'A selflessness unknown to most, especially at a time like this, when everyone's killing everyone.'

And a warm brother? Hermann had asked the new Kommandant who had answered, "That is putting it politely."

Having been a prisoner of war, Kohler was impressed. Madame Chevreul didn't live in just one room but in a third-storey suite that, beyond the floor-to-ceiling drapes, must overlook the Parc Thermal from the Hôtel Grand's western corner. Léa Monnier guarded the entrance, but so too did the cook and the maid who also occupied that first room, Madame the third and most spacious, and with a reception room between and another beyond, this last door being closed. And locked? he had to wonder, ignoring her and going over to try it. Locked tight, all right, but probably only because she had the present company.

Under blankets and a coverlet most would have sold their souls for, she was propped up with feather pillows in a four-poster that must have cost a fortune. The powder-blue dressing gown had been newly laundered, pressed, and thoroughly dried, a miracle in itself. The fair, shoulder-length hair had been brushed to a sheen by the maid. Pensively the dark-blue eyes took him in with a mixture of disdain and indignation.

'Really, Herr Kohler, I must object. Such impertinence at such an unmentionable hour does not become you, nor the cause you pursue. I never rise before ten. To do so would be uncivilized.'

'Detectives have to get up earlier.'

Was the belligerence deliberate? she wondered. He had had to wait a good twenty minutes and now stood impatiently on the carpet before her and not a centimetre closer to the foot of the bed than the two metres Léa had insisted on.

'To what do I owe this visit? A few small questions, is it? Nothing difficult, or have you a better line of balderdash than that partner of yours?'

'Louis hasn't been here, has he?'

Ah, mon Dieu, she had caught him out. 'Moves quickly, does he, your partner? Oh, please don't look so unsettled, you foolish, foolish man. He hasn't. News simply travels, but I do expect a visit from him, though at a more civilized hour. It would be unseemly of either of you to ignore me. Rumour is rife enough as it is. Will you take tea?

'Léa . . . Léa, dearest, would you oblige?

'Sugar, Inspector? Milk, is it?'

'Black is fine.'

And still impatient. 'Sit over there in my chaise longue where I can see you. Were there daylight, a little sun, though fledgling at this time of year, might have warmed you further than the fires in my stoves. I've three of those. Smoke if you wish. You'll find cigarettes in my case on the dressing table. I don't indulge until noon. It's best to build up one's ability to resist temptation, I think.'

He ignored the put-down and immediately found her cigarette case. Anxiously lighting one, he let her see him in the table's mirrors, but didn't turn to face her. Instead, he ran that gaze of his over everything, knowing that his looking so closely was bound to unsettle her.

'They've said things, haven't they, some of those in the dining room?' she asked, a modest quaver betraying her feelings.

Still he didn't answer, and neither did he turn to face her. 'Art Deco silver frames, you ask of the photos, Inspector? Childhood friends—sisters, even? An estate in Kent, perhaps? A millpond where three young women, each with all the joys and sorrows of their tender lives still ahead of them, are in a rowboat, me at the tiller, age twenty-three, if you must know. Rebecca Thompson is in the bow and dangles fingers into the water looking as if she wants to strip off all the finery society insists on and take the plunge. Judith Merrill is at the oars and about to do just that. Guests . . . were they guests of mine, you wonder, or was I the guest? How deep is a past you cannot yet know nor ever fathom?'

Her voice had risen to an edge that, ignoring her further, would only sharpen. The cigarette case was, of course, from Van Cleef & Arpels, the jewellery the same as Louis and he had noticed Léa Monnier wearing when at the head of that mob in the foyer of the Vittel-Palace late the day before, but had Madame known her henchwoman had borrowed it, and why leave it lying about like this when they both knew things were being stolen?

The tea was brought in a willow-ware cup and saucer, Herr Kohler giving Léa the coldness of a once-over.

'What mob?' he asked her.

'Tut-tut, Inspector. Léa is to leave us now. Ours is to be an interview in the privacy of my room. Having insisted upon it, I think it best you deal only with me for the moment.

'Léa, dearest, I'll ring when I've finished with him.'

There wasn't a speck of jewellery on Léa Monnier, the grey house dress similar to that of a *Blitzmädel* but without the flashes. Retreating, she shut them in.

'The Old Bailey?' asked Herr Kohler, cigarette in hand and cup and saucer clumsily balanced. Unfortunately he would pursue his questions as a dog does buried bones. In this he was no different from St-Cyr except, perhaps, for the degree and manner of persistence. 'The Old Bailey, you ask? Léa chose duty to king and country over prison, that is true. Léa Easton then, Inspector. Abused as a child—taught the harsh lessons of a male-dominated world at a very early age, I suspect, though would never ask. Couldn't even vote, though too young at the time, and of course women didn't have the vote anyway. Arrested due entirely to a mistake, she having become caught up in some street demonstration and carried along into the truncheons of a battalion of mounted police. She had, I believe, chosen a most unfortunate moment to go on an errand for the mistress of the house in which she was employed as kitchen help, hence her arrest—was this what they told you, those who would whisper vindictiveness out of envy?'

He didn't answer, knowing this would only upset her all the more, but waited, his tea still untouched. Datura . . . Was it that he actually *thought* Léa had those missing seeds and would poison him here?

'Léa does have her enemies, Inspector, and they, poor souls, will say the most uninformed of things.'

Cigarette ash was tapped into his saucer—would he drown the butt in the tea or pinch it out and put it away in the little tin most carried whether they used tobacco or not?

He would *drown* it, she thought, and leave it for Léa to find, but was there not something to overcome the impasse between them? 'Life hasn't been easy here, Inspector. I do miss my lovely home and the Percherons we bred. They're the most noble of creatures. Do you know of them? You must. There are pictures on my bureau. Please look at them. I've no secrets.'

Ach, and get the hell away from her dressing table, was that it?

'My husband loved the breed and knew our stables so well he could walk there unaided. Understandably he was very distressed by all we had had to let go to the war—we only had two mares and one stallion left by 1919. Gun carriages and supply wagons took the others instead of the plow and cart. Isn't it a downright disgrace the idiocy you men will get up to? Come, come, you knew that war. Fighting over virtually nothing? Killing? Destroying so much? Had even one woman had the vote, none of it would have happened. No sons would have been lost, not the millions and millions; no lovers, either, or our beautiful Percherons.'

Votes for women, and how the hell did she know he must have experienced that other war? Kessler, the former Kommandant, was that it? A last parting word from him, or Weber but the information via Berlin?

The stallions in the photos were magnificent dappled greys, the mares too, and of at least seventeen hands. Big, heavy, strong, docile, and intelligent, the ploughman's constant friend, the artilleryman's *Kamerad*. 'I knew them on the farm and at the front. None are better.'

But did he think it a matter of mere coincidence or divine predestination that he might well, as an artillery officer in that other war, have used Percherons from the Château de Mon Plaisir? 'When this war is over, Inspector, you must pay me a visit. Indeed, I insist.'

'I'd have to bring Louis.'

Ah, merde, he had gone right back to the dressing table but what, please, was he searching for? Intimacy? Understanding? Doubt still crowding all else? 'Is it all a con, Inspector? Is that what you're still thinking?'

The hairbrush, mirror, and powder case were of enamelled silver and decorated with naked goddesses—Cérès among them? he must wonder.

The accessories were of Baccarat. Perfume in one crystal phial, oil in another, the portrait photo of Rebecca Thompson—that of a slim, dark-eyed beauty also of twenty-three and looking defiantly into the lens as she stood straight, though turned all but sideways to the viewer, hands folded demurely in front and below the waist, eye shadow deepening the depth of her look. A woman with a mind of her own, Inspector? Is that what you're thinking, or simply, as most men would, are you wondering what it would be like to have sexual intercourse with her? The fucking, I think you would call it.

The empty perfume bottle in Caroline Lacy's pocket had been

by Guerlain, remembered Kohler, a 1925 Exposition presentation, Baccarat having made the bottle in an Art Deco style, and much favoured by this one, but he'd leave it until Louis and he had had a chance to talk things over. Judith Merrill, in the other portrait photo, was the oldest and maybe six years senior. 'Élizabeth what?' he asked of her own maiden name, not turning.

Unfortunately such things couldn't be avoided. 'Chevreul née Beacham. Inspector, those photographs are from a long time ago and have no bearing whatsoever on the tragedies here. They are but fond memories of a past I still treasure.'

But there were none of her family and only two of the husband—one as a boy of eighteen driving a piebald mare and cart, and the other as the blind French soldier he had become. 'Did you spend time in the Old Bailey yourself?'

He was watching her too closely in the mirrors, but had he seen her tremble? 'Was that what they whispered? Well, was it?'

He nodded. Without asking permission, he helped himself to another of her cigarettes. 'And from truck driver to ambulance driver, for Léa was but a step?' he asked, waving out the match and leaving it on her dressing table.

In another day, at another time, she would have turned her back on him! 'Léa and I met time and again throughout that war, Inspector, for she tirelessly brought wounded to the various stations where I was on duty, including the ward where in July of 1916 I first met my André. War smashes social conventions, isn't that so? War collapses time and brings the distant into instant contact with the result that associations unheard of before suddenly become the norm.'

'And then?' he asked, still unwilling to leave the matter.

'An exploding artillery shell destroyed her ambulance, killing all five of the wounded and the orderly she had in the back. Sent to Paris to recover in the early autumn of 1917, she met Claude Monnier at one of the canteens. Abruptly we lost contact but war came again in 1939 and . . . '

Had he anticipated this too? 'We didn't meet until 3 December, 1940, when we were rounded up and sent first to Besançon. Terrible . . . the conditions there were shameful. Léa . . . Léa looked after me when I came down with flu and then pneumonia. I "owe" her, Inspector, as our boys used to say of one another—yourselves, too, I suspect.'

He still hadn't touched his tea but had set it on her dressing table. 'Madame de Vernon?' he suddenly asked.

Was this safer ground or a minefield? 'Irène de Vernon soon discovered that Caroline Lacy and Jennifer Hamilton wanted to become sitters. She wouldn't reveal why she objected so vehemently. Caroline didn't understand her, she said, and was being wayward. I was to refuse all further approaches. At first an offer of payment in postdated cheques was made—forged, I concluded, on Mademoiselle Lacy's account at the Morgan Bank in Paris. When I refused, as I should have, she then threatened me. Violent . . . *Ah, mon Dieu,* even Léa was afraid of what that woman might do.'

'And must have, is that it?'

'Inspector, please!'

'Yet you finally agreed to let Caroline become a sitter.'

'Only if Jennifer Hamilton would wait outside the Pavillon de Cérès to accompany the girl safely back to her room, if such an exception to the curfew could have been made. If not, they would have had to stay the rest of the night, which would have been fine by them. They were lovers, Inspector. Everyone knew it, for they hid nothing. Their love was pure, but Madame de Vernon spat on it and hated that Hamilton girl.'

'Lovers . . . Why didn't you inform my partner and me of this when we first spoke?'

'I . . . I didn't think it appropriate—polite, damn you!'

'And earlier, when asked what Caroline was to have brought along, you told my partner that it was only what that girl desperately wanted to know.'

Men . . . Why must they be such irritating pigs! 'The wording of our invitations is always couched in ambiguity, but I'm sure that partner of yours will have discovered what it was the girl was to have brought. A photo of Madame's former villa in Provence. Caroline Lacy wanted me to ask Cérès to contact Monsieur de Vernon. She was determined to find out what had really happened to him.

Madame had been left a widow but the leaving needed explanation. I agreed, finally, to take the girl as a sitter but, of course, that became impossible, last night's séance having been held without her.'

And we'll never know the answer, was that it, wondered Kohler, or was Madame de Vernon now to be blackmailed with it *and* the murder? 'Things have been stolen. Did you suspect either Caroline Lacy or Jennifer Hamilton? They were here often enough—seven times, I understand.'

One would have to try. 'But not here, Inspector. In there,' she said, pointing to the room whose door he knew was locked. 'Neither would have had an opportunity, since there is an entrance off the corridor. Léa showed them in. I came through from here. They held hands as they sat before me on the divan. Always the hands. Caroline needed constant reassurance; Jennifer perhaps just as much, for she's a strange one. Outwardly very confident, then suddenly inward and introverted.'

'And with Nora Arnarson?'

'The mistake I made was to let that girl accompany Mary-Lynn Allan. With Caroline, I decided once was enough. Belief is in the believer, not in the skeptic.'

'Vocal was she, our Nora?'

'Very.'

'And was this Jennifer Hamilton also a skeptic?'

'Again I must ask, is it that you think it all a con, or am I truly opening doors for those who seek a peace of mind and happiness far beyond anything they've known? Yours is not just an inquiry into two unfortunate deaths. Whether you wish it or not, my very being as a medium has been put on trial. All are watching and waiting for the outcome.'

'What did you really lose?'

'My talisman—is this what they whispered, those dreadful harpies who gossip at every opportunity? What I lost was an empty perfume bottle of no consequence. A piece of trash, nothing else.'

'Describe it for me.'

'I have already forgotten any details of it. You've recently lost two sons in the Battle for Stalingrad. If you would like to become a sitter, I could ask Cérès to contact them.'

'If that was an offer of peace, forget it. I haven't anything tangible of them, not even a photo. Nothing.'

'But yourself. Cérès will understand and accept.'

'And my aura?' he asked.

How dare he? 'Mary-Lynn's was vibrant. Electrified by danger. Yours . . . well, if you must know, is even more vibrant and not unlike that of the aurora borealis at its greatest excitation.'

'Good, then tell me, what's in that other room?'

The bell was rung, Léa entering to clear away as the cook brought in Madame's soft-boiled egg, toast made from white bread, and a conserve, the maid her *café au lait*. Somehow Louis and he were going to have to turn this house of dreams inside out. And yes, he had just heard another bell ring, if only for tea.

Though the darkness still intruded, St-Cyr could see that the forehead was high and broad, the hairline well receded, the goatee a prominent ear-to-ear fringe that set off what might have been a wrestler's build, but apart from the smells of various herbs, the cowshed and all, eau de cologne wafted pungently. Startled by it, he had to wonder if Brother Étienne had deliberately drenched the cloak or if it was but the norm.

'Chief Inspector,' came the booming from the depths, 'how good of you to come out to meet me. An extra pair of hands, is it? *Ah, bon*, take these and I will get my box.'

The burlap sacks were thrust into the *sûreté's* hands and weighed far more than thought, the patois that of the Vosges.

'Indoors, Inspector. *Vite, vite*. We mustn't let you catch cold. I've enough to treat as it is.'

Was concern to be masked by bluster and humour, or were these but a defence behind which to hide nervousness?

The snow was brushed off, the heavy homespun cloak unhooked, the shout he gave echoing up from the foyer to staircases and railings that were crowded.

'*Mes chères amies*, your melancholy is with me. Our Caroline? Give me but a moment with the chief inspector and I am totally yours until noon.

'It is this way, Inspector. The consulting room I never use except to leave my things. *Merde,* what a trip. Ice on the road, my Angèle slipping so many times I had to lead that wonderful creature down the hills at the pace of the snail. A Percheron. One of Madame Chevreul's, we are certain. *Absolument.'*

The door was closed.

'Now, what can this humble servant do for you? A few small questions—*Ah, oui, oui,* I think that you have those. Begin please.'

The cloak was thrown off, the soutane just as heavy, of a dark-brown homespun, its many pockets bulging but having far fewer of the odours, especially that of the cologne.

The overboots, high and enviously dry and warm, were unlaced and removed, the big toes wiggled beneath heavy woollen socks.

'I make this trip as often as possible but believe Untersturmführer Weber is determined to put an end to my visits, hence my having come today and brought more than usual.'

Somehow a handkerchief was found, its red that of field and harvest or cowshed, felt St-Cyr. The nose was blown, the dimpled cheeks and chin mopped of its snowmelt, the big, dark-brown eyes as well, and wary. At thirty-eight, the brother would have been too young for Verdun but more than acceptable for 1939. Had he hidden behind the cloth, as some might wonder if succumbing to the invective typical of veterans of that other war who sought to find those to hold accountable for the nation's failure in this one?

Having sat down, facing him across the table, felt Brother Étienne, this *sûreté* took out pipe and empty tobacco pouch, gesturing at the hopelessness of such a situation.

'Frankly, *mon Frère,* I don't know where to begin. Two murders and a petty thief.'

As well as a visiting monk who was supposed to arrive next Wednesday but had told them all he would come today, a Sunday, and early at that—was he wondering this also or had he accepted the excuse? 'And almost a thousand souls to question here, and nearly seventeen hundred in the Grand.'

'And one missing capsule of *Datura stramonium.'*

The massive fists were clenched.

'Madame de Vernon, that most persistent of creatures, was robbed?'

'But not, I think, by our petty thief.'

'Who seems only to have impulsively snatched the visible and all but worthless,' muttered Brother Étienne, running his hands over the table between them. 'Kleptomania . . . They say it can't be treated with herbs or anything else. Believe me, I've searched. I even went back to Culpeper, the British herbalist who died in 1654.'

'It's a disease of the mind, though invariably ignored by psychologists and little studied.'

'But in a place like this, is it that those so afflicted subconsciously demand of themselves that they acquire some little item which then defines each of their victims? Items, *mon cher* chief inspector, with which to identify their owners and possess a tiny part of them. Is it power over others that is desired, the afflicted not even knowing this of themselves?'

The depth of thought and sincerity were evident, the conclusion not easily arrived at, the expressions and gestures reinforcing these, the initial cloud of cologne very at odds with them. 'You've lost things too, have you?' asked St-Cyr.

'Often I must empty overloaded pockets to find an item.'

'And?'

How anxious this *sûreté* was, though waiting pensively now to look beyond the answer. 'A bent, hand-forged nail I kept to remind me of the Cross. It could not have been easily straightened and was of no use otherwise, lest one had magnetized it, of course, which I had.'

'To pull grains of iron oxide from sand?'

'*Ah, bon,* Chief Inspector. Magnetite which I then grind for those needing it, just as a prisoner of war will file a nail or bit of wire to place the filings on the tongue each day. The body needs its iron but such a thing is too often overlooked.'

Hermann had done that very thing during the more than two and a half years he had been a prisoner in that last conflict, but had this one known of his imprisonment? 'Anything else?'

'The woven string I used to wear at all times around my left wrist. Its knots were to remind me of the sister who had woven it for me when I entered the priesthood. Celibacy, she said, would be the hardest task of all. If I had any doubts at any time, I was to touch each knot and think of her. The string had worn through long ago but I couldn't part with it, for she was very dear to me. Put plainly, Inspector, our father couldn't afford to keep either of us. Marie became a nun, I being given to *les* Pères Tranquilles.'

A light knock at the door was repeated.

'*Entrez, ma chère,*' he called out, assaulting the ears as he quickly leaned over the table to whisper, 'A little nourishment in a house where not a morsel can be spared.

'Mrs. Parker, how many times must I tell you I have eaten, that the journey was far from long and tiring, yet still you never forget?

'A little soup, Inspector. Blow on it. Don't burn the tongue. We'll share, the two of us. It's best that way. Friends at once. Comrades.'

Urging that the soup be dealt with, he took her hands in his and ran big, work-worn fingers gently over the backs of them before nodding. 'Twice each day. You've been very good about it.' His whole being was intent on her and her alone. 'But still a little more is needed, don't you think? Once on waking, after the morning's wash and a good dry. Not too rough now, you understand? First warm the towel over the stove, then pat lightly with it. Give the healing every opportunity but use the lotion only twice. You've marvellous hands. A fountain-pen maker's daughter, Chief Inspector. Remarkable instruments I first encountered as a boy when wounded Americans were brought here to these very hotels and were writing letters home. The Treaty of Versailles was, I believe, signed with a gold one President Woodrow Wilson donated.'

Colouring, this spokeswoman blushed at the recognition and, taking one of the burlap sacks, quickly fled the room to softly close the door.

'One tries, Inspector, to find that most responsive chord. She has, I believe, no relation whatsoever to that family but dreams of it.'

And before coming here the brother had found out all he could about Hermann and him. 'Don't touch the soup.'

'*Ah, mon Dieu,* you can't think she would poison me? Not Eleanor.'

'Perhaps, but did she fill that canister whose smell, unless I'm mistaken, is far stronger than it should be?'

'*Datura stramonium* is very bitter and needs masking. In India they mix the seeds with curry, or with figs or dates but not to kill, only to incapacitate so as to rob or rape.'

A well-read man. 'Just don't eat or drink anything but what you've brought yourself or can get in the guards' canteen.'

'Surely you must have been made aware of the brush with which I've been tarred? With that cloak of mine reeking as it does, I would be most unwelcome in that canteen and subject to both verbal and physical abuse.'

'Welcome or not, the warning is clear.'

'And I, the healer, knowing each of the inmates intimately, must have much to tell you.'

'But plainly our killer or killers can't allow it.'

Filling the tin cup, the Brother drained it. 'The soup is perfectly fine, Inspector. All my life I have dreamt of this task God has prepared for me, and now again I must rise to its challenge.'

5

Kohler noted the ripe smell that emanated from the room in which this ringer of bells sat with Louis. Closing the door, he leaned back against it to block all exit while lighting yet another of Madame Chevreul's cigarettes.

'A nothing monk, eh, Louis, who stinks to high heaven? Comes here hot on the heels of two detectives to have a look at them and see what's up? Made sure our first victim had the eggs, milk, and cheese the child inside her needed yet helped her try to abort the mistake? Always brought the former Kommandant a little something to grease the wheels. Was full of juicy gossip that he embellished for Colonel Kessler's benefit. *Ein Spitzel, ja?*'

'Herr Kohler . . . ' began Étienne.

'It's Herr Hauptmann Kohler to you, my fine one, or Herr Detektivinspektor Kohler, and don't forget it.'

'As you wish, but what makes you think I wasn't acting on Colonel Kessler's requests? He was fully cognizant of Mary-Lynn's mistake, as you put it, and that her health, as that of everyone herein, was in jeopardy. Could he not have asked me to do both?'

'Feed her and abort her without telling her he'd asked you to?'

'Hermann . . . '

'Louis, let me handle this one.'

'He wasn't the father, not in so far as I knew, Herr Kohler, but if you must make that assumption and think what you will without further evidence, so be it. And as for my coming here today, I was late on Friday and couldn't attend to all who needed my presence.'

A smartass and defiant as well. 'Then understand, *mein Lieber,* that Untersturmführer Weber has it in for you. If not a charge of dealing on the black market, then one of bribing the former Kommandant into letting you come and go at will.'

There was no response. 'Have I rung his little bell enough, Louis, or do we need more?'

The cigarette was remembered and passed to his partner.

'*Merci, mon vieux,*' said St-Cyr, 'but he has already informed me that he believes his days of coming here are numbered.'

'If I'm not first poisoned,' said Étienne with a shrug. 'But Herr Weber has it in for the Senegalese as well, has he not, Herr Hauptmann *und* Detektiv Aufsichtsbeamter?'

'*Ach, sprechen sie Deutsch?*'

'Is Alsace not just on the other side of these hills and mountains or have I been mistaken all my life?'

'Louis . . . '

'*Doucement,* Hermann. Brother Étienne has many to attend to and very little time.'

'Madame Chevreul, eh?' asked Kohler, still not budging.

'The one who blasphemes by claiming the goddess Cérès speaks through her?' demanded Brother Étienne rising to the bait.

'The very one.'

'*Schlaflosigkeit, mein lieber Detektiv Aufsichtsbeamter. Schlaflosigkeit.*' Insomnia.

That did strike this belligerent Gestapo in the balls, thought Étienne, but had Élizabeth said the opposite? 'After one of her so-called séances the Lord, I know, will forgive, Madame Chevreul is so excited sleep will not come since the goddess, still having her ear, keeps on pouring it at her.

'She dreams, Inspector Kohler, if you will allow me to use a shortened title for you. She awakens with a start at some sudden revelation only to drift off until interrupted again by another juicy bit of news. In desperation this humble monk before you has prepared infusions of betony and skullcap; of lady's slipper, oats, and skullcap; a decoction of mistletoe, lime flower, and hawthorn; and infusions of lemon balm, hyssop, and lavender, and yet again, a tincture of St. John's wort. Though she has repeatedly begged me for a stronger sedative, and such things can become addictive and are oft-dangerous, I now have her on a tincture of valerian before bed, and an infusion of it with mistletoe and skullcap, but she is not, I repeat, to take too much of either.'

'Like the thorn-apple seeds you gave Madame de Vernon?'

'Hermann . . . '

'Louis, how many times must I tell you never to interrupt a member of our glorious Führer's Gestapo when he's in the process of questioning a murder suspect?'

'Madame de Vernon, Herr Hauptmann?' said Brother Étienne, reminding him and ignoring the accusation.

'The very one.'

'Is a hypochondriac that would try the patience of Saint Bénédict himself. If not the headaches, the migraines; if not those, the neuralgia and/or the rheumatism—I never know ahead of time, you understand: the shoulder, the hip, the spine, the knuckles of the left hand. Did you know she used to play the piano for the ballet studio her ward attended in Paris? Ah, I thought not. Currently I have her on a tisane of the Herb of Grace.'

'*Ruta graveolens,* Hermann. It's good for many complaints not just neuralgia and rheumatism. Brother, why the extra datura?'

They had every reason to want an answer, though temptation demanded that one not be given; however . . . 'She rightly claimed that the dried leaves and stems stank, but of course, having hung the bunch I had given her above her bed, would not listen and insisted that I powder and bottle them. This I did, but she claimed they were not enough. Since the contents can and do vary from leaf to leaf, not just from plant to plant, I was forced to let her use a little of the powdered seeds as well, but of course she then demanded more of those than I felt safe. The war, she said, the uncertainties of it. I might be called away and not allowed to return—what would she do? The child would have an uncontrollable spasm and die. Inspectors, can it be that you have yet to encounter Madame de Vernon? If so, let me tell you that one can only surmise she has been put-upon and is very angry at what the world and life have dealt her.'

Their looks were questioning, the cigarette butt carefully pinched out by the *sûreté* and returned to Herr Kohler for that one's little tin. 'All right, I worried because I felt she might well misuse them. Madame de Vernon hates those with whom she has to share a room and blames them for her plight, as much if not more than that dead husband of hers.'

'Who sold her villa out from under her and ran off with his mistress, Louis, thereby losing the cash.'

'Having gambled it away, no doubt, Hermann. Apparently Caroline Lacy thought there must have been a problem with his death in 1920.'

'As did Jennifer Hamilton, the girl's lover whom Madame de Vernon must have hated with a passion,' added Kohler.

Ah, bon Dieu, de bon Dieu, thought Étienne, the husband a gambler but did neither of them know of the nocturnal fire that had destroyed the casino here on Saturday 17 July, 1920?

'Brother, what's the problem? You seem to have thought of something,' asked the *sûreté*.

'I was just thinking of my patients and wondering when I might be allowed to attend to them.'

'Perhaps. On Friday last, at about 1530, Caroline Lacy went out-of-doors. You must have met her. You were, I believe, among the last, if not *the* last, to have spoken with her.'

And the prime suspect, was that it? 'I had arrived late. A flat. My *petrolette.* I'm always having trouble with the tires. These days one can't find a replacement for the inner tubes when needed. Mine date from 1938, or was it 1936? One of the Senegalese offered to patch it and I had wheeled the bike over to him and another.'

And so much for his *also* having had a flat and arriving late on the last day of Mary-Lynn Allan's life, thought Kohler. 'Their names, please?'

'Sergeant Senghor and Corporal Bamba Duclos. Caroline motioned to me, and I went over to her first before leaving the bike with them. Inspectors, I have been given to understand that the girl was killed in the Chalet des Ânes. Is such a terrible thing possible?'

'Who else was nearby?' asked Hermann.

'Or did I follow her inside that stable and kill her with a pitchfork, I who have the hands and strength that could have done the job far more easily? A child, the hesitant lover of Jennifer Hamilton? *Ah, mon Dieu,* you two seem so in the dark it frightens me. Caroline *needed* the comfort of another human being; Jennifer *offered* it, and what was that lonely, desperate girl of nineteen to have done when she found herself a friend just along the corridor from her own room and in a hotel where most had shunned her? Certainly one thing led to another, but for the first time in her short life, she thought she was being valued by another. She had found, if I must put it bluntly to you, that sense of worth which is so necessary.'

'Was Jennifer Hamilton predatory when choosing her relationship with Caroline?' demanded Louis.

Ah, bon, Chief Inspector. *Bon!* thought Étienne, but I will not give you the benefit of the answer you appear to want. 'That I could not say nor think.'

'But when you met her on that last afternoon, Caroline was uncertain?'

'Hesitant. Upset and very depressed, which caused me to believe she had lost her lover and was brokenhearted. I gave her what she asked for and said she needed most, which was God's blessing, and then a little snack and the few things I had brought for her.'

'The nettles, Louis.'

'The Host wafers and that small bar of soap, Hermann. Beechnut oil.'

'Alfalfa seeds,' said Herr Kohler.

'A seashell,' said the *sûreté*.

'I didn't give her that, inspectors.'

'But you knew of it,' said Louis.

Ah, merde, without so much as a hint, the two of them had worked together to lay a trap for him. 'A creamy white to yellowish, oval seashell with coarse, short teeth along its aperture, but only because the girl had shown it to me.'

'But did she show you anything else?' asked Hermann.

'Nothing, Inspector, nor did she tell me why she had shown me the seashell. I think perhaps that she had simply been feeling it for reassurance.'

Like the buds of that beechwood sprig, but fair enough, thought St-Cyr. 'It was near the end of the day, Brother. Most of the other internees would have gone indoors. A few were about but not too near?'

Ah, nom de Dieu, how much did they really know? 'All right, Becky Torrence was near. I . . . May God forgive me, I felt the girl might well have been following Caroline, for she stood some distance from us among the trees on the other side of the clearing where they used to walk the donkeys.'

'Was Caroline aware of her?' asked Louis.

'I don't think so. Her back was to her.'

'Anyone else?' asked Hermann, not taking his gaze from this healer for a moment.

It would have to be chanced. 'Is it that you want me, Herr Hauptmann *und* Detektivinspektor, to name anyone, or am I to tell you how it really was?'

'Don't get too cocky.'

'*Zut,* why would I? Nora Arnarson was some distance away and homeward bound from one of her forages.'

'Trapping rabbits, Brother?' demanded Louis.

Brother Étienne's fists were again instinctively doubled.

'*Ah, mon Dieu, mon Dieu,* so what if she traps a few of them in a place like this? Look, I know it's illegal and that there are either three years forced labour if caught, or prison, but here . . . Surely you would overlook such a thing?'

Or would they? They gave no hint.

'Did Mademoiselle Arnarson wave, pause, or start towards you and Caroline Lacy?' asked Kohler.

'Nora was cold and, seeing that I was occupied and late, pressed on.'

'Nora, Louis. He knows her well enough.'

To have used the informal. 'Must suspicion run constantly in your veins, Inspector? Nora looks after Angèle when I bring her, as I have today. She will have stabled her, rubbed her down, talked to her, thrown the buffalo robe my great-great Uncle Marcel brought home from the Western Plains of Canada and the United States of America over her, and forked out a plentiful supply of hay.'

And able to use a pitchfork—was that it? 'Where, Brother?'

Ah, cher Jésus, these two! 'The former riding stables.'

'Behind the former polo and jumping grounds, now the soccer field when weather permits, Hermann, and not all that far from our lodgings. Near to the fencing pavilions and the *tir aux pigeons.*'

The clay-pigeon shoot, but was St-Cyr, having been in Vittel recovering from wounds prior to when the American wounded started to arrive in 1917, the more dangerous of the two since he was still able to remember the locations? 'Colonel Kessler, the former Kommandant, liked to ride and kept two geldings there and a plentiful supply of hay. On the days that Angèle was with me, he felt a little comfort should be allowed. Today is fortunately no different. Mademoiselle Arnarson will be looking after her.' But could Nora really handle St-Cyr or Kohler if either should go after her? wondered Étienne. Would it be possible to get a warning to her? 'Now, may I leave, inspectors, and go on my rounds since I have nearly a thousand to deal with in this hotel alone?'

'Aren't there four French doctors in the hospital and one Scot?' asked Hermann.

'And do such ever really listen to their patients, Herr Hauptmann *und* Detektivinspektor? I do, and therein lies the rapport I have with each.'

Reluctantly Kohler stepped aside, the brother hoisting the heavy, iron-bound wooden medicine box of his surgery on to a shoulder and even closing the door after himself.

'An ammo box, Louis, stamped with the First American Army.'

And another leftover from that other war. 'He knows of Mrs. Parker's supposed fountain pens, having encountered them here as a teenager.'

'And probably knows of a hell of a lot of other things, having lived in the area all his life. Isn't a homosexual and never has been,' said Hermann, still not happy about having let him go.

'Yet is somehow able to use that cologne, the herbs, sour milk, and cow shit that cling to this cloak of his to suggest otherwise, but does Brother Étienne have more than an idea of what must have happened to Madame de Vernon's husband? Knowing of the casino fire here in 1920, he was taken aback by my mention of the husband's probably having gambled her money away, but refused to tell us what had troubled him.'

'It smells about as strongly as he does, Louis, since he just happened to mention that Madame de Vernon played the piano in Paris for a ballet studio. Did he learn that with his vows or just out of idle curiosity? And while we're on him, is it that he came here today just to have a look at us and find out how far we'd got?'

'Perhaps, but for now let's consider this. Caroline Lacy wanted Madame Chevreul to ask Cérès what had really happened to Madame de Vernon's husband. The girl had borrowed a photo of her governess's former villa from that one's locked suitcase and was terrified the woman would discover it was missing before it was returned.'

'But Madame de Vernon didn't lose that little perfume presentation box and bottle.'

'Madame Chevreul did?'

'And claimed she slept like a baby after every séance and was so emotionally exhausted she dropped right off,' said Hermann.

Yet suffered from insomnia. 'Was it stolen by our kleptomaniac?'

'No doubt, but according to Madame Chevreul not by Caroline or Jennifer, who held hands through seven preliminary interviews, each needing reassurance from the other and having had no access to her bedroom, they being interviewed in the next room which was kept locked and still is, but supposedly has an entrance off the corridor. Frankly, I didn't believe her. Why not interview them in her reception room, given that I had to walk right through it to get to her?'

'A sleight of hand then, better even than that of Houdini?' asked Louis.

'Certainly as fast as Madame Chevreul's cigarettes disappeared without her noticing the extra ones I took.'

'*Bon!* And on the evening of Mary-Lynn's death, they were alone in Room 3–54 when an enraged Madame de Vernon came to get Caroline and had the door slammed in her face.'

'By Caroline, who was in tears, Louis, and very upset.'

'Enough for Madame de Vernon to claim that the couple had broken up, and for Brother Étienne to now echo it, but did things go far beyond that?'

'A wad of chewing gum . . .'

'A substance Madame de Vernon claims she has no taste for, Hermann.'

'Becky Torrence knowing that woman couldn't have been asleep, since neither was she, the others having gone off to play poker.'

'Nora Arnarson publicly deriding Madame Chevreul's success, both at the séance and later when the two dropped in to tell the poker players. She and Mary-Lynn argued vehemently, the one then running ahead and up the stairs in tears.'

'Only to be shoved by Madame de Vernon, who was really after Caroline to put a stop to her enquiries?'

'It's possible, Hermann, but then . . . *Ah, mais alors, alors . . .*'

'Louis, if that woman's bed was empty, Becky Torrence must have known of it, hence her nervousness when I first encountered her.'

'And then her interest in Caroline's whereabouts late last Friday afternoon, if the brother was telling us the truth? *If,* Hermann, but why wasn't Jennifer Hamilton with Caroline, if for no other reason than reassurance, since that girl, if still a lover as Jennifer has claimed, would have confided in her?'

'Women, girls . . . Caroline *was* wanting to tell the new Kommandant that Mary-Lynn's death hadn't been an accident and that she'd seen her being pushed.'

'But was convinced, Hermann, that she herself had been the intended victim.'

'Jennifer must have known who Caroline was to have met in the Chalet des Ânes. I'll look forward to seeing her.'

'But you already have? The girl said so.'

'A soup-and-bread carrier?'

'With a childhood scar on her chin.'

'She's one of Weber's informants. I'm certain of it.'

'Then chase after our healer. If my guess is right, he'll either be in Room 3–38 or Room 3–54. I think I'll take a walk and have a word with that horse of his. Nora Arnarson tried to lie to this chief inspector, and the others in that room of hers, knowing that she was, went right along with it to shield her. Instinctively the female herd closes round to defend the threatened.

'There's another thing, Hermann. Brother Étienne is also treating Jennifer Hamilton. The girl's a tidier with her own things, but did she lay out and tidy Mary-Lynn Allan's last effects, or did some, as yet unknown, fanatic tidier have access to that room and reason beyond that of the others?'

'What's he treating her for, an irrepressible desire to steal little things?'

'Find out.'

'Two flat tires, Louis. Each causing him to arrive late, but hours before Mary-Lynn's killing, the second too damned close to Caroline's.'

'*Bien sûr,* it's a puzzle, especially since a man like that can't be suffering from memory loss and wouldn't have forgotten that he had already used such an excuse.'

'Have you had breakfast?'

'Not yet.'

The riding stables had the look of the long-abandoned, the stock having been requisitioned by the Wehrmacht and used for transport to the Russian front or sent to farms in the Reich. Apart from one stall, halfway along the central aisle and chosen for its maximum shelter, there was no other sound save that of the mare moving about as she enjoyed the hay the girl had thrown down from the loft above.

Of Nora Arnarson there was no sign, but was she watching him? wondered St-Cyr. Patting the mare's neck, he ran a hand over the robe of the brother's ancestor. Was it a tidy arrangement, the mare being used on those days the *petrolette* wasn't?

Beneath the fur there was a moth-eaten backing of wine-coloured, faded velvet. The seam had been torn open long ago—an arm could be slid well in-between the two, though by now anything that had been left would have been removed.

The loft was empty but for the remains of the winter's hay and a wooden-tined pitchfork that leaned against a nearby wall. Had she gone off on one of her traverses? Had she sensed she might be followed here and taken precautions?

Out across the open expanse of the polo grounds there was no sign of her or of anyone else, nor across the former racecourse beyond it and right to the three-metre-high barbed wire of the perimeter. The golf course on the other side gave only winter, the Hôtel de l'Ermitage, that of luxury and temptation. It had to have been the source of the golf balls and wallpaper, but the road that led up to it from the Parc Thermal had not been plowed, and neither was there any sign of wheeled tracks or of chimney smoke.

Sacré nom de nom, where was she?

As he started toward the Institute of Physical Education, the sound that came was that of the persistent: a thump, a pause, a thump, the three repeated with a constancy that puzzled until he found her in the first of the fencing pavilions, which was open on three sides and facing the polo grounds. Lacrosse stick in hand, the hard rubber ball was being flung against the inner wall only to bounce back, be caught and returned. She had even marked out the size of the goal net and could put that ball wherever she wanted. Sometimes she threw it so that it bounced on the floor first, just ahead of the goal; sometimes it hit the top-left corner or the lower right, but with a swiftness and surety that impressed. She never missed, always caught the rebound, worked ball and stick both before her and above her head as she sometimes ran in to turn and put it into a corner behind her imaginary goalkeeper.

The three-quarter-length brown anorak had its hood thrown back. The dark-brown toque fitted snugly.

'Inspector . . . '

Ah, merde, she'd been crying, had been startled by his sudden appearance, and was wary.

He didn't come closer, this *sûreté,* Nora noticed with a wince. Instead, he stood and searched the pavilion's floor where she had shovelled the windblown snow away, and when at last he found what he wanted, he crouched to examine the spot.

Then he pulled off a glove and ran a finger over the concrete.

'Ashes, mademoiselle. What, please, did you burn?'

Ah, damn him, damn him! *'Une cigarette.'*

'The butt, then, since you were in hock for weeks. The firewood purchase, *n'est-ce pas?'*

Shit!

'First, mademoiselle, we now know that you were seen by Brother Étienne late on Friday afternoon, and shortly before Caroline Lacy was killed.'

Étienne must have had to tell him. 'It was late. I was cold. I . . . I didn't even wave.'

'Who was with him?'

He would persist until he got the answer he wanted. 'Caroline, I think.'

'But Becky Torrence was nearer to them than you were?'

'Was she? I didn't notice.'

And lying again, was it? 'Would Becky have followed Caroline from the Vittel-Palace?'

'To kill her? Becky? You must be crazy. Inspector, I'd been out for hours. I *had* to get warm. The ground fog that hangs over the valley here had come in. Visibility was poor. Tree trunks were in the way. How was I to have seen anything?'

The lacrosse stick was now held lightly with its curved and open end just touching the floor at her feet, the ball in her left hand, the girl seemingly at comparative ease but poised like a coiled spring.

The short-cropped hair protruded from under the toque, giving its wisps of amber-to-blonde; the dark blue eyes assessed all possibilities and risks as the throat, beneath its woollen scarf, constricted.

'A moment ago you were crying, mademoiselle. Even as you threw the ball.'

'Am I not allowed to?'

'Bien sûr, but were the tears from relief or despair?'

Over something Étienne had left for her—this was definitely what he was thinking. Beyond him, the footprints of the path he had trod showed plainly enough, but there wasn't anyone else's that she could see.

The note Étienne had left had burned in but a few seconds, the ash falling grey and crinkled and very fine, and she *had* tried to remove it and hide the evidence. The match had been buried in the snow she'd shovelled away, but if he wanted to he could find it.

And in the room early this morning he had asked if Mary-Lynn had been Jewish and was Jennifer, had said that neither he nor his partner would do a thing about it if true. He'd taken one hell of a chance with them, would have to be told something—he had that look about him, but could he be trusted? These days one never knew.

A brief grin would be best and then, 'All right, you win. Early this morning the Marines and the Forty-Third Division took the Russell Islands in the Solomons. They're going to build fighter aircraft landing fields there in but a few days so as to hit the Japs well before those people get to our boys and our ships.

'Last Thursday, German U-boats intercepted a convoy in the North Atlantic sinking another fifteen merchant ships. In Tunisia, British and American forces are taking heavy losses because Rommel has a new tank against which nothing seems to work.* But last Tuesday . . . last Tuesday, the Russians reoccupied Kharkov and are now six hundred kilometres to the west of Stalingrad. Tears of joy, Inspector, and tears of grief.'

She bounced the ball and caught it, swung the stick out and pulled it back still with the ball. Again and again she did this. Easily, fluidly, teasingly, threateningly, silently saying, Are you now going to turn me in? If so, tell me and see what happens.

'Is the brother of the FTP?' St-Cyr asked, unruffled.

The Francs-Tireurs et Partisans. 'A devout Catholic, Inspector? One of the Pères Tranquilles? Aren't the FTP communists?'

'Some of them, but you're well informed. Perhaps it is that you are also aware that the Vosges and this whole region are known for its partisans. The Franco-Prussian War, the Great War, Mademoiselle Arnarson, and now again, Alsace having changed hands once more.'

She shrugged. She took to throwing the ball against the wall. He would get no further with her on the matter, decided Nora, but he

---

* The Mark VI.

hadn't mentioned that Étienne must be listening to the Free French broadcasts from London—a highly illegal act—and he would have mentioned it if of the enemy.

'Two murders, mademoiselle, and now some answers, please. Apparently you frequently went through the Hôtel Grand not only in search of Caroline Lacy and Jennifer Hamilton but asking where those two had been and with whom they had talked. Did you suspect either of having stolen that good-luck penny your father sent?'

Did he never forget anything one said? 'In a place like this, superstition thrives, Inspector. People believe others can contact the dead and learn all kinds of secrets from them or simply get words of endearment and reassurance. Others seek to find out when the next shipment of Red Cross parcels will arrive, or if a parcel from home will come or a letter or postcard from a prisoner-of-war husband or fiancé.'

'While still others believe they are prima donnas of the gods?'

Madame Chevreul. The ball had best be kept bouncing. At least then she wouldn't have to look at him. 'Lots of us are playing roles of one kind or another. How else are we to survive?'

'But dream? Is yours that of the trapper?'

She swung the stick.

'The loner? Even in a cage like this, I've found ways of being by myself.'

The ball hit the upper left corner of the goal. 'And what, please, have you learned that is enough for someone to want to kill you? Come, come, mademoiselle, put that stick down and talk to me. This little presentation box of Guerlain's was stolen from Madame Chevreul and found in Caroline Lacy's pockets. Was Jennifer Hamilton the thief?'

She would stop. She would have to, decided Nora, but had they found the Star of David? 'Wouldn't a kleptomaniac have kept it all to herself?'

'Was Caroline the thief, then?'

Throw the ball again, she told herself. *Again!* 'Or neither of them, Inspector? As far as I and the others know, Madame Chevreul gave that little box to Caroline to tell her everything was fine and that she could count on being a sitter at the séance that was to be held last night and wasn't even cancelled because of her death. Caroline couldn't resist showing it to us. Madame de Vernon came into the room and tried to snatch it from her. There was a scene. The girl was slapped several times and took to shrieking, which only made Madame angrier until the four of us parted them and faced up to her and she cursed us and gave it back to Caroline but with a warning to us. The Kommandant was going to hear about it and what we had all been up to, but that is why Caroline had it with her. She *knew* Madame de Vernon would smash it or throw it in the stove.'

And not stolen at all?

The ball was stopped. He must long for his pipe and tobacco, thought Nora, for he took them out as one would from compulsive habit, only to quickly tuck them away as he spoke his thoughts aloud: 'My partner was informed otherwise, mademoiselle, and we will have to deal with it when time allows, but with Madame de Vernon we have a woman whose husband had stolen everything and left her to eke out a living playing the piano in a ballet studio.'

Had Madame Chevreul told his partner that or had Étienne? wondered Nora. 'Where she met and saw a chance to get a meal ticket and maybe enough for her retirement? All Caroline ever wanted was to dance, and being the youngest of a very wealthy family, she went to work on her daddy, as girls will, until he agreed to let her study in Paris and let that woman be her guardian and mentor.'

'But it never happened, the dancing career.'

'Not with Poland in September of 1939 and the Blitzkrieg in 1940. The villa in Provence must have looked pretty good then, it being in the *zone non occupée.*'

'Was it empty?'

Had he experience of such? 'It was but they couldn't stay there. Even though the caretaker knew her from before, he wouldn't let them, so they found a place in the village until the call went out for Americans and someone turned them in for the reward.'

Again she began to throw the ball. 'What really happened to the husband?' he asked.

She would put it into the lower right corner. 'All Caroline really knew was that he had come from a very wealthy family in Barre, Vermont.'

'Tombstones and polished granite slabs for monuments and buildings.'

'Maybe his is in one of the graveyards in town—Caroline did wonder, and taking a chance, even asked some of the women who came in to do laundry in the afternoons and offered to pay them if they'd find out for her. If you ask me, Caroline thought he wasn't any good, Inspector—that he had run off to Paris as a young man, to the girls, the fun, the booze, and the drugs. Too much money, too little sense. It happens all the time. You must have seen it lots.'

'And the gambling, mademoiselle?' he asked as the ball hit the floor and went into the upper-left corner.

'She thought that too, since after he had sold the villa, he must have then lost the whole bundle. He did join up in 1917 and was wounded on 29 September, 1918, and sent here to recover—that much Caroline was pretty sure of.'

'Only to die in 1920 in a fire, mademoiselle?'

On 17 July of that year. 'Caroline didn't know but wanted to find out, I think.'

'And you have been trying to piece it together.'

'Wouldn't you if you were bored out of your skull in a place like this? All the records were lost. The debts, the names. I'll bet arson was suspected, but I don't know. Caroline might have whispered that to Jennifer, since she confided everything to her. I'm sure of it.'

'And Madame de Vernon is aware of this?' he asked, she having stopped the ball only to throw it again and again.

'Probably.'

'Then Jennifer Hamilton is also a target—is this what you think?'

The ball couldn't be stopped now. 'I haven't had a chance to talk to her. Things have been happening too quickly.'

'But it's possible?'

'Yes!'

'Did the couple have a falling out?'

'Caroline was upset after Mary-Lynn fell, but then so were the rest of us . . . and still are.'

A cautious answer. 'Is Jennifer the thief, mademoiselle?'

'Jen? If she thought I felt that way she would be here now, facing right up to me.'

'Perhaps, but you are also hiding too much. Is Herr Weber aware of this?'

The ball was *missed*! 'That *Nazihund,* that bastard? He's pointed me out three times in the lineups we have, chooses one here, another there, then I've had to wait for hours outside that damned office of his. Twice while Caroline was in there being grilled—the poor thing coming out in tears. Once while Jen was in there, then he showed me a spread of the anonymous letters he had received about me. My name was misspelled. Some of them couldn't even get their grammar straight, never mind the spelling.'

'British?'

The ball was returned to the net. 'Mostly, but not all unfortunately.'

'And what were they denouncing?'

'My independence, my loneliness, my long hikes even in the bitterest of weather.'

She stopped to look out over the golf course, to the Hôtel de l'Ermitage and the forest beyond, and as the tears came again, she said, 'It's a perfect day for cross-country skiing and snowshoeing especially. Every time it's like this, I think of being with my dad. I was five when he first took me with him. Five years old, Inspector. We had to camp out. The blizzard lasted for four days. Never have I felt so close to someone before or since. I loved him with a passion that was crazy.'

'Did they complain about your trapping rabbits?'

She mustn't look at him now. 'Everyone knew of it soon enough, and forgive me for wanting to take the Lord's name in vain, but the others come into our room as if they own it. They stare at you even if they've nothing to say, or ask the dumbest of questions. If you're at all different in this life, watch out, and the closer the community, the tighter the grip the others have on you. Beware of *les originaux ou originales,* Inspector, and I am definitely one of them.'

The odd ones. She retrieved the ball, deftly picking it up off the snow as if both stick and ball were parts of her. 'Did they object to your looking after Angèle?'

'Here the aspergillum doesn't just sprinkle holy water but kindness. Brother Étienne is a saint and everyone knows it and knows what would happen to them should they speak out or point the finger at him. Granted, he's like a hairdresser at times and some idiots will tell him the most scandalous of things while others seek his advice and reveal far too much.'

'Does he gossip?'

'Is he an informant—isn't that what you really want to ask? A man who risks his life time and again to bring a little happiness and sometimes, as today, food that is desperately needed and hasn't been tasted in years?'

When he gave no answer, Nora found she still couldn't stop throwing the ball, because it really did help not to have to face him. *Chacun pour soi,* Inspector? Is that what you still think?'

Everyone for him- or herself.

The lower-left corner of the net received five direct hits.

'It's the catechism of the times, isn't it,' Nora continued, 'so why shouldn't it be even worse in here behind that bloody wire? Lying, cheating, stealing—did you know we had a terrible bout of underwear theft from the laundry lines and had to post guards? Can you imagine waiting while the damned laundry *dried* in a place like this? But now it's only the little things.'

Wanting that pipe and tobacco of his, he again took out the one and clenched its stem between his teeth for comfort.

'Which brings us right back to Jennifer Hamilton and Caroline Lacy,' he said, gesturing with the pipe.

Ah, damn! 'All right, I *was* suspicious of Jen but really only because of her relationship with Caroline. It was out of character, I felt at first, and then opportunistic because Caroline's family has a whopping lot of money. Jen had tried and tried to get Mary-Lynn to speak to Colonel Kessler about her flat in Paris. She needed to get there—everyone agreed that she did, and exceptions here are being made every now and then. Some do buy their way out or have it paid by someone else. *Bien sûr,* Jen could have sold some of the things in her flat if she had been able to get there. The prices are fabulously high now for Old Masters and antiques, especially if the latter were originally from the Third Reich.'

'Where's the cache of petty thefts?' he asked so suddenly the ball was caught but not thrown. 'Come, come, out with it, mademoiselle. If you know that, then you are in more than just danger.'

'Kleptomaniacs don't kill, Inspector. As far as I know, it's not in their nature. They're usually quite gentle and retiring. Look, if I knew where it was, do you think I'd still be wondering who was taking things?'

The ball was again thrown.

'Whoever it is, Inspector, she's uncanny about it. No one has ever seen her steal anything, so why should anyone be able to find out where she's been hiding the loot, such as it is?'

'And the missing datura seeds, mademoiselle?'

Was he close to the truth? she wondered. 'All of us in that room of ours knew where that Frenchwoman kept a spare key to that suitcase. Caroline, me, Jill, Marni, and Becky. We're all terrified, isn't that so? Now, if you don't mind, I'd like to be by myself.'

'Before you broadcast the Brother's news bulletin?'

He *would* ask and she would have to tell him. 'At first it only goes out to a very few. You've been privileged.'

'*Ah, oui, oui,* but does Herr Weber suspect this breech of security has been happening?'

'He might. I really don't know. Often the Free French broadcasts are jammed, or the weather's too off and Étienne can't get a thing.'

Étienne. 'Yet all must be hungry for the news he brings.'

'We let it out only in little bits and with days between and as rumours.'

'Aren't you afraid of informants?'

'Always.'

'Was there anything else in the note he left for you?'

Why had he asked? 'Nothing. How could there have been?'

'Let me try the stick. I used to play soccer. Left centre forward.'

'You'd only lose the ball and I haven't got another.'

'Then for now, enjoy your dream. Hermann will be wondering

where I've got to. I think I'll tell him I attended a lacrosse game in which so many goals were scored, I completely lost count.'

The furor had died down; the door to Room 3–38 had been closed for maybe five minutes, maybe ten.

Kohler took another look around, wishing Louis were with him. Louis would have picked up on things this Kripo might well have missed.

Jill Faber sat silently on her cot against the wall nearest to the kitchen corner with its stove leaking trails of woodsmoke, for she'd built the fire up too high and the sound of its crackling pine and smell permeated. Marni Huntington, the redhead, was to his left, against the inner wall, the girl sombre too, as if, in having Brother Étienne in the room, demureness was best.

Becky Torrence, the blonde from St. Olaf College in Northfield, Minnesota, held the slimmest wedge of Port-du-Salut in her lap, the room's share, a treasure, while the camp's nothing monk consoled Madame Irène de Vernon on that one's cot.

Gone was the *bonheur,* the booming bluster, the open-armed gestures. Instead, this Pied Piper of Hamelin who had climbed the stairs with the whole of the Vittel-Palace following now held that woman's hands and let her pour out her heart to him.

'Me, I told Caroline not to go outside so late in the day, *mon Frère.* I begged her not to. The chest.'

'Yes, yes, madame, you did as you should have.'

'She was determined, was still very upset—had been that way for the whole week since that . . . that other one had fallen. I asked her who she was going to meet, and she said . . . *Ah, Sainte Mère, Saint Mère, mon Frère* Étienne, she said, "It's not what *you* think. You'll find out soon enough." Soon, Brother? Soon?'

'Now, now, Irène, please try to calm yourself.'

'It was that Jennifer Hamilton. Caroline went to meet her, to tell her their affair was over. *Over,* you understand. I'm certain of it. Who else would have killed my child? She was always after Caroline and followed her everywhere just as that one over there did.'

Uh-oh, thought Kohler.

'Becky Torrence?' asked the brother, startled.

'*Oui*. I've seen the way she looked at my Caroline when a glimpse of flesh was revealed while having a wash. That one would seek her out, *mon Frère*, Caroline embarrassed by the look, me quickly closing the gap in the curtain. Lust, I tell you. Lust!'

Louis should have heard it.

'The child did not understand at first, but that Jill over there who talks so lewdly of the Senegalese is very aware of what that Torrence girl felt for my Caroline. Ask her. She knows. Look how she tries to stare me down now. She once caught that other one trying to kiss my Caroline who was so innocent, the Virgin herself would have been astounded. Caroline pulled away in shock. Instinctively, I tell you. Instinctively, while that one, that *garce* Jill said . . . '

'Yes, yes,' managed the brother, all ears now no doubt, felt Kohler.

'She said, "Better luck next time, eh, if that's what you really want."'

'I *didn't*!' swore Jill. 'That's all a pack of dirty lies.'

'Lies, is it?' spat the woman. 'Then who was it, please, who went after Caroline the night that other one fell?'

'I . . . I felt sorry for her, that's all,' said Becky. 'I was worried, yes, but I definitely wasn't secretly in love with Caroline, nor did I kill her in a fit of jealousy. It's horrid of you to suggest such a thing.'

'Horrid, is it?'

The two were all but shouting now.

'Caroline lived in hell because of you, Madame, and as for my glimpse of bare flesh, it's hard to avoid in such cramped quarters.'

'You *wanted* to see her nakedness. Her *cul*. You enjoyed it.'

'Inspector, I lowered my eyes as quickly as I could, but guess who was telling that girl how to wash herself?'

'You would have lain with her if she had let you,' spat Madame de Vernon, 'and then . . . then I would have had to listen to the two of you!'

'Becky . . . Becky, leave it,' cautioned Jill, getting up to reach out to her. 'Marni doesn't think it's true, and neither do Nora or I.'

'*I didn't kill her, Jill. I swear I didn't!*'

'*Jésus Christ,* Madame, look what you've done,' Jill said shrilly. 'Destroyed us all!'

'Mesdemoiselles . . . mesdemoiselles,' urged Brother Étienne, 'a moment of privacy. Inspector, somehow I must calm Madame. Her pulse, it is racing.'

'Pull the curtain and tell her to hold her fire or a charge of murder will.'

Jill swiftly closed the curtain, then went back to Becky to brush the backs of calming fingers over a tearstained cheek.

The hand was seized and pressed to those lips. Becky Torrence was a mess, felt Kohler. Nervous as hell, afraid—terrified, but of what? Death—they all were, but was it also of something else, something far worse, like the shame of being discovered having been the thief of things of no consequence except in a place like this?

After Caroline, she was the youngest. Maybe twenty-three and missing home and everything else.

The Port-du-Salut had been splashed by Becky's tears, Jill setting it aside as Marni Huntington went to join the two.

Now both comforted the room's littlest one, death having passed that title on. Together they hugged her, putting foreheads against hers as if girls of ten consoling one after some terrible trouble at school.

'We're all boiling, Inspector,' said Jill, drawing away a little. 'That bitch behind the curtain has made our lives hell.'

Kohler found the last of the cigarettes he had taken from Madame Chevreul's case and, lighting it, took two drags before gently placing it between Becky's quivering lips. 'Not too much,' he said softly, gently lifting her chin to give her a smile. 'The others need a little. It's always good to share.'

Jill looked at him; he looked at her, he to ask and she to answer straight enough. '*Oui,* I translated that note for Caroline. Look, I didn't know whom she was hoping to meet or who had arranged it, but when she begged me to put it into *Deutsch,* I did. "*Bitte sagen Sie dem Kommandanten, dass es kein Unfall war. Ich sah wie es passierte und wer es war.*"'

Please tell the Kommandant that was no accident. I saw it happen and know who did it.

Becky dried her eyes and wiped her nose with the back of a hand. 'I really only wanted to help her the night Mary-Lynn was killed, Inspector. She was very upset about something and had been coughing and wheezing like crazy. I felt she'd die if I didn't. She couldn't find her cigarettes, had panicked. I grabbed her in the dark and said I'd help. I found the light switch and turned the room light on.'

'Madame's bed was empty, was it?'

'I . . . I think so. The cigarettes weren't anywhere near where they should have been. Jill found them on that thing we call a coffee table. Marni had been looking too. Caroline . . . Caroline *knew* she was being punished by that woman behind that damned screen.'

'*Garce!* Masturbator! The widow, the wrist, eh? I heard you earlier that night! I did. I really did!' yelled Madame de Vernon.

Ach, mein Gott, did the hatred run so deep?

'Were you really listening, madame?' asked Jill. 'Did she make you envious, our Becky, you whose life has been so dry you would leave that bed of yours to try to kill Caroline only to make a terrible mistake?'

'Fucking bitch, you'll get yours, too. The settling of accounts!'

All this time Brother Étienne had been urging calm, but at last he said, 'Irène, what did you do with those missing datura seeds? Come, come. I gave you three of those capsules. Oh for sure, you were in the hospital being attended to. I have my sources and know you were, but you could easily have returned without the others in this room knowing. You would have had the times they'd be away, the daily round of things that always have to be done. The roster.'

This was hotly denied, but it was Jill who said, 'This room of ours is often empty, except for her, Inspector.'

And wasn't *dénonciation* a favourite French pastime? 'Hand it over, madame. Save yourself a lot of grief.'

'And someone else—is that what you think, Inspector?'

'I'm waiting.'

'Then wait, for I haven't stolen it from myself.'

Stubborn . . . *Ach,* the woman was pure poison and should have been the one to have fallen. 'Come on, you three. Let's find us a quiet corner in that dining room that's never used.'

Except for lineups. 'I have to lug the hot water,' said Jill. 'There's always one hell of a crowd and I'm late enough as it is.'

'I've got to see if there's any mail,' said Marni Huntington, who all this time had continued to rub the back of Becky Torrence's neck only to pause as something had been said that had struck her, the three of them in this room by then that night. The three of them, then Caroline coming back to find her cigarettes.

'And I'm supposed to be waiting outside Herr Weber's office,' said Becky. 'Am I for it this time?'

Hermann was deep in conversation. Tense, subdued, and not liking their being kept from things, Jill Faber, Marni Huntington, and Becky Torrence sat across the table from him, Brother Étienne's cloak to one side.

'The Senegalese, Louis,' he said, but nothing else.

Out in the cold, on the terrace of the Hôtel Grand, the lineups were long. Breath billowed, feet were stamped, cigarettes cupped for their meagre warmth. Interspersed, in small groups or as singles, the British and Americans each muttered and bitched just as others did in Paris and Lyon or outside the shops of any other city, town, or village, but here . . . here where there had been the shops of the elegant—of Hermès, Molinard, Coty, Boucheron, and Cartier, of Elizabeth Arden, too, and Barclay—there were now root vegetables and dried herbs, an occasional very worried rabbit, a solitary hen, and pieces of another.

Rope-soled sandals were on offer, with canvas-repaired leather shoes whose laces were of dyed Red Cross parcel string waiting for the owners to pick them up if they had the cash or something with which to barter. Buttons, pins, some even rusty, were with thread and needles and the unravelled, rewound wool from worn-out sweaters and skirts. Much of it had been gleaned, no doubt, from Vittel's citizenry, either by purchase beforehand or placed on consignment. Squares and lengths of cloth were in another shop; in yet another, the flea-market leftovers of a nation down on its luck and desperate for cash since potatoes alone were at 600 francs per kilo if available on the black market.

But women did love to shop. Even without the wherewithal, they could still peruse, and it did alleviate the boredom, yet all who looked at him as he threaded his way among them seemed to say, 'How could you people do this to us,' and then . . . then, 'It wasn't me, damn you, but am I next?'

'Where can I find the Senegalese, mademoiselle?' he asked. She had the look of the embittered.

'Behind the church. They did it, didn't they? Those bastard blacks took turns while one of them held her down.'

'Then they stabbed her to death to shut her up,' said another.

'They're sex-starved,' yet another went on, suddenly turning on him. 'They're not allowed to use the brothel that's reserved for the guards, so they keep an eye out and try to buy it if they can.'

'The officers go into town, Inspector,' said another.

'Caroline begged those blacks not to rape her, Inspector, but they couldn't wait, could they? What they had thought for sale wasn't, so they took it anyway.'

'She didn't scream because she couldn't.'

'Soap,' said one in another line. 'She had a bar of Lifebuoy to sell or trade, but they shoved it into her mouth.'

'Chocolate,' said another. 'Hershey's Milk. Two bars.'

'A fortune they didn't even think to steal when they were done with her.'

'They'll be shot if caught, so you and that partner of yours had better watch your backs.'

'Cracker Jack Nut Candy Popcorn,' said yet another. 'Garden seeds. Packets and packets of them.'

'She must really have wanted something from them but they couldn't have understood her French—was that how it was, Chief Inspector?'

Her brown eyes had the look of the disgusted. 'Your name, please?' asked St-Cyr.

'Madame Élaine de Charbonneau, formerly of Paris Mondiale Radio, but originally from Hartford, Connecticut. A Vassar graduate, not that it matters here, and with a doctorate in Elizabethan Literature from Cambridge. My husband was killed during the Blitzkrieg, the Ardennes breakthrough. Where were you when that was happening?'

Running away with all the others?—so many still had to ask it. 'Madame, I'm sorry you lost your husband.'

'Are you?'

The firewood compound was well behind the church and separated from it by a treed area, the barbed wire of the fence running along the rue Charles Garnier, that of the architect of the Paris Opéra. A habitué of Vittel, Garnier had brought everything together here in 1884 and had built the original casino and its theatre, for he had designed the one at Monaco. Out went the old baths, in came those with their wonderful mosaics of tile and walls of white marble. Byzantine, oh for sure, but of Caracalla too, Vittel was then very much on the map as one of the preferred destinations of *la haute et grande bourgeoisie urbaine.*

But then, during the fin de siècle, from 1890 to 1910, they had what was called the Crisis, as the market for spa-goers became saturated and many Vittel regulars drifted to Baden d'Outre Rhin and other such places. A complete reconstruction was called for, with eight new hotels, fifteen villas, the racecourse and stables, a new promenade, two bottling plants and such for the sale of the waters. All well and good except for the intervention of that war to end all wars, but then . . . then *la Cité Blanche,* the White City of 1920 to 1936 ushered in the concept of the man of action. Fencing, swimming, physical education, tennis, golf, but concerts, too, and gambling of course. No longer were the waters to be taken simply for their healing powers but for toning and cleansing the psyche as well as the body. Art Deco became the norm, but throughout the years Bouloumié's original concept of open vistas across the landscaped park was kept.

Yet no one could have envisaged it as a prison, or even, for that matter, as a hospital for wounded soldiers.

Among the Senegalese, the Bambaras, originally from Mali, had been the backbone of African bravery in the Great War. Sergeant Senghor, with his Croix de Guerre with two palms, had to be part Bambara. And the rest of his parentage? wondered St-Cyr. Was it of the Serer, the Mandinka, or Wolof, these last being sensitive to every nuance but known as the black Corsicans because one moment's gentleness and good humour could be fiercely followed by the opposite.

Six of them were splitting logs they'd sawn to firewood size, the compound fenced in to prevent theft, the gate open but under a guard that had obviously attracted considerable attention.

A brisk trade was in progress, the Oberfeldwebel, the sergeant-major, his rucksack open, quickly ducking the profits out of sight as Wehrmacht razor blades, boot grease, notepaper, black bread, matches, meat and potatoes, and even items from the Russian Front were whisked away in exchange for cigarettes, chocolate, soap, and chewing gum. Canned condensed milk, too, and pork and beans.

'Inspector . . . ' blurted one middle-aged British woman, aghast at having been caught dealing.

'Actually, it's Chief Inspector. A word with the woodcutters,' he said in *Deutsch* to the Oberfeldwebel. 'I won't be long and you can carry on here as usual. *Ach,* nothing said and no one the wiser.'

'*Verdammter französischer Schweinebulle,*' cursed Ewald Reinecke. '*Alles raus, schnell machen!*' Get out of here fast.

They vanished.

'*Papiere, bitte,*' he said with a smile, the facial scars of battle stretching. '*Den Passierschein auch.*'

The letter also that was to have been signed and stamped by Herr Weber. *Merde,* but the Germans loved their papers. '*Liebe Zeit,* Oberfeldwebel, I only want a few words.'

'*Gut,* now give.' The stumpy fingers were snapped, the Schmeisser that was slung over the left shoulder gripped.

One hundred francs were found—fifty would have been too little. Hermann would have simply handed over a thousand just to pin the *salaud* down later if needed with a little blackmail.

Again the fingers were snapped, and again. 'One pays for everything these days, doesn't one?' said St-Cyr with a sigh.

'But that provides for my corporals here and allows you ten minutes without the necessary documentation, *mein lieber Oberdetektiv.*

Please use the shed and keep out of sight. We'll call you when your exit is clear.'

Hermann should have dealt with him. Hermann wouldn't have taken any of his humiliating *Quatsch*!

They weren't happy, thought Kohler, still closeted with the three of them from Room 3–38. They were definitely hiding something. Becky Torrence kept touching the edge of Brother Étienne's abandoned cloak and then gripping it as if she couldn't stop herself.

Conscious of the girl's nervousness, Jill Faber, the saucy one with the grey eyes and jet-black hair, finally broke.

'All right, I did trade with the Senegalese. One pays off the guards at the wood depot and those boys look the other way. Marni and I often went together. She would talk it up with the guards and watch out for things like Weber or any of the officers while I went in to deal with the others.'

'Jill's better at it,' said the redhead.

'And doesn't mind that they're blacks?'

'Niggers? Why should she? They're men, aren't they? Sometimes a gang of us would be trading, sometimes only Jill.'

They glanced at one another.

'Weber knows of the trading post. He must,' offered Jill.

'It's one of the ways he finds things out, so he lets it happen,' added Marni, watching him closely now.

'He has informants among you, has he?'

If Herr Kohler felt he'd trap them by playing dumb, he'd best think again, thought Marni, but she'd give him an innocent glance, would finger the back of her left wrist in doubt and then lean forward a little before letting him have it. 'We don't know who his informants are, Inspector. How could we?'

'They change,' said Jill, spreading her hands on the table and moving them slowly toward him. 'He keeps getting new ones.'

'And when Colonel Kessler was Kommandant?'

She'd best smile a little whimsically, thought Jill, and let him see that light in her eyes so as to keep him from getting at Becky. 'It was better then. There would only be one German corporal and the Oberfeldwebel with the glasses, or no guard at all.'

'And you, Mademoiselle Torrence, did you ever join in?'

'*Me?*' yelped Becky, dropping her gaze as she gripped the edge of the brother's cloak. 'I don't do trades. I . . . I can't.'

'Because they're blacks?'

She shook her head and glanced desperately at each of the others. 'I'd . . . I'd be no good at it. They . . . ' Oh damn, damn! 'It's just the way I am.'

This one was their weakest link and the other two were aware of it, but had there been an element of truth in Madame de Vernon's accusation?

'They get us extra firewood sometimes, Inspector, and bring us hot water,' she went on, unable to keep her voice from being brittle. 'Having a bath is always difficult. Jill or Marni watch out for me and . . . and hand the buckets in, then I do the same for either of them or for Nora.'

They would have to do something to distract him from Becky, thought Jill. 'The Senegalese installed our stove when we first got here. Nora told them where to put it and how to fix the chimney. She's really very good with them.'

And wasn't here to answer for herself. 'Friendly?'

She would catch a breath and hold it, thought Jill, would make him think she'd been letting those boys fuck her and would give him a knowing look then say, 'Nora's easy, Inspector, and isn't concerned in the least that they're black. Nora knows how to get along with working men. I didn't. Not then. I had to learn.'

And if that wasn't saying something, what was? But not only about Nora.

'Can I go now, Inspector?' asked Becky. 'Herr Weber will be in a rage, but if I don't show up, he'll . . . '

Either Weber was already using her or still trying to get her to cooperate. 'First tell me if the three of you ever went into that woodshed of the blacks together?'

'Once.'

It had leapt right out of Becky and now he would want to know why they'd done that, thought Marni. 'There was a gang of us,' she said, placing her hands on the table before her as Jill had done. Jill would be looking at him in that way a girl would who wanted things to happen between them.

'We'd a bet on, Inspector,' said Jill. 'One of them tells fortunes but doesn't need a goddess to intervene and ask a dead relative or friend what can be seen from above or what's going to happen.'

'He's supposed to be very good, better even than Madame Chevreul and a heck of a lot cheaper,' added Marni, giving him a grin.

Becky was vulnerable; Becky had to be sheltered, felt Kohler. 'What gang?'

Shit! 'Mary-Lynn and everyone else from Room 3–54, and us with Caroline and Nora,' said Jill. 'Bamba Duclos is known for it, Inspector. A thing like that can't be hidden for long, not in a place like this where gossip is nine-tenths of everything.'

She had better add something, thought Becky. She couldn't just sit here and say *nothing*. Herr Kohler would only become more and more suspicious of her. 'He . . . he has a little wicker basket from home. It isn't any bigger than a soup plate and just as deep. There . . . there are all kinds of strange things in it.'

And wouldn't you know it, she'd been rubbing shoulders with those boys. 'He shakes the basket, does he?'

Why was it that Herr Kohler now looked at her in the way he did? wondered Becky. Emptying the light completely from his eyes as if he *knew* the truth about her and was only waiting for her to confess?

She felt herself falling, felt absolutely, totally out of control, heard the breath rush from her and had to shut her eyes.

'He shakes it, doesn't he?' came the reminder, startling her.

'*Oui,* and then he . . . he let's everything settle and . . . and reads the way the things have fallen.'

A juju man in a land of juju ladies.

'I got a parcel from home that very day,' said Marni quickly. 'He had said I would. New underwear. A slip, a pair of nylons I sold within seconds. Six packs of cigs.'

A fortune, but Duclos had probably lugged that mail sack into the camp office and set the parcel out for Weber and the censors to examine.

'Bamba said Jennifer's maid would come late that very afternoon and she did, Inspector,' interjected Jill. 'He said that Becky wouldn't have to see Weber for three whole weeks and she didn't. The Untersturmführer laid off pressing her to cooperate and she . . . she was a lot better for it, weren't you, Becky?'

They touched hands, the girl blinking away the tears, only to blurt, 'Then he started pulling me in again, Inspector. I can't stand it anymore, Jill. I know he's trying to break me.'

'Easy,' said Kohler. 'Easy.'

'Sorry. Please forgive me.'

She touched her chest and blanched, looking as if totally ashamed of herself.

Herr Kohler was a big man with very strong hands and Becky would be concentrating on those, poor thing, thought Marni. 'Nora brought the hooch, Inspector,' she said, forcing herself to fiddle with the top button of her shirt blouse while giving him a look even Brother Étienne himself couldn't have mistaken.

'It was just good fun,' offered Jill, leaning forward again. 'We laughed for days. Bamba's got the biggest dark brown eyes and when he rolled them up to the ceiling of that shed, we thought the worst until he flashed us that great big grin of his, knowing he'd caught us out. Then he'd tell whoever's fortune it was that everything was going to be OK.'

'Sometimes,' muttered Becky.

'And Jennifer Hamilton was with you?'

'Jen wanted to know if everything in her flat was still there and if it would be safe.'

'That's when Bamba told her Thérèse, her maid, was coming for a visit,' said Marni quickly. 'He took the longest time with that basket of his and had to shake and shake it before poring over the way the pieces had fallen.'

'He was worried,' said Becky. 'He said things could be difficult for Jennifer and that . . . that she should leave offerings of food in scattered places outside our hotel. We would have to come back again because the little piece of ivory with the holes in it that looked like a miniature game board indicated the trouble needed all of us to work together to conquer it.'

'The crystal of quartz was upside down,' Marni went on. 'Jennifer tried to get him to tell her what that must mean, but he wouldn't.'

'It was really weird,' said Jill. 'It was almost curfew.'

'We were still in a huddle on our hands and knees . . . ' began Becky.

'The firewood was piled all around us,' interjected Marni, quickly giving Jill a nudge and silently telling her to let him know she wanted him—anything to keep him from getting at Becky.

Kohler held up a hand to stop them.

'They were watching us,' said Becky, gripping the edge of the brother's cloak. 'One of those blacks was touching me.'

'And Jennifer Hamilton, how did she feel?'

She must look steadily at him now, thought Becky. She must square her shoulders and show Jill and Marni that she could. 'Jen had gripped Caroline's hand.'

'Had the ballet dancer already asked what had happened to Madame de Vernon's husband?'

She wouldn't shake her head. She would just let him look at her in that way of his as she tried to shut everything else out. 'Caroline was thinking about it but . . . but wanted to wait. It . . . it was the first time for all of us.'

'When?'

'Just after the Christmas party the British threw for us.'

'And have there been other attempts to get Bamba to read your fortunes?'

Had he no feelings? 'Jill took me once more, and once I . . . I went alone, all by myself.'

'Becky, you didn't?' said the others, both caught off guard.

'Why?' asked Herr Kohler.

It would have to be said plainly. 'Because I thought Herr Weber was going to have me deported.'

To a concentration camp.

The ax had stopped, the log that had been split, falling on either side of the chopping block.

Sergeant Matthieu Senghor gave it a moment for he could see that this *sûreté* was determined.

'The blond, blue-eyed young American, Chief Inspector. The one called Becky, from Mademoiselle Jill's room. The timid one. She was nearer to the Chalet des Ânes than the one who traps. Brother Étienne looked towards her once and then again while talking to Mademoiselle Lacy. Perhaps he thought she was following the ballet dancer, perhaps only watching from among the trees nearby to see where she went, but we didn't see her go into that place, nor did we see Mademoiselle Lacy enter it either. We didn't go in there ourselves, I swear it.'

'I wheeled the brother's bike away,' said Bamba Duclos, carefully choosing his words. 'Always the punctures, always the need for a patch. That thing has to have new inner tubes but those are impossible to get unless God answers the brother's prayers.'

Hermann would somehow have produced a cigarette to share with them. 'And no one had asked any of you to meet with that girl?'

'No one, Inspector,' said Senghor. 'The timid one came here three times, though, to see what the basket held. First with several of the others. A dozen maybe, then with only the one, Mademoiselle Faber, and then once and alone. I tried to discourage her. *Bien sûr*, Mademoiselle Torrence was terrified of being alone with us, but also of something far worse, though she refused to say of what and begged the corporal here to look into her future. Bamba's grandfather and father were both known for their skill in divination, so the talent and responsibility fell naturally to him.'

The shorter of the two, but bigger across the shoulders, Duclos's gaze was wary but then, at a sudden thought, he flashed a grin. 'She paid me well, Inspector. Two cans of Libby's pork and beans, one packet of Oxo beef-tea cubes, one of raisins, two packs of Lucky Strikes, two bars of chocolate, and some of the chewing gum those people eat . . . but me, *ah, mon Dieu,* I knew I shouldn't have touched that stuff. I pulled a filling and the sergeant here had to yank the tooth. The pain . . . the blood . . . '

'Yes, yes, please continue.'

'Some may think they want to see what the sun will bring them in the morning or in a few days, a week, or even a year or the years, but when they find out they go all to pieces if it's bad. She was like that. A twist of hair.'

'Untersturmführer Weber was putting the squeeze on her,' said Senghor. 'We were certain of it. One can always tell. Bamba took her into the woodshed while the rest of us worked and kept a watch.'

'The sergeant told her she would only be with me, Inspector, but even then, it worried her. Is she afraid of men?'

'What about the other internees? Did any of them see her going in there with him?'

Talk. Had there been talk? 'Some must have, the guards most certainly.'

'The shed, then, and the basket. Get it and show me.'

Made of dark-brown, tightly woven cane more than fifty years old, the basket was frayed around its rim and had doubtless been with Duclos throughout that other war.

Taken from its skin bag, the contents were then emptied into it. Several polished bits of turtle shell; some tiny gourds, all quite different; a little piece of ivory with rows of holes as in a gaming board; a dead iridescent beetle, a wood-borer perhaps; a short length of copper wire badly coiled; a lion's talon, the middle digit; a wooden spool without its thread, three brass cartridge casings, one from a Lebel Modèle d'ordonnance, the 1873, an officer's gun. A Mauser 9mm Parabellum lay nearby, again from the gun of an officer. Had that one shot the French officer and Duclos then shot him?

A British tommy's .303 calibre was yet another cartridge casing. Fighting alongside them, or over ground once taken and then lost, Duclos would have had plenty of opportunity to add such things to his little collection. A sharpshooter's cloth insignia, French Army and certain death if captured, lay beneath a gold wedding band and photo of a dead *poilu*, a French soldier. There was a scattering of shrapnel; one lens from a pair of eyeglasses; a bent compass needle; several teeth from a small animal, a monkey perhaps; then small, white bird bones; a spent shotgun shell being incongruously next to the dried, coiled bit of an umbilical cord. Several polished pieces of various woods in unusual shapes were also present, as was the cork of a champagne bottle, Moët et Chandon; three scimitar-shaped pieces of silver, each about five centimetres in length and strung together with finely-linked silver chain; a confirmation medallion; a piece of amber with an embedded fly and once the fob off some German officer's pocket watch no doubt; a nurse's cap badge, British and that other war yet again; a brass tunic button too; a small pocket-knife with Swiss Red Cross symbol and extended, opened pair of scissors; a tiny brass bell to ring the future or, if hidden on the person, give that one away. *Ah, merde,* had Colonel Kessler been to see these boys himself? Was *this* where his use of 'bell ringer' had come?

There were several small scraps of tightly rolled wallpaper, a rooster's beak and foot, the ebony carving of a naked woman with a child on her back, a gunflint, a twist of fine blond hair—Becky Torrence's?

Several short feathers from a chicken, beach pebbles, and bits of water-worn glass joined a few sou, some pfennigs, a one-mark bill from the time of the Kaiser and several centimes from Senegal, and beads, too—lots of beads from home.

'A money shell,' said the *sûreté.* 'A cowrie once used in trade and found virtually all over Africa. Slaves were bought with them. Gold, ivory, and diamonds, too.'

'It was stolen right after Christmas, Inspector. I've looked everywhere. I know I didn't lose it. One of those ladies must have taken it, but unfortunately some of the British also came to consult me at about the same time, and for me to accuse a white woman . . . '

Overcoat pockets were dredged, and when he had it, the detective laid it on top of everything, porcelain-white to creamy yellow and with its rows of short, stubby teeth.

'Grandfather will thank you, Inspector, as will my father.'

'I think Caroline Lacy was about to return it,' he said. 'Now, show me what you do.'

'I shake the basket, Inspector, and the things leap up to settle of their own accord.'

'And in their arrangement lies the future. What was Becky Torrence's?'

The detective was pointing to the twist of hair but did he really need to know? 'The thigh bones were crossed, Inspector. The twist of her hair was beneath them and the lion's talon hooked overtop with the cock's foot leading away to the spool of lost thread, which indicated a long journey. The empty gourds told of a terrible thirst, the eleven millimetre cartridge casing of the cold for some of those shells, they simply didn't fire in that other war because of being stored for so long in a damp place. The sharpshooter's insignia told of the loneliness among many others, the scimitars of demons.'

Duclos had the look of one who absolutely believed he had the gift and the concern, too, for Becky Torrence.

'She was shattered by what the sun had to say, Inspector. I tried to tell her that if she would come again we'd have another look, but she . . . She just turned and walked away without looking at anyone.'

'*Ah, bon,* I'll be in touch. For now let me keep the cowrie and borrow the twist of hair.'

6

Through the trees, the artistry of nature seemed everywhere. Vista after vista, thought St-Cyr, snow cascading from a branch, sunlight glistening, wind drifting. No wonder Monet, Manet, Pissarro, and the other Impressionists saw such things the way they did. If only time were available to enjoy them; if only Hermann, who couldn't have cared less about such, could find him some pipe tobacco. Dried, ground nettles, herbs, carrot tops, and beet greens—no doubt available in various combinations in either of the hotels—would be of absolutely no use. *Merde,* but the craving just wouldn't go away. Like an infernal itch, it was distracting when inner calmness and a quiet think were imperative.

Several of the curious had gathered near the Chalet des Ânes. Though the victims were under guard, the resident questions, jeers, and demands would not be. The bodies would have to be moved and that meant, of course, the presence of this *sûreté,* but first a request to Herr Weber would have to be made, an order given by him since nothing could be done without the latter.

Entering the casino was not difficult. Everyone was far too busy to take note of one lonely French detective, the invited guest of a then-to-be-absent Kommandant. The building was entirely different from the one he had known while recuperating here during the Great War and prior to the Americans using the Parc and its hotels for their hospital, yet the memories couldn't help but come.

Films had been shown in the theatre—this had been saved from the disastrous fire of 17 July, 1920. One couldn't forget Charlie Chaplin in *Police,* Charlie frantically refusing to go along with his fellow robbers and *protecting* the damsel in distress.

In *The Floorwalker,* the chase had been on escalators; in *The Rink,* on roller skates. Tears had freely run with the laughter these American 'silents' had brought. Senegalese had been sprinkled throughout the audience, Moroccans, Berbers. Algerians and Cochin Chinese, all in uniform as well as the others—all French citizens, members of the Colonial Army and united with the rest by that common bond of the front.

But then had come the Treaty of Versailles and the occupation of the Rhineland and then that of the Ruhr, and with them charges that France had deliberately used its 'black and yellow' troops. One rape, one incidence of a brutal mugging would probably have been enough to set off the passive resistance of the Germans. The firm of Krupp had even sent in an investigative reporter. While several unfortunate incidents had been uncovered, others had revealed coloured troops enthusiastically helping with the grape harvest. Yet the stigma of the 'black terror' had spread, and of course as time went on this stigma had only become worse.

In 1937 the Nazis had ordered the compulsory sterilization of the 'Rhineland bastards,' the children of German women and these occupation troops, and now, of course, Herr Weber was free to take it out on the camp's Senegalese.

As God would have it, and He did do things like this, the Untersturmführer's office was adjacent to the entrance of the theatre, the lineup to see Weber long but silent, and here, too, was none other than Becky Torrence.

The surgery was simply Room 3–54, noted Kohler, the audience a crowd at the door. Lisa Banbridge, the twenty-two-year-old, ponytailed brunette with the hazel eyes and degree from Duke University, was ready to give assistance. Candice Peters, the forty-year-old with the frizzy brown hair was still tidying herself—a rash under the arms, her worries of erysipelas having proved false. The soap she had paid plenty for had been bought on the black market in the Reich by one of the guards on leave and was to fault, though relief would come slowly and there was also the chagrin of having been taken to the cleaners.

Jennifer Hamilton stood beside him. Although the bed Mary-Lynn had used still held its fastidiously tidied array of last effects, they had the look of having been tidied again. Unfortunately Louis hadn't given him the sequence. Now the suitcase, closed and flat, lay beneath precisely folded blankets and the two sheets each inmate would have been given every month in exchange for their others. Then came the pillow; next to these, the shoes and precision again, the one pair toe-to-heel behind the other; then the coats, folded with the arms tidily crisscrossed over the front, but here, too, they had that look, as if whoever had first done it hadn't been satisfied, or perhaps some other compulsive had come along to redo the lot.

Out of spite? he wondered. Louis would have too.

Boils can be painful, the brother's touch that of the sensitive, the naked bottom of Barbara Caldwell, the auburn-haired thirty-two-to thirty-six-year-old graduate from Rhodes College in Memphis, Tennessee—rather nice were it not for the inflamed, now lanced and erupted volcano just to the left of the crack.

'We have no secrets,' said Jennifer softly, not looking up at him but still at the patient. 'We can't have. We know *everything* about each other. It's been weeks and weeks, poor thing. She avoided asking Brother Étienne to deal with it, even the last time he was here.'

The brother didn't waste time. Using a wooden mallet from that toolbox of his, he pounded a root, warmed it and its juices in a pot on the electric ring, added a goodly splash of cider vinegar and handful of coarse salt, then juggling the hot poultice, clapped it on her bum.

There was a yell, but he held her down. 'You'll thank me,' he said *en français*. 'Three times a day for the next four days, then once a day until the inflammation has completely disappeared. I don't want that coming back.'

An appreciative sigh ran through the crowd.

'What did he use?' Jennifer whispered, still mesmerized.

'Comfrey. The soldier's friend. Louis would be able to tell you better, but I think it's been in use since the Middle Ages.'

Lisa placed a towel over the poultice, then helped Barb to yank up her slacks but leave them unbuttoned. 'Just lie there,' she said. 'Give it as long as possible.'

They looked at each other, these occupants of Room 3–54. Dorothy Stevens, the tall, thin, thirty-six-year-old brunette and graduate of Ohio State had bared her feet, the sores between the toes being a classic example of the usual fungal nightmare of communal living.

'Who tidied that?' asked Kohler quietly.

Ah no, thought Jennifer; he was pointing at Mary-Lynn's things yet watching her so closely she could feel it. 'Becky. I . . . I think Becky must have. I saw her ducking out of here about four days after Mary-Lynn fell. When we passed in the corridor, she . . . she said she was looking for Nora.'

This informant of Weber's was panicking. Now a glance up at him, now away to the bed, then back up to him in doubt, the soft brown eyes furtive.

'Was it tidied more recently?' said Kohler.

Why had he to ask? 'I . . . I don't know. It . . . it looks the same to me.'

The scar had tightened on that chin of hers, the fair hair falling forward over a knitted brow. He'd have to ignore the others, felt Kohler. 'Why was she looking for Nora in this room?'

Under such scrutiny Jennifer felt her stomach muscles tighten. Vomit began to rise. 'Maybe she was looking for Caroline.'

'Because Nora had been dogging the footsteps of the two of you, was that it, eh?'

So he had found that out. Again the muscles tightened, harder this time. Harder. 'Nora thought Caroline might have been stealing things. I told her she was crazy but she persisted. Caroline had lost things too. One of the pink satin ribbons from her practice shoes, a pebble she'd kept because it was interesting. A trachyte porphyry, Nora had called it.'

She swallowed, but it didn't go down well, noted Kohler. 'Anything else?'

Had she winced? wondered Jennifer. Had that been what had caused him to ask? 'A glass marble—a cat's-eye. It had been her "shooter" in grade school and was, I think, the only thing she had left from home. Madame de Vernon kept throwing Caroline's things out. Caroline . . . '

Swiftly she turned away to hide her tears in panic.

'Inspector, how could you?' seethed Lisa Banbridge. 'You know Jen can't have done a thing. None of us have.'

Candice Peters of the frizzy brown hair wrapped her arms about the girl. 'That was cruel,' she said. 'And here we all thought you were different from Weber and the others. Jen has been holding in her grief terrifically. We're all upset, but she was in love with Caroline. Love, damn you!'

'Love,' said another.

'OK, OK, I'll back off, but there are things I have to ask her. Nothing difficult. Just a few questions.'

'Like *what*?' asked Lisa suspiciously.

'Like, what is the brother treating her for?'

'Anxiety,' sighed Brother Étienne, having used the rest of the comfrey to prepare a hot footbath for the case of athlete's foot. 'I should have thought that evident, Inspector. An infusion of lemon balm taken twice daily, morning and night, and with a little of the honey in that cough syrup bottle she's still clutching, or hadn't you noticed?'

'The tea of France?'

'*Oui.* You should try it instead of longing for tobacco. It relaxes the nerves, calms the heart, and is but a mild and pleasing sedative.'

'Ask her if she left this room the night Mary-Lynn died.'

The eyes and nose were wiped, the look valiant. 'I didn't. Caroline left, as I told you, at about midnight.'

'A terrible attack of asthma,' said Lisa, still not convinced he was going easy.

'I was afraid to accompany her because of Madame de Vernon. Caroline . . . Caroline said she would be all right once she had found her cigarettes.'

'You'd been having an argument—that right?'

'A disagreement, nothing worse. We'd patched it up by the time she'd left.'

'But hadn't. Caroline had still been in tears and very upset.'

'Was she?' asked Jennifer.

'And the photo that one had borrowed from Madame's suitcase?' demanded Kohler.

Did he really *think* she would have kept it when she had *told* him she hadn't? 'I burned it in the stove, like I said.'

Although in better control of herself, there was still anger. 'But you only did that *after* Caroline had been killed.'

She mustn't smile, felt Jennifer, must simply be firm. 'Really, Inspector, I wouldn't have done so before. We were to have taken it to the séance last night.'

All well and good and tough, was she? 'You could have returned it instead.'

'Could I?'

'Caroline must have told you where Madame had hidden the spare key. Everyone else in that room of hers knew of it.'

'But I didn't. *Bien sûr,* there were things Caroline would tell me— lots of them—but there were also those she wouldn't and didn't.'

And that was one of them. 'What did you lose to the resident kleptomaniac whose speed of filching things reminded you of Houdini?'

She mustn't waver, felt Jennifer, must face up to him even if his partner had remembered that comment of hers and had passed it on. 'Am I that person—isn't this what you really want to ask?'

'Just tell me.'

The urge to rattle off two dozen items was almost more than she could bear. Lisa would be quick to add things, Barb, too, but she'd best use anger. 'One of these.'

Snatching at the blue Bakelite butterfly pin in her hair, she dragged it free and snapped off its spring-loaded alligator clip before handing the butterfly to him. 'It was broken, but I had kept it because I only had this one left. Sure they were teenage, little-girl things, but I wore one when dealing to give that impression of inno-cence and naiveté. Women will do such things—you should know this as a man. Even though times were very difficult for the sellers, the paintings and antiques I was buying didn't come easily.'

She shrugged, forced a weak smile, and said, 'They still asked far too much, but a touch of innocence was useful, and of course I emphasized the new home they'd be getting. What I did wasn't illegal, Inspector, and what I finally paid was simply less than had been asked.'

The sellers had been Jews and others on the run. 'That why you stuck around until it was too late for you to leave France?'

'Partly, but I also couldn't manage the shipping. The Occupier and the French kept throwing up the roadblocks.'

Reichsmarschall Göring being the biggest of them. 'How much is the stuff you've got in that flat of yours worth?'

'In Boston and New York, or in Paris and Berlin?'

She seemed to thrive when talking business. 'Both.'

'Lots, then. There's an early Corot landscape that I bought for myself in the autumn of 1940, paying 28,000 francs. In June of 1941, I could have sold it for 1,210,000, today . . . ' She shrugged. 'And it's only one of several pieces I have, or had.'

The official exchange rate was 50 francs to the dollar, or 200 to the pound sterling, the black bourse rate being the more usual and at 110 to 120, and 350 to 400, a worry to be sure and maybe the reason entirely for the anxiety attacks, but one had to ask, wasn't it being a little too free with the info? 'Did our kleptomaniac take anything else of yours?'

'Inspector, please don't blame me for buying from the desperate. If it hadn't been me, it would have been someone else, and at least they knew, or thought, that the pieces were going to a place of safety and to owners such as themselves who would value them. The Paris market is everything in the art world—surely you must know this. I was just a little fish in a big and very turbulent pond.'

Excuses . . . they all had their excuses. Time and again Louis and he had come up against these 'buyers,' Göring especially. 'Just answer what I asked.'

Were Herr Kohler and his partner really on the side of the persecuted as everyone was saying, even Untersturmführer Weber? 'The key to my flat. It . . . it was on a string I would wear around my neck. When taking a shower downstairs, I had hung it on a hook, but when I got out, why, it . . . it had been taken.'

'Why a shower downstairs?'

'Because one was free, and for which I paid two cigarettes.'

'Was anything else of yours stolen?'

'A lipstick. The tube was empty—I'd even used a matchstick to get at the last of it—but one keeps such things as reminders of what we once had. One has to here.'

That was fair enough, but she was still too wary. 'You and the others asked the Senegalese to look into your futures.'

So he had found that out too. 'Just after the Christmas party. We all thought it would be a lark and were still in a partying mood.'

'You asked about your flat?'

'Bamba . . . That was his name. He said Thérèse, my maid, would come soon and she did, that very afternoon.'

'Was that all?'

Had he talked to Bamba? 'I was to leave offerings of food—crumbs, really—and . . . and was to come back for another reading. My fortune wasn't good, but I haven't been back yet.'

'Was anything taken from that little basket of his?'

'By me, or by Caroline?'

He waited. He didn't and wouldn't say another thing, thought Jennifer, until she had answered him, but she mustn't let apprehension get ahead of her. 'Or by neither of us, Inspector? Caroline did keep nudging me to watch Becky. That one wasn't just tense. It was as if something exciting were building up inside her, but we . . . we didn't see her take anything. Was something missing?'

'Don't worry about it. Tell me about Mary-Lynn and Colonel Kessler.'

'Why not ask what you really want? Mary-Lynn had been left in the lurch by her "fiancé."'

'An SS, a Sturmbannführer.'

'*Oui*, Karl Hoffmann. She wanted to get even—lots of girls feel like that. Colonel Kessler was friendly but not a lover, not if you ask me. It was more the friendship of one who wanted to practice his

English and who enjoyed her knowledge of books and appreciated her support at the séances. Mary-Lynn wanted to find out where her dad's remains were. It . . . it had become an obsession with her.'

'One that Madame Chevreul played upon?'

'Really, Inspector, I'm not the doubter Nora is. Caroline *wanted* to become a sitter and I . . . why, I *wanted* whatever Caroline wanted.'

'Did she steal that L'Heure Bleue box and bottle from Madame Chevreul?'

'And claim that Madame had given it to her?'

'Just answer.'

'Then no. Madame Chevreul pressed it into Caroline's hands to cement the goodwill between them.'

'And seal the payment of five hundred greenbacks?'

Would his questions never stop? 'That, too, since you ask. Madame Chevreul knew only too well that Madame de Vernon had been getting after Caroline for wanting to become a sitter. The presentation box was something Caroline would love to have for the thoughts it would bring, and of course having it would strengthen her resolve.'

'Picked up from Madame's dressing table, was it?'

Why had he to ask that? 'It . . . it was near the photos of the friends Madame had left behind when she came to France. A Rebecca Thompson and a Judith Merrill. Léa Monnier used to work as kitchen help for Mrs. Merrill. That's . . . that's how Madame Chevreul first met her.'

'Léa Easton.'

'Yes, but Madame Chevreul wasn't married then. Her maiden name was Beacham. You . . . *Ah, merde, merde!* You don't know, do you?'

Herr Kohler took her by the arm and, leading her out of the room, walked her along the corridor toward that elevator shaft with everyone looking at them. Just *everyone*. 'No place is more private,' he said. 'Now, you start telling me what I don't know and should.'

The gate to the elevator had been locked again, and using another chain, and he saw this as they stopped, would know that Mrs. Parker had insisted on it, but wouldn't know how sick she, herself, still felt at the thought of it having been left open. 'They were suffragettes. Judith Merrill took Léa Easton to their meetings and convinced her to join. Léa was only sixteen at the time but soon found herself leading a screaming mob of umbrella-wielding, vote-demanding women. She would have, wouldn't she? She's a natural.'

He said nothing, this Gestapo detective. He just looked at her, she with her back now to that gate. 'Léa wasn't the only one who spent time in prison, Inspector, in London's Old Bailey, where they were force-fed in the summer of 1914. Judith Merrill, being the oldest, was accused of being the ringleader. A bomb had been set off in Oxted Station on 4 April, 1913, four houses torched on the third in the suburb of Hampstead Garden, then later, I think, the Yarmouth Pier pavilion. It had just been built at a cost of 20,000 pounds, but the police and Scotland Yard didn't catch up with Léa and the others until 1914.'

Still he waited, saying nothing but giving no further hint of what he was really thinking. 'When Lord Merrill finally got his wife out of jail, he sent her to the remotest of his country estates and kept her there without her ever being able to see their children.'

Still he didn't say anything. 'She killed herself with an overdose of white arsenic.'

Rat poison. 'And the other one?' he asked, but only after seeing that they were still quite alone, though some along the corridor were watching them.

'Rebecca Thompson was twenty-three years old. Separated from the mob, she had run up a narrow lane to avoid the truncheons but was caught, beaten, and then savagely raped by no less than four men, each of them a bobby. The judge was solicitous and committed her to an insane asylum.'

'While Élizabeth Beacham and Léa Easton volunteered to go to France for king and country.'

'Eventually, yes, that is correct, insofar as I was told. The one as a nurse, the other as a truck driver.'

And now resident head juju woman and her number-one flunky. 'So how is it that you know all this, and do the others in Room 3–54 and Room 3–38?'

She winced. She couldn't help but do so, looked desperately away to the distant onlookers, then at his shoes, and only when her chin was lifted, at him. 'I . . . ' The tears couldn't be stopped. 'I was told it by two of the British. They . . . they grabbed me in the Hôtel Grand and forced me into the darkness of the cellars where they . . . they said that if I ever told anyone who had said it to me, they would see that I never told anyone another thing.'

'And Caroline, did you tell her of the suffragette past?'

'I couldn't. She . . . she wanted so much to go to that séance, I had to keep it all to myself.'

'How many times did you wander about in the Hôtel Grand by yourself?'

'Lots, but . . . but not after that happened. After that, I avoided the hotel like the plague and only later went there with Caroline.'

'And did those British women ask if you had broadcast that choice bit of news about Madame Chevreul in the Vittel-Palace as they would have wanted you to?'

'Twice, but I . . . I told them I had to wait for an appropriate time.'

Both of her hands had been gripping the gate and she felt him freeing them, but all he said was, 'Don't be telling anyone else, not until I give you the OK. Now, I'd best find my partner.'

The lineup outside Herr Weber's office was that of the silent and subdued. Becky was third from the far end, and when she saw St-Cyr approaching, she panicked and turned away, and when he came near, she flinched but still kept her back to him.

The aroma of spearmint was clear, her left hand surreptitiously opening near to that thigh to drop the crumpled sleeve from a stick of chewing gum.

'Wrigley's,' he said, having picked it up. '*Ah, bon,* Mademoiselle Torrence, while my partner is probably now upstairs questioning others, a few small questions for you; nothing difficult.'

'*Here?*' she bleated, desperation registering in sky-blue eyes that rapidly moistened as she glanced at others in the line, others who had now taken a decided interest in the proceedings.

'I won't detain you long.'

'But Herr Weber wants to see me.'

Ignoring her panic, he smoothed out the wrapper and its covering, folded them precisely in half, unbuttoned his overcoat, and tucked the silver paper and the other away in a waistcoat pocket.

'We'll let him wait if necessary.'

'But . . . but I haven't done anything! I really haven't.'

Pale and quivering, she was vulnerable. The cheeks were fair, though sunken, the lips those of the young, the nose not aquiline or overly Roman but dusted with freckles the colour of which the pallor increased. In all such things St-Cyr knew he searched for answers, and yes, Hermann's accusations of being overly harsh were true at times, but answers were desperately needed. 'Let these two go ahead. The theatre is empty. We'll go in there.'

'The theatre . . . ?'

Seat after seat was covered in wine-purple fabric, worn and faded by the years, the cigarette burns and spills all too evident, and from the seats came the stench of sour sweat and old tobacco smoke. Art Deco flames seemed to leap and fan out from along the side aisles and from the stage itself, above whose closed curtain hung a huge portrait of the German Führer and two swastika flags, one on either side of him.

'Smoke damage from the fire in 1920 necessitated redecorating,' he said. 'Not bothering to replace the seats must have been a cost-saving measure.'

He indicated one of these next to where he was standing, then took the one directly behind, forcing her to awkwardly turn to face him.

'The thefts, mademoiselle. What did you lose?'

'Me?' she yelped.

He waited. Not for a moment did he take those dark brown, ox-eyes of his from her, felt Becky. The mustache was bushy and wide and badly in need of a trim, as was the hair. Had he no time for such things?

There was the mark of a recent bullet graze on that broad brow. The nose had been broken several times but not recently. A boxer?

she wondered, the smell of anise, wet wool, and old pipe smoke coming to her now.

Again he asked.

'Me?' she yelped again. 'A photo from home of the dog we once had. A beagle. Harry . . . his name was Harry. The fake gold compact my brother gave me on my sixteenth birthday. Its mirror had broken long ago and the catch was no longer any good but I couldn't part with it, not here . . . not in Paris, either. A letter from my mom. A button. It . . . it was pink, from the cardigan she had knitted for me before I left for France in 1939, fresh out of college. I had set that button aside and was planning to sew it back on, but then . . . then it was gone.'

'Were others in the room at the time?'

'*Others?* Caroline and Jennifer—yes, yes, Jennifer was there, and . . . and Jill.' What did he *really* want from her?

'Madame de Vernon wasn't present?' he asked.

'Jennifer wouldn't have dared come if that woman had been in the room.'

'And at that first session with Bamba Duclos, mademoiselle?'

'We all went, all but Madame. Mary-Lynn had wanted us to try it. Nora . . . Nora said, "Why not?" Marni . . . Marni agreed. Jill set it up.'

'Tell me about the items in his little basket.'

'Was something stolen?'

'Just tell me what you can recall.'

'So that I can trip myself up if I'm the thief? I'm not, Inspector. I'm not!'

Hermann would have said 'Go easy, now,' but Hermann could sometimes let concern for the suspect intrude when least needed. 'Was anything stolen from it?'

'How would I know?'

'But you went twice more, mademoiselle. You would have seen if something was missing.'

'*What?* What was taken?'

He waited. He didn't back off. 'And I was near Mary-Lynn when she died, wasn't I, and near Caroline too—that's it, isn't it? You think

I did it. You're just like Weber. Demanding everything and thinking the worst. He has a list he keeps. Did you know that? Names are crossed off, but mine keeps coming up and I'm being asked back again and again. I *won't* squeal on my friends. I mustn't. Sure we have our arguments—who doesn't in a place like this, but I'd never rat on anyone. Everyone in that room of mine has been good to me except for Madame. I'd . . . I'd kill myself if I did a thing like that to them or to anyone.'

'Yet Herr Weber keeps asking.'

'He doesn't just ask, Chief Inspector. He tells me my papers aren't very good and that a delegation from Berlin is coming to examine all those in the Hôtel de la Providence, and that he's going to get them to check mine thoroughly. I . . . I was late getting my visa, the last time I had to, and once one is late for such a thing in France, it's on one's record, isn't it? Well, isn't it?'

He didn't answer.

'Later I . . . I was arrested but simply because I was an American.'

'Why didn't you leave when you could?'

'I had a job with the Foyer International in the boulevard St-Michel. We had exchange students from South and Central America, the States, and other countries. I . . . I stayed because I felt responsible.'

'Even after the Führer had declared war on America on 11 December, '41?'

The Foyer's purpose had been to bring students together to help prevent wars, but did he already know why she had stayed? 'There weren't many of us Americans scattered about. I did plan to go into the *zone non occupée* when our embassy moved from Paris to the town of Vichy after Germans declared war on us, and later I did have to check in with the local *commissariat de police,* but no one seemed to worry too much about me being in Paris.'

'Then the net suddenly closed.'

Had he really believed her? *'Oui, c'est correct.'*

'Mademoiselle, it will go no further.'

Ah, Sainte Mère, Saint Mère! 'All right, I had a lover. A French boy.'

'Age?'

Why did he have to know that? 'Twenty-five.'

'Eyesight, health? Come, come, Mademoiselle Torrence, at that age he should have been in our forces and, therefore, most probably in a prisoner of war camp in the Reich.'

She turned away but there was nowhere to look but the rows and rows of empty seats and the Deco lights. 'As a child, he had had tuberculosis. That "Army" of yours didn't want him. He tried and tried but they . . . they wouldn't listen.'

'But you wanted him.'

'Was that so wrong? He was every bit as French as you are, probably lots and lots more.'

To insist on it was one thing, to emphasize it further, another. 'And on 29 May, 1942, mademoiselle?'

'*Why must you ask me a thing like that?*'

'Because I must if Hermann and I are to help you and get to the bottom of this.'

Salaud, she wanted to shout at him, but would have to tell him. 'I made Antoine give me his jacket, damn you. I unstitched that thing you people had forced him to wear, then I told him to go south into the *zone libre,* that I would follow as soon as I could, but . . . but one thing led to another and I had to wait because the Kommandantur in the avenue de l'Opéra wouldn't let me have the necessary *laissez-passer* and *sauf-conduit.* I was being *kept* in Paris.'

'And the star, mademoiselle?'

'I'm not a thief. I wouldn't have stolen a thing like that from myself. I'd have left it in my sewing basket, where it had been hidden away tucked under the lining for months and months.'

She'll hate you now, Louis, Hermann would have said, but weren't sewing baskets often borrowed by others? 'Did this boy ever send you a postcard?'

Her lower lip was bitten, the eyes clamped shut to hide her tears but then she turned away, resting her forehead on the back of the seat in front of her, which she gripped with both hands as if he were laying into her with a rawhide *Schlag.*

'The postcards, mademoiselle?'

'Two. They were also stolen. Each was so blacked out I could hardly make sense of them. *Am well*. Blank, blank, blank. *No news of my family*. Blank, blank, blank. *Am going to work*. Blank, blank, but where, please. Where?'

The urge to be compassionate would have to be resisted. 'And then nothing?' he asked.

She nodded, then blurted, 'He didn't even have a Jewish name! His great-grandfather had changed it but now . . . now Herr Weber must know. He must, but he never says. He just smiles and tells me my papers need looking at when I know they don't!'

At a glance, Kohler could see that Louis had broken Becky Torrence but Weber, having heard of what had been going on behind his back, had drawn his pistol and had had Bamba Duclos brought to the office by two strongarms. That one, his future having flashed before him, had politely dropped his gaze to summon what courage he could. 'Mam'selle,' he said, 'I didn't tell him you had come to me to read your fortune. Someone else must have.'

'SILENCE!' shrieked Weber in *Deutsch*.

Leaping to his feet, he smashed Duclos in the mouth with that pistol. *Gott sei Dank,* a shot hadn't gone off.

'YOUR PAPERS, FRÄULEIN. PAPERS!'

Everything was going crazy. Terrified, Becky tore at pullover, blouse, and undershirt, but the uncovered waist-pouch just wouldn't open.

'HURRY, WHORE!'

'THERE'S NOTHING WRONG WITH MY PAPERS. NOTHING!' she cried in French.

Pouch ripped open, papers and passport were flung onto the desk. Backhanded, knocked all but senseless, she reeled and held her left cheek in shock. 'You . . . you . . . ' she began.

'*Schiesse,* Untersturmführer, leave it.'

'*What was that you said to me, Kohler?*'

'Knocking her senseless isn't going to help.'

'HELP, IS IT?'

The papers were snatched up. Turning swiftly away, Weber

crouched to spin the dial of the safe that sat on the floor behind and to the left of that desk of his, and below the board on which hung the keys to every other lock in the camp: two for each, by the look, and labelled underneath, and if one were missing, would its absence be noticed?

Abruptly the most valuable things anyone could own these days were pitched into the safe, the door slammed and dial spun.

'There, now we shall see,' said Weber, noting that St-Cyr had stepped in front of the slut. 'Very well, *mein Lieber*. Very well.'

Upending the hessian sack that had been brought with the black, tins spilled across the desk. 'Cans of Klim and Borden's Sweetened Condensed Milk, Kohler? Others of Maple Leaf Creamery Butter?'

'Bovril, too. *Ach,* I can see that, Untersturmführer.'

'*Zigaretten?* Camels, Chesterfields, Players, Woodbines?'

'Those tins of Kam are probably similar to the American ones of SPAM. Ground ham and pork.'*

'And half-kilo bars of Neilson's Chocolate, with those of Hershey's, Kohler?'

'Atlas and Del Bey raisins, too, Hermann,' said Louis, still perched on the balls of his feet and ready to deal with this obnoxious little desk tyrant who was damned dangerous since he still had backup Schmeissers standing guard over Bamba Duclos.

These *Schweinebullen,* these two from Paris, thought Weber. They were *known* to cause trouble. The American was fingering her cheek and lower jaw. Gingerly the *Schlampe* explored her lips for possible splits, the hatred in her gaze all too clear. Naked, what would she do if she had six of the blacks at her? Scream? Go crazy? Fight certainly.

Two cans of Libby's pork and beans were selected by him and set aside, two packets of Lucky Strikes, one packet of Oxo cubes, one of raisins, two bars of chocolate, and some chewing gum. 'You paid this one, Fräulein. Now you will tell me why.'

'I . . . I have nothing more to say to you.'

'*Don't!*' said Louis in *Deutsch*, grabbing Weber by the wrist as the gun was swung at her. 'Listen instead, Untersturmführer, and I'll

---

* Ground ham and chicken.

tell you why this young woman, a prisoner in your care and therefore under the rules of the Geneva Convention, met with this one.'

'Louis . . . '

'Hermann, if I have to break his arm, I will!'

'VERFLUCHTER FRANZOSE HAU AB!'

Cursed Frenchman, fuck off. Louis had yet to notice the memorial to Weber's dead sister on that desk, the swastika-bedecked photo a constant reminder.

The arm was released, the gun came up, but so did a *sûreté's* forefinger.

'Orders are orders, Untersturmführer. We are here on those of the Kommandant von Gross-Paris and those of Gestapo Bömelburg, Head of Section IV.'

The Gestapo in France and two old acquaintances, but how deep was this thing going to go? wondered Kohler.

'Sit down and let's talk,' said Louis. 'For myself, I'm sorry I didn't first ask your permission to withdraw the Fräulein from your lineup but things were moving too quickly and the need to settle matters had become paramount.'

'I have letters that prove everything,' seethed Weber. 'Letters, Fräulein.'

Again the safe was opened: three turns to the right to land between the 52 and the 58, thought Kohler, two to the left and between the 27 and the 35, and then back around to the 11 or thereabouts. 'The First American Army again, Louis. Another leftover.'

One by one the anonymous letters were thrown down, the door to the safe left open.

'Do you deny what they say?' demanded Weber. He'd show these two who ran things here. He'd not have them going over his head.

Becky knew he was going to send her to a concentration camp. There was now no longer any hope. 'My name is Becky Torrence, Herr Untersturmführer, not Frau Rebecca Tarance or Torance, and the room number is 3–38 not 2–38 or 3–28.'

Would he hit her again or shoot her? she wondered. 'I think if you look closely, Herr Untersturmführer, you will see that those which use my correct name have largely been written by Madame de Vernon, a few of the others by girls in the Vittel-Palace, yes. One gets blamed all the time for things they never did in that hotel you people keep us locked up in, and one has to defend oneself against unwanted advances, too, so hatred is born. But the other letters . . . especially those who have called me Rebecca and not spelled my last name correctly, have been written by girls and women in the Hôtel Grand. Again perhaps because I fiercely rejected their advances. Was Léa Monnier, who insists on looking at me the way she does, among your letter writers? She's been here a lot. I've had to line up next to her time and again and suffer her closeness, and you know this!'

'And you, Fräulein? You? Kohler, this is the lover of a Jew. She helped the boy to escape to the free zone that no longer exists. Antoine Rochon, mademoiselle? I have the proof.'

And Becky, her enemies, sighed Kohler inwardly. Again Weber went to that safe of his. An unopened tin of fifty Will's Gold Flake cigarettes rolled out, another of Woodbines and then one of . . . *Ah, merde,* fine-cut pipe tobacco.

The telex on the regional office-to-office paper contained but a single line of heavy type and the name of none other than the Obersturmführer Klaus Barbie, Head of Section IV Lyon, and another old acquaintance they would rather not have met.

Kohler, having seen the name, thought Weber, had given that partner of his a warning glance.

SUBJECT ANTOINE ROCHON ARRESTED LYON EINSATZKOM-MANDO 22 NOVEMBER 1942, DEPORTED MAUTHAUSEN KZ. HEIL HITLER.

Becky was going to go all to pieces on them. Louis had extended a steadying hand. Obviously she had got Jill Faber to teach her a little *Deutsch,* yet still, one had best try to be gentle. 'He's in Austria, Becky. Working in a factory.'

'Not a stone quarry and a concentration camp? Isn't *KZ* the short form for *Konzentrationslager*?' she asked, letting the tears fall freely.

'Look, don't do anything crazy, eh?'

'Like throwing myself down an elevator shaft?'

Schiesse, what the hell was this?

'Maybe Mary-Lynn didn't want to live, Inspector. Maybe she felt having a child here was just too much. Maybe Nora had convinced her that trying to reach her father was simply stupid.'

'And Caroline Lacy?' asked Louis.

'Caroline . . . ?' she asked, startled and turning to face him.

'Did she know about Antoine, mademoiselle?'

Ah, no . . . 'Jill did, Nora did, and Marni, too.'

'But not Caroline?'

'Not unless Madame de Vernon had somehow found out.'

'The bodies, Untersturmführer,' said Louis firmly. 'Have Corporal Duclos bring a stretcher to the Chalet des Ânes first, and one other to assist him. This young woman will identify each victim, as is necessary, you to be a witness.'

The snow was everywhere and through the trees the Chalet des Ânes looked as if it could never have been the site of a murder. To the northeast, Becky could see right across the Parc Thermal to the boundary fence beyond the soccer field the British insisted on calling the football field as if all Americans were simply ignorant of such fine distinctions.

To the west and northwest, and much nearer, were the casino from which they'd just come, then the Grand and the Vittel-Palace. The Établissement Thermal, whose round pavilions at either end marked the fountains that gave forth the waters of La Grande Source and La Source Salée, was but a short walk from the Vittel-Palace. These pavilions were joined by the covered promenade that was always popular. There were lots of internees about now, some even peering in through the spa's windows in hopes of catching a glimpse of something to alleviate the boredom even though the Fermé sign was clear enough and they must have looked in there countless times. Surely the Germans could have opened that up, giving the girls such pleasure and employment too, but no, and as for Jill getting the swimming pool filled this coming summer, they'd best forget it. With Herr Weber advising him, the new Kommandant would never agree.

'Inspector, do I really have to do this?'

'A glimpse, that's all,' said Kohler. 'I'll be right with you.'

Had he thought she would bolt and run, a Gentile who had had a Jewish fiancé, a girl who had inadvertently kept the Star of David she had removed from his coat? 'Caroline would have felt the chalet offered no threat, Inspector. Corporal Duclos was to have met her. On Friday afternoon I . . . I only followed her from the room to see that he did.'

'And then?' he asked.

He was watching her closely now because those brief moments when Brother Étienne had left Caroline and walked the *petrolette* over to Duclos and Sergeant Senghor for repairs were critical. 'I was satisfied they had seen her. I . . . I turned away and went back to our hotel.'

'Meeting Nora on the way?'

He'd be sure to ask Nora. 'I . . . I didn't see her then. I . . . I don't know where she went. She must have been cold, had been out a long, long time, walking the perimeter fence. Always she gets as far away from everyone and everything as she can, but . . . but I didn't meet up with her.'

And maybe did. 'Went back to the room, did you?'

He wasn't going to leave it. 'I went into the shops on the Terrace of the Grand.'

'Weren't they closing?'

In time for the curfew for visitors and shopkeepers. 'We had about an hour.' There was nothing in his eyes now, absolutely nothing.

'"We"? Who was we?'

Ah, merde! 'I meant me. Collectively the others. British and . . . and Americans, and some from the Hôtel de la Providence. They're now allowed only the last hour once a week, on Fridays. Colonel Kessler used to let them go there just like the rest of us but Herr Weber, he . . . he made the times for them far more restricted.'

'Can you name any of them who could vouch for you?'

'Me? For obvious reasons I tried always to keep my distance. I had to, didn't I?'

'But not on that Friday, not when Caroline was killed. Stopped about here, did you, before turning back to those shops?'

Would he miss nothing? wondered Becky. They were still among the trees, had yet to reach the circular clearing the donkeys would have trod. 'Here, I think. Yes, here. A bit of the bark had been torn off this beech tree. Look, someone's been at it again.'

'Fire starter?' he asked.

Nora had been the one to tell them that the inner bark could be eaten, but she would just nod and say, 'We're always in need of it.'

'Nervous was she, this most recent bark puller?'

'All right, it was me.'

Duclos, Senghor, Weber, and Louis were now at the chalet, the two guards opening its doors, the stretcher being carried in. A last glance from Louis said, *Don't be long but don't spare her even though she's young and vulnerable.*

'Who opened that padlock? You must have arranged for that as well.'

'*I didn't know!* All I was asked to do was to get someone to meet her in that . . . that place, that Caroline had something she absolutely had to tell the new Kommandant, and that . . . '

'*Something,* mademoiselle? Wasn't it that she was certain Mary-Lynn had been pushed?'

'Yes, oh yes!'

'And the padlock?'

'I . . . I think Jill must have arranged it with one of the guards. He was to unlock it, but leave it hooked through the hasp as if still locked. Duclos would then duck in and wait for Caroline who didn't at first know whom she would be meeting. French or German, until I told her Corporal Duclos had agreed.'

'So at the last moment she *did* know whom she would be meeting?'

'Yes, but . . . but she must have seen Sergeant Senghor and the corporal walk away with the bike towards the wood compound.'

'And Brother Étienne?'

'Did he duck into the chalet?'

'Or did you follow her in and deal with her? You had every reason, mademoiselle. More, no doubt, than anyone else.'

'Even the killer of Mary-Lynn?'

'Especially that one, if both are the same.'

They started out again and only then did Herr Kohler say, 'Before

Louis and I got here from Paris yesterday, you must have gone to have another look. After all, Caroline hadn't returned to the room on Friday evening, had she? Madame de Vernon would have been beside herself with worry.'

A little of the hard, crystalline snow blew from the chalet's roof. Underfoot, it had been trampled. 'At first Madame thought that Caroline was with Jennifer, but when Jen was found, that . . . that wasn't so.'

'Out with it, please. Better here than in there with Weber.'

She nodded but could no longer face him. 'I . . . I went out early Saturday morning, as soon as we could leave the hotel. The doors to the chalet were closed, the padlock hooked through the eye of the hasp, but open and probably just as it had been left. I waited. I picked at the bark of that tree. I dreaded what I would have to do. No one was about, not even Nora.'

'And then? Come, come, mademoiselle.'

'I ducked inside, but . . . but it was too dark to see anything. I whispered her name and . . . and when my foot touched hers, I stumbled.'

'And?'

He wasn't going to believe her, but she would have to try. 'I ran. I got back to the Vittel-Palace and went down into the cellars, then up into the laundry, where I'd left the things I had told the others I was going to wash. I didn't tell anyone about Caroline. I couldn't. I . . . I hid that because I knew I would be blamed if I didn't.'

But would she, as the killer, have returned at all? wondered Kohler. Louis would have said it's possible, but then . . . Yet that Star of David had been crammed into Caroline's pocket as though in anger. The hurried use of the only weapon available had been there, the impulse of it, the fierce determination of that moment—didn't all of these seem to say she had done it?

'Nora didn't know I'd arranged for Caroline to meet Bamba, Inspector, nor did Marni or even Jill. Earlier Caroline had asked me to find someone and knew that I would because before Bamba told me my fortune that last time, she had caught me taking things from our pantry to pay him for it.'

Weber having then singled out those very items, which had to mean that he either had been told of them by Duclos after the fact, or by someone else, yet the others in Room 3–38 had genuinely expressed surprise when Becky had said she'd gone back for a third reading all by herself. Jennifer Hamilton, then—she must have told Weber, Caroline having let her know.

'Somehow I would have explained to the others that I'd taken those things, Inspector, that they'd not been stolen as they'd thought. Somehow I'd have paid them back, but Caroline, she . . . she didn't blackmail me into asking Bamba to meet with her. She didn't even know who would until just before it happened.'

But if Weber had known beforehand of the meeting, what would he have done?

Louis was waiting for them, the corpse laid out as before. Weber, the collar of his greatcoat up, stood in the aisle in front of that middle stall, having impatiently lighted a cigarette.

Duclos and Senghor kept their distance as much as possible but obviously didn't like being there. Neither of them dared to look toward the victim, nor did they look directly at Becky or anyone else.

Nudging the girl forward, Kohler laid a steadying hand on her right arm.

To gasp in shock and turn away was normal, to want to be sick too, thought Becky. There were livid blotches on the lower parts of Caroline's face and neck. Blood had run from a corner of the lips but had since been frozen.

'Mademoiselle,' said Chief Inspector St-Cyr.

There was a tearful nod, a faintly blurted, 'Yes, it's Caroline.'

'She spent time getting herself ready for the meeting,' said Louis, not sparing her. 'You must have watched.'

A moment had to be given.

'Caroline . . . Caroline had wanted to look her best in case she'd be taken straight to the new Kommandant. Yes, I watched her, as did Madame, who kept asking her why she had to go outside at such an hour. "A *cold* . . . you are coming down with another," she said. "That chest of yours is far too weak and you know it!"

'Caroline answered, "It's not what you think. You'll find out soon enough."'

'She was raped, wasn't she?' seethed Weber, flinging his cigarette down at the foot of Senghor and Duclos. 'You and those others from Room 3–38 set it all up. This one held her, while this one went at her, then they took turns.'

As implied earlier by Madame de Vernon, thought Kohler, but *lieber Gott,* he was serious! For all his life since the age of ten, Weber must have dreamt of just such a moment.

Becky Torrence was now a wreck.

It was Louis who said, 'Raped and then tidied afterwards, Untersturmführer?' A *sûreté's* hand was held up to silence the sergeant and his corporal.

Contemptuously Weber said, 'It's of no consequence. Someone else must have done that. These two are guilty. One look at them is enough.'

'We didn't touch her, Boss,' said Senghor to Kohler but evasively flicking a glance at St-Cyr. 'Corporal Duclos told me what he had agreed to do but, as he was under my orders, I advised against it. We took the brother's bike to the shed and repaired its flat.'

'But first you made use of her,' said Weber. 'A white girl, a virgin.'

'There was no evidence of a struggle, Untersturmführer,' said Louis, giving Senghor a look that said *Don't ever lie to me again.* 'Though she's been tidied as before, it's common practice for us to take a victim's temperature so as to estimate the time of death. When I did that, I checked for semen. I am also certain that whoever does the autopsy will find she was still a virgin.'

This cursed, interfering Frenchman would say anything. 'Then whoever tidied her must have interrupted these two.'

'And then killed her before the tidying, thereby giving them the identity of her killer? Sergeant, did you see anyone enter this building?'

Though the chief inspector now knew he had earlier been lied to about any of them having been asked to meet with that girl, he was still on their side, thought Senghor. 'No, I didn't.'

'Corporal Duclos, did you?'

Senghor threw him a look that said a lot, thought Kohler, but the corporal concentrated on the dung at his feet and lost himself in God only knew what.

The sun had risen, thought Bamba, but Grandpapa and Papa had said one must never read one's own future; nor should the gift ever be used for profit or in competition with another such as Madame Chevreul, even though the desperately needed food and cigarettes would pour in; nor should one *ever* claim to be able to go beyond the future to speak to the dead and hear what they had to say.

'Well?' demanded Louis.

'Bamba, *mon ami,* you must tell them,' said Senghor.

The sharpshooter's insignia, his own, thought Bamba, had been upside down, the blanket pin of the dead French soldier hooked through the gold wedding band of the woman who had died of a bomb blast in that other war and given birth to twins they had then had to bury.

The points of the scimitars had touched the little brass bell as if to ring it one last time, the cock's foot had been turned inward, the thigh bones scattered.

Herr Weber would see that both Senghor and he were beaten to death. Not today, not tomorrow, but soon. The receiver of the gift and the giver of it would be no more, and the juju lady of the Hôtel Grand would win. 'I did look back once as we neared the church. I did see that one enter this place.'

The victim.

'Though in a hurry, Mademoiselle Lacy glanced our way,' said Duclos, 'and I knew then that things would not go well for her.'

'There, you see.' Weber smirked. 'Others were waiting in here, weren't they? Others of you blacks. You *knew* what they were going to do to her. They grabbed her from behind, didn't they? They shoved a filthy rag into her mouth, tore at her clothes, forced her down and pushed her face into the ground before flipping her over so that she had to look at them as they raped her, one after the other, before stabbing her to death with that pitchfork.'

Gott im Himmel, would nothing convince him otherwise? wondered Kohler.

'And wiped it clean, Untersturmführer?' asked Louis, defying the odds.

'Ask them, don't ask me.'

'Hermann, be so good as to take the mademoiselle to the Vittel-Palace. We'll join you when we've moved this one to the morgue.

'Untersturmführer, who reported the killing and what did you find here? Please go over everything as closely as possible.'

'Louis, are you sure you don't need me?'

One look said it all: *Merde, mon vieux,* why must you ask? Just bugger off and make use of the opportunity.

The safe was not as easy to open as it was thought. Kohler spun the dial again, bringing it to between the 52 and the 58. Listening for the tumblers, he moved it a degree and then another and another before leaning back to look at the *verdammte* thing.

There was no mistake. It was the basic, three-tumbler combination locking mechanism, a Yale, though that really wouldn't matter much, for all such had about a million possible combinations. Oh for sure he'd narrowed the range down, but still . . .

A frantic search yielded nothing, not even behind the photo of Weber's sister, but then tucked inside the cover of der Führer's *Mein Kampf* was a slip of paper: *3 right to the 57, 2 left to the 32, and back around to the 11.*

Again he listened for Weber's approach. Again he realized that there could be no reasonable excuse for his being there.

Beneath the cartons of cigarettes, tins of the same, and of pipe tobacco, there were the files the Untersturmführer had gleaned from the former Kommandant's desk before Colonel Jundt had arrived. Telex after telex laid it on from Colonel Kessler to the Oberkommando der Wehrmacht, the OKW, the High Command of the Army: 'The men are desperately needed here. Already I have had to send far too many. Barely enough remain to adequately guard and patrol the camp. I can let you have three and no more.'

For the Russian Front, and guess whose name was top of the list? 'Untersturmführer Weber is most anxious to prove himself in combat.'

And in another file, this one not from Colonel Kessler to the OKW but from Weber to Obergruppenführer-SS Kaltenbrunner, head of the Reich Central Security Office in Berlin and a drunkard, a sadist, and an anti-Semite if ever there was one but, worse still, an intriguer who was suspicious of everyone and everything.

'Attention, most secret. Kommandant Kessler is a traitor to his country. His cosy friendship with the Americans indicates he is convinced the Reich will lose the war. Having taken a mistress from among them, he has made her pregnant, which unfortunately has led to her suicide on the night of 13–14 of this month. The padlocked gate of an elevator shaft was tampered with and the third-storey gate opened by the victim who then jumped to her death.

'Easy on the Jews who hide here with false passports, Colonel Kessler continually rejects my urgent demands that the Reich Central Security Office be asked to have their Honduran and other papers examined.'

Another file gave the deaths of the Senegalese while out in the forest cutting and hauling logs. 'Killed during an escape attempt. Death from heart attack,' this last a favourite with SS and Gestapo interrogators.

Three such notices stretched back to well before Kessler had been recalled, but there were also telexes from the former Kommandant to the OKW complaining of the Untersturmführer's 'attitude.'

Weber didn't just have that photo of his sister with its tiny swastikas at the upper corners of the frame. There were others in an envelope in the safe that, judging by the stamps on the backs, could only have been taken by the police photographer in Koblenz. Overcoat and dress were in disarray and well above the waist, the girl flat on her back, legs slack and spread widely, arms thrown out, blood on the snow near the head and thighs, mouth open, eyes staring, shoes and stockings lying under the shadow of the Schutzmann who must have found her, those of the district's Polizeikommissar and one of his detectives falling on the white woollen bloomers the mother had insisted on.

She'd been a student, having completed the first year of what would have been a six-year program to become a home-economics teacher. Dead, Friday 23 December, 1921, at 1807 hours, age eighteen years, four months, and eleven days.

Kessler had had good reason to be worried and Weber plenty to have gotten rid of him, but there was no sign of the directive Kessler would have left for Louis and this partner of his.

An envelope gave Jennifer Hamilton's Paris address on the avenue Henri-Martin, the full name of her maid, Thérèse Marie Guillaumet, an often-added-to list of the paintings and antiques, the address of the Head Office of the Paris ERR, the Einsatzstab Reichsleiter Rosenberg—the covetous collectors of all such things—and a telex from Weber to them stating that when in Paris on leave in mid-April he wished to meet to discuss a matter of common interest that had come up in the course of his duties.

This boy was a climber who could rightly claim that the valuables had been bought from Jews on the run and for others who were clients in America. Jennifer Hamilton didn't have a hope in hell of leaving, and as for Becky, if her papers and passport were removed, Weber would be the first to realize it and to telex Berlin about a certain two detectives.

Reluctantly he replaced everything only to take up the girl's papers and passport again. Convinced that Louis and he had judged her guilty, she had stood all alone outside this office, hadn't known what he would be doing in here, only that should Weber come along she was to have given the door a damned good thump.

Unfortunately Louis wasn't present to vote on the matter but a can of pipe tobacco might help, along with six packets of Lucky Strikes and a good 10,000 Reichskassenscheine, the Occupation marks at twenty francs to the mark.

'And a wad of American dollars just in case,' he muttered to himself.

Only then did he see the chewing gum. Four packets of Wrigley's spearmint, one of them open and missing two sticks.

'Louis . . . ' he blurted, for Louis wasn't going to like what he'd found, that was for sure.

As he looked up, Kohler saw the keyboard again and this time his heart really did sink, for there definitely were two keys to every one of those *verdammten* locks, and certainly the lift-gate lock hadn't been tampered with but opened with its key. Weber would have checked the board after learning of Mary-Lynn

Allan's death, but could well not have noticed beforehand if one had been missing.

The same for the Chalet des Ânes. It was that or Weber himself who had used them, the chalet killing then having taken care of everything.

'And two missing sticks of chewing gum . . . ' It was not a happy thought.

To all questions there had been but obstruction, thought St-Cyr. *Bien sûr* it had been a mistake to have grabbed Weber's wrist and threatened to break his arm, a greater one to have insisted that Hermann make use of the opportunity and leave them, but now . . .

Matthieu Senghor and Bamba Duclos, terrified of what the Untersturmführer might well do to them, still waited to lift Caroline Lacy's body on to the stretcher. Weber, the flap of his holster unfastened, smoked yet another cigarette, the two armed guards ready at the wide-open doors. Clearly he was trying to decide what to do: kill them or leave it.

'Untersturmführer, since you feel Colonel Kessler should have called in detectives from Vittel's Kripo nearby, why, please, did he not do so?'

This souvenir of Verdun, this irritating, infuriating *sûreté* was going to pay for what he had done! '*Verdammter Schweinebulle,* ask him, don't ask me.'

'He left no note of advice for us on the death of Mary-Lynn Allan?'

Desperate now, this *sûreté* was waiting for it, as were the blacks. In Paris, Gestapo Bömelburg would lift an eyebrow at their loss, those of the SS on the avenue Foch giving little other than grateful smiles, since their two most hated troublemakers in France would have been conveniently dispatched, such was the reputation of this flying squad of Bömelburg's, these seekers of the truth. But there might be questions.

'Well?' came the insistent demand.

'None.'

'Untersturmführer, is it that you no longer wish to assist Hermann and me with this investigation?'

'*Gott im Himmel,* I am head of security here and must be consulted at every step and yet am simply to be ignored and then manhandled?'

'I'll speak to Hermann. When we move Mademoiselle Allan's body, we'll tell you everything.'

'But only what you want. Admit that the delay in your getting here caused the death of this one.'

The corpse was nudged with the toe of a jackboot.

'*Gut,* we understand each other completely,' said St-Cyr. '*Bitte, mein Lieber* Untersturmführer, where were you on the night Mary-Lynn Allan was pushed?'

'*LIEBER CHRISTUS IM HIMMEL,* DO YOU WANT A BULLET?'

'Please just answer.'

'La Maison de Roussy on the avenue de Châtillon. It's very good. They look after you. No taste is discouraged. Little birds of fourteen and fifteen can be found because they want to be, but since you and Kohler are confined to the camp, you will have to take my word for it.'

Patience . . . one must have patience with one such as this. 'A name—someone who can state under oath when you arrived at that brothel, how long you dallied, and when you left.'

'After fucking two little French girls who were only too willing?'

'Please just answer.'

'Noëlle and Brigitte wouldn't want to have to swear to anything, not after the time I gave them.'

And smirking now. 'Madame de Roussy then?'

The head was tossed as if struck. 'That old boot? *Ach,* she doesn't write anything down but numbers because she can't and has been told not to anyway. All she does is hand out the yellow cards each *putain* has to sign and date.'

In case of venereal disease. 'Then those will have to do.'

'Unfortunately I no longer have them. Our resident doctor has, but since he is home on leave, you will have to take my word for it.'

'Then please tell me if you knew beforehand that this girl was to have met someone here. You have your sources.'

'My informants?'

'Isn't Jennifer Hamilton among them?'

Kohler would have let him know this. 'Her lover—isn't that who you mean?'

'Of course, Untersturmführer.'

'*Ach,* I did hear of a possible meeting and that this one had thought the death of Fräulein Allan no accident, but in the constant flood of gossip I'm subjected to, I paid no attention.'

'Even though it was forbidden for any inmate to enter this or all such other buildings?'

'Girls will be girls. Contrary to what Colonel Kessler thought, they are not able to police themselves—a matter Kommandant Jundt and I are taking steps to rectify.'

'Yet this girl was not only convinced Mary-Lynn had been pushed. She saw what happened, Untersturmführer, and was convinced that she not only knew who had done it but that she, herself, was to have been pushed.'

The blacks hadn't moved a hair but had shuddered inwardly at every word. 'Perhaps it is that she confided in the wrong person—have you and Kohler even thought of that?'

Weber had constantly moved from Matthieu to Bamba and back again, often standing close to them. 'What really happened after Caroline Lacy went missing, Untersturmführer? As head of security you must have been made aware of the girl's absence.'

Thinking it had gone unnoticed, this Frenchman had dared to undo that shabby overcoat of his and the jacket so as to make the Lebel 1873 he was carrying a little more accessible. It would do no harm to answer, but was he really ready to die while defending two black *Kammeradin* from that other war? 'Frau de Vernon got Frau Parker to speak to Kommandant Jundt. That had to wait until morning and only then was a search of the grounds made, the girl soon found.'

'By whom?'

The fun could now begin. 'By one of these blacks.'

Ah, merde. 'Which one?'

'That one.'

'Sergeant Senghor, please run through it for me. Leave nothing out, no matter how insignificant.'

Weber wasn't going to like it, thought Matthieu. 'One half of the chalet's door was slightly ajar, Chief Inspector, the padlock hooked through the eye of the hasp but obviously open and as if replaced in a hurry. I knew at once that it wasn't right. I entered, found her, and touched nothing.'

'Was she just as she is now?'

There was a nod. 'I reported it to the Untersturmführer Weber, who then went to see for himself.'

'Touching nothing?'

'That I do not know. Like the rest of my men, he simply kept me waiting in the cold. He entered, took a long time—fifteen minutes at least, maybe twenty—and then came out but said nothing to us, only walked along our line, pausing to stare at each of us and demanding that we look at him before ordering that the chalet be placed under guard to await your and Herr Kohler's arrival.'

'You and your men were then sent to get on with your other duties?'

The head was shaken. 'We were left at attention. Two hours later, I dismissed the men myself and we went to get warm even though we had things we should have been doing.'

'Corporal Duclos, did you kill this girl?'

'No, I didn't, Chief Inspector.'

'Then for now, please assist your sergeant. Take her to the hospital. Ask Sister Jane to show you where to leave the body. Request that she make certain no one touches it—not any of the doctors nor any of the sisters. Just a clean sheet placed overtop.

'Untersturmführer, a moment. Since you entered this building to find her, please be good enough to take me through things step by step. It is required.'

'I haven't time. I have duties I must attend to.'

'And this is definitely one of them. Did you touch anything?'

'Why would I?'

'You took a good fifteen minutes in here all by yourself.'

'That is only the word of a black. If it was five minutes, I'd be very surprised. Two would have been more likely.'

'Did you question the lock's having been open?'

'Of course, but as all keys are on the board in my office, I would have known right away if one of them had been taken. Colonel Jundt and I went through everything before you and Kohler arrived. Let me tell you, he is just as dissatisfied with your being called in as I am. Berlin is going to hear of it.'

'When in your office earlier, Untersturmführer, I noticed, as my partner will have, that each lock on that board of yours has a pair of keys. Some are American, most, though, are French, especially the pin tumblers and other door locks. Are you completely certain all of them were there at all times?'

'Have I not just said that?'

'Then for now that is all. Please see that this building is locked and guarded twenty-four hours a day. No one is to be allowed in unless with Hermann or me, and that includes you and the Kommandant. Something is not right.

'Oh, there is one other matter. Everyone seems to have lost a little something. Since you have had to interview many of the inmates, and often several times, has anything been taken from you? Some small, personal item of no value to anyone other than you?'

How could this one even begin to understand the loss? 'The bloodstained ribbon that was once in my sister's hair. Her attacker had tried to use it to tie her wrists. It was always kept neatly folded in front of her photo on my desk.'

'But at first you didn't notice that it was missing?'

'I often touched it.'

'That is not the answer.'

They were alone now. There was just the two of them. 'One day it was there, then it wasn't. I immediately thought of the cleaning staff, who come in from town for an hour or two, but as would be expected, those bitches denied taking it. I had already searched the floor, my pockets, the drawers—the safe, even. Occasionally I would have it in hand only to set it aside to get on with something. I felt it must have slipped to the floor and then been swept up. No one would have wanted it for a ribbon.'

'Because of the stains, of course, but please, the length, the original colour?'

Did he doubt the loss? 'Prussian blue. Twenty centimetres by two, and with a thin, very fine white lace border on each side. Silk from the old days before that other war and the Occupation it brought, which led to her defilement and murder by your blacks. Our grandmother gave that ribbon to her. Sonja wore it often, always with pride.'

'And of those who are among your informants who might have taken it?'

'Have I been trying to discover that on my own—is this what you think?'

'Please just answer.'

'None of them would have dared. I, too, have ways of twisting an arm, even if it breaks.'

7

Both from within and outside the once-elegant shops of the Grand, Becky was certain people stared at her. They thought her guilty as Herr Kohler hurried her along the terrace toward the Vittel-Palace. They accused her, asked silently, *How could you have pushed Mary-Lynn and then* stabbed *Caroline? You* lied *when first asked by Herr Kohler about Mary-Lynn. You tried to* deny *having followed Caroline out into that corridor but had to admit it when Marni and Jill reminded you.*

The looks from the British were by far the most damning, those from the Americans as though betrayed, she having let down their side.

'Inspector . . . '

It was Jill, it was Marni, it was Nora.

'Inspector, Becky wouldn't have killed anyone. Not our Becky.'

Jill had said that. Jill. They'd been watching for her. They held her tightly, clasped her mitten-covered hands, made him pause only to then be confronted by Léa Monnier, who, porkpie hat cocked to one side, sable collar up, flashed a hideous grin and rasped, 'Caught you, eh, did he, ducky? Bet that black number, that mumbo-jumbo man you went to, didn't tell you you'd get pinched. Bet he told you life was going to be a bed of roses, if only you'd give him a can or two of pork and beans, a couple of packs of Lucky Strikes, one of raisins, two chocolate bars, and some gum, but Cérès has it differently. Cérès says that little ballet dancer was killed by you to shut her up.'

All who were around looked at them, all stood still, but then . . . then from a distance came the creaking and sighing of frost-gripped branches.

'Cérès was consulted last night, was she?' asked Herr Kohler cautiously.

In for a penny, in for a pound, felt Léa. 'Perhaps if you and the chief inspector were to consult the goddess, you might find the answers. Unlike the dancer having been stabbed by that one, Mary-Lynn told Cérès she had been pushed by this one!'

A fist whacked Nora on the shoulder, she turning so swiftly on Léa, one would have thought her lacrosse stick in hand.

'Ridiculed Cérès, did you, luv?' taunted the woman. 'Told Mary-Lynn that she was being hoodwinked, that Bamba Duclos was every bit as good as Madame Chevreul but that neither of them spouted anything more than bullshit? Well now, we'll see, shall we?'

Nora didn't back off. Nora stood right up to her and said, 'I didn't push Mary-Lynn. I would never have done that.'

Léa's bushy, dark-rooted hennaed eyebrows arched. 'But you thought the lift gate closed and locked, luv? You didn't think she'd fall, and when she did, you had to lie.'

Mein Gott, this place, this den of females, thought Kohler. 'Well?' he asked Nora.

She would have to tell him. 'I chased her up the stairs. She yelled at me that I was being unfair, that all her life she'd heard stories about her dad and that she had needed to know where his remains were lying and had wanted and wanted to speak to him and finally had.'

'Admit it, luv, you tried to grab her in the dark and instead she stumbled and fell and that is what Caroline Lacy told Cérès last night, Inspector, when Madame made contact with her and the other one.'

A week ago that corridor light had been on and then had gone off, but not before Caroline had seen what had happened to Mary-Lynn Allan, or thought she had. 'You went back down the stairs a bit to avoid being seen by anyone else, did you, Nora?' asked Kohler.

'It wasn't like that, Inspector. She's lying. I was on the stairs and, yes, we were yelling at each other and I was chasing after Mary-

Lynn, but she was my friend. I had even loaned her that last fifty to pay off this . . . this greedy cow's incessant demands for the cash or cheque up front.'

'Cow, is it?' began Léa, only to be shushed by Kohler.

'Fifty American?' he asked.

'Yes! Otherwise Mary-Lynn wouldn't have been at that séance, even though Colonel Kessler would have been waiting for her to sit beside him.'

'And hold his hand?'

'Yes.'

'Cérès can tell you who the father was, Inspector,' said Léa. 'All you and the chief inspector have to do is ask. Madame Chevreul will be only too willing.'

'And the fee?'

'Peace and an end to the matter.'

Herr Weber, the Senegalese, and the chief inspector were waiting in the cellar near the elevator, thought Becky. Livid, Mary-Lynn's face was swollen. Her eyes, once of the loveliest shade of grey and often full of concern for another, were horrible. Her nose and teeth had been smashed, her lips broken. Deep, yellowish-green to copper-red, the skin at the base of her throat was now putrefying. Soon the stench would be unbearable.

'Mademoiselle,' asked St-Cyr, the corpse having been lifted out and placed on a stretcher in the corridor.

Herr Weber was watching her closely. Swiftly Becky turned away, Herr Kohler grabbing her as she bent double to throw up, choke, and blurt, *'Dear God, why did you have to make me look at her?'*

'Ah, bon, mademoiselle. Now a few answers.'

'Louis, those had better wait. We need to talk.'

'Sacré nom de nom, Hermann, what now? Sergeant Senghor, please see that Mademoiselle Allan's body is also taken into Sister Jane's care. *Vite, vite.* Away with the two of you.'

'A moment, Louis. Corporal, for the record, tell us what the sun revealed of Mary-Lynn's future when those of Rooms 3–38 and 3–54 paid you to read the basket for them in December after that Christmas party the British held for the Americans.'

Herr Weber smiles knowingly, Inspector, thought Bamba, but if one were to draw attention to this and refuse to answer truthfully, one would only suffer ten times the usual. 'In addition to her future, she asked if Cérès would reveal where her father's remains lay and if the goddess would convince him to speak to her, but through Madame Chevreul who would relay his words.'

'And?'

'I told her that such an impenetrable fog as surrounded her father on that battlefield would only part if she believed absolutely in me and the basket and no longer went to Madame Chevreul, but that she would have to come back alone.'

'And did she?'

'Three times, Boss.'

Somehow Becky found her voice. 'They compete, Inspector. Ever since the one started speaking to an asteroid, Corporal Duclos and Madame Chevreul have known about each other. At the party several of the British girls made a point of tormenting Léa by saying to others how good the corporal was and that he could, if pressed, even reach one's ancestors. Léa . . . Léa said she would have to see about it. We thought no more of it except to agree that we'd all go together for a session with him.'

No lies could be told, not now, thought Bamba, not with Herr Weber knowing what his informants must have told him. 'Each time I saw the sun rise for Mary-Lynn Allan in the basket, Boss, I saw her falling down a deep, dark well. I couldn't understand this, since we had no such wells but couldn't tell her what had been revealed.'

'But you did tell someone else?'

'Yes, Boss, but only because that one paid me well. Two boxes of Del Bey raisins, a bar of Lifebuoy soap and four packs of Camels, three tins of Klim, two of SPAM, and two of the Hershey's nut-chocolate bars.'

'A lot, so what about the name, Corporal? Come on, out with it.'

'The lover of the one who was stabbed.'

* * *

'Jennifer Hamilton . . . ' began Louis. 'But why would she want to know the future of Mary-Lynn, Hermann? Oh for sure a little curiosity, but to pay far more than necessary? Certainly Corporal Duclos and Sergeant Senghor were wary because of Weber's presence, but both were also hiding something we might desperately need to know.'

'The fierce competition between jujus and that Weber knew exactly what had been going on. Jennifer couldn't have supplied all those things, not from Room 3–54's larder without a lot of explaining. Someone had to have given them to her, and that someone has to have been Weber.'

'Hermann, this isn't good.'

'He needed a suicide, Louis. Now, back off for a moment and eat. I can't have you flagging out on me because of low blood sugar, not with what I have to tell you.'

'*Ah, bon,* Inspector, although we've apparently little time left to enjoy life if what you've said is true, I always knew my partner was clever and myself indeed fortunate, but now you're also a medical doctor, or is it an herbalist?'

Admittedly the biscuits from a British Red Cross parcel were as hardtack, thought Kohler, the Hôtel Grand at 1435 hours, an all-but-empty dining room down the length of which, between its Art Deco columns, a muted group of four in overcoats, fingerless gloves, hats, and boots smoked cigarettes to the butt while playing whist as though damned to it for the rest of their lives. 'Just eat. Don't argue. We're going to need each other.'

With deliberateness Louis opened a can of SPAM from an American parcel and deftly ran a knife around the contents before upturning the tin and shaking it out onto a sheet of collabo newsprint. Then he sat back to survey the corpse with the eye of a connoisseur who had just been betrayed.

'Fried with onions, peppers, and mushrooms, it might be all right, Hermann, if a sprinkling of parsley and a little thyme were added, but cold and alone on those as a last meal?'

The hardtack was white and heavy. 'Put a little of this chutney on it.'

'*Ah, mon Dieu,* it's comforting to know you want to play nurse-maid as well, but those are orange-juice crystals.'

'Oh.'

A can of cold pork and beans was opened and, after hammering the hardtack with a fist, a slice of the SPAM was laid to rest and covered, spoonful by spoonful with the other.

'*Bon appétit,*' said Louis. 'Now, please enlighten me.'

The Wehrmacht's cooks had refused entry to the kitchens, having locked all doors to prevent contamination by datura. Apparently the rumours were rife.

Kohler leaned forward to confide the worst. 'Weber and Kessler were at each other's throats. The one, having put the other up for the Russian Front, was targeted to Berlin-Central as a traitor soft on the Americans and the father of Mary-Lynn's unborn, the girl having unfortunately—now get this—tampered with that padlock and then committed suicide.'

Immediately causing the abrupt recall of Colonel Kessler, but caution had best be urged. 'The Untersturmführer kills her to establish the necessary proof?'

The missing sticks of chewing gum were mentioned, Louis choking on a bit of biscuit.

'Hermann, if this is true, we'll never get out of here and you know it. Granted, Jennifer would have had to tell him beforehand that Mary-Lynn would be attending yet another of Madame Chevreul's séances and that Nora would again be with her, the others off playing poker, except for herself and Caroline.'

Becky having stayed in her own room, a fact not likely known beforehand. 'Entry for Weber wouldn't have been a problem, Louis. It was the most distant wing of that hotel and late at night.'

'But, *ah, merde, mon vieux,* one lone male—an SS at that, and head of security—among 992 females, any of whom could get out of bed or leave that poker game to walk the corridors or climb those stairs at any moment?'

'He was desperate. He had to get rid of Kessler before that one got rid of him. They'd probably been at each other's throats since the British first got here.'

'But couldn't have known when those two would come back from that séance, Hermann, nor even which staircase they would take.'

Louis could be difficult. 'Just listen, will you? These aren't bad, by the way.' The spoon was given a flourish. 'We both know that padlock wasn't tampered with. The corridor lights were blinking off and then on, something Weber need not have engineered, since it happened often.'

'Good. Your opinion is comforting, but all we really have is Jennifer Hamilton's word that Caroline Lacy left Room 3–54 at about midnight to return to Room 3–38 for those cigarettes. A lover's tiff that was soon settled, according to Jennifer, the couple parting on good terms, Becky claiming otherwise and that Caroline was distraught, Madame de Vernon telling me that when the girl left her on Friday afternoon, two days ago, she felt Caroline was going to meet Jennifer to end the affair.'

'That woman was still out in the corridor, Louis. I'm certain of it.'

'Perhaps, but what, really, did Caroline see, Hermann?'

'Since she absolutely must have seen something.'

'And wouldn't otherwise have done what she did.'

For beverage there was tea made with cold water and sweetened with Borden's Condensed Milk courtesy of a Canadian parcel, for dessert, a Neilson's chocolate bar, eight ounces or 226.8 grams.

'Let's set Weber aside for the moment. Was the wrong one pushed, Louis?'

'Madame de Vernon hating Jennifer.'

'Who repeatedly went along with Caroline to beg Madame Chevreul to let her become a sitter.'

'So that Cérès could be asked to contact Madame de Vernon's unfaithful husband.'

'Caroline hoping to find out exactly what had happened to him.'

'Something Madame de Vernon definitely did not want.'

'Did she steal that datura from herself, Louis, as Brother Étienne accused, she hotly denying it but now waiting to put it to use?'

If so, they were in even deeper trouble, since Weber would be only too willing to blame them for having let it happen, and Berlin-

Central only too eager to hear of it. 'That monk knows far too much for his own good, Hermann. A nocturnal fire destroys the casino here but he fails to mention it?'

'And twenty-three years later Madame de Vernon finds herself back in Vittel at the very scene and enduring five confrontations with our head juju lady, demanding that she not let that ward of hers into any séance.'

'A request Madame Chevreul refuses.'

'While probably taking great delight in so doing, Louis, because she can use the publicity, or Léa has convinced her she can.' *Ach,* the tea was exactly like the bilge water they'd often found in the over-run trenches of the British.

'And everyone lies, Hermann, if not to protect one another and the herd, then to protect themselves.'

'With or without the others realizing it, but secretly thinking it in any case. Women, Louis. *Girls!* Why the hell must they be so difficult?'

Apparently the orange-juice crystals didn't help the tea. 'Mary-Lynn was shoved, Hermann, of this there can be little question.'

'But was the shoving meant for her or for Caroline, as that one repeatedly claimed, or for Nora Arnarson who fears she will be next?'

'Weber knew about Becky Torrence's fiancé, Hermann, and was secretly using that information to get her to cooperate.'

'So that he could have an informant in each of those two rooms and was planning to get rid of Mary-Lynn so as to pin the paternity and death on Kessler and be free of him.'

'Caroline claiming she had been the intended victim in order to hide behind that, Hermann, until she could tell the Kommandant what she had really seen.'

They ate in silence. They didn't know where to turn, and certainly they'd need absolute proof, felt Kohler, but something else would have to be mentioned. 'Jennifer has let everyone know the contents of her flat.'

'A fortune. Granted, it's curious for one to be so open, especially if cognizant of the huge inflation in such things, but . . . '

'Guess who has a list and has invited himself to Paris in April for a little look and a tête-à-tête with the ERR?'

The Einsatzstab Reichsleiter Rosenberg.

This definitely wasn't good. 'Then are we dealing with one or two killers, Hermann, and is that not the question we most need to answer?'

'Whoever killed Caroline must have known the Chalet des Ânes' padlock would be open and had either been waiting inside for her or had stepped in right after her.'

'But did her killer know ahead of time, Hermann, that Sergeant Senghor would be bound to order Corporal Duclos not to meet with that girl?'

'Maybe Brother Étienne knows more than he's saying.'

'Then let's hope he doesn't fall prey to his own medicine.'

'While treating a certain juju lady and her henchwoman. Jennifer told me she was hauled into the cellars here, Louis, and given the lowdown on Madame Chevreul and Léa. Those two were suffragettes, something she has yet to broadcast in the Vittel-Palace. I've told her not to until we're ready.'

'But a past that caused them to volunteer for active service . . . '

'They knew each other from London's Old Bailey in the summer of 1914, but before that too.'

'The street riots, Hermann, the smashed windows, the bombings, and the arson. That battle with suffragettes had been going on for years in Britain.'

'Madame Chevreul claims to sleep like a baby after every séance but is being treated by the brother for insomnia.'

'A lie we were most certain to uncover.'

'She also claims that Guerlain sample box was stolen by our kleptomaniac but that neither Jennifer nor Caroline could possibly have done it, the former then claiming that Madame had given it to Caroline to cement things.'

'Knowing full well, Hermann, that Caroline would show it to everyone, Madame de Vernon in particular.'

'And another lie that Madame Chevreul must have known we'd be bound to uncover. Maybe she wants to draw attention to herself or to Madame de Vernon. Maybe, too, she really does want us to ask Cérès for answers, since that would bring acclaim. She did lose her talisman—at least, that's what one of her "dreadful harpies" told me when I was reviewing the troops here with Weber.'

'Her gris-gris. That's Wolof, I think—Senegalese—for talisman.'

A can of corned beef, probably from Argentina via Britain, was opened and sampled.

'She must really have her enemies,' said St-Cyr.

'And competes with Duclos. *Ach,* she did tell me that her powers were being questioned and that whether I liked it or not, all were watching and waiting for the outcome.'

'And right after that séance a week ago, took the trouble to publicly warn Mary-Lynn to take great care.'

'Nora having constantly derided Madame's efforts, Louis, which could only have been bad for business.'

'Léa, then, Hermann, which causes Nora to worry if she herself was the intended victim or soon to be.'

The corned beef was really quite tasty. 'Why choose to meet at the Chalet des Ânes? Why not simply in the open, or at the wood compound?'

'That chalet can't be where the resident kleptomaniac hides her loot, Hermann. It's far too visible and would have required borrowing the key time and again or making a copy of it.'

A packet of Lucky Strikes was opened, one lighted, and after two deep drags were taken, passed over.

'Mary-Lynn's things were tidied, Louis. When asked, Jennifer claimed Becky must have done it that first time, but to me they looked as if they'd been tidied again, and recently.'

When given, the order they'd first been seen in was definitely not the same.

'Jennifer, then, and not Becky, Hermann? Please don't be too soft on Mademoiselle Torrence. She refuses to go along with Weber's request that she become one of his informants but knows Caroline is to meet with Corporal Duclos because she was the very person who had set that meeting up.'

'And can't have Caroline telling Colonel Jundt that she helped her fiancé to escape to the free zone, something she couldn't have known Weber already knew.'

'The Star of David then being crammed into Caroline's pocket and the pitchfork seized and driven home on impulse.'

'But by a killer, Louis, who then returns to the scene to find her victim and then, after lying to me about her having had a look, admits that she did?'

'That cowrie shell, *mon vieux*. Was Caroline planning to return it to Corporal Duclos with an apology, and if so, was she the thief or given it by the same so as to get him to agree to take that note to the Kommandant?'

'Given it by Jennifer who would have told Weber who Caroline was to have met and when and where. We'll have to ask her.'

'But first, Madame Chevreul and Léa Monnier. Since the house visits have been somewhat delayed, let's hope the brother is still with them.'

Three birds with one stone and a locked room too. '*Ach*, I almost forgot. I found something.'

Not until the pipe was packed and the furnace going did St-Cyr heave a contented sigh and say, '*Merci, mon vieux*, I knew I could count on you.'

'As can Becky.'

There was choking, coughing, wheezing as the passport and papers were set before him—tears, too. 'I couldn't leave them, Louis. We might never have got another chance.'

Alone, worried about Weber, for if true, Hermann and he couldn't withstand another run-in with the SS, St-Cyr drew on his pipe. Before him were the windows of Madame Chevreul's reception room. Already the ground fog, that bane of Vittel's existence, had returned to sweep slowly in and up over the snow-covered ground and all but hide the tree trunks and pavilions. *Bien sûr*, there was still a view—magnificent if earlier in the day. The Chalet des Ânes could still be seen. Caroline Lacy had headed for it at 1530 hours Friday, Nora Arnarson had been over by the perimeter fence . . .

'Something,' he muttered softly to himself. 'We are missing something so simple, it's right before us.'

Off in the distance, against the wire and seen, then not seen, the lone figure of that girl prowled the edge of her cage like a trapped cougar.

'She must know this park better than anyone yet claims not to have found the hiding place but has admitted to suspecting Jennifer Hamilton and of not only tracking that girl and Caroline Lacy into this hotel but also of asking others where the couple have been and to whom they've spoken.

'Has said of the relationship between the two that at first she felt it was out of character of Jennifer and then opportunistic because Caroline's family were very wealthy and yet . . . and yet she lies. She confesses only when confronted with the hard and inescapable truth. Is still hiding something.

'Will be twenty-six years old on Wednesday. Isn't married. Doesn't even have a fiancé anymore.

'Why not?

'Claims to have seen Brother Étienne on Friday but claims not to have waved. When asked who was with him, answered, "Caroline, I think."

'"Becky?" he had asked, Nora answering, "Was she? I didn't notice."'

Had mentioned the very ground fog and the poor visibility, that the tree trunks had been in the way, and then had said, "How was I to have seen anything?"

And knowing that, had she then gone to the chalet to confront Caroline Lacy?

Few if any would have seen her. Caroline must have entered the chalet at close on 1600 hours, would either have found someone waiting for her or would have waited herself for that person.

Had somehow acquired that cowrie shell.

The time of death, though calculated to be 1600 hours, could well have been somewhat later. A time for confrontation? Argument?

Nora Arnarson would have had no problem getting in there, but what had she found? Caroline simply waiting to be met or already dead?

It would have been all but dark inside, a light needed, a candle, a flashlight? But these last had been confiscated on arrival at the camp and were illegal.

A match, then, a simple match. But if so, the burned stub had been pocketed. Hadn't she since taken care to dispose of just such a thing?

Like a wraith, the trapper had lost herself and though he searched and searched, she could not be found. But had Madame Chevreul watched the proceedings from her windows late on Friday afternoon as he was now, and where, please, had Becky Torrence really been, Becky who had gone out there early yesterday morning to find Caroline's body and yet had said nothing of it until forced to by Hermann?

The aroma of smouldering rosemary, the incense, felt St-Cyr, of medieval monks that had perfumed the otherwise saturated air of their abbeys, filled the bedroom, instantly clearing the mind with its flavourful sharpness and competing with the lingering eau de cologne. Léa Monnier had just been attended to. With evident propriety, Brother Étienne hurriedly tugged the grey Blitzmädel dress and flannel slip down over the last of that backside to swollen ankles, cracked toenails, and bunions.

Madame Chevreul, her timing all but perfect, had opened the door, only a glimpse of the patient's state of undress having been offered.

'Chief Inspector, how good of you to have been patient. Léa, dearest, perhaps a few of your delightful *canapés de raifort à l'anglaise* and a glass of Brother Étienne's magnificent elderberry wine to polish off the inspector's lunch of cold pork and beans and SPAM.

'Really, Inspector, we would have heated it for you had we but known.

'Léa, dearest . . . '

A dark look was given this *sûreté*, a beet-red fist wrapping itself around a corked brown medicine bottle, the admonition breathed.

'*Couillon,* you didn't arrest the little one. How many times must I tell you it was her?'

Becky Torrence. 'Léa, Léa, I won't have this. Please don't be vulgar. The chief inspector is a guest, *n'est-ce pas*? Be the eminently polite and capable woman I know.

'Inspector, you must forgive her upbringing. Léa has been in terrible pain all morning, last night as well.'

Washing his hands in a large cut-glass bowl, the same as was used in the séances, no doubt, and uncertain if he should say anything in the presence of the *sûreté,* the brother did. 'Madame Monnier, please have whomever rubs you down use a glove. No cuts or scrapes in your skin or theirs, you understand, otherwise it will enter the bloodstream and we do not want that.'

The hands were dried, a doubtful glance given before taking hold of Madame Chevreul by a forearm, as one would an old and dear friend.

'I must emphasize its danger, Élizabeth. Oh for sure it will work like a charm. Our brother, the abbot, swears by it and blesses the day it was first administered, but I must urge extreme caution. Only a little at any one time, and rubbed in only until the numbness is felt. The skin will tingle. There will be that welcome sensation of warmth, but all in moderation and with great care, as emphasized.'

The Art Deco and other jewellery that Léa Monnier had worn when first encountered caught the light, setting off the fair hair, dark-blue eyes, and perfectly made-up cheeks and lips of this medium whose powder-blue woollen suit and soft grey silk blouse were magnificent.

Earrings matched the bracelet and one of the rings. The high heels were of dark-blue patent leather and worth an absolute fortune in themselves.

'Isn't he wonderful, Inspector?' she said, having noted with pleasure his scrutiny. 'Léa suffers terribly from sciatica and lumbago.'

'Gout, too,' grunted the woman defiantly.

'Hence the horseradish canapés?' he asked, gesturing with pipe in hand: thin slices of buttered black bread with chives and mustard to which had been added a topping of finely grated horseradish.

'The goutweed poultices are better,' grunted Léa.

'And a tincture of juniper, Inspector,' hastily added the brother to avoid further unpleasantness. 'A teaspoonful thrice daily, with a little water.'

'*Juniperus communis?*'

'Of course.'

Juniperus sabina being occasionally fatal, if taken internally. 'And the monkshood rub?' asked St-Cyr.

The wolfsbane, the blue rocket of gardens, the little turnip, and *sûreté* thoughts that would not be good. '*Aconitum napellus,* first used by Welsh physicians in the thirteenth century. Dissolved in alcohol and mixed with belladonna.'

Deadly nightshade. 'A liniment, then, of not one but two poisons, Brother, the first one of the most deadly.'

The latter containing atropine, hyoscyamine, and hyoscine, as did the *Datura stramonium,* the belladonna having been favoured by Venetian ladies in waiting whose pupils would then be dilated by beautifying draughts.

'Belladonna, itself, is nothing to play with. A hallucinogenic and a sedative, Brother? Respiration and body temperature increase until, with restlessness and giddiness, numbness leads to a comatose state, usually causing death, albeit delayed for some hours, even days; the former, the aconite, if but 0.00405 of a gram is ingested, one-sixteenth of a grain, within two to six hours, sometimes less.'

It was clear that this *sûreté* thought him imprudent, but one must be firm. 'The aconite giving a most agonizing death, Inspector. Hence my urging the utmost caution.'

'You don't fool around, do you? A bitter taste, after which there is that tingling and numbness you mentioned, but on the tongue and lips. *Ah, mon Dieu, mon Frère,* as little as 0.0000324 gram—one two-thousandth of a grain—will give the taste test, but that alone is sufficient to kill a healthy mouse in but a few minutes.'

'Inspector . . . Inspector, shouldn't you be more concerned with those missing seeds? Brother Étienne and I both agree that Irène de Vernon must have them. Caroline Lacy was terrified of her and very clear about the hatred that woman bore her and her roommates and, I must add, Jennifer Hamilton.'

'One capsule of four pods, each of which will contain from fifty to one hundred seeds, each in turn of about 0.1 milligram strength, one hundred seeds at most yielding the ten milligrams that are needed,' said Brother Étienne, sadly shaking his head. 'Caroline Lacy, I am certain now, must have been in danger of it, Nora Arnarson also, and Jill Faber, and Marni Huntington.'

'And Becky Torrence, Étienne. We mustn't forget her,' said Madame Chevreul.

'Each seed is but from two to three millimetres long, Inspector, and all can be easily hidden if removed from the capsule and its pods.'

'Jennifer Hamilton is in the greatest danger, Inspector. That is what Cérès said Caroline Lacy had insisted when the goddess spoke through me last night. Léa can confirm. We are all, as a result, extremely worried about that girl. Please make certain that nothing untoward happens to her. I have this feeling, and it makes me tremble.'

Jennifer then. A wineglass was brought and filled, the canapés offered, Léa Monnier's expression remaining grim and unrelenting.

The brother gave a nervous smile. 'Since I uncorked it myself, Inspector, I think you will find it untainted.'

'*Ah, bon, merci.* And did Caroline Lacy give the name of her killer?'

'Léa has already told you,' said Élizabeth.

Becky Torrence. 'A fait accompli, then?'

Time . . . was it an opportune time? she wondered. 'That girl was seen entering the Chalet des Ânes on Friday afternoon at around 1600 hours, Inspector, and all but on the footsteps of the Lacy girl. Perhaps Becky Torrence chose not to tell you this, but should have known that from here there is an excellent view which neither the gathering dusk nor that wretched ground fog entirely obscured. Léa and I were earnestly awaiting Étienne's arrival as, I dare say, were many others. Would this dear servant of the Lord bring the oft-promised liniment or again "forget" due to his deep concern over its nature? We saw him speak to Caroline first, giving her a few items, which she gratefully tucked away in her overcoat pockets. Then, as he would have done, he blessed her.'

'And wheeled my bike over to Sergeant Senghor and his corporal before coming in, it being the Hôtel Grand's turn to receive the first of my visitations.'

'Becky Torrence spent no more than seven or eight minutes inside that chalet, Inspector. Certainly when Cérès contacted her last night, Caroline anxiously stated that she hadn't expected Becky to confront her. I, of course, have no recollection of what was said, for when in clairaudience, it is only my voice that the goddess uses to reach the needy.'

'They argued violently,' said Léa, again passing the canapés. 'She said she had been wrongly accused of something, a star perhaps. The Milky Way was mentioned and that when she had denied any wrongdoing, the Torrence girl had seized a pitchfork and pinned her to the wall, demanding she confess.'

'Really, Inspector, if only you and Herr Kohler would agree to become sitters, all would be made most clear.'

And they had known precisely, felt St-Cyr, what had been found with Caroline—that Star of David that would have worried Becky the most.

Quickly at a signal from Madame, lunch was served to avoid further questions. *Oeufs brayons,* a favourite in Normandy: baked eggs with crème fraîche on crusty white bread, the last of the sauce then being added, with butter, salt and pepper, and chopped parsley. A warm potato and frisée salad with bacon would follow, *une salade au lard champenoise,* the frisée being winter's curly endive.

Unfortunately there was just enough for Madame and the brother, and one had to settle for the canapés and wine.

'Your partner, Inspector?' she asked. 'Where is he?'

'Hermann? Interviewing your maid, I think, and now your cook.'

'Léa . . . '

'Stays, Madame Chevreul. For now just trust to the gods that nothing untoward will be revealed.'

It was a room like no other, for the signs of the zodiac, half-moons, asteroids, comets, stars, and other things in silver and gold paper covered its walls and hung from the ceiling, and when he had closed and locked the door behind himself, Kohler stood looking down at this 'maid' of Madame Chevreul's, this former waif with the jet-black hair who had somehow, in that first crush of a mob encounter, slid a hand inside a greatcoat to steal his Walther P38.

She was like a sparrow yet a merlin, and her soft violet eyes looked up at him from under naturally curving, long black lashes as if from adventure's doorway. Not that of a room on the other side of Les Halles or even one from around the Carrefour Vavin in Montparnasse, but rather that of the 5th arrondissement, the rue St-Jacques or rue St-Germain and the Sorbonne. Innocence, then, and intelligence, but the dream of both and the memory.

'Cosy,' he said of the room. She wouldn't smile, wouldn't say a thing, thought Marguerite Lefèvre. Men like this had wanted to use her often enough in the past and she was certain she knew exactly what he was thinking.

The tent, the 'cabinet' that blocked the doorway into Madame Chevreul's bedroom, was both circus and child's playhouse, yet neither. From its inner sanctum, behind its dropped curtained doorway, the resident medium could conjure up anything she liked while the sitters pensively waited all but in darkness and with eyes tightly closed, holding hands in a semicircle around the table out front.

'Wallpaper,' he said. 'That of flowers, birds, Chinese pagodas and sampans, glued and pinned to cloth. Louis could give you the makers even if from a hundred years ago, but where did they get it?'

'They?' she softly asked, blinking up at him but only once.

'The blacks. The Senegalese.'

Her French was Parisian and perfect, her age not more than twenty-five, though she would definitely, with the Brother's help, keep that youthful complexion for years—the figure, too.

Block printed and of eighteenth- and nineteenth-century design, the wallpaper had been patiently stripped from opulent walls, dried, coiled, smuggled in, and sold to Madame Chevreul or simply handed over in return for a favour.

'The Hôtel de l'Ermitage?' he asked, now fingering an uncoiled curl of the paper as if a silk chemise he would trail down a girl's thighs before teasing off her step-ins.

She must shake her head and shrug, felt Marguerite. He looked inside the cabinet, the tent, saw that the door to Madame's bedroom was curtained off but easily accessible, saw the armchair she used, the throw rug on the floor, all such things, the luminescent gauze as well, the white ectoplasm that would appear to issue from Madame's throat when in a trance.

'Phosphorescent paint,' he said, fingering the gauze now and smiling that smile of his, for, on drying, the gauze had been crinkled repeatedly to make it again soft and pliable.

Curbs and crosswalks in Paris and elsewhere were painted with its whiteness to aide pedestrians during the blackout, thought Marguerite, but Madame wasn't going to be happy with her for having allowed him in here. Madame was going to tell Léa to see that she was punished severely, but what Madame had still not realized, or perhaps she had, was that such a punishment could be exciting in itself. *Une flagellation.*

And anyway there was nothing she could have done to have stopped him, a Gestapo.

'Léa gets things from time to time,' she said of the paint with a shrug.

'In trade?'

'Or by purchase.'

'And if one of those guards asks for a little comfort?'

Another shrug, but curt this time, would be best, the glimpse of a smile, now shy and defenceless. 'Don't you want me to gaze into my crystal ball?'

This item was on another table, and of smoky quartz, about twelve centimetres in diameter. Damask-covered, the table would have seated two, with one chair against the wall that faced the tent.

'You are a doubter,' she said, her pulse quickening at the thought. 'It's best then to start with such a ball. Once that negativity has been banished, clarity will come. You will definitely be surprised by what I see. The instant I set eyes on you, I knew.'

They read palms and tarot cards too, and the Ouija board, and places for each were set about the room. 'Caroline Lacy and Jennifer Hamilton were interviewed in here, amongst all of this?' he asked.

'If Madame has said so, then it must be.'

'Where's the divan?'

'What divan?'

'The one the two of them sat on while holding hands and being interviewed.'

No one had warned her of this, not Madame or Léa or Hortense, the cook. A lie would be best, then, but given with complete innocence and abandon. 'We haven't yet been open for business here, and are only now ready.'

'But have to wait until things have been settled?'

It would be so easy to seduce him. Men like Herr Kohler exuded a sexuality over which they had but little control, though, unleashed, would it all be one-sided as Madame continually insisted of men? she wondered, but thought not, for he had both an emptiness to those pale blue eyes of his and a light that was gentle and kind.

In short, he was a man no woman should trust. 'Please sit, Inspector. Let me gaze deeply into the ball.'

He did so, she too, their knees touching, he even setting notebook, pencil, cigarettes, and matches to one side, but a banging at the door into the corridor saved him and he knew this, for he smiled that smile of his and said, 'Maybe we'd better wait for another time.'

Hortense *would* interrupt things. Hortense was *always* interrupting things, but Herr Kohler had also set one of those little phosphorescent lapel buttons the Nazis doled out to those in Paris and elsewhere who would wear them in the blackout and her hand had closed about it and his had closed over hers.

'*Ah, bon, ma chère mademoiselle. Bon,*' he said.

'Actually it's *Madame* Lefèvre, and my husband is in one of your prisoner-of-war camps. Which one, I'm never sure, for he's a bit of a troublemaker and they seem to keep moving him around, but then . . . *Ah, mon Dieu,* he and I have been apart for so long now, I think we both must feel as two entirely different people, each perhaps having found their true self but due to circumstance of course.

'*Sacré nom de nom,* Hortense, I'm coming! Please don't break the door down with that fist of yours. You will only disturb Madame and her guests.'

'And Léa, of course,' muttered Herr Kohler, having at last released her hand. Would he have *crushed* it if she had resisted? she wondered.

Steam rose from the baked eggs and cream that had only just given a first, well-savoured morsel. Alerted by the banging next door, the three of them had paused, Brother Étienne darting a glance at Madame Chevreul and then at Madame Monnier, they avoiding his questioning look of alarm.

'Léa . . . ' began Madame Chevreul, her knife and fork still poised.

'Answers, madame. Answers!' insisted St-Cyr. 'A suffragette, Madame Monnier? A mob leader before the Great War and now again?'

Dieu merci, the banging had at last stopped, thought Élizabeth, but it had to mean Marguerite had been forced to let Herr Kohler into that room of rooms. 'Léa, you needn't say a thing. Inspector, I won't have this. Please show some respect if not manners. We are at our luncheon, late though it is. I told you and Herr Kohler not to listen to the harpies in this hotel. Whether Léa was a heroine of that cause or not has no bearing whatsoever now.'

'But it has, madame. It has, and were you not a part of that cause as well? It was all about power, wasn't it? Males dominating females to the point of not even letting women have the vote or as here in France where even a bank account or the freedom to travel without a father or husband's sanction is still necessary, but now what do we have? Females dominating females. A suite of four rooms at the top of the heap when six are forced to share each of the other rooms? Three stoves with plenty of wood and even coal and a choice of foods most in the country, not just in this internment camp, have not seen since the autumn of 1940?'

How dare he question her like this? 'Men. Why can't you all be like Étienne? Kind to a fault, gracious to every woman no matter how demanding or objectionable? Always considerate, always gentle and concerned, never hesitating for a moment, Inspector. Always valuing the very crucibles of humanity, for without us, where would you men be?'

Ah, bon, challenged she had let past feelings and beliefs come swiftly to the fore. The eggs would become cold but could be reheated. 'You never went home to England, madame? Why, please, was that?'

He had taken an educated guess, but she would not demean herself by giving him so much as a dismissive gesture. 'I was married, was I not? My first duty, under God and the law, if no other, was to care for my husband, a badly disabled veteran. Blind, wasn't he?'

Who had died in 1919 and likely couldn't have given her the Art Deco jewellery that had come into fashion in the 1920s, they being a time for unleashed gaiety and relief from that terrible war as well as for the breeding and sale of Percherons. *'Bien sûr,* but there are no photographs of the family you left behind, only those of the two friends who were arrested with you.'

He hadn't seen those of André, but how *could* he treat her this way? 'We were force-fed. Tied, Inspector, each in her cell—bound hand and foot to those atrocious iron cots of the Old Bailey. *Forced* to suffer the indignity of male hands while a rubber hose was thrust, I tell you, *thrust* down our throats. One chokes, one vomits, one tries to catch the breath but thinks she is about to drown, and all the while it is men who are doing this to us, to God's most delicate and intelligent of creatures? *Men,* I tell you. *Men!'*

The eggs were definitely getting cold. 'Surely there would have been a matron present?'

'Inspector . . . '

'Brother, stay out of this. Let her do the answering.'

'We were suffragettes, you silly man. The worst of the worst to those ignorant boors. Léa, who was but three cells from mine, had just turned seventeen. Repeatedly she fought them. Repeatedly they savaged her and then laughed at her nakedness and despair. *Laughed,* I tell you, while they turned the hoses on her.'

Brother Étienne urged caution and, reaching out to her, took hold of a hand but it was definitely not the time for calmness, felt St-Cyr. 'Is this why you let her wear your jewellery when she leads a mob here?'

'My jewellery? Léa, what is this he is saying?'

'Drugged was she, Madame Monnier? Given a little more than a droplet or two of that tincture of valerian while having a nap before confronting my partner and me last night and leading us to the Pavillon de Cérès?'

'*Espèce de salaud,* Madame was in the bath. I was only trying it on when the call came to lead that demonstration. We couldn't have the Americans telling you we were to blame for the killings!'

'Léa . . . ' began Madame.

'Élizabeth, I . . . '

'It is Madame Chevreul, please, and let us never forget it.'

Brother Étienne had set his plate aside, the eggs still swimming in their sauce, but the parsley looking lonely. 'Madame,' said St-Cyr, 'though you claim to sleep like a baby after every séance, Cérès doesn't let you.'

This *sûreté* was going to cause trouble unless stopped, thought Léa. 'The goddess frequently insists that Mrs. Judith Merrill, my former employer at the time, still has things to tell Madame, Inspector. What it is like when one passes over, whom one meets and how one recognizes others. They were very close and always Madame is anxious for word even when in her sleep. To her great joy, her André is no longer blind, yet she tosses and turns.'

'At the thought of his watching her?'

Quick to seize his frightful little moment, felt Élizabeth, the chief inspector snatched the portrait photographs from her dressing table.

'This one?' he asked.

'White arsenic,' whispered Brother Étienne with caution, again reaching out to her, the eggs now like a raft between them.

'A most unpleasant death, Brother.'

Tears were rushing down Madame's cheeks. 'I knew, damn you. Immediately after Judith had taken it, I felt a loss that wouldn't leave me. Weeks later, the return of the letters I had written to her from France only confirmed my worst fears, for Lord Merrill had chosen to include the death notice. Twenty-nine unopened letters, one for each year of her tender life, and nothing else but three puny lines of type in the *Times* and the lie of it: "*Dead of an illness.*" I hated him for what he had done to her, to all women. Is it any wonder, then, that we struck for our rights?'

There had been those in France who had wanted the vote and a say in other matters that concerned their everyday lives, felt St-Cyr, but there had never been the collective will to organize as strongly as there had been in Britain. 'And your family, madame?'

Léa's look was one of caution, Étienne's that of heartfelt concern. 'The father that I loved as a young girl does evermore had disowned me. Neither Nanny Biggs nor my two brothers who were much older than me would go against his will, those two especially since they stood to inherit my share of his estate.'

Bankrupt then, and in 1914, a volunteer. 'And now, madame?'

This *sûreté* wouldn't stop until he had uncovered everything. 'Thanks to Colonel Kessler, we rule ourselves. Léa, please see what is happening next door.'

A worry to be sure. 'A moment, Madame Monnier. You have your sources, as does your mistress. Has anything been stolen in the Hôtel Grand since the deaths of either Mary-Lynn Allan or Caroline Lacy?'

Was he ready for it, this grunt of a cow? 'Nothing since the Lacy girl, the same for the Vittel-Palace.'

'You have informants there as well?'

'I hear things.'

'Then Caroline Lacy was the petty thief—is this what you're implying?'

'Inspector, we were all but convinced of it,' interjected Madame Chevreul.

'But that is not what you claimed to my partner, madame. You told him neither Jennifer Hamilton nor Caroline Lacy could have been the thief.'

'I was mistaken.'

'You interviewed them in that other room, madame. They held hands, were never in here—had no access to this room and yet you are mistaken?'

That Guerlain presentation box. Jennifer Hamilton must have told him differently. 'Léa, please go. Hortense and Marguerite may need you.'

'Am I forgiven?'

'Of course and as always, but never covet what can never be yours.'

A hand was touched, a cheek given a decisive peck.

'Now, eat your lunch,' said Léa. 'Don't let this *vache* spoil things. Hortense will only be upset if you do.'

The boot-snatcher, the 'cook,' had flung the door wide. Fists doubled, she came on in, reminding one of a difficult birth: no fault of the child's, none of the mother's, simply circumstance that had governed everything since.

She wasn't just off a butcher's block in some poverty-stricken London lane near the East India Dock; she was swift, deceitful, loyal to her mistress, and one hundred percent determined.

'You are not to be in here unless Madame has given the permission!'

The rush of breath was fierce. 'Even though I'm from the Gestapo?'

'One of those? Pah! Briefcase men with nothing better to do than to interfere in the lives of others. Get out and we will discuss it in the corridor after I have locked the door.

'Marguerite, has he interfered with you?'

'Jésus, merde alors, I only wanted my fortune read.'

'Your fortune? It's a *zéro.* One can see this at a glance.'

'I was about to read it for him,' said the dove with utter innocence, 'but now have no need since he is convinced. Desperate, *ma chère* Hortense.'

'What did you try to take from him?'

'A button.'

Hurriedly crossing herself, the cook turned away to close the door, giving herself a moment to swallow.

'A button is nothing,' she said, her back still to them. 'Buttons go missing all the time. They are necessary.'

It rang when he spun it on the Ouija board. Only when it had stopped did he say, 'This one's not necessary.'

'She is not the thief, monsieur. She simply took it to tease.'

'You will forgive me?' asked that one, stepping close to brush against him and finger his lapels, the clean, sweet smell of her and of lavender all too clear.

Hortense was now behind him, so good, yes good, thought Marguerite. 'We read people in here, Inspector. We come to know all their secrets and desires.'

'Right now I want some answers.'

'To *what*, please?'

Hortense tapped him on the left shoulder. 'It is to me you are to speak. To me,' she said.

The other one let go of him but not before giving him a tiptoed brush against each cheek and the lightness of a brief embrace.

'*Merci*,' Marguerite whispered, leaving him perhaps with the lingering thought of more to come if he would but forgive her.

'How much do you star-gazers rake in a week? And don't be telling me this room hasn't been up and running since you got here and probably well before that circus in the Pavillon de Cérès downstairs.'

The cook's off-blond hair of fifty-five years looked as if self-cropped before a broken mirror, the bags beneath uncompromising grey eyes sagging to hard-cleaved pale cheeks and unpainted, grimly set lips.

'Any fool could see that it must have taken us months and months to organize.'

'Open a year, then?' he asked. She was getting the measure of him, was not as tall as the dove but at least twice as wide and ten times as strong.

'A year? It means nothing.'

'Simply that Jennifer Hamilton and Caroline Lacy were interviewed in here by Madame Chevreul, but there's no divan.'

'There was for them. They sat before that.'

The tent, the cabinet. 'With the curtain drawn and Madame inside?'

'Questions needed to be asked, answers given.'

'First the palms, Inspector,' dared Marguerite, 'then the tarot cards and my crystal ball, and only after those, the Ouija board and Hortense, and finally *le cabinet de* Madame Chevreul, *médium des médiums.*'

'Madame Chevreul sitting in judgement of them behind that screen?' he asked.

'Things had been stolen. Little things,' said Hortense. 'So many we were all wondering who was doing it.'

'But then Madame's talisman vanished and wonder of wonders, things turned ugly, is that it?'

Hortense would tolerate no more from her, thought Marguerite, but Herr Kohler would demand it. 'Jennifer couldn't have stolen anything, Inspector. It's simply not in her nature, not after what I have seen of it in my crystal ball. That, however, could only mean Caroline Lacy, her . . . her little companion.'

'Her lover?'

How quick he was to say it. '*Oui.*'

'Who must have gone through the curtain that hides the door behind that thing when Madame was no longer in conference with the goddess and was known to also be absent from her other rooms?'

And on a visit to Untersturmführer Weber, was this what he meant, or was he just fishing?

'Well?' he demanded.

'If you say so, then yes.'

'Marguerite . . . '

'Hortense, *ma chère,* I had better tell him. Jennifer first came here alone, Inspector, and several times. Me, I read her future in my crystal ball. To begin, I used the smoky quartz, as I would have with you and for much the same reasons, but then it was the rose quartz and only after that the clear crystal, for her worries drive her to anxiety and one must search deeply for the reasons. Always I cleanse each ball before and after a reading. This washes away all evidence of former images, ensuring each new reading is uninfluenced by them. I also magnetize the ball by passing the hands over it, though never touching it. I burn incense: apple blossom to sharpen the symbolic visions if those are being received; lavender to release myself from my own past, which might hinder intuition; lilac to stimulate perception. With Jennifer there were so many things clouding the ball and troubling her innermost psyche, but before we could reach total clarity, she was taken from me, only to then return but with Caroline.'

'Hand in hand, eh, and well after Jennifer's having been hustled into the cellars here and telling the truth about that one's past and Madame Chevreul's?'

Léa had come. Léa filled the doorway. Having heard what Kohler had just said, she was not happy.

'Caroline was such a shy and repressed creature,' continued Madame Chevreul, she and Brother Étienne having started in again on their lunch. 'Trampled, Inspector, by that dreadful woman who had dominated every facet of her tender life.'

The brother, having entrusted that very woman in total with enough datura to kill from six to twelve, was clearly haunted by the thought of what had been stolen—a third of it—but where, really, did he sit in things, this healer, this gossip, this courier of BBC Free French broadcast news, this bell ringer?

'Your talisman, madame?' asked St-Cyr.

'My gris-gris—isn't that what some would call it? A black who tells fortunes is better than me, Inspector? A man who is not only poor and uneducated but one step from the savage?'

'Élizabeth, I must caution you.'

'Étienne, please eat and then tend to the others. I'm sure we have kept you long enough.'

'He stays.'

'I think I had best, for the moment.'

A generous morsel was taken, the dark goatee of this nothing monk given a hasty wipe with a napkin.

'Laughter, Inspector,' she asked, causing that napkin to be impatiently crushed in a fist. 'Snide remarks? Whispers about my abilities? I who have done so much for so many and have freely given of myself? I who had as one of my most loyal and strongest of believers Colonel Kessler, the very Kommandant of this camp?'

'Élizabeth, he was asking about your talisman.'

'A mere trinket of no consequence, so please be kind enough to help yourself to the warm potato salad, Étienne. Time and again, Inspector, Colonel Kessler came to me, at first at the urging of Mary-

Lynn Allan, though he knew, of course, of the interest in spiritualism in the camp, and even of some of its mediums, having paid a few visits to them out of curiosity.'

'*Ah, mon Dieu*, Élizabeth, he was a doubter,' muttered Brother Étienne, shovelling salad onto his plate.

'Certainly, and certainly, like so many after that terrible war of 1914–18, he was curious but also, Étienne, Beate Kessler née von Hennig, his wife of thirty-seven years, having lost her father and two brothers in it, had long ago become a devout believer and practitioner. As you well know, it was really she who convinced him to find out more.'

Knife and fork were lifted in a resigned gesture. 'This is nonsense, Inspector. Élizabeth, repeatedly I have warned that what you claim is against the laws of the Church.'

'Nonsense, is it, to reach those who have passed over, Étienne? To talk to them? Ask questions of import and be given answers? Doesn't the inspector need to know why Colonel Kessler was so distressed and what he wanted desperately to ask that wife of his and their little maid?'

'A girl, a child of twenty,' whispered the brother. A forkful of the salad was taken, a bit of the bread brusquely torn off and used to mop up sauce that had been missed. 'Continue, Élizabeth, if you must.'

Étienne *would* use the bread like that and eat like a peasant! 'Cérès was asked by him to contact Frau Kessler, Inspector, I having placed before the other sitters the wedding ring his wife had given him and the photos and letters from her that he had brought along. Initially he wanted proof, and asked things only his wife could have known. The name of their first dog? Mädy. The breed? A dachshund. The number of puppies in her first litter and why a new maid had been needed? Five. Their names? Johann, Käte, Christina, Jörg, and Erik.

'After that, his doubts began to leave him. He did ask Cérès if his wife could give his former rank, the date and time of their wedding. A captain, she said, 15 June, 1906, a Friday at 1600 hours, the drawn swords of his hussars catching the sunlight as they had formed the

archway over them and cheered. Fortunately his commanding officer had managed a small task for him to perform in Paris, but the
couple didn't stay at the Ritz, she said when asked. They had only
had one evening's meal there. Instead they had stayed at a small inn
on the quai Voltaire, in the very house where Voltaire and Richard
Wagner had once stayed. Across the Seine there had been a magnificent view of the Jardin des Tuileries, he having thrown the French
windows open and stepped out onto the balcony every morning on
waking. Visits to the Louvre, the theatres and galleries, shops, and
gardens had occupied the fortnight they'd spent there and only on
the last day had he had any diplomatic duties to perform. All such
details poured from her in a rush of joy at being able to reach him,
he dumbfounded at first, then shedding tears of joy himself and
begging her forgiveness.'

'Emmi Lammers hadn't been the first of their house daughters,
their maids, but the sixth,' snorted Brother Étienne, giving a massive shrug.

'And the colonel's distress?' asked the inspector, ignoring
Étienne's implication.

She would like to let this *sûreté* wait, thought Élizabeth, but had
better not since the look Étienne had given her had as much as said,
I've done what I can to save you from yourself. 'Cérès . . . Cérès was to
ask her if she'd had any more visits since her last letter of 5 September of last year.'

'Élizabeth . . . '

'You can *think* what you will, Étienne, but I know Frau Kessler
was questioned by the Gestapo, first in her own home and well
before the Americans came here to stay with us, and that this had
been greatly troubling him. Visitors at such a time? Had the Gestapo
seen over the house? he had asked her. Had they spoken to Emmi,
this new maid? Had either of them been taken for a drive in the
country—a drive when petrol is so short and automobiles reserved
only for those with special permits?

'They had stopped for tea along the way, Inspector, and had
spent two hours over it. Tea, at a time of such shortages?'

'Herr Weber, Inspector. Colonel Kessler was convinced the

Untersturmführer had been contacting Berlin behind his back and saying things he shouldn't have.'

To the Reich Central Security Office. 'And Emmi Lammers wasn't the first,' said St-Cyr.

'Young and pretty and needing a father figure—isn't that what you think, Inspector?' asked Élizabeth tartly. 'Alone, despondent, and vulnerable, is what I would say, just as was Mary-Lynn Allan.'

'The father, was he?'

'*Absolument!* That is why he insisted Étienne take care of it.'

'Élizabeth, your choice of words is shameful, and while I must insist they are untrue, they can only lead you astray. Inspector, the colonel's home was in Düsseldorf. Beate Kessler wanted to join her sister in Duisburg nearby, but he insisted she was far safer where she was.'

'Then on 9 September of last year, Inspector, his words came back to haunt him.'

'The RAF dropped the first of what have since become known, apparently, as "heavy incendiaries,"' said Brother Étienne. 'Fifteen-kilo bombs of solid or liquid phosphorous that do not explode on impacting the roofs of buildings but first penetrate below.'

'The house was gutted, its walls all but collapsing,' said Madame, seizing the moment with relish, which only caused the brother to raise his eyebrows in despair and say:

'He went home on compassionate leave on 15 September to see where what had been left of them had been buried. Now, I really must get on with my patients.'

'You told Mary-Lynn to eat parsley, Brother, and you brought her enough to do the job.'

'He wasn't the father, of this I'm certain.'

'But that is *not* what you whispered to me, your confidante, Étienne.'

'All right, he was! Does that satisfy you?'

Their voices had risen. 'The parsley, Brother?'

Ah, merde, this was not going well. 'I gave it to her because she couldn't face having a child here and out of wedlock. It had been a mistake, she said, a moment of weakness brought on by despair. She pleaded with me for help and I . . . May God forgive me, but I felt she could be suicidal.'

'You couldn't face up to the laws of the Church yourself, Étienne. Is this what you are admitting?' asked Madame forcefully.

The plate, the knife and fork and napkin were pushed away, the look one of resignation.

'The greater sin must always take precedence, Élizabeth. Please try to understand that to prevent the one, I had to help the other.'

She would reach out to him in comfort and forgiveness, she must! 'As you now help me, *mon chèr,* whose only sin is to believe in both the God you serve unquestionably and the goddess whom I, alone, am able to reach.

'Inspector, as the séances progressed, so did the questions. Colonel Kessler asked of the suitcase he had left in the cellars of their house. Had any of the visitors inquired of it? Beate Kessler told him one of them had looked the house over while the other had questioned her; Emmi Lammers, though, said that the suitcase, in spite of its having been seen, had not been lifted from its place on a top shelf and was now much safer.'

'Under all the rubble of a burned-out house,' said St-Cyr.

'*Oui.*'

'Élizabeth . . . '

'Other currencies, Brother? Gold coins, family silver, and pieces of jewellery?'

'I have absolutely no idea. He would certainly not have confided that.'

'Especially since to hide such things from the Nazis and not declare them would have been against the law, but with memories of the mark at 4.2 to the American dollar in 1914 and at 4,420,000,000 to it at the close of 1923, a wise move, considering that the Reich was again caught up in a war that looked more and more as if it would also be lost.'

Sex and money, Hermann would have said, and always some *salaud* lurking in the shadows to take advantage. 'You were treating him for what, Brother?'

'Rheumatism. It had plagued his knees since that other war.'

As it had Hermann, to whom poultices of boiled, mashed horse chestnuts—a Russian remedy—had been applied by this partner of his when in search of a little peace of mind. 'Madame, did Léa Monnier convey any of this Cérès dialogue to Herr Weber?'

'Lea . . . ?'

'Is one of his informants.'

'Léa would do no such thing.'

'But probably did, so now will you tell me when she left that séance the night Mary-Lynn was killed?'

Oh dear . . . 'Léa . . . Léa's sciatica had started up again. Though she was needed, I had excused her from attending.'

'And when you returned to your rooms here?'

Before going downstairs again to try to reconnect with the goddess because of being worried about that girl's safety, but one didn't need to remind him of this. 'She wasn't in her bed. The toilets, I assumed.'

'How long did you spend while trying to reconnect with the goddess?'

Had he believed her? 'An hour, two hours—three, perhaps—how could I possibly know?'

Time enough, in any case. 'Through self-hypnosis and breath control, Inspector, Madame Chevreul goes into a trance,' said Brother Étienne.

'While Léa Monnier is free to do as she had been ordered by Herr Weber, Brother?'

'Ordered? But . . . but surely the Untersturmführer wouldn't have wanted that girl to fall to her death?'

The brother had been genuinely taken aback, Madame Chevreul's knife and fork merely hesitating as if intrigued. 'At the moment, it's but one of several avenues since Madame Monnier has accused Nora Arnarson of having chased up the stairs after Mary-Lynn and, not realizing that the lift gate was open, of having tried to grab her only to have caused her to stumble forward and fall.'

'That Arnarson girl, Inspector. I knew she disbelieved. I felt it right from the first—one always does. Time and again, at Colonel Kessler's urging, I would try to reach Mary-Lynn's father only to fail because of her friend.'

'Yet you tolerated Nora's presence?'

'She had witnessed Colonel Kessler's joy. I thought her doubts would have ceased.'

'But in spite of this, finally had success.'

'Profoundly so. At 0200 hours on the night of 26 September, 1918, the sky over that battlefield to the northwest of Verdun was filled with flame and the deafening roar of the American artillery barrage. Men who had never been in battle and were soaked to the skin and cold from having had to wait in the open in their trenches for more than a week soon found themselves advancing uphill through dense fog and machine-gun fire.'

'The east bank of the Aire River and just to the east of the Forêt d'Argonne, Inspector,' said Brother Étienne. 'The First American Army, Thirty-Fifth Division. Mary-Lynn Allan's father was killed on the twenty-sixth, Madame de Vernon's husband wounded on the twenty-ninth but at Cierges-sous-Montfaucon, which is about five kilometres to the northwest of that hill, the advance of the twenty-sixth having been against Montfaucon itself, on which stood a heavily defended barracks.'

'Their luminescent compasses failed,' continued Madame Chevreul. 'There was so much buried metal in that old Verdun battlefield it threw them off. When she spoke to Captain Edward Bruce Allan, Cérès said he had told her he lies buried beneath the tank he had destroyed. A knoll was to his right, Inspector, another to his left, the true bearing on a line of sight of 42 degrees to the south, southwest or 222 degrees from north. He and his men had been advancing up the defile between those knolls when the mustard gas was encountered, causing the men to panic further, but then . . . then out of the fog and not ten steps away, the muzzle of that German tank appeared, it immediately firing at them, the shell exploding in a cloud of shrapnel which cut the air, instantly killing his sergeant and two others, he seizing their grenades even as they fell, Sergeant Davies crying out to him, "Don't, Cap," but it was of no use.'

'Élizabeth . . . Élizabeth,' began Brother Étienne, gesturing at the impossibility of reasoning with her, only to be ignored.

'He lies about three kilometres to the south-southwest of Mont-faucon, Inspector, near the foundation of a ruined barn. The defile is, of course, much overgrown. Bracken covers the knolls, but there are two cedars on the one and a young oak on the other, each with the strength of many. Armour plate and tank treads cover him and these are to be found beneath a metre of thrown-up earth. A digging machine will have to be used. Mere pick and shovel will not suffice.'

And never mind the use of a compass! thought St-Cyr. 'Any unexploded gas shells?'

'A danger to be sure, but Cérès didn't say. *Ah, pardonnez-moi.* He didn't say to Cérès.'

'Nor tell you, madame, that the tank would have been American, for the Wehrmacht, throughout that war had so few, they had had to use captured ones when available, though not, I think, in that battle, and as for the poisoned gas you say was used, it was the Americans who fired it at the Germans then, not the other way round.'

'The confusion of battle is always terrible.'

'But as a nurse and an ambulance driver, you and Léa Monnier would have heard plenty of what the front was like and would have driven over past positions of it many times, and certainly after that war, the bereaved sought solace in spiritualism right through the '20s and well into the '30s.'

Millions had died, so many of them between the ages of nineteen and twenty-five. 'Comfort, Inspector. News of loved ones, a word or two. Those are what I bring. Colonel Kessler was convinced I possessed that rarest of gifts.'

'Whereas Bamba Duclos, though he doesn't appear to often contact those who have passed over, will do so if pressed as he reads the fortunes of present lives and is a charlatan?'

'That black told Mary-Lynn that I would *never* be able to get Cérès to reach her father or find where he lay buried, that only if she believed totally in his powers—his!—could he read her future in that little basket of rubbish.'

'But he did read it?'

'And kept it from her because he saw her falling down a deep, dark well but couldn't understand this because there were no such wells that he knew of in the camp.'

'How is it, please, that you knew of this, madame?' Brother Étienne had taken to folding his napkin again and didn't look at either of them, having done all he could to protect her from herself.

'Léa told me,' she said.

'Léa who is so loyal she would find out for you?'

'*Oui.*'

To shout for Louis would do no good, felt Kohler, to try to back away and through the medium's cabinet to reach him but a bad gamble. Léa Monnier didn't just fill the corridor doorway to this room of rooms; behind her, a mob had silently gathered. Broomsticks, mallets, pots, ladles, and knives were in hand, hair in the eyes of some, chewing gum in the mouths of others, fags clenched between the lips of still others.

Hortense, the cook, was immediately to his left, having stealthily taken a few steps to get into position, the maid, Marguerite, to the right and still over by the Ouija board, that one watchful to the point of being intensely so, the tip of her tongue caught between the whitest of teeth, her breath short and fast, her pulse racing as if just after having stolen something.

'*Couillon,*' said Léa softly, 'you have no right to be in here. We didn't kill either of those bitches.'

'Streetfighter, mob leader, and defender of the realm, is that it?' he asked.

Her grin was huge. 'I broke a few heads, if that's what you mean, and crushed the balls of others.'

'They must have enjoyed having you all to themselves in the Old Bailey.'

'And now, what now?' she said, letting him see the pearl-headed hatpin in her palm.

Ach, du lieber Gott, the damned thing was at least twelve centimetres long. The maid sucked in a breath at the thought, her gaze flicking anxiously from Léa to him, to Hortense and the table that lay between him and the cook, ah yes.

The crystal ball was hefted, the girl fighting down the urge to step forward and cry out in alarm, a hesitant hand being extended only to resignedly drop.

Hefting the ball, he set it not on its little brass stand but on the damask tablecloth that was embroidered in a circle round with the symbols of the zodiac. 'Month by month,' he said. 'A Libra, a Scorpio—which are you?' he asked of Léa, the ball rolling a little until at last it had come to a tentative stop.

'Please don't,' managed Marguerite.

'Then start talking.'

'Not here, and not without Madame,' swore Léa softly, and she meant it too.

'Things have gone missing, haven't they? Little things. Jennifer Hamilton pays visit after visit and becomes a suspect only to cease coming and then show up again but with Caroline Lacy.'

'Madame interviewed the couple time and again,' said Léa.

'And was finally satisfied that neither was the thief, eh?'

'Yes.'

'And Caroline was to have become a sitter while Jennifer was to wait for her outside the Pavillon de Cérès—is that right?'

It was. 'All alone?' he asked.

Herr Kohler had moved and in so doing had carelessly jostled the table and rumpled the cloth. 'I . . . I did ask Madame if I could wait with her,' said Marguerite, 'but was told that would not be allowed.'

'Why not?'

The ball was again beginning to roll, but he hadn't noticed this yet, had taken out his cigarettes and was placing two of them on the cloth facing Léa. 'My partner borrowed those,' he said. 'Now I'm returning them, but without interest.'

'My ball . . . ' managed Marguerite. 'Please don't let it fall.'

'Like Mary-Lynn, eh?' he asked, and, reaching out, snatched up the ball as it left the table. 'Now, you start talking like I said.'

'Marguerite, I'm warning you,' whispered Léa, her octagonal glasses catching the light.

'Jennifer . . . ' began the girl.

'You were lovers,' he said with a finality that hurt and, setting the ball down, paused to light himself a cigarette and to drop the spent match on a cloth that had taken her months and months to embroider.

Still she didn't leap forward. She mustn't. Ashes soon fell.

'Why did you break up? Come on, mademoiselle. If lovers, why the sudden split?'

'Madame—'

'Thought Jennifer might have been stealing things?'

'Yes!'

'And after you, Jennifer then takes up with Caroline. That must have been hard, or was it merely a necessity since Jennifer was then able to come here again?'

'Those American bitches with their Ivy League crap,' grunted Léa.

'Alpha Beta Theta bullshit!' shouted someone out in the corridor.

'Pi Beta Phi!' said another.

'Sororities?' he asked.

Léa let him have it with a laugh. 'If that's what they're called, we've got the biggest of them!'

The ball began again to roll, Marguerite Lefèvre to hesitate with fingernails to her lips and eyes rapidly moistening, yet still she didn't step forward—couldn't, wouldn't, Léa having given her a scathing look.

'Please,' she wept. 'Herr Kohler, I beg you.'

'Smoky quartz, wasn't that what you started Jennifer on?'

'Yes! Then the rose and . . . and then the clear.'

'And in between sessions, the simply being together.'

Again he caught the ball, snatching it up in midair, but this time he placed it securely in her trembling hands and she . . . why, she could only let him see her tears and hear her gratefully whispering, '*Merci.*'

He stepped away from her, began to close the gap between himself and Léa, said, 'I think I've seen enough for now,' but turned at the last, as Léa and the others began to make way for him, Herr Kohler to catch sight of her frantically examining the cloth and brushing the ashes away to fastidiously tidy it before passing a final smoothing hand lovingly over it, only to then pause as he continued to look at her, she now steadily at him.

Then he was gone and Léa was saying, 'You little fool. Wait until Madame hears of this.'

8

They were moving now as detectives should; they weren't wasting time but all along the corridors of the Grand, crowds lined the walls and the shrillness, the shrieks, the jeers, and banging of pots and pans was deafening.

'Léa Monnier, Hermann. Cérès knew of that Star of David,' managed a visibly harried Louis, for several had tried to hit him.

More couldn't be said until, at a shout from a clearly ruffled Brother Étienne who had ducked out of a doorway, the uproar died as suddenly as the nod from Léa had started it up.

Now the pots and pans were lowered and the rabble, dressed in separates often of the most incongruous kind, some sucking on their fags, others wishing they had one, fell to a watchful silence and then . . . then, as these two detectives hurried past, a whispered hiss, *'None of us did it!'*

'We're clean,' said one whose breath alone claimed otherwise; another, 'Caroline Lacy was the thief. Becky Torrence was seen going into the Chalet des Ânes after her.'

'Nora Arnarson, inspectors. Ask Nora why she tried to grab but shoved Mary-Lynn.'

'Her friend . . . Some friend.'

'Ask Angèle,' whispered another. 'Ask that nag of Brother Étienne's what Nora likes to share with her.'

'Oh yes, to share when there is so little.'

'Louis, what the hell are they talking about?' asked Kohler.

'Something so simple I should have seen it.'

Out on the terrace, the light of day had left and the shops were closed.

'That sprig from a beech tree, Hermann, and three curls of the inner bark. Though mention of these implies Cérès knows what we found with Caroline Lacy, who else in the camp but Nora would think to nibble on them?'

'Not Caroline?'

'Not Jennifer either, nor Madame de Vernon or even Becky.'

'Caroline wasn't just going to tell the Kommandant who had pushed Mary-Lynn, Louis.'

'Nora saw her being followed by Becky and must have thought Caroline would tell Colonel Jundt about that girl's fiancé, but that Becky wasn't strong enough to have dealt with her.'

'And that's why Becky came back the next morning to find out what had happened.'

'Nora having told me that at first she had thought it out of character for Jennifer to have taken up with Caroline, and then opportunistic.'

'Jennifer having been in love with our kleptomaniac, Louis, with Marguerite Lefèvre, Madame Chevreul's maid, something Nora may well have known.'

Had Hermann really pinned the thief down? 'The evidence?'

Kohler told him, Louis muttering, '*C'est possible, mon vieux, but . . .* '

'*Gott im Himmel,* why must you continually doubt the obvious? I caught her red-handed!'

'And she made a visible impression on you.'

'Deliberately?'

'Hermann, how many times must I tell you not to be putty in the hands of the female sex? You share yourself with two women in Paris, can't bring yourself to decide between them and they know this yet live together in harmony and have become fast friends.'

'They've left me, and you know it. Giselle to become a mannequin, Oona to . . . '

'Yes, yes, but they'll be back as soon as you are.'

'And Marguerite Lefèvre?'

'Could well have sized you up and seen right through you.'

'No crystal ball needed?'

'None.'

'Then she was trying to shield Jennifer.'

'Her former lover, Hermann? *If* still former, Madame having been kind enough to have warned me that Cérès has claimed Jennifer is in great danger.'

'Since Madame had stopped her from seeing Marguerite until Caroline came along. Two days, Louis. That's all Jundt and Weber are giving us, and one of them's gone. If we don't come up with answers today they'll call in Berlin-Central and we both know what that means.'

Unlike the Grand, the Vittel-Palace was as silent as a tomb. All doors were closed, the smells still everywhere: ersatz perfume and pomanders but especially those of burning rutabaga steaks, boiling cabbage, and frying SPAM, or the smoke from innumerable stoves, some with the taint of refuse, others with that of the caramelized sweetness of toasting black bread, then too, the pungency of over-heated electrical wires and the reminder, of course, that the damned place was nothing more than one hell of a fire trap.

A knock at Room 3–54 brought nothing, the room uninhabited, that of Room 3–38, the crowded waiting looks of apprehension. Clearly the two rooms had gotten together to discuss things.

Becky Torrence sat on her cot with Marni Huntington to one side and Jill Faber to the other. Dorothy Stevens, the tall, thin brunette from Ohio State with the uncooperative hair, was standing by the stove, where she had been eagerly licking a cone of what looked to be some sort of ice cream.

Candice Peters, the all-but-forty-year-old with the frizzy brown hair from North Carolina State, was sitting on Nora's cot. Droplets from the newspaper-covered cone she held fell to her slippered feet.

Barbara Caldwell, the auburn-haired thirty-two- to thirty-six-year-old from Rhodes College in Memphis, Tennessee, was standing beside Marni's cot on which sat Lisa Banbridge, the twenty-two-year-old brunette from Duke with the lovely hazel eyes and pony-tail.

There was no sign of Nora, none either of Jennifer or of Madame de Vernon.

'The washing, Louis. *Diese Pariser.*'

The condoms. Three of these hung limply from the curtain cord that had shut Caroline Lacy and Irène de Vernon off from the others.

'It was just fun,' confessed Jill with a shrug. 'All we wanted was to be by ourselves for a little like it used to be when Mary-Lynn was with us.'

'*Une veillée,* inspectors,' offered Lisa. 'For centuries such evening gatherings of women have been a tradition in France, a chance to talk things over, to recall the past while doing a little sewing or mending. Jill was telling us about Madison, Wisconsin, and the farmers' markets she used to go to every Saturday morning as a student. The apples . . . '

'The McIntosh,' said Marni, that chocolate thing of hers all but gone.

'The Red Delicious—tart yet sweet,' said Dorothy with longing.

'The cheese,' said Candice. 'Muenster, Gruyère, caraway, brick, and Havarti, but best of all, the farmer's. Little cubes on toothpicks were always given away, inspectors, slices of apple too, sometimes a whole one if a girl smiled and flashed her eyes the right way. It would be snatched up and quickly handed over to be tucked out of sight in a pocket or ravenously bitten, the farmer's wife giving her husband the elbow.'

'Maple syrup,' sighed Becky, unable to stop herself from smiling and crying at the same time. 'Mary-Lynn *loved* maple syrup.'

'Popcorn,' said Jill, giving her a tight hug. 'She liked that, too.'

'Pumpkins at Halloween,' said Candice. 'We used to fry the seeds in a little salt and butter and then eat them while they were hot. They were *so* delicious.'

'Honey,' said Marni, as if reliving the memories of a ten-year-old. 'Clover, basswood, wildflower, buckwheat, and black locust, inspectors, the sweetest of all and softest of golden yellows. The beekeepers would let you have a sample. If you wanted to try any of them they'd dip one of the twigs they'd whittled into whatever jar you chose even if they knew you weren't going to buy a thing.'

'You could have your *whole* breakfast or lunch that way just by going from stall to stall,' said Becky, having regained her composure. 'There would be the smells of freshly baked bread and buns from the bakers' stalls—those of chestnuts, too, sometimes—and fudge or pull taffy from the candymaker's. Certainly those of burning hickory and grilling sausages, and of the winter, spring, summer, or autumn. Maybe a little sharpness in the air or even falling snow but that wonderful, wonderful tingling feeling of just being outdoors and absolutely free to do whatever one wanted. No guards, no war, no internment.'

'Yes, yes,' said Louis impatiently. 'Where is Madame de Vernon?'

They looked at one another. It was Lisa who said, 'Jill was telling us about the Red Gym—the Armoury Gymnasium that is on Langdon Street down by Lake Mendota and had been built in 1893. She used to have a beau in the Badgers Rowing Club and had taken to getting up at five to row with one of the girls' crews just for a chance of seeing him. From its redbrick walls and heavy, oaken door you can look uphill to see the sun glistening on the beautiful big white dome of the State Capitol. It's built of blocks of Bethel granite.'

'From Vermont,' confessed Jill.

'And Madame, knowing of Barre, Vermont, and her former husband, was convinced you were taunting her, as indeed you were with those.'

The *Kondoms*. It would be best to shrug and to tell them, thought Jill. 'Bango, she flew into another of her boiling rages. Oh, sorry. Bango means "right away."'

'And left us to ourselves,' managed Becky. 'I didn't kill anyone, inspectors. I swear I didn't. Gosh, all I ever wanted was to help Antoine.'

'Her fiancé,' said Marni, tightly gripping the girl's right hand. If an arrest was to be made, it would have to be of all of them.

'And Nora and Jennifer?' asked Hermann.

'Nora's gone to get some more clean snow so that she can make us another of these glorious snow ice-cream cones her dad taught her how to make, though he liked the raspberry best, Nora the blueberry. Jen's doing her laundry.'

'We always have to make sacrifices,' said Dorothy of Jennifer's absence. 'Everyone in this hotel tends to eat early because we're hungry by four and positively ravenous by five.'

Which would mean, of course, that when Caroline Lacy was killed, all but a few had been in their rooms doing that after having, like Madame Chevreul and Léa Monnier, just watched Brother Étienne arrive.

Blue eyes, green, dark olive-brown, hazel, and dark grey impassively looked at St-Cyr and Kohler as if, when they eventually left the room, there would be a collective sigh of relief and they'd go right back to what they'd been doing, discussing the simple things that everyone had taken for granted before this war.

It was Jill who said 'The laundry's behind the kitchens and about as far from here as you can get. Sometimes at this hour there's still a little hot water but it'll be lukewarm at best. It always is.'

The room was cavernous but of electric lighting there was only that from two widely spaced forty-watt bulbs. Leaking bronze taps, above the rows of zinc-lined drain tables yielded the periodic patience of ice-cold droplets that would, in the early hours of a still-distant morning, freeze.

Oak-framed, truss-backed washboards hung above the tables. Only one of them was being used—a lone occupant—and from it came the irritable clash of buttons on rippled brass as invective was muttered. The smell of ivy leaves, stewed and drained in desperation to give a liquid hopeful of soap, was clear enough. Sand could be used, and there was evidence of it.

At regular intervals, cast-iron, rubber-roller clothes wringers were clamped to the tables, but of the washing machines and bench ironers of the interwar period there wasn't a sign. All would have been removed and placed in storage. The Hôtel de l'Ermitage? wondered St-Cyr.

'*Curtis,* Louis,' said Hermann, giving the manufacturer's name of the clothes wringers. 'It's like taking a step back in time.'

Those twenty-six and -seven years since the wounded of the First American Army had been in residence. 'Soldiers everywhere have no need of the complicated, Hermann. In any case, the simple copper wash-boiler, a mere tub, didn't come into general use in France until the late '20s and early '30s. Washing machines and other such labour-saving devices were but objects of curiosity in catalogues.'

Hand cranks turned the rollers and these were all but as long and heavy as tire irons, thought Kohler. Jennifer simply wasn't present, only the small heap of wet underclothes that she had left on a distant drain table along with a bottle of what must be Brother Étienne's lavender wash water.

The nearby wringer roller's hand crank had also absented itself, a worry to be sure.

'Madame de Vernon,' said Louis to her back, 'what have you done with that girl?'

She wouldn't turn, thought Irène. She would concentrate on the scrubbing. 'Me, Chief Inspector? Nothing, but why not ask that *garce* yourself? I arrived and she fled.'

'Where to?'

'I didn't notice.'

'Madame, you hated that girl. She was terrified of you.'

'Terrified? For raping the innocence of my Caroline? *Bien sûr,* I wasn't happy with what she was doing to that child of mine but as to her being terrified of me, that I couldn't say.'

'Have you killed her?'

The scarf-swathed neck stiffened as the head was tossed. 'You accuse without a shred of evidence? You arrest without the magistrate's warrant? That door leads to the Hôtel Grand, the stairs nearby, to the cellars. Please take your choice.'

'And leave you to your laundry?'

She had him now! 'It's Caroline's. Are laundered clothes, freshly ironed not necessary when the dead are to be buried, or have such considerations been dispensed with, and if so, how, please, am I to inform that girl's parents of such a desecration?'

Releasing the blouse, she hastily crossed herself, then rigidly waited for the proceedings to continue.

Hermann went to check the door and to leave it open, momentarily disappearing toward the Hôtel Grand. Such ease of alternate access had not been anticipated.

'A mortised pin tumbler deadbolt, Louis, no doubt with a key Weber takes from that board of his every evening and hands to the designated guard.'

That one then leaving the door unlocked if paid enough; if not, the key itself having been purloined and perhaps even copied—Hermann didn't need to say it, only, 'She could be in the Grand.'

Since both doors had yet to be locked.

'Madame . . . ' began Louis.

These two from Paris hadn't realized that such comings and goings had been possible and would now have to think about it. 'As I've told you, Chief Inspector, I didn't notice.'

'The cellars, Hermann. Leave me to deal with this one.'

'Why should I tell you anything? You both protect the Jews, isn't that so? One snap of the fingers and Herr Weber learns of what you, a *sûreté*, said to the others in that room I must share. You asked, Chief Inspector, if any of them were Jewish and you said . . . '

'Yes, yes, that neither Hermann nor I would report them.'

She must keep the pressure up! 'Even if Jennifer Hamilton were a Jewess, you would have kept silent? A submarine, I believe that Jill Faber said of such filth. Oh, please don't look so dismayed. Gossip is everything in a place like this. Those bitches I have to live with whisper in English to each other, and me—I listen! Now, if you don't mind . . . '

'Louis, bring her with us. Let her point the way.'

'*Je refuse catégoriquement!*'

'Filth, madame?'

'*Untermenschen*—is this not what *les Allemands* call such people?'

Subhumans. Inadvertently she had revealed that she also knew how to speak *Deutsch*.

'Me, I repeatedly told Caroline exactly what they were like. Taking the jobs from others, charging far too much for things, *cheating* at every chance.'

Hermann had gone down into the cellars. '*Ah, bon,* madame, let's discuss the matter, but before we do you'll tell me why you didn't want that girl asking questions of the husband who had taken you to the cleaners in 1910 and died in 1920.'

'Laurence? In a place like this, where gossip is but food for regurgitating vultures? As was my right, I demanded that she obey me but that . . . that *salope,* Jennifer Hamilton, told her otherwise and now . . . now look at what has happened. My Caroline taken from me and everyone whispering that I thought to kill the child but *pushed,* I tell you, the wrong person? I who was asleep. Asleep!'

'Having hidden the datura cigarettes she would desperately need.'

Ah, merde, this had gone too far, but there was no turning back. 'I did not *hide* them, as those bitches are saying. I simply set them out in a more convenient place since there had been trouble with the electric lights.'

'That girl refused to leave Room 3–54 and Jennifer Hamilton, madame. She had slammed the door in your face and yet now you claim you were asleep?'

'Lies . . . it is all lies. Oh for sure I tried to put a stop to Caroline's attending one of those séances of Madame Chevreul's. I begged that woman to reject her. I offered far more than the usual fee but even that was refused. Why? I ask you. Why was I to have had my most private affairs aired in front of a gang of so-called sitters, I who have given *everything* for that child?'

'You threatened Madame Chevreul. Even Léa Monnier was afraid of what you might do.'

'*Bon!* She should be!'

'Laurence Vernon, madame. Let's dispense with the prefix of *les hautes* that you must have added.'

'Why should I not have done? Everyone else here dreams of something and lives it. My father was of the de Marignanes of Aix, the same as the daughter the great orator and writer Mirabeau took to wife in 1772.'

After having scandalously deflowered Marie Emilie, her unhappy father then cutting off the couple's allowance, Mirabeau plunging them into debt with equal scandal. 'The fire, madame?'

This *sûreté* wasn't going to leave it. 'Did you think I didn't know what those bitches were trying to prove? The casino here, arson on the night of Saturday, 17 July, 1920, a corpse charred but not beyond recognition, I tell you, and one missing adulterous husband who had stolen everything from me including one of the villas of the de Marignanes? How else was I to have put a stop to such maliciousness? Was I to have let Caroline, in all her innocence, have that . . . that charlatan of a woman ask a *goddess* about my Laurence?'

'How did he die?'

'I wasn't here. I was in Paris. Caroline . . . Caroline knew this, but that . . . that bitch Jennifer Hamilton wouldn't leave well enough alone.'

Kohler didn't really know what he'd find in the cellars, but a third murder, especially that of a lead informant, would definitely be to Weber's advantage, since the son-of-a-bitch could then claim them incompetent and put a call in to Berlin.

Louis and he couldn't withstand another run-in with the SS. Vouvray in early December had been bad enough, Paris often far worse—Lyon, too, and Vichy more recently. A legacy then of hatred: two honest cops who were stupid enough never to look the other way when pointing the finger of truth.

Had Madame de Vernon crushed that girl's skull? Was that informant of Weber's lying in some darkened storeroom, blood all over the stone floor but freeing up a flat full of valuable antiques and paintings?

The main breaker box was at the foot of the stairs and handy to anyone who could have ducked in that side door. By simply pulling the breaker, whatever lights were on would suddenly go off and no one else the wiser, especially as the damned thing had a padlock on it, another Harvard six-lever, long-shackled relic.

Liebe Zeit, but the First American Army had sure left a lot of stuff. Weber knew of the séance that Mary-Lynn and Nora would be attending with Colonel Kessler. Perhaps he had even known or suspected Kessler would escort them to the front entrance afterward. He'd have known of the Saturday-night poker sessions but not if those two would then drop in or when they'd actually climb that far staircase to Rooms 3–54 and 3–38.

But with Mary-Lynn's 'suicide,' the threat of Kessler's sending him to the Russian Front would have been over.

Then why that Star of David in the Chalet des Ânes, unless Caroline had also intended to tell the new Kommandant about Becky and by so doing, admit that she knew who had been stealing things?

Jennifer or, better still, Marguerite Lefèvre.

Overloaded, the electrical wiring tended to dim and then to blink the intermittent lights, and in every room or corridor upstairs that same on and off would be happening. Weber would have had no need to touch the breaker box. He could simply have let himself in that door and come down here to make his way through to that wing before climbing the staircase to then open the lift gate and wait on the way up to the attic.

The girl wasn't in any of the nearest storerooms, all of which were empty. She wasn't in the immediate corridor, and when he turned on to the main one, there was still no sign of her. *Verdammt!*

Doors were open, others closed, and at each of the latter he had the feeling he'd find her behind it. Not having a flashlight was a problem. Strings dangling from the ceiling would, when pulled, have turned on each light, but all had lost their bulbs, the Americans having a better use for those in their rooms, the string as well.

When he reached the foot of the main staircase, he couldn't help thinking of Mrs. Parker and all 990 of them waiting in silence, there having been not one, as originally thought, but two murders.

All would have known the cellars well enough, and hadn't Nora Arnarson made apricot brandy down here somewhere?

'Arson, Madame Vernon.'

Was the chief inspector afraid she might torch the hotel with everyone in it? wondered Irène. Certainly he was still suspicious of her having been in Paris at the time of the casino fire, and certainly Herr Kohler had yet to return from the cellars, and now this one was beginning to also believe that the worst had happened to that girl, a filthy lesbian who hadn't been able to keep herself from stealing Caroline's heart and innocence.

'Early in October 1920 I was notified of the fire by two detectives from the Sûreté Nationale. Their names and the exact date or day escape me, of course. The lack of vitamins here, the memory loss that happens because of such a thing. Many others are afflicted and forget even to whom they've just been speaking. Perhaps the chief inspector's name was Lafarge, perhaps Lafleur. Perhaps it was in the third or fourth week of September instead, a Wednesday. I'm certain it was midweek, but me—I simply can't remember after so many years. But I do know that they came to my flat—I was living in a single room on the rue Moncey at the time. After telling me what had happened, they asked me to pack a bag and to accompany them.'

Two detectives, a senior one at that, and a long and tedious journey by train to the provinces—she could see him thinking this and concluding that they must have had good reason, especially as the corpse had been kept on ice for so long and they must have had difficulty locating her, the address given being in Pigalle, she well down on her luck and moving unannounced every time the rent came due.

'Laurence had lost an arm, the left, to shrapnel. When we got to the morgue in Vittel, the corpse I was shown was the same but only in that regard. I thought him taller, bigger across the shoulders but they . . . they said the fire could well have shrunk him.'

'He'd been gambling, had he?'

'*Ah, mon Dieu*, what did that monk tell you? That my Laurence had been here with his latest floozy? That his family had finally overlooked his squandering his life away on drink and women and gambling and had let him inherit 356,750 American dollars from the estate of his mother, not a franc of which would then be left for me?'

Beyond taking out his pipe and tobacco pouch, then searching for his matches, the *sûreté* gave no indication of interest in what she had just said.

'As a boy of fifteen, Inspector, Brother Étienne had been here among the curious on the morning after that fire. Monsieur le Père, the abbot of that order he serves, had been summoned to give the last rites, but ever since then that boy, now a man, has tried, unsuccessfully, I must add, to find out why anyone at all should have perished when the inquest itself could find no possible reason other than an accidental fall brought on by far too much drink in an attempt to forget the losses at the tables.'

Ah, bon, there's flesh on the cinder—she could see him thinking this, but better that she tell him than that monk.

'A gossipmonger, that is what Brother Étienne is! Whispering insidiously of things he can know nothing of, but doing so to curry favour especially with that . . . that Madame Chevreul. A woman, I would not be surprised if you were to discover, who had poisoned her blind husband just to be free of him and get her hands on his money.'

'And then come to Vittel in July of 1920 to take the cure?'

Ah, merde! 'That . . . that I couldn't say, but if the one is wrongly thought, why not the other? Here everything is blown out of all proportion and the truth forgotten.'

Jennifer was down here in the cellars somewhere. Kohler knew it, felt it, yet couldn't find her. Frost clung to the stone walls, dampness hugged the air and through the dim and distant ceiling light of a lone electric bulb, fog hung and with it came the stench of the drains and the sounds of scurrying little feet.

Lighted matches, now running short, had revealed that Nora Arnarson didn't just trap rabbits. There was still no sign of Jennifer. Louis would have said, *It's curious you should be thinking of Nora at such a time,* but the silence did suggest the trapper and she could easily have come down here to check on her traps. She would have been outside getting fresh snow for her ice-cream cones, would have come in by that side door to the laundry and seen what was going on or sensed what must have happened. No Jennifer present, but Caroline's things also in a heap waiting to be washed. Had she heard Jennifer crying out or come down here only to catch sight of Madame bludgeoning the hell out of that girl?

The door was ajar, the room beyond it dark, and he knew that he had at last found her.

*   *   *

'Madame Vernon,' said the *sûreté* as if he suspected the worst and would persist until he had what he wanted, 'I will ask one more time. What did you do to that girl?'

'Beat her to death with that clothes wringer's armature—is this what you think?'

'You know it is.'

Bien sûr, the soggy little heap of laundry the girl had left did look neglected, thought Irène, but if she were to stand her own ground firmly, the chief inspector could never prove a thing. Fingerprints? she asked herself. Blood spatters on her slippers? *Ah, merde,* he had ducked those eyes of his to them and was now searching upward. Her woollen socks, the hem of her skirt—was there blood on those, she could see him asking himself.

'They taunted you,' he said, watching her closely now, too closely. 'On the night of the thirteenth, fourteenth, when you stormed down the corridor to Room 3–54, the door was closed but not locked, was it? You entered, *n'est-ce pas*? You flung on the overhead light and found them together. Kissing, madame. Fondling. Did you yank the covers from them?'

'*Salaud,* they were arguing as I have already told you! My Caroline was in tears and very upset. I begged her to come back to the room but she . . . she shrieked and flung her fists at me. *À moi!* She pushed me out into the corridor, slammed that door in my face, and held it shut, I tell you. *Shut,* against me!'

Ah, bon, her blood pressure had rocketed. 'And from then on, the shouting only became more vehement. Others, in the nearby rooms, must have heard you.'

'*Imbécile,* it wasn't the first time! They had heard Caroline and me yelling many times. Soon they were all telling me to shut up, all shouting, "Oh, for God's sake, let her decide for herself!" To them I was nothing but a stupid, interfering old woman who was so insanely possessive I would destroy Caroline's happiness!'

She caught a breath, glanced hurriedly about for something with which to defend herself and, realizing that nothing was close to hand and that he had swiftly moved in on her, swallowed hard, relaxed her clenched fists, and said more moderately, 'What was I to have done? Let that bitch Jennifer Hamilton patch up the affair? I had to put a stop to it. She didn't love my Caroline. Having stolen whatever else she could from me and everyone else to gain power over us as Brother Étienne insists such a thief would do, she had to steal the ultimate, the heart of an innocent child, the one and only treasure I have always held above all others. *Always.*'

For some time, felt Jennifer, and she was certain it must be Madame de Vernon, there had been no further sound of the woman's lighting a match before cautiously stepping into each storeroom to see if she was there, but now . . . now there was nowhere left to hide. Now Madame would find her. Madame had killed her husband—Caroline hadn't known this for sure but had become convinced of it, convinced too that Laurence Vernon had been in Vittel at the casino and had again taken up with another woman. Vivacious, witty, intelligent, and wealthy—recently a widow perhaps, but not grieving. A girl out for a good time: the spa, the relaxation from all cares but those of pleasure, the casino and its theatre, the dancing too, and the meals . . . such meals. He had just inherited a bundle and would have been boasting of it, but unfortunately for him, Madame had learned of it from his family in America, and had come here from Paris to confront him.

Caroline had been certain of this too, certain that if Cérès was to be asked, the truth would come out and everyone in the camp would know exactly what Madame was like and why she could no longer stay in the same room with the woman.

Laurence Vernon must have died in the casino fire of 17 July, 1920. He had often been 'under the empire of alcohol,' as the French were fond of calling alcoholism, and before Madame could stop things from happening, had lost a second fortune.

She's going to kill me, thought Jennifer, bracing herself, having backed right into a corner. If she's not stopped, she'll grab me by the throat, is far too strong. Caroline had always warned that Madame's temper could flash to violence, that too often she, herself, had been the victim. Gentle, timid, hesitant, naively innocent Caroline, whose awakening had been so sudden and complete. Caroline who had asked that a meeting be arranged in a place no others would think of, Herr Weber then demanding of her that he know everything ahead of time. Just *everything*.

Caroline, who had held her hand so tightly when sitting on trial before that medium's tent of Madame Chevreul's. 'Have either of you been stealing things?' that woman had asked of them from behind the screen.

Caroline had lost her 'shooter' marble to this . . . this thief of theirs and had been found with a Star of David. A sprig from a beech tree and three curls of the inner bark had been in that stall, a tidied corpse. Why tidied? Why laid out like that? She would have known the shame such a thief would have felt when exposed to the stares of everyone else in the camp. The shunning that would follow, the total silence of everyone spoken to, their looking away not just for a day or two but forever.

Caroline, who had wanted to tell Kommandant Jundt not just who had shoved Mary-Lynn Allan, or even that Becky Torrence had helped her fiancé to escape to the free zone, but that she had inadvertently discovered who the thief was.

Caroline, who had been pensive when facing Marguerite . . . who had played the imp before gazing deeply into the last of her crystal balls as only she could, the clear . . .

Caroline, who had been so upset and had felt so betrayed.

Kohler waited. He could hear someone softly, tensely breathing. When he nudged the door, whoever it was held her breath and he wondered, was she waiting with that armature wound up and ready to kill him?

Ach, there was only one way to find out. Sacrificing the last seven matches in the box, he flung them one by one into the room.

They fell like star shells over a battlefield, thought Jennifer, each arcing through the darkness only to finally go out and leave her biting back the tears.

When he lifted her chin and took the armature away, Jennifer knew that Herr Kohler had found her, not Madame. Not yet.

*   *   *

Louis wasn't going to spare the girl, even after what she'd just been through. They couldn't—Kohler knew this, yet it saddened him to see her so stressed and going to pieces in front of them.

'My apartment,' she blurted. 'If I don't get back to Paris, what's to happen to all of those precious things I bought for my father's clients? An oil on panel by Lucas Cranach the Elder, inspectors. It's magnificent. I would sit for hours in front of it and never tire of feasting my eyes. There's a sketch by Jan van Eyck for his *St. Barbara*. The folds of her gown cast such shadows they set off the whole piece—its mood, its purpose, its divine purity and poise—and I just know it was done in charcoal first and then in pen and brown ink, for the shadows tell me this as much as does the fine detail. She has an illuminated breviary in her lap but is not reading—she knows it all by heart and one can see this in her peace of mind as those beloved words come silently to her. There's another sketch by Delacroix—*Ah, mon Dieu,* words fail me. It's a preparatory for his *Descent from the Cross,* after Peter Paul Rubens. It, too, is in pen and brown ink on paper. I'm certain the ink was made from oak galls—that's one of the first things we question when examining such works, for forgeries are everywhere in the art world. I acquired it for the Levy family in Boston.'

She paused. It seemed to calm her to tell others of these things, thought Kohler. Even Louis was listening attentively and perhaps had begun to realize just why the poor kid was so concerned.

'There's a collection of snuffboxes that I had spent nearly a year building for Mrs. Anna Blumenfeld Senior. German gold and enamel, by Daniel Baudesson, circa 1765: a countess at her *toilette* with ladies in waiting. She's just come from the bath and though it is in miniature, you can see how pink her skin is and feel how hot the scented water must have been. Another German box is of gold and bloodstone, with a stag on the run and being set upon by ferocious hounds. Why must men who hunt be so unforgivably cruel? The box is circa 1750, but though exquisite, is not a favourite of mine.'

'You've exceptional taste,' murmured Louis, somewhat mollified.

She brightened. 'I've Swiss boxes with enamelled silver birds that spread their wings and sing when the boxes are opened. Naturally they're favourites, and I know I will feel a terrible sense of loss when they've finally been shipped home but'—she shrugged—'one has to learn to bear such feelings if one is to be a dealer.'

'And your favourite of favourites among the snuffboxes?' asked Louis, as if they had all day and night.

Those soft brown eyes took him in, strands of the fair hair being tidied, for they'd fallen over a still deeply furrowed brow. 'A gold and semiprecious stone box by Johann Christian Neuber that is inset with 107 stones and is from Dresden, circa 1780. I paid 2,500 francs for it but know it's worth at least thirty times as much.'

Twenty-five American dollars on the black bourse becomes $750.00 at home. 'A bargain,' muttered Louis who had yet to even find that pipe and tobacco pouch of his.

'Please don't think me opportunistic, Chief Inspector. With that 2,500, the Meyerhof family of four made it to the *zone libre*. I know this because, in their gratitude, they sent me a postcard. They had "found employment." There was "plenty of food." These brief words filled in places among those the censors had blacked out and they told me that the family had reached Marseille as planned and were about to board a ship. To Tangier, I think.'

'And the card, mademoiselle?'

Was it proof he wanted? 'It . . . it was unfortunately stolen—taken.'

'Like others, Hermann,' Louis said with a sigh as if totally absorbed in the tale or resting up to gather steam, especially as she hadn't bothered to mention the card before.

Again she found the will to uncertainly smile at him, thought Kohler, but then grew serious. 'Each piece bears a certificate, Chief Inspector, with the letterhead of my father's shop in Boston. Each gives details of the piece, the date purchased, the price negotiated, the name of the seller and to whom the item is to be delivered. My father, I know, would be very proud of me and would say to my mother and to my uncles who are partners of his, "Hasn't our Jenny the eye?" Ever since I was a little girl, I've been among such things.'

And Weber knew it—Kohler could see Louis thinking this but

all that *sûreté* said was, 'There's a bench of sorts near the boiler, Hermann. Let's sit a moment.'

'Sometimes it's still a little warm at this time of day,' Jennifer managed.

Madame had fled, and they were both worried about what that woman might now do, thought Jennifer, but the one from the Kripo, the criminal police, took out his cigarettes, the other a pipe and tobacco pouch and they shared a match, she accepting a cigarette though shaking still.

'*Merci*,' she said softly. They would push her now. They wouldn't let up until they were satisfied she had told them everything.

Was the vulnerability but a subterfuge? wondered St-Cyr. She wasn't beautiful but perfectly capable of using the charm of her eyes and faintness of a smile to plead innocence and overcome whatever doubts Hermann might have.

With him, he suspected, she knew that no such ploys would work. The tobacco did, however, calm her a little. 'Mademoiselle, you were billeted with the British when you and the others first arrived at the camp. Things must have been chaotic.'

Merde, he was even watching the way she smoked her cigarette! '*Ah, mon Dieu*, those first few weeks were so overcrowded we were constantly tripping over one another. One couldn't have the briefest of washes in privacy or even share a bath without several looking in to say hello, ask for something, or tell a person to hurry up and make sure they didn't leave a ring but scrubbed it out, nor was there much to eat.'

'The British had to share their parcels with them, Louis.'

'Fights broke out, animosities grew so deep they still fester.'

She'd been grateful for Hermann's interjection about the parcels, had seized on it, but would now have to face the truth. 'Things went missing, did they?' asked St-Cyr.

'A bar of expensive soap, a tube of toothpaste, slippers, socks, and underwear—all such things unless kept well hidden or guarded. Shoes, even, but in October we were moved here. It . . . it was then that the theft of little things was first noticed.'

'But they'd been going on while you were in the Grand?' asked the *sûreté*, gesturing companionably with that pipe of his.

'*Oui,* I think, but how were we to have known? The British now say they hadn't lost a thing before we arrived but . . . but as to its being the work of a kleptomaniac, I . . . '

She shrugged, had mastered the art of that gesture perfectly, her gaze falling fully on Hermann, of course.

Concern had best flood his eyes, thought Kohler. Warmth, too. 'Photos, postcards, letters from home, Louis, and bits of ribbon.'

She mustn't flinch, thought Jennifer, though having had to sit in front of Herr Weber's desk so many times, she knew well enough the ribbon to which he was referring. 'Buttons, but only those that wouldn't have easily been recognized had an attempt been made to use them.'

'With whom were you billeted?' asked Herr Kohler.

Cold now, was he to her? wondered Jennifer. 'With Léa, Hortense, and Marguerite Lefèvre. Madame Chevreul said that it was the least she could do, given the circumstances. Everyone must double up, except for her, of course.'

Herr Kohler flicked a glance at his partner, then said to her, 'That spare room with the crystal balls and such . . . Was it emptied out and taken over?'

He'd been in it, then. 'They . . . they kept it locked but we all knew of it soon enough and that the British had been reading palms and the Ouija board and holding séances in there at ten and twenty francs per person—less perhaps, or the equivalent—and for some time.'

And one hell of a lot cheaper than for the Americans! 'But not in the Pavillon de Cérès?'

First Herr Kohler would go at her and then the other. 'The Pavillon . . . Not while we were billeted in the Grand. It was simply far too crowded. I slept on the floor beside Marguerite's cot. There were so many things we had to learn—she helped me a lot, let me tell you, would lend me things, a towel, a pair of slacks. In turn, I shared my toothpaste, perfume, lipstick, and hand-soap with her, for they hadn't had anything so good in ages.'

'You got to know her well, then,' said Herr Kohler.

How well, was what he wanted, the *sûreté* simply sucking in on that pipe of his, the tobacco mixture sweet yet spicy, its aroma reminding her of Colonel Kessler but also of home, her father, and the shop. 'Wouldn't anyone who had slept beside you for weeks?'

'Were you lovers?' asked Herr Kohler.

Again she would shrug. 'Such things happen, especially in places like this. We were afraid, confused, lost, lonely . . . Ah, so many things, I . . . '

This time the shrug was defiant, thought St-Cyr.

'Really, inspectors, my private life, such as it is in a place like this, has nothing to do with what has happened.'

'Or everything,' he said, watching her even more closely now.

She would stub out her cigarette, but with infinite care so as not to waste a grain of unburned tobacco. 'We saw each other daily even after I moved here.'

'Until?' he persisted.

It would have to be said quite simply. 'Until one day, early in December, Marguerite broke things off and wouldn't even look at or speak to me, but I . . . I think Madame Chevreul had told her she had better break it off or else. I . . . ' *Ah, merde,* she would have to tell them. 'I was suspected of stealing things. My feelings were hurt, of course. Terribly, but . . . but Madame, she wouldn't listen. I was to be banished. Marguerite was to . . . to find another but hasn't. Not yet, not that I know of.'

They were making her angry and she couldn't have that, she mustn't, felt Jennifer. Anger would only play right into their hands, but her cheeks were already warm and inadvertently she had clutched the cigarette butt she had been going to return to Herr Kohler for his little tin and it had crumbled to dust.

'Caroline Lacy, mademoiselle,' said the *sûreté.*

'Caroline . . . Because I had roomed with Marguerite and the others, she . . . she wanted me to help her to become a sitter. At first Madame Chevreul refused, but Léa . . . Léa finally spoke on our behalf.'

'Things were still being stolen,' said St-Cyr.

'*Oui,* but Caroline and me, we passed the severest of tests. Madame was satisfied.'

'But then came the loss of her gris-gris, Louis.'

'Only now have Hermann, Madame Chevreul, Léa Monnier, and everyone else, it seems, in the Hôtel Grand become convinced Caroline Lacy was the thief.'

'But . . . but Caroline *was* to have become a sitter, inspectors?'

'At a séance, mademoiselle, which for her just never happened.'

'I didn't kill her. I swear I didn't! Caroline was convinced that Cérès would reveal Madame de Vernon had hit her husband with an empty champagne bottle, a Moët et Chandon. Not a full one, for otherwise it . . . it might have exploded and sent flying glass into her eyes and Madame, she . . . she would have known this could happen.'

'And then set fire to the casino here?' asked Herr Kohler.

'*Oui.*' Jennifer nodded. 'We . . . we spoke of it often. It was all just supposition but . . . but the more she thought about it, the more my Caroline believed, and me, I . . . I joined in because it pleased her.'

Were the tears real? wondered St-Cyr. 'But you did have a falling out with her on the night Mary-Lynn died. Caroline was very upset and had a severe asthma attack as a result.'

The eyes were wiped. 'We . . . we patched things up, as I've told you.'

'But you did tell Herr Weber that Caroline desperately wanted to arrange a meeting with someone so as to let the new Kommandant know what she'd seen, and prior to this, you did tell him the future Corporal Duclos had predicted for Mary-Lynn Allan.'

Ashen now, Jennifer knew she couldn't look at either of them and was in danger of stammering. 'He told me that if I didn't tell him things and find out everything he asked me to, he'd see that I never left Vittel. He doesn't like me, inspectors. Indeed, he hates what I've become and ridicules me, while I . . . I have to sit in front of that desk of his and must not look anywhere else but straight at him. He . . . he enjoys humiliating people like me, but says he has to make allowances, as he does with Brother Étienne, until the Führer orders otherwise.'

'Louis . . . '

'Hermann, we'll deal with Herr Weber later. Mademoiselle, who arranged the meeting at the chalet?'

'Becky, but she . . . she has already told you this. Jill . . . Jill didn't get one of the guards to open that padlock. Caroline . . . '

She couldn't face them now, thought Jennifer, but would have to say, '*Ah, mon Dieu,* inspectors, I know she must have found someone who had a key.'

'Louis . . . '

'Not yet, Hermann. Had Caroline found out who the kleptomaniac was, Mademoiselle?'

A nod was given. 'She must have, but . . . but why *didn't* she tell me, inspectors? I would have gone with her. Together we could have stopped whoever did that to her.'

'A fanatical tidier, Louis.'

'One who visits back and forth, Hermann, just like everyone else.'

'But also goes for long, long walks in the Parc, in the freezing cold, inspectors, all by herself. Who else has the capability of hiding things every day in a place no one else would find or even think of? Caroline really did see something the night Mary-Lynn fell, but she wouldn't tell me. She was afraid that if I knew, it would then put me in danger.'

Already the Ouija boards, the cards, and such were out in the Vittel-Palace, and in nearly every room of this giant dormitory it was as if each occupant was secretly wondering if she would get through another night. So muted were the conversations, thought Kohler, he and Louis could hear a throat being cleared several doors away. Lots read in bed, all bundled up and knowing that one by one the stoves would go out and the temperature plunge. Some thought they could already see their breath and would look for it as a page was turned. Those who had gloves wore them. Others clutched mugs of hot water, and of course all the hot plates were fully on, and what lights there were already blinking.

Nora Arnarson had still not returned to Room 3–38.

'She's probably gone to check on Angèle,' said Jill Faber, somewhat subdued. 'Nora's very conscious of that mare and loves her almost as much as does Brother Étienne. He'll be wanting to get away soon. Nora usually likes to say good-bye to him.'

'As a young girl, she loved to ride the plow horses they used when hauling logs out of the bush,' said the redhead, Marni Huntington, trying to smile at the thought. 'Her brothers would dare her to ride bareback and even to stand on her hands.'

'She has two brothers in the services, inspectors,' said Becky. 'One's in the USAF, the other in the Navy. P-51 Mustangs and anti-submarine patrols on a destroyer, but she hasn't heard from either in well over three months and is afraid both have been killed as well.'

'As whom, mademoiselle?' asked Louis.

'As her fiancé, Einar. He was in the Marines and was killed in action on Makin Island in the Gilberts, 17 August of last year.'

'Hermann, I'll find her.'

'You'll need my scarf.'

And a flashlight. 'Try to pry some answers out of Herr Weber. Let's meet in the foyer here.'

'What if he's opened that . . . '

'Safe of his? Better the gamble now, Hermann, than later.'

And wasn't the office in the casino?

'Find Nora, inspectors. Please find her,' said Becky, unable now to look at either of them, simply twisting her hands in despair. 'I don't know what we would do without her. Madame de Vernon hasn't come back either.'

Jennifer Hamilton had wrung her laundry out by hand and had climbed the stairs with Louis and him but had gone on alone to her room. 'Maybe we'd best stay together,' said Hermann.

It was almost 1800 hours Sunday, 21 February, 1943, and they had been here since the day before at 1522 hours. 'Weber, *mon vieux*, and I out there.'

'The curfew for us internees is at six in winter, inspectors,' said Jill. 'The entrance doors will be locked in a few minutes. Nora . . . '

She left the thought dangling, couldn't bring herself to say it: a night outdoors in weather like this.

*   *   *

The wind from the northwest was punishing, thought St-Cyr. Caught in the Valley of the Petit-Vair, with the Butte de Sion to the north, Vittel and its internment camp had the Haute-Saône and the Vosges Mountains to the south and the east, and not that far. Simply put, it was damned freezing and dangerous, for it blew in such unforgivable gusts, he was in fear of becoming lost.

'*Merde alors,* mademoiselle, where the hell are you?'

She wasn't in the stables, but he did find the leftovers from some sprigs of beech. Each stem had been clean cut with a knife that was very sharp. 'An Opinel,' he muttered. 'The peasant's constant companion. Wooden-handled and cheap.'

Rubbing the mare behind the ears and caressing her, he discovered that the forelock had been gently tied and patiently undid the knot.

Things weren't good—indeed, Nora's absence was terrible. 'Mademoiselle,' he sang out, wishing the wind wouldn't pluck his voice away even inside the stable.

She wasn't in the first of the fencing pavilions, nor in the second, though why she should have been in either at this time made no sense. Recent footprints hadn't been encountered, but would they have all been quickly filled in?

Something must have happened to her.

In spite of the concern, he had to ask himself, Why does a nonbeliever bother to make a Ouija board? There had been one under her bed when Hermann and he had first had a look around that room.

When and why had she come to France and why hadn't she got out before it had become too late for her?

She *had* been looking for the thief and had been following Caroline's and Jennifer's steps or retracing them, and had been asking questions: whom the two had spoken to and where they had gone.

Had she finally found the hiding place? he wondered. She did know the camp like no other, and had doubted Jennifer's sincerity with Caroline, had felt her opportunistic—must have known of the previous affair between Marguerite Lefèvre and that girl, would have spoken to the former, yet had so far said nothing of it.

And as for the *Datura stramonium,* only Brother Étienne had been as knowledgeable of the hazard.

Had even lied to this *sûreté,* had chased up those stairs after Mary-Lynn Allan, who had been in tears because of what her friend had been yelling at her. Derision.

Was being used by Brother Étienne to relay news of the war. Had seen Caroline go into the Chalet des Ânes and had known Becky had followed the girl.

'*Sacré nom de nom,* this investigation!' he cursed and, turning his back to the wind, pulled up the collar of his overcoat, having returned to the stable.

'Is she out on her trap line?' he asked Angèle. 'Has she fallen and become lost?'

Outside again, the intermittent visibility was terrible. '*Pour l'amour du ciel,* mademoiselle, how many metres of fence line have you forced this poor detective to walk in such weather? What am I going to find when I come across you?'

Had she become so desperate she had gone over the wire? Had she tried to leave a message for Brother Étienne, had that been why the mare's forelock had been tied?

'Even now I can't ask myself if she's been murdered but she always did wonder if she would be next and if she had been the intended victim on the night her friend had fallen.'

A fortune's worth of cigarette butts was heaped in the ashtray, the Untersturmführer with hands folded in front of him.

'That Arnarson girl, Kohler. What do you make of her?'

Clearly Weber was on to something. 'A loner.'

'Guilty of causing the death of the mistress of Colonel Kessler?'

Was the bastard about to back off on claiming it a suicide?

'Well?' he demanded, his voice rising.

'We don't know that yet, Untersturmführer.'

Still on his feet in front of the desk, this disloyal Kripo, this

266

doubter and 'partner' of a Frenchman who would think to manhandle an SS, was now to learn the hard way. 'Colonel Kessler's court-martial is in three days. I was hoping . . . '

'His *what*?'

'Yes, yes, Kohler. I assumed you knew. Since you didn't, perhaps you had best look at this.'

A chair was indicated. Berlin-Central had responded to Weber's latest query and had sent the Untersturmführer a telex, but would he now think to file it in that safe of his only to discover certain items were missing, or was he already aware of that?

Arnarson, Nora Ingibjorg, born 24 February, 1917, Clearwater Lake, Wisconsin, U.S.A. Entered Michigan Technological University, Houghton, Michigan, September 1935; graduated with honours in Geology, May 1939; postgraduate studies in Biology, Chemistry, and Extractive Metallurgy, September 1940 to May 1941. Entered Vichy France via Marseilles 13 September, 1941, on a six-month student visa.

In June 1940 the French Government had moved from Paris to Vichy, but then on 11 December, 1941, the Führer and the Italians had declared war on America. Until then Vichy had been courting the Americans, who had been sending much-needed quantities of food and other supplies to France through the British naval blockade. This had all been stopped, of course, but Nora must have arrived on one of those ships, though would since have had to have that visa extended only to have been finally rounded up in September of last year with other Americans.

'Why, please, does a young American student—a girl, no less—travel to France at such a time?' asked Weber.

'There's no mention of Paris. Did she stay in the unoccupied zone?'

The Free Zone, which the Reich had overrun on 11 November of last year, the American embassy, then in Vichy, having been immediately closed. 'Berlin-Central are most interested. At their request, I have just sent Paris and Lyon a photo of her.'

Thoughts of promotion must be dancing in this pseudo-schoolmaster's head. A forefinger tapped the side of that nose just as his Kommandant would have done.

'My experience as a cell leader in the Party tells me she is not what she claims, Kohler. Apparently no one here has yet been told by her why she really came to France. Instead, she has said "to study Roman and more recent ruins." A girl who had, on two occasions, requested of Colonel Kessler that a microscope be found so that the lectures she has been giving others might be better illustrated?'

'Brother Étienne seems to get along with her well enough, as do her roommates, except for Madame de Vernon.'

And you have just dug yourself an even deeper hole, *mein Lieber.* 'We'll get to the Frenchwoman soon enough. That monk, Kohler. There can be no radios in this camp, but lies from the BBC Free French and Voice of America broadcasts are being whispered. Kharkov is another disastrous defeat for our glorious armies? The Führer likens it to Stalingrad, from which the Soviets are now six hundred kilometres to the west and unstoppable?'

On 3 February the Battle for Stalingrad had ended, on the sixteenth, that of Kharkov. Along the Eastern Front, which stretched for more than 2,400 kilometres, the Wehrmacht apparently was either in a holding pattern or in retreat. The supply lines were simply far too long, the winter the harshest in the past fifty years, the Luftwaffe busy defending Berlin and other cities and towns in the Reich and losing far too many aircraft.

'There is no rout, Kohler, no defeat, and there will be no more of these whispers. If it is found that the monk was involved, as I suspect he was, he'll be shot. As will the person to whom he gave such lies.'

Was the warning clear enough? wondered Weber. 'Find the killer or killers. You have, I believe, until tomorrow before I call in experienced detectives from Berlin-Central.'

'Frightened, are you, of what Louis and I might find?'

'*Ach,* you've not even found the thief—a kleptomaniac who now possesses a deadly poison?'

'We're not certain of that.'

'But still fail to register such a concern with this head of security, one who has his finger constantly on the pulse of this internment camp?'

'We're working on it.'

'Do you still persist in claiming the thief must have stolen the key to that gate's padlock from this board of mine?'

A hand was flung up and behind to point at it.

'Stolen like Houdini, Kohler, while I was sitting right here interviewing her, one of my informants? That partner of yours asks the occupants of Rooms 3–38 and 3–54, I tell you, if there is a *Jude* among them? Is it that you also think I wouldn't have been aware of such a thing?'

'*Liebe Zeit,* Untersturmführer, it's *Jüdin.* You've been listening to Madame de Vernon.'

'*Jude oder Jüdin,* they're all the same. Berlin-Central are going to hear of what she has to say. Shall I put in a call to them? It'll take a few minutes. There may be a bombing raid in progress. One never knows now, does one, what with the Americans by day and the British by night.'

'Lies and then the truth, Untersturmführer?'

'*Ach,* maybe now you'll see exactly where that so-called partner of yours stands, but please don't bother to tell me you'll talk to him. Colonel Jundt and I will discuss the matter over supper. I take it you'll be dining with us, or has the thought upset your stomach?'

Between the gusts there were lulls, pauses through which, on the cold, clear air, came the distinctive, if distant, rhythm of an ax that did not falter.

Puzzled—alarmed—St-Cyr was torn by what to do, for if the sound entailed what he thought it must, the trapper was bent on only one thing. The distance from the casino and the main gate beyond it would have been taken into consideration by her—perhaps two-and-a-half kilometres. The windchill alone and relief in the evening meal would also have offered possibilities of preoccupying most of the guards of whom there were few enough because of the demands of the Russian Front, but still it was a terrible gamble.

Infuriatingly, another gust drowned out all sounds of the ax, but then, as the wind tailed off, the unmistakable falling of a tree came, and with it the sound of its hitting the fence and bouncing from the ground.

'*Ah, merde,*' he managed, 'what has made you so desperate?'

Angèle was cooperative, but harnessing her to the cutter took needed time, finding Hermann all the more. '*Vite, vite, mon vieux.* An emergency!'

'Inspector, what is going on?'

'Stay put, *mon frère,* and that is an order!'

It didn't take long to locate the tree. Its stump was beyond the rose arbours and the tennis courts, was beyond even the snow-covered vegetable plots of the British that had been raided and torn up by the Americans last autumn in retaliation, but wasn't far enough from the perimeter wire that overlooked, through the night's darkness, what had once been the racecourse but was now the 'football' field.

She had gauged the wind and had taken another desperate gamble by timing its lulls so as to have the immediate help of a final gust.

The once-healthy spruce, perhaps fifteen metres in its former height, had become her ladder to freedom.

'We've got a problem, Louis.'

'Which we will now have to settle.'

Fortunately, the lone guard on the gate, having heard the approaching sleigh bells, was already opening the barrier.

'Domjulien is this way, Hermann. It's the road Brother Étienne would have taken.'

'The Hôtel de l'Ermitage, Louis. The source of those *verdammte* golf balls and that wallpaper.'

Out of the wind, behind the hotel, footprints in the snow led to the east and there seemed only the prospect of pitting themselves against a girl who, alone of all, would know how best to use the weather against them or anyone else. *Bien sûr,* she must have planned to wait here until Brother Étienne had come by to pick her up, but hadn't.

'*Courage, ma fille,*' said Louis with evident admiration. '*Merde,* Hermann, the only thing that might stop her, and I emphasize the "might," would be dogs.'

'No one has mentioned them and we haven't heard or seen any. Maybe they were needed in Russia.'

Beyond an open woodland of beech, etched against snow and sky, the forest thickened to spruce as it climbed the hills until becoming a forest, the Bois de la Voivre. She would have kept the ax, wouldn't have even needed matches, would have made certain she had dressed warmly, but still, what had tipped her off, for she couldn't have gone back to the room to pick up anything?

'She would know exactly what she faced out there, Hermann,' said Louis, indicating the forest. 'Before you went to talk to him, Weber must have told someone to send her to him. Perhaps he waved that telex in front of one of his informants, or that one managed to read it.'

'Or Nora was warned by someone who simply wanted to cover herself.'

'Jennifer Hamilton?'

Who had left them outside Room 3–38 and had gone along the corridor alone to her own room. 'Was Nora in there, having a look at Mary-Lynn's things?' asked Kohler.

It was only as he turned the cutter around that Angèle objected, tossing her head and snorting as she pawed at the snow.

'She's excited, Louis, is refusing to leave.'

A nearby alcove window had been broken in and a woollen toque had caught on a spine of glass.

'Nora must have seen that there were two of us in the cutter and concluded that she couldn't outrun Angèle,' said Louis.

'Yet she still had the presence of mind to try to lead us astray. The electricity will be off.'

'And she'll still have that ax and her Opinel.'

9

Luxury was draped in white sheeting and as the beam of the flashlight searched about the seeming vastness of the Hôtel de l'Ermitage's foyer, it finally came to rest on a staircase of marble whose Art Deco railing curved gracefully upward.

The damp, the cold, the smell were penetrating, this last of mouldy wool mingled with long-spent cigar and other tobacco smoke, dust, and perfume, thought St-Cyr. Built in 1929, the hotel was in four sections, placed in a gentle zigzag. One wing faced onto the golf course, then there was the one he and Hermann were in, and then, end to end, two others facing the forest close in on either side. Nora Arnarson could delay them and then try to leave with Angèle and the cutter, and they both knew this.

'Four storeys, Hermann. Two more in the attics for the help. One hundred and twenty-two rooms and suites for the guests, plus kitchens, dining room, lounge bar and café, front desk, and offices.'

'And we've only one flashlight, which is likely to give out on us at any moment.'

Hermann didn't always tend to worry and was simply in need of reassurance. 'Weber will soon know where we are and come running.'

'Maybe we should tell her that.'

All of the furnishings from the Vittel-Palace and probably from the Grand had been stored in the Ermitage. Narrow passages, often cluttered and dead-ended, threaded through the mountains they would have to negotiate if she refused to answer.

'Mademoiselle,' called Louis, only to have, if possible, the silence plunge even deeper until, through it, came the gusting sounds of the wind outside.

The alcove she had broken into was behind them, a once-pleasant and no doubt much-sought-after recess from which the comings and goings of the clientele in the foyer and at the front desk could have been watched while quietly perusing a newspaper.

Angèle snorted, the sleigh bells jingling their reminder. 'Stay here, Hermann. Let me flush her to you.'

'She'll have already figured that out.'

'Mademoiselle,' called out Louis, 'your best chance is with us. If guilty, we'll insist on taking you to Paris; if not, and I must emphasize this, we will guarantee that Herr Weber doesn't use you to cover up his own guilt.'

'*Louis, we can't yet prove he's guilty!*' hissed Hermann.

'*But she doesn't know that.* Mademoiselle, Herr Weber had reason enough to have killed your friend.'

Friend. . . . The echoes rebounded. 'Inspectors, please let me go. I didn't do anything.'

She was on the first landing of the main staircase, was briefly caught by the beam of their light.

Louis switched it off and indicated that they should spread out. 'You left a knot in Angèle's forelock,' he called.

'Brother Étienne always comes and goes this way,' she blurted in despair. 'He wouldn't have stopped to tell me he knew I had escaped. I wouldn't have ridden in the cutter. That would only have implicated him. Once in the woods, I'd have followed a stream. There's a pair of skis waiting for me three kilometres from here, a deserted farm in the hills ten more and to the east of that over a rise, a woodcutter's shack. I . . . I was to have stayed there until he had arranged to send someone. *Ah, merde,* you won't arrest him, will you?'

'An accomplice, Louis.'

Silenced by that, she blinked when the beam of the light again briefly caught her.

'That knot, mademoiselle,' said Louis. 'Even chief inspectors make mistakes. Had I but known . . . '

'You would have let me go? Me, a key piece of that investigation of yours and now suspected of murder?' They had moved and were by the heaped and cluttered front desk and a lot closer to her.

'Please don't do anything we would all regret,' said Hermann. 'Please just come down.'

'Let's discuss it—is that what you mean?' The *sûreté* had kept the light off. The Kripo must now be at the foot of the stairs.

'There isn't much time, mademoiselle,' said St-Cyr. 'A few minutes at most.'

They wouldn't know until it was too late. They couldn't, Nora warned herself, and taking the stairs two and three at a time, went up through the pitch-darkness, leaving Herr Kohler far behind.

'She'll use that ax, Louis, or cut her wrists.'

'But is guilty of what, Hermann?'

'Admit it. That monk's with the Résistance. Weber's going to have a field day making mincemeat out of all of us.'

The first floor was crowded with furniture—beds taken apart and leaning with their mattresses against the corridor walls, rooms filled to overflowing. No order, just a jumble, and done in haste since the Grand had become vastly overcrowded and the Vittel-Palace urgently needed.

Nora listened. Nora tried to hear them, but they moved silently as a team. First one would go ahead, and then the other. Only then would the flashlight come on briefly and she would know for sure that it was but a matter of seconds until they found her.

They wouldn't understand that she and Mary-Lynn hadn't just argued about Cérès talking to the father Mary-Lynn had never known. They couldn't know that Mary-Lynn had yelled, "You're afraid of what Einar is going to say to you if Cérès *does* get through to him as she did with my dad. You *didn't* let Einar have you, Nora. You told him to stop making love to you and buzz off. You stupidly shouted that if he really, really *did* love you he would have to wait!"

Einar had been blazing mad, had sworn at her, a thing he had never ever done before, and had run off to join up, and later she had agreed to come to France.

When the beam of the light found her, she blinked but didn't lower the knife, could feel the blade already cutting into her throat.

'Don't, mademoiselle. Please don't,' said Louis gently.

She was in one of the rooms, jammed between two bureaus, with knees up tightly and back against a wall. The Opinel was at the jugular and once cut, thought Kohler, how the hell were they to stop the bleeding?

'I did try to grab Mary-Lynn earlier on the stairs but tripped and fell and she got well ahead of me. I heard her scream. I cried out to her in confusion and despair for I didn't know what had happened, only sensed it, for when someone falls like that, they . . . Caroline did see me when I finally got to that gate to look down the elevator shaft but . . . but it could only have been a glimpse because the lights then went off again.'

She wasn't going to listen, felt Kohler. She had that ax leaning right beside her but must have told herself she couldn't use it on anyone, not even to escape.

'I'll be shot, won't I?'

Louis had lowered the light and was now shining it toward the other side of the room and back a little.

'Not if we can help it,' said St-Cyr. Hermann wasn't going to get any closer unless she could somehow be distracted. 'The wallpaper, *mon vieux*.'

'The Senegalese, Louis.'

The light was now shining fully on that far wall. 'With the dampness, it's come loose and they've been peeling it off,' said Nora, finding the will to faintly smile at the thought. 'Madame Chevreul needed to decorate that tentlike cabinet of hers and Léa . . . Léa made them find her something no one would know of until seen. I'm not the only one who has broken into this place, but they've been into it lots and lots. They must have.'

'Weber will only use it against them, Hermann,' said Louis sadly.

The flashlight blinked as flashlights will. 'He's on to me, isn't he?' she asked. 'When I met Jennifer on her way down to the laundry this evening, she said Marguerite had told her he had received a telex from Berlin about me and that he'd been very excited by it and wanted to see me. I . . . I worked for our Intelligence Department, inspectors. They'd been canvassing the universities and said I might be useful.'

A spy, thought Kohler. As if they didn't have enough trouble already. The knife was still determinedly at her throat. She'd die if either of them moved.

'Ever since I was little, my mom has always spoken to me in her own language. I did tell them that my accent would be far too off, that even the local patois I'd have to deal with wouldn't cover that up, but they didn't think I'd have a problem if I worked on it, not back then in '41 when they needed people quickly and Vichy still had the carpet out.'

'Mademoiselle, what . . . ' began Louis.

'Did I do? Look, I didn't kill anyone. I was sent here to help us get an independent estimate of the size and grade of the deposits of aluminum the Compagnie des Bauxites de France are mining.'

'The valley of the Argens, Hermann. The Département de la Var, near and at Brignoles to the east and northeast of Marseille.'

'Where I handed my reports and field samples in, either to my boss or to our contact person.'

'And the valley of the Hérault, in the Bas Landguedoc,' said St-Cyr, 'to the northwest of Montpellier.'

Louis was obviously dismayed at what they were up against, but the girl seemed relieved to be finally telling someone.

'I even went to Les Baux to see where it had all begun. I fell in love with your country, Chief Inspector, and was, I felt, doing something that would not only be useful to the war effort but to France as well.'

Les Baux-de-Provence, a place of troubadours and knights, was about twenty kilometres to the north of Arles and a ruined hilltop town and ancient fortress where bauxite had first been discovered in 1821 and given that name.

There was blood on her neck and she could feel it.

'Aluminum equals fighter aircraft and bombers, inspectors.

France has by far the world's largest source of high-grade ore. The Germans haven't nearly enough of their own and must get it from here and from Hungary.'

'An earthy-red, chalky ochrous rock, Hermann.'

'But not ochre, which has far more iron,' she said. 'Though formed in essentially the same way in tropical climates of the past, bauxite is a residual deposit caused by the chemical and physical breakdown of rocks that are high in alumina.'

St-Cyr hadn't taken his eyes off her for a split second and Nora knew she couldn't keep the acid from her voice. 'You French, Inspector, are letting them take seventy to eighty percent not only of the mined bauxite but of the refined metal.'

Whose smelters were in the Savoy, in the valleys of the Arve, the Isère, and the Arc, where plenty of electrical power was being generated. 'You certainly got around.'

'The Germans tried to control the price paid for the ore and metal. Vichy wanted more, of course, but what did the Compagnie des Bauxites do but worry they wouldn't sell a thing and accept seventy-five francs a ton, which was far less than even the Reich's Vereinigte Aluminium-Werke had offered. In 1941 Germany took 230,000 tons of ore. At four to one of metal that alone equalled nearly 60,000 of the refined, but Vichy also allowed the sale of 34,500 of that. In 1942, up until I was arrested and brought here, it was worse. The only problems the Germans were having were the distance to the Reich, the extreme shortages of railway stock—since they had stupidly shot themselves in the foot and had taken far too many locomotives and railway cars—and the lack of labour, since they had locked up far too many of the miners as prisoners of war.

'Now, please let me die in peace. I didn't kill anyone and I didn't steal anything and I've no reason now to lie to you or to anyone.'

'But you do know who the thief is.'

'The klepto? Not really. I suspected Jen and then Caroline but never accused either nor told anyone else.'

Her fingers were sticky, the blade not quite where it ought to have been, thought St-Cyr, but was she beginning to realize this?

'That crystal-ball gazer?' asked Hermann. Somehow he had reduced the distance to her by half.

She would give Herr Kohler a faint smile for such an attempt, thought Nora, and would tell them both. 'To me, Jen's still head over heels with Marguerite, who may or may not give a damn about her anymore. I simply don't know her well enough nor why they split up. Jen's never said a thing about it, not to me and not to anyone else that I know of, nor has Marguerite.'

'But Jennifer then took up with Caroline, Hermann.'

'Leaving the other one homicidally jealous, Louis?'

'Perhaps, but then . . . '

'Caroline really did want to find out what had happened to Madame de Vernon's husband, inspectors. Jen . . . Jen was always encouraging her to.'

'How much traffic goes back and forth from hotel to hotel?' asked Louis.

'Lots. Every day, and lots of overnights, too. If Marguerite's been stealing things, tell her I hope that Indian Head penny brings her the luck my dad wanted me to have.'

The flashlight went off and then came on, the wrist being caught, the knife hand pulled back, Hermann having grabbed the girl in a bear hug.

Finally she stopped struggling and just let him hold her. '*Ah, bon,*' said St-Cyr, 'now we'd best get to work. We've company.'

'*ACHTUNG, ACHTUNG!*' came the call from Weber, given over a loud-hailer. '*RAUS, ALLES! KOMMEN SIE! SCHNELL! SCHNELL!*'

'*NICHT SCHIESSEN, KAMMERAD!*' yelled Hermann. '*NICHT SCHIESSEN!*' Don't shoot.

'COME DOWN. IT'S ALL UP WITH YOU, KOHLER.'

'Stall him, Hermann. Keep him occupied.'

'Are you crazy?'

'There's something I have to do. Mademoiselle, come with me and don't try anything other than what I tell you.'

'Louis, I'm not hearing this, not from you. You can't leave me and try to make a break for it in that cutter. He'll have left at least two men holding that nag by the harness.'

Hermann loved horses and would normally have used the mare's name but it wasn't a time to quibble. 'Just tell him we're not going anywhere until I have what we need.'

Weber hadn't come in force but could have and should have if he had been wanting to make a big show of things. Instead, there was the baksheesh-taking Oberfeldwebel whom Louis had encountered at the wood depot and one very recent, teenage recruit who had awkwardly slung his Mauser and, having taken the loud-hailer back, was now nervously manning the floodlight.

It was blinding, and a forearm had to be thrown up to shield the eyes.

'WHERE IS SHE, KOHLER?'

Maybe fifteen metres still separated them. Shoulder-high mountains of furniture were on either side, Louis and the girl now well behind, Weber just inside the front entrance, the Oberfeldwebel to his right, but that Schmeisser and the stance spoke of the Russian Front and absolutely no desire to return to it.

Reinecke had been his name, and even from here the shrapnel scars below the helmet were clear enough. Louis and the girl would be caught in the crossfire—was that really what Weber wanted, having drawn his *Polizei Pistole*? Dead they could give no answers and Berlin-Central wouldn't give a damn. Indeed, they'd be pleased, and Weber must know it too.

'Kohler . . . '

'*Ach,* there's no problem, Untersturmführer. The little imp is with my partner.'

'That slut is wanted, Kohler. Wanted!'

To duck would not be wise. '*Liebe Zeit,* Untersturmführer, admit that we saved you a hell of a lot of trouble. Those woods are probably infested with partisans who would only have welcomed her and smeared egg on your face in Berlin.'

Kohler still hadn't moved. Beyond him, behind the front desk, St-Cyr and the girl were hurriedly searching for something. '*Komm'* here, Kohler. Now!'

A grin would be best. 'I've twisted an ankle. You'll have to be patient.'

'Your gun, then. Toss it out.'

Weber would shoot Louis first—was that it? 'Ach, my hands are full. Look, there's really no problem.'

'Where did she get that ax you're holding?'

'This? It's a leftover from that other war and branded right on its handle. Probably the ax was rusty as hell when she found it but it's been beautifully cleaned and is as sharp as a razor.'

'That monk . . . He threw it over the wire to her, or one of the blacks sold it to her.'

Weber couldn't have discovered that his safe had been broken into, or maybe he had and that was why he'd brought so few with him. 'We'll have to ask the brother and those boys, Untersturmführer, but didn't you tell me you knew everything that was going on around this camp? Who was meeting who and where and why, and who would be attending that séance on the night of the thirteenth and where they'd go afterwards before they climbed that staircase. A bell ringer . . . wasn't that what Colonel Kessler said over the telephone to the Kommandant von Gross-Paris? You did listen in, didn't you?'

'IT WAS A SUICIDE, KOHLER. A SELF-MURDER!'

'You knew Nora Arnarson and Mary-Lynn Allan would be attending that séance with Colonel Kessler and you knew you had to pin something substantial on him. What better than the suicide of the young woman he'd made pregnant?'

'She jumped, Kohler. He drove her to it, and that is among the charges Berlin-Central will be presenting at his court-martial.'

Louis had best be ready. 'Then the key to that padlock must have been stolen from that board on the wall behind your desk.'

'STOLEN RIGHT IN FRONT OF MY VERY EYES?'

'If not, Untersturmführer, then who the hell opened it other than you?'

Weber and the others were coming for her, thought Nora, panicking. Herr Kohler hadn't been able to stall them any longer. There was now no hope unless she could make a run for it, but how? Boxed in, she and the chief inspector were behind walls and walls, having gone beyond the front desk through crowded office after office frantically searching until, at last and on the floor at their feet, the beam of his light had settled on two dusty registers.

The fake marbling of their heavy covers sickened her but not just because of the time needed to look through them. Someone had stolen the leather jackets such books would always have. Shoe repairs? she wondered. Boots, gloves . . . would it really matter why the Senegalese had stripped them off or that they would have even been under guard? They'd been doing all the heavy labour and would have carried the registers in.

'There are strongboxes, too, Inspector.'

The registers had been on top of them, and both of the two boxes had been broken into.

'*Ah, merde,*' swore St-Cyr, dismayed by the thought. 'The house detectives,' and flinging up the lid of each, he found the empty holsters that should have held two of the Lebel Modèle d'ordonnance 1873s just like his own.

'Say nothing of this, mademoiselle. *Nothing,* do you understand?'

Nora knew she had to nod but that his mind must be in a turmoil, for if the Senegalese had stolen them, and they must have, it could only have been for one reason.

The register he handed her was thick and heavy. There were pages and pages of names, dates, room numbers, signatures, amounts paid, and far too little time.

Shoulder-to-shoulder, they began.

'Saturday 17 July, 1920,' said St-Cyr. 'Madame Élizabeth Chevreul, the Château de Mon Plaisir near Mortagne-au-Perche in Normandy.'

Nora had the Vittel-Palace's register, he the Grand's, he having set the flashlight between the two books so that it shone toward each of them and both would have as much light as possible. If worse came to worst, she knew he would douse the light, push her to the floor, and draw his weapon.

Built in 1899, the Vittel-Palace had opened in 1900 for the season on 1 June. Page after page had to be turned just to find the right year. Nora knew she couldn't do it fast enough. Often pages stuck together, whole clumps of them. The dampness . . . A gap. Page after page of nothing but empty spaces and blue lines. In 1915 the French Army had turned Vittel and its Parc Thermal into a huge hospital for their wounded. In July 1917, the first trains of American wounded had arrived, the French having decided to turn it over to them. By August 1918 there had been more than 1,300,000 dough-boys in France.

Her heart sank. There was no Madame Chevreul, not in the Vittel-Palace's register. Not that she could find in the weeks prior to 17 July, 1920, and right after it; nor was there in that of the Grand. She could have stayed in any other of the hotels in town.

Instead, there was a Mademoiselle Élizabeth Beacham who, hav-ing arrived on 1 July to "take the three-week cure," and having paid fully for it, had stayed at the Grand in a suite of rooms on its top floor only to have left in a hurry on the morning of the eighteenth.

She had used her British passport.

'Vernon, mademoiselle. A Laurence Vernon. Please hurry.'

Floodlight bathed the jumble of things that had been shoved and heaved aside nearest to a door that had somehow been hastily shut. Louis was in there with the girl. Louis . . .

Had it all come down to this? wondered Kohler. The years of working together, him out here with Weber's pistol at his back and the Oberfeldwebel about to let off a burst from that Schmeisser?

Nora could hear them clearly, as could the chief inspector whose hand had gently but firmly come to rest on her left shoulder, his flashlight having been extinguished.

'*Tell them to come out, Kohler!*' shrieked Weber.

'So that you can have them shot for resisting arrest?' yelled Kohler angrily.

A silence intruded, Nora's heart hammering, the chief inspector catching a breath.

'*Ach,* Untersturmführer,' said Herr Kohler, 'since there are two keys to each of those padlocks on that board of yours and no one could have borrowed one without your knowledge, or so you have repeatedly claimed, who did you give one to the Chalet des Ânes to, or did you open it yourself like you must have the other one?'

'I didn't open anything!'

Abruptly Weber fired twice into the ceiling above, showering plaster chips and dust as the sound reverberated and the smell of cordite came.

'Hermann . . . ' blurted the chief inspector from behind the still-unopened door, his voice a torn whisper. *'Ah, mon Dieu, mon vieux, why didn't you let me know how serious things were?'*

Nora felt him shudder at the thought of what must have happened, but then he dragged out his revolver and she heard its hammer click once on the half-cock and then on the full, sounds she had known since childhood.

'You to the floor at my feet, mademoiselle. Me to deal with them, but please don't try to run. Give life every moment you can.'

Kohler could see that the kid with the floodlight had pissed himself, but the Oberfeldwebel had anticipated that, with one good shove from him, the kid would have dropped the light, so there was nothing for it. 'Was it Jennifer Hamilton you gave that key to?' he demanded of Weber.

'Jennifer would never have killed Caroline, Inspector,' whispered Nora.

'She was desperate, mademoiselle. Alone and terrified,' said St-Cyr, 'but we still don't know that he actually gave her that key.'

'Kohler . . . ' began Herr Weber.

'Jennifer told you everything, didn't she, about Colonel Kessler and her roommate Mary-Lynn Allan?' shouted Hermann. 'Where the couple had been or were going, who they had been with or would be, and what he had given her.'

One couldn't help but feel triumphant, felt Weber. 'One teases, Kohler. One offers a little reward and then withdraws it. Fräulein Hamilton was so afraid I would renege on my promise to let her go home to that flat of hers in Paris, she begged me to use her. Begged, Kohler, and often went down on her knees.'

The son of a bitch! 'You had to find out how close Colonel Kessler was to Mary-Lynn. He'd a history of such affairs, so you made damned certain you planted a *Spitzel* in her room.'

And the room not far from those attic stairs and elevator-gate— was this what was now going through Kohler's mind? wondered Weber. 'Kessler was an arrogant fool and insufferable. *Mein Gott,* he wouldn't listen to a thing I said and thought he knew everything there was to run a place like this and that he could do as he pleased. Play golf when he wanted, shoot clay pigeons or go for a ride on one of his horses—horses that were needed on the Russian Front, Kohler—and afterwards, ah yes!—dine with that slut in town or stroll with her here in the Parc Thermal while talking to her as one would to a friend. One of the enemy?'

'Admit it. He knew you had been going on and on about him behind his back to Berlin-Central so he recommended you for the Russian Front. You had to get rid of him. What better way than to blame him for the suicide of that girl and make sure it happened?'

Had Kohler been into the safe?

'Afterwards you must have wanted to know what she had said through Cérès in that séance, Untersturmführer. Was it Léa who told you, or Marguerite Lefèvre?'

'The crystal-ball gazer. Is it that you fancy her? Let me tell you, she thinks you must and is willing.'

'Even though she may still be in love with Jennifer Hamilton?'

'Is she, Inspector?' asked Nora softly. *'If so, then Marguerite must have hated Caroline.'*

'Hermann, please don't push your luck. Go easy,' whispered St-Cyr.

'Love . . . is that what you would call it, Kohler?' shouted Weber. 'Oberfeldwebel Reinecke . . . '

'Wait!' cried Herr Kohler. *'Ach,* think about it, Untersturm-führer. Von Schaumburg, the Kommandant von Gross-Paris, is asked for our help by an old and much valued *Kamerad* from that other war, a former schoolmate as well, but a man you're now intent on putting up before the firing squad . . . or is it the piano wire you want them to use? A man who would have left us a directive on what must have happened to Mary-Lynn Allan, you then realizing you'd best destroy it. *Mein Gott, Dummkopf,* isn't von Schaumburg bound to demand a full enquiry should anything happen to Louis and me? It won't just be you who's grilled, SS or not. Reinecke, here, will come in for his full share, as will that boy.'

The light dipped, the light flew up. 'I'm not a boy! I'm a soldier!'

'Call them out now, Kohler. Now!' yelled Weber.

Reinecke had heard enough and had swung the Schmeisser round and jammed it into his back. 'OK, OK, Oberfeldwebel.' Damned if that door Louis was behind hadn't a calendar pinned to it: 15 September, 1939, and circled; an end to the season as usual but the start of yet another war.

'Louis, he's got my gun.'

Though muffled, that voice soon replied. '*Zut,* Hermann, I wish you wouldn't keep losing it. A moment, please, Untersturmführer. We were looking for an essential piece of evidence when you interrupted us.'

Nora tried to focus on the pages as the flashlight was switched back on and his revolver slid away.

'Hurry, mademoiselle,' he whispered. 'We need it.'

Down page after page her forefinger fled. There was nothing. It seemed all such a waste but then . . . then, 'The Vittel-Palace, Room 3–15,' she heard herself whispering. 'Arrived 3 July, 1920, but couldn't have left or paid his bill.'

But had lost another fortune at the tables, thought St-Cyr. There wasn't any need for Nora to search for Madame Irène Vernon's name. The woman wouldn't have tried to renew old vows or have stayed in any of the hotels, couldn't have afforded a room here in any case or wanted to.

She would have watched him from a distance, picked him out from among the crowd, seen who he was with and who was interested in him, and even heard his voice and laughter, having sat in that alcove whose window Nora had broken.

'The Chalet des Ânes, Hermann,' he called out. 'Please inform the Untersturmführer that it is necessary we search it now.'

'That can't be where the hiding place is, Inspector,' whispered Nora earnestly. 'It's far too open to view.'

'Agreed, but we'll search it anyway so as to buy us a little time.'

*   *   *

Nora didn't know if she would ever leave this place. Bathed in flood-light, they crowded around where children used to see the donkeys resting. The two who had been on guard outside the chalet and the one who had remained with Angèle had been dismissed and that wasn't good. It couldn't be. The chief inspector stood to one side of her, Herr Kohler to the other, their weapons having been taken from them. Herr Weber and the Oberfeldwebel were keeping them covered, and she as well.

Matthieu Senghor and Bamba Duclos, having been summoned, had cleared away the dried straw and dung and were now lifting the iron grill of the sewer in the centre of the hard-frozen, earthen floor.

Caroline's body, though earlier removed, had been just behind them, in that stall. Try as she did, Nora knew she couldn't help but glance into it. The pitchfork was still leaning against that far wall, the overturned water bucket was still to her left. There had been only two other items beyond what had been in Caroline's pockets, and these were now in the chief inspector's hand.

Sickened by the sight of what he held, she waited, knowing he had noticed her reaction.

'There's nothing in this drain but ice, Boss,' said Senghor to Kohler.

'Search all the stalls but that one,' said the chief inspector.

'*Schnell!*' shouted Weber. Hurry!

Now the Senegalese had their backs to him and to the Oberfeld-webel, felt Nora. Would they be shot and left in one of the stalls? Weber did intend to kill them—why else his having dismissed the guards and that other man and then accused these two yet again of having raped and killed Caroline?

'*Einen Moment, bitte, Untersturmführer,*' said St-Cyr.

'Did I not tell you fifteen minutes and that was all?' demanded Weber.

'Of course,' the chief inspector went on, companionably ges-turing with pipe in hand, 'but I need to ask you something. Why would one of your *Spitzel* have stolen the ribbon of your dead sister? Surely that was a dangerous and very foolhardy thing for her to have done.'

On entering the chalet, the Oberfeldwebel had embedded the ax in one of the uprights. Fortunately it wasn't far from her, thought Nora. It was just behind Herr Weber and within easy reach. The boy with the light was nearest to it and in partial shadow.

'Danger's the thrill, Louis,' said Herr Kohler, taking another drag at his cigarette and gesturing with it. 'That's what drives our klepto to steal.'

These two, thought Weber. They wouldn't be missed by Berlin-Central or by Gestapo Paris. '*Ach,* I've no idea why it was stolen, only that it was a loss I personally felt and still do.'

'But could it have been that something of your sister's was needed so that Madame Chevreul could use it to reach the goddess during one of the séances?' asked St-Cyr.

'Who would then question his sister Sonja, Louis, to find out exactly how she had died.'

'Haven't I told you Sonja was raped by one of those black bastards?' demanded Herr Weber.

'And they've been paying for it ever since,' insisted Kohler, 'but just suppose Cérès says it differently? Suppose Sonja tells her she had a crush on one of them?'

No one moved. Everyone waited.

'*DAS IST SCHEISSE, KOHLER! SCHEISSE!* YOU'RE INSANE!'

'*Lieber Gott,* Hermann. Sonja Weber had given the boy a cup of hot soup—an act of kindness, that is all. Isn't that correct, Unter-sturmführer?'

They were simply trying to rattle him, but why? wondered Weber. 'When arrested, he confessed readily enough.'

'Yes, yes, but have you never asked to attend one of those séances?' persisted Herr Kohler. 'You who loved your sister and still miss her every day? You who still want revenge?'

'Hermann, he was only ten years old at the time, or was it eleven?'

'Friday 23 December, 1921, Louis, at 1807 hours and the Occupation of the Rhineland, the Americans having moved out of Koblenz.'

'Leaving the Senegalese to do their duty, is that how it was, Hermann?'

'Big buck niggers, Louis. Sex with them and lots of fine young *Mädchen* enjoying it, too, judging by the number of illegitimate births, eh, Untersturmführer? Admit she had taken an interest in the boy and that it could well have gone a little further than your father felt decent.'

In a rage, Herr Weber had taken aim at him.

'Inspectors . . . ' managed Nora. 'Listen, please. Can't you hear that sound?'

Senghor and Duclos paused, the boy with the light hesitating, Herr Weber smiling cruelly at her now.

'Perhaps it is you, Fräulein, who should get it first.'

The Senegalese had slipped into a far stall but would it happen now? wondered Nora, looking up to the ceiling above to frolicking wood nymphs the children would have loved.

Again the smell of pipe smoke came to her, the aroma soft but warm and spicy, yet sweet too, like honey. 'My dad . . . ' she said, the memory close. 'He would often smoke a tobacco mixture like that. Virginia tobaccos with a touch of perique, a medium blend from England, sometimes from Scotland.'

Please don't do anything foolish, said St-Cyr silently to her. 'Untersturmführer, since you hold all the cards and Kommandant Jundt will require adequate explanations, why not let us see this thing through?'

Had Kohler found the police photos of Sonja? wondered Weber. Had he been into the safe and read Colonel Kessler's telexes and his own?

That pipe tobacco . . . When they had arrived yesterday, St-Cyr had had none, Kohler not even a cigarette, yet now both had plenty.

'You've five minutes left,' he said. It was now 2035 hours.

Senghor and Duclos could no longer be seen by Weber and Ober-feldwebel Reinecke, thought St-Cyr, but Mademoiselle Arnarson had been torn between glancing at the beechwood sprig and curls of inner bark in his hand and at that ax, and had already tried once to distract them by mentioning the sound and looking up to the ceiling above.

Weber would kill her. Reinecke would deal with Hermann and him. Secretive at times, Senghor and Duclos had used eye contact to signal to each other. Both had brought along their hessian satchels as if heading off into the woods for a fortnight's woodcutting. Both must be armed and had but one task: Reinecke first, then Weber, then that boy. They knew they had no other choice. Duclos would have brought along his little basket, Senghor his medals.

'Mademoiselle, this sprig of beech,' said St-Cyr. 'Did you leave it in that stall?'

'Me?' managed Nora. 'I swear I wasn't here when Caroline was killed. I did notice that Becky had followed her.'

'A fact which you denied when asked.'

'Yes, I know I did. I . . . I was afraid for her and for what Caroline might well say to the new Kommandant, those I won't deny, but I didn't kill her. Not to save Becky, nor myself, not for any reason. I did know Caroline was to have met someone but . . . but as she had just spoken to Brother Étienne, I . . . I felt everything must be all right.'

'And this sprig? It, too, has been cut in exactly the same way as those I found in the stable at Angèle's hooves.'

'Someone must have picked it up.'

'To pin the murder on you?'

'Lots know that I nibble on those buds and the inner bark from time to time and also share them with Angèle.'

To break her would be hard after what they'd just been through with her, but she gave every indication of being guilty, had even dragged off her toque and bowed her head, had closed her eyes and was now silently moving her lips in prayer.

Weber was smirking, Hermann lighting yet another cigarette, having begged another match from the Oberfeldwebel.

'Boss . . . ?'

'Well, what is it, Sergeant?' asked Herr Kohler.

Bamba was as ready as he was, thought Matthieu. They were never going to get out of here alive but somehow they had to get that girl and St-Cyr and Kohler to move aside. 'Ask the girl to step into that stall where she killed the other one, Boss. Ask her why Bamba and me, we saw her earlier opening that padlock. Ask her to show you how she used that pitchfork and to tell you why she took the time to tidy things and hide what she did.'

Weber had turned to face Senghor and Duclos, Kohler noticed, but Reinecke hadn't. Nora Arnarson was now deathly pale, the boy with the light holding it as steadily on her as he could.

'Aircraft, Louis. RAF bombers. Those are what she was hearing.'

They'd flown over Vittel before but was it Munich that would get it tonight, wondered Kohler, or Augsburg again? On 17 April of last year, in a daring daylight raid, they'd hit the MANN U-boat diesel-engine plant there, a first for the Lancaster which could, it was reported, carry a bomb load of 6,350 kilograms.*

'Four Merlin engines, Hermann.'

'Cruising speed of 338 kilometres per hour, Louis; range when loaded, of 2,675 kilometres. Nothing's safe anymore, *mon vieux*. No wonder Colonel Kessler had his doubts about the Reich, eh, Untersturmführer?'

The boy with the light knew his duty yet hesitated, waiting for the command until at last he blurted, 'Untersturmführer, what shall I do? There are windows. The light will be seen.'

'You and you, into that stall, inspectors,' said Reinecke, motioning at them with the Schmeisser. 'The girl to stay where she is.'

And that ax? wondered St-Cyr.

Nora felt herself being pulled and thrown to the floor. Flame flashed through the pitch-darkness, shots filling the chalet, the Oberfeldwebel turning to fire burst after burst at the Senegalese; Herr Weber firing once, twice, and then again; the sound of each weapon harsh and very different from each of the others until silence intruded.

'Hermann, are you all right?'

'And you and Nora?'

For ages, it seemed, they waited. The boy whimpered for his mother. Someone gave a sigh. Something metallic slid to the floor as the smell of cordite came to her.

Finally the flashlight came on briefly. Nora blinked, and as she did, the chief inspector gently brushed the back of a hand against her cheek, then got to his feet and helped her up.

---

* Later, about 300 were modified to carry up to the 9,979-kilogram (22,000 pound) "Earthquake" or "Grand Slam" bombs, the largest of the European war

The boy was slumped against the upright under the ax, the Untersturmführer had been hit twice, once in the forehead, once in the chest—horrible messes where the slugs had exited.

Cut to pieces, Duclos and Senghor lay in the stall from which they had fired the revolvers they had found in those boxes.

Oberfeldwebel Reinecke had been hit in the chest but only once. Sickened, Nora waited.

Picking their way through the dead, the two collected their own weapons, St-Cyr the satchel of Duclos, leaving everything else for others to find, others who would be there all too soon.

'Hermann, find Jennifer and bring her to Madame Chevreul. I'll take this one to the Grand. We'll pick up the brother on the way.'

'Angèle, inspectors. You can't leave her out in this weather.'

'The stable, then. The two of us. We can't let this girl escape, Hermann. I wish that we could, but it's just not possible.'

Louis had the bracelets out and had already clamped one on her and the other around his *sûreté* wrist.

Outside, on the cold night air, the sound of aircraft was even louder and then, from the Hôtel Grand and the Vittel-Palace, their voices rising first in a cheer, and then in song, *'Bless 'em all, the long and the short and the tall . . . '*

The revelry on hearing the RAF continued in the Vittel-Palace, the corridors crowded with every type of sleeping garb: scarves, toques, overcoats and fingerless gloves, nightgowns or pajamas but with heavy woollen work socks pulled all but to the knees, hair in paper twists or nets, hair with all the pins and ribbons out. Brother Étienne's face creams were on some, their eyes like saucers in the dim light, their lips unmade as they faced the grim countenance of Mrs. Parker, who pushed her way through them.

She climbed the stairs. Kohler was right behind her, and as they went up, the hush they left behind followed.

Obviously anxious and very troubled, Jill Faber, who had urgently summoned the woman, met them outside Room 3–38. 'We're holding her, Inspector. She isn't going anywhere.'

Irène de Vernon, her hair in curlers, sat propped up in bed with her own and Caroline Lacy's pillows behind her and a cigarette she was obviously enjoying.

Marni Huntington stood guard with Nora Arnarson's lacrosse stick.

'OK, so what the hell has happened?' he asked of Madame de Vernon, not liking the look of things.

The grey eyes behind their wire-gold frames coldly took him in. Ash was flicked. 'They accuse, but you will find that it wasn't me.'

'Jennifer . . . ' began Marni. 'She's been poisoned by that one.'

'Pah! A plague on you! I did no such thing, Inspector. *Bien sûr,* I might have suggested it, but me, a killer? *Cher Jésus,* forgive them. *Mon Dieu,* such bitches. Look closely.' She tossed the hand with the cigarette. 'It could have been any of them.'

They all began to talk at once.

'The caramel pie with the Del Bey raisins,' blurted Marni, so close to tears and sickened by what had happened, she wanted to bash the woman.

'The stew,' said Becky, shattered by the thought.

'We were all in here having such a good time talking about home,' said Jill, 'we didn't even notice that that bitch had hurried past the door.'

'*Garce,* is it?' shouted the woman.

'Later, after that one had come back, Jen ducked in to say she'd be with us just as soon as she'd had her supper,' said Marni, threatening her with the stick. 'The . . . the others had left it in their room for her. That's how Madame was able to poison it.'

'A stew that Dorothy had made with potatoes scavenged from this morning's soup ration and two cans of pork and beans,' said Jill, knowing it must have been the stew.

'And SPAM,' said Marni. 'Diced and fried first to give it a bit more taste.'

'Candice made the pie,' said Becky, as if in the telling there was reassurance. 'You burn the sugar first, Inspector, then add the gently cooked raisins and stir like mad before gradually thickening with powdered cracker crumbs. The pie crust is made from those as well, with marg' and Klim and water. Packed down firmly and baked just a bit beforehand. Warmed, really.'

'Barb Caldwell made the tea,' said Jill, having calmed herself a little. 'Dried, roasted carrot greens we stole from the vegetable plots of the Brits last autumn. Nora made us all snow ice cream, but Jen hadn't had hers. That's why Nora went for more. Where is she?'

'Busy,' said Herr Kohler.

'Snow and condensed milk with sugar and chocolate,' said Becky. 'It's a real treat.'

'And the datura?' he asked.

They glanced at one another.

'I think you had best come this way, Inspector,' said Eleanor Parker, adjusting her glasses. 'First there was a terrible thirst water wouldn't cure, if I understand things correctly. Then an excruciating migraine and pronounced feelings of faintness—the onset of vertigo, I suspect. The pupils dilating.'

'She couldn't seem to catch her breath, or even stand,' said Marni. 'It was pitiful.'

'Her pulse was racing,' said Becky. 'She was quivering like a leaf and kept trying to tell me how worried she was about her flat in Paris.'

'But couldn't quite find all the words or string them together,' said Marni. 'You bitch!' she shouted, turning on the woman.

'Don't!' yelled Kohler.

'Girls, *please*! Try to remain calm,' said Eleanor Parker. 'Apparently she muttered to herself as much as to anyone, Inspector, but was terribly disoriented, poor thing, and couldn't seem to find her sense of balance.'

'Was seeing things,' said Becky, greatly distressed by it all. 'Her face was flushed. She kept trying to grab something that simply wasn't there.'

'Kept falling asleep,' said Jill. 'Had pulled off all her clothes when we found her. Why *didn't* she come to our room right away after having eaten?'

Had emptied herself. Barbara Caldwell was holding her upright while Candice Peters and Dorothy Stevens were trying to keep her feet in basins of water as they washed her off.

Asleep, right out of it, the girl constantly twitched and jerked her head while muttering things to herself in terror and opening and closing her hands as if still trying to grasp something illusive.

'She said bats were crawling all over her,' wept Becky, 'and that her guts had spewed out and they were feeding on them. Bright orange and green lights were flashing, red ones were burning her eyes.'

'Spiders were crawling inside her,' said Barb. 'I heard her saying that.'

'Monsters,' said Dorothy.

'How long since she ate?' asked Herr Kohler.

'Two hours, maybe a little more,' said Jill. 'Ten minutes, fifteen . . . How long does it take before that stuff begins to hit someone? She ate and then she stayed here for maybe a half hour or more until Barb came to find her like this. Naked as a banshee and shitting herself.'

'Jen!' cried Lisa Banbridge, shaking her. 'Jen, please wake up!'

There was no time to get Brother Étienne to help, no time to reach the camp's hospital to get one of the damned doctors to do something useful like pump out her stomach. Even if they did, and the ingested seeds were evacuated, enough of the poison could still be left to kill.

'She's going to die, isn't she?' said Becky.

Holding the girl by the shoulders, Kohler stuck his fingers down her throat and bent her over, Jennifer panicking as she coughed and threw up and again evacuated herself.

'Ah, no!' cried Barb. 'More water, someone! And another towel.'

It was only as he looked down that Herr Kohler saw the seeds and felt his heart sink, thought Jill. Maybe there were only fifty of them, more likely well over a hundred, but some had been hastily broken in that woman's mortar. Madame de Vernon . . .

'It isn't good,' said Herr Kohler, and she could see that he was really feeling it. 'All you can do is try. At least two enemas, maybe three. Warm water, not hot. Add a little salt, if you have any. That can't hurt, but I really don't know.'

The food was there on the tiny kitchen counter where she'd had a hurried, stand-up meal, having heated the rest of the stew and eaten it right from the pot.

The pie was glazed and had lots of raisins that would have masked the datura's bitterness.

The tea might also have helped. 'Who made the cake?' he asked, startling them.

In the shape of a small loaf, and heavy, it was dark brown and chock-full of raisins, prunes, apricots, and bits of apple, all of which would have been dried when received in Red Cross parcels.

'It . . . it wasn't here when we left to go to the other room,' said Lisa. 'Jen must have been given it.'

'By whom?'

'The Brits make it,' said Jill. 'It's a favourite of theirs. Butter, sugar, and powdered crackers instead of flour.'

'It's called pound cake,' said Dorothy.

'Is that why Madame was gloating?' he asked Jill.

They all looked at her but she had no answer, and he said, 'OK, I'll borrow it and the rest of the meal and take Madame along with me.'

Though he cared deeply, he would have to leave them to it now, felt Jill, but as he turned away, he paused and she saw that he was intently looking at Mary-Lynn's things, which were still neatly piled on her bed.

'Who tidied these again?' he asked, and she could sense that he was deeply disappointed in himself, though she couldn't know why.

The suitcase was now under the blankets; the shoes, placed side by side on top of the raincoat, the rest precisely positioned just as Louis had seen them.

'Jen must have,' said Barb. 'Every once in a while she gets a tidying craze and goes at her own things, but then it passes and she's just like the rest of us. Hit and miss and toss again.'

'She ate and then she waited while she did that,' said Dorothy. 'Had she come to see us right away, we'd have got to her a whole lot sooner.'

Mary-Lynn Allan's suitcase was not heavy and when opened, the meagre clothing that it still contained had been neatly arranged. A couple of blouses atop two sweaters and under them, a length of lace-fringed, bloodstained ribbon and a whole lot of other things, all precisely arranged in rows and protected by clothing both above and below.

Herr Kohler picked up a broken, blue Bakelite barrette, a bow. Replacing it, he chose a bent, hand-forged nail, then a string bracelet with knots in it, and finally an Indian Head penny.

'She wasn't,' blurted Lisa. 'She couldn't have been. Not our Jen. Not with all of those beautiful things in her flat.'

'Take care of her. Do your best.' Louis would be looking for the hiding place, Jennifer having transferred everything here so that it would be sent away and she wouldn't have to worry about it anymore. Jundt would have called the guards.

'Answers!' shrieked Jundt. *'Verfluchtes französisches Schwein,* why did you not report the shootings immediately to me? You and Kohler did nothing to stop them. *Nothing,* I tell you!'

Jundt had come in force; three harried Schmeissers and his own Mauser covered Louis and the girl and Brother Étienne, all of whom had their backs to the reception desk in the Hôtel Grand's foyer.

'Colonel, we couldn't have done anything,' said Louis calmly in *Deutsch.* 'Herr Weber had demanded our guns and we had handed them over.'

'He knew you were up to something. He had caught you out!'

'Not at all. Sergeant Senghor—'

'The blacks!'

'Had stolen two revolvers we knew nothing of, Colonel, but the Untersturmführer most certainly should have and had them removed when the camp was first opened in March 1941. Those two men were bent on escaping. When Fräulein Arnarson and I overheard them chopping down that tree, I realized what was happening and alerted Herr Kohler and we immediately gave chase in spite of the need for us to attend to our investigation here.'

'Another murder was in progress, Colonel,' said Hermann.

'Ach, Kohler, what is this one saying?'

'That in spite of the urgency of our own concerns we caught the blacks on the run in deep snow, me then alerting the Untersturm-führer. Unfortunately he was as unaware of their having armed themselves as we were and refused to believe they hadn't raped and murdered Fräulein Lacy.'

'That is why he insisted on taking them to the Chalet des Ânes,' said St-Cyr.

'You're handcuffed to that girl.'

'She's a suspect, Colonel.'

'And is that woman also a suspect, Kohler?'

'I didn't poison anyone, Herr Kommandant,' insisted Irène Vernon shrilly. 'I am innocent, I tell you. *Innocent!* It's all a terrible mistake!'

'Fräulein Jennifer Hamilton isn't likely to live, Colonel,' said Kohler. 'Let us settle this business, then, as is my duty, I will gladly give you the report we will be submitting to my superior officers, the General von Schaumburg, Kommandant von Gross-Paris, and Gestapo Bömelburg.'

'Berlin-Central will have to be notified.'

'As will the High Command, Colonel. Perhaps for now, though, it would be best if you were to telex them an urgent request, asking that they immediately suspend your predecessor's court-martial since new and important information has come to light.'

'Suspend . . . ?'

'Until the whole matter is cleared up and the planets are in conjunction,' said St-Cyr.

They sat in silence and they waited, and all around them, felt Nora, the Pavillon de Cérès, with its blackout drapes drawn, was like being in a little Art Deco forest. Brother Étienne was chewing anise and gathering his thoughts beside her, Madame de Vernon to his left, Herr Kohler's handcuffs around both of the woman's wrists to keep her quiet.

Together, the one his pipe in hand, the other a cigarette, the chief inspector and Herr Kohler sat apart from them in hushed and urgent consultation. Jen had been poisoned by Madame—Nora was certain of it, though couldn't help but feel for Barb and Lisa, Candice, and Dorothy. A kleptomaniac right in their midst, a roommate and friend they had trusted absolutely. Still, all would sympathize, none would want Jen to die. All would miss her even now, and even though Herr Weber had been forcing Jen to spy on them.

St-Cyr's handcuffs were around both of her own wrists and for herself she had to wonder what the future held yet couldn't thank them enough for what they'd done: gambled that Kommandant Jundt hadn't been told by anyone that it had been she who had tried to escape and that he wouldn't immediately check for tracks in the snow.

Cautiously she opened a clenched fist and, nudging Brother Étienne, showed him the Indian Head penny Herr Kohler had returned.

The Boche wouldn't be satisfied with just Senghor and Duclos, thought Étienne. Others would be blamed. Berlin-Central would rush to incessantly hound everyone. None would escape. All would be questioned hour after hour, Nora tortured—she would be, and he, too. Would he be able to withstand it and not give anything away, a healer of healers, a dreamer of dreams, and brother to a maquis of twenty-seven? Some were but students on the run like the others, but in total fifteen of whom were mere boys of eighteen and twenty from Paris and other cities and towns. *Bien sûr,* when they had first come, and most of them alone, they had been merely wanting to hide out from the STO, the Service du Travail Obligatoire, as the forced labour draft for the Reich was now called, les Pères Tranquilles sheltering them in the woods and not all in one locale. The internment camp here was to have been a listening post from which to keep an eye on the Boche, though it also became a place for him to have lived that dream. Colonel Kessler, having suspected nothing, had come to welcome the visits. Colonel Jundt would be but a disaster.

Nora didn't know any of this but must suspect some of it—hadn't that been why she had summoned the courage to confide in him and beg his help? Hadn't that been why he had readily agreed, even without having first consulted the others, the brother abbot among them?

Gently he wrapped a hand about hers and, feeling her tremble, closed her fingers over the penny. 'Irène might see it,' he said.

They could prove nothing, thought Irène, but to handcuff her like this was to have her tell the new Kommandant everything she knew about them. They'd soon see. They'd suffer for what they were doing to her, these two from Paris. Detectives—is that what they called themselves? Cérès . . . was it that they were planning to get the Chevreul woman to call upon the goddess for answers? Was that why they had kept the bracelets on the other one? Caroline really had seen something the night the other one had fallen. Never had the girl been so convinced of anything, other than her life as a ballet dancer. Though she, herself, had tried to caution the child to hold her tongue and stay out of trouble, that slut she had taken up with had encouraged her not only to speak out but to demand to see the new Kommandant.

But it couldn't have been just for that reason Caroline had been silenced. A yellow star had been found in one of her pockets. A star . . .

Leaving his chair, Herr Kohler came over to her and, taking out his cigarettes, placed one between her lips and lit it. 'They'll be here soon,' he said.

They were going to ask that Chevreul woman to contact Laurence and from him find out exactly how he had died in that fire when no one should have.

They were going to ask the goddess about that Jennifer Hamilton, for by now that one must surely have died. Hadn't Brother Étienne given warnings enough of those seeds, even to having accused her of having stolen them and lied about it?

'Louis, are you sure this is going to work?' said Kohler.

'Ah, *mon Dieu,* Hermann, must you continue to doubt the powers of clairvoyance? Thanks to Jennifer Hamilton we have what is needed. Let's leave the rest up to the goddess.'

Pensively Nora remembered other séances, other times. To the mirror of the cut-glass bowl of water there were now, again, but tiny ripples, to the circle of sitters, but the flickering of the three oil lamps from whose reservoirs braided wicks of Red Cross parcel string protruded, the Pavillon de Cérès being otherwise darkened.

Marguerite Lefèvre tended the lamps and the censers as a priestess would before taking her place among the sitters. Everywhere the balsamic aroma of smouldering St. John's wort fought to overcome that of the fish-oil margarine in the lamps, the *herba Sancti Ioannis* being perhaps the herbalist's most useful plant. Effective for treating wounds, bruises, and burns, it was also a sedative and remedy for colds, coughs, and fevers.

Étienne would, of course, know all of this. Refusing to become a sitter, he had taken a chair among the silent onlookers who had crowded in after Madame Chevreul and the sitters, and now sat with rapt attention as in a courtroom whose doors had been firmly closed.

Léa Monnier stood directly behind Madame Chevreul, a pillar of strength and loyalty throughout all the years of their having known each other. Hortense Gagnon, Madame's cook, was among the sitters, the chief inspector choosing not to be at Madame's right but directly opposite, with a now-silent yet still-enraged Madame de Vernon between him and Herr Kohler.

Freed of the handcuffs too, Nora sat alone among the other sitters. Jill and Marni had Becky between them and were directly opposite her, the seating arrangement being such that she could see them at all times if her eyes were opened, and they and others could see her.

Jen had died; Jen had been poisoned, but had it really been by Madame de Vernon?

There had been no sign or mention of the things Jen had taken, nor of the meal she had eaten, yet was that what worried Madame de Vernon so much or rather, was it that Madame Chevreul really did know what had happened here in the casino on the night of 17 July, 1920?

Caroline had been silenced, Mary-Lynn had been pushed, but of Weber and the Senegalese and the other two who had been killed in the Chalet des Ânes, none here knew but her, Madame de Vernon, and the two detectives. St-Cyr had warned the woman to keep the information close, just like everything else if she valued her freedom and supposed innocence. He and his partner would let Cérès have a say and then would, if necessary, challenge the goddess.

Madame Chevreul knew only too well that her reputation as a medium had been deliberately put on trial and that all the privileges that had been earned with the position, the rooms upstairs and such, could be lost. Wearing a superbly embroidered robe of closely woven white wool that trailed to slippered feet, her jewellery starkly evident, she had dipped the wineglass and raised it as one would a chalice. All eyes were now to be tightly closed, hands held and heads bowed—Léa would do her best to see to this, but of course one could catch a glimpse now and then if one persisted.

There was a pause that extended as though an intense inner struggle were in progress, the words not coming easily but finally as if lifted from Madame Chevreul. 'Then a spirit passed before my face,' she said, the voice other than her own, 'and the hair of my flesh stood up.''

Herr Kohler would probably be silently asking his partner if this was necessary, thought Nora, St-Cyr cautioning him with a 'Patience, *mon vieux*. Patience.'

'It stood still, this spirit,' the woman went on, 'but I could not discern the form thereof: an image was before mine eyes; there *was* silence, and I heard a voice saying . . . '

Again there was a lengthy pause, again a different voice but as if from a great distance and saying, 'Call now, if there be any that will answer thee.'

A sip was taken, the water from La Grande Source cold. 'Cérès,' she began. 'Cérès, can you hear me?'

There was dead silence. Not a soul moved. Again the question was asked, and again. 'It's of no use, inspectors,' said Madame Chevreul. 'I greatly fear there is a doubter in our midst.'

'But you're convinced Becky Torrence killed Caroline Lacy to protect herself?' asked St-Cyr.

'*Oui.*'

---

* From the King James version of the Bible: Job 4:15–16 and Job 5:1.

'And that Nora Arnarson accidentally . . . '

'Or deliberately, in the heat of argument.'

'Pushed Mary-Lynn Allan, not realizing that the lift gate was open?'

'That is correct.'

'Perhaps Cérès needs the sound of your bell.'

Taken aback, she tossed her head. 'Really, Chief Inspector, I am earnestly committed to obtaining the answers you need. Cérès can and will provide, but all must be in trine. None must doubt. Even Étienne, though the teachings of the Mother Church condemn what I do, still has the will to respectfully remove himself from the circle while listening with eyes closed, and I would earnestly suggest that you and Herr Kohler do likewise.'

'But of course. It's only that throughout this investigation we had been given to understand we should consult a ringer of bells. At first we thought this must be the brother who, in addition to those on Angèle, rings the one for vespers.'

'And you rang one for Léa to bring your breakfast while I was there,' said Herr Kohler. Opening the hessian sack he had brought from the chalet, he took out Bamba Duclos's little basket and rang its bell to emphasize things further.

'Duclos is nothing but an impostor, inspectors. The very idea that he could even begin to compete with my powers and cause me the slightest concern is ridiculous. The mere posturing of a fraud. I alone possess the ability to cross the threshold and, through Cérès, to reach those who have passed over. I who sit here before you in this circle of circles, bring back word from them. Words, need I emphasize, not only of endearment, but words that have been proven true and absolute.'

'But there is only one bell that will work, isn't there?' asked St-Cyr. 'And I have it here.'

'My talisman . . . '

'Your gris-gris, madame.'

Four-sided, it was as if two isosceles triangles had been placed base to base, thought Nora. In all, it was about three centimetres in length, by half that across, and was flat and no more than a few millimetres in thickness. Some kind of polished stone, perhaps, or enamelled surface.

'An Art Deco pendant,' said St-Cyr. 'When first seen, I thought, as you have claimed, Madame Chevreul, that it was but a bit of costume jewellery of no consequence, for that is the impression a first and hurried glance might well give, depending on the lighting and circumstance. The chain, however, is of very fine, cubic silver links each of no more than a millimetre to a side.'

He waited. He dangled it in front of himself.

'A trinket, as I stated, Chief Inspector. A chain was needed and I took one I had.'

'Élizabeth, surely there can be no harm in telling him?' asked Brother Étienne.

'So that he can make a fool of me?'

'So that he can help you, I think.'

'You see,' said St-Cyr, 'Colonel Kessler firmly believed that Cérès could give us the answers you claim she can. Why else his desperately shouting "a bell ringer," as he must have, to the Kommandant von Gross-Paris when the telephone line to Paris began to fade after urgently requesting our presence? A man, I should add, who had, against his every effort, been hastily recalled to answer certain charges and face a court-martial.'

There was shock and then a chilling and defiant silence, thought Élizabeth. None glanced questioningly at another, all eyes remaining on her. Everyone was waiting. Everyone would believe her an absolute fraud if she failed to go through with it.

'Very well. It shall be as you insist, but the Arnarson girl is to leave the circle.'

'She's welcome to my chair,' said Brother Étienne. 'I'll stand at the back.'

'With her and where you belong, Étienne.'

'Of course.'

'Mademoiselle Arnarson, *un moment s'il vous plaît,*' said St-Cyr. 'Examine this talisman closely and give us your professional opinion.'

Iridescently mauve and mottled, it was lovely in a curious way, and was backed by sterling silver, and as she held it, Nora couldn't help but say, 'I always wondered but could never get a close enough look because Madame dangles it in front of herself until séance contact has been initiated and then lets it and its chain coil into her left hand, which closes about it until again needed.'

'And?' asked St-Cyr.

'It's of alexandrite, a type of chrysoberyl from the Urals.'

'Which was discovered, Hermann, in 1833 and named in honour of the teenaged boy who would later become Tsar Alexander II.'

The chief inspector had switched on the flashlight, under the beam of which she now held the pendant.

'Chrysoberyl is very hard, and next in hardness after diamond and corundum,' said Nora. 'When cut and polished as this is, or simply uncut, it's iridescent but dominantly emerald green in daylight or, as now, in artificial light, mainly reddish. Hence it was thought of as being magic. In daylight, the emerald, but at night the amethyst, this one of a pale pink to violet. Inspector, if you look closely at this mauve area, you'll see that there are many parallel striations, all of which are very close and equally spaced. Those are minute cleavage planes—there are three sets of them and along the dominant one the stone can most easily be cleaved. They pick up the light, absorbing and refracting it and changing the colour, depending though on the source and nature of that light.'

'A magical stone. Is it valuable?'

Mary-Lynn wouldn't have wanted her to look at anyone but Madame Chevreul. 'It's very rare and much sought after.'

'*Ah, bon, merci.* For now please join the brother. A trinket, madame?'

'Élizabeth, did I not tell you what was best,' came that basso profundo voice.

'All right, damn you, I purchased it because I fancied it. Was that a crime?'

'Purchased when Art Deco was beginning to come into vogue?' asked St-Cyr.

'Yes!'

'Purchased after that husband of yours had passed over, leaving you a healthy estate?' asked Hermann.

'Really, inspectors, I do not need nor wish to answer that or any-thing else. This séance—'

'But had best, madame,' said Louis.

'All right, that, too, is correct but I didn't kill him as some have maliciously suggested.'

'We'll get to Madame Vernon soon enough,' said St-Cyr. 'Like your rings and bracelet, Léa Monnier saved this for you when the internment camp was first at Besançon in the old French Army bar-racks on the plateau above that town. Like many, you fell ill that first winter. The conditions were utterly deplorable and shameful to me as a Frenchman, some of whose fellow citizens were entirely responsible—open to the winter's wind and weather, vastly over-crowded and with only three latrine pits outside and far too little to eat, but somehow she managed to nurse you back to health and all the while, and especially when your suitcase was searched on arrival and such jewellery would most certainly have been confis-cated and a worthless receipt given, she hid them.'

'In my bras, my step-ins, and inside of me,' snorted Léa. 'Was that a crime?'

'As far as Hermann and I are concerned, not at all, but the pen-dant found a new use here. To induce a trance, the medium uses self-hypnosis and breath control. Chevreul, the nineteenth-century hypnotist, popularized the use of a pendulum. The subject to be hypnotized was told to concentrate on its gentle swaying.'

'Inspector, really. How has this any bearing on your inquiry?' asked Élizabeth. 'How I reach clairaudience need not concern us.'

'Were it not for one aspect, madame. The chalice, please, and a little water. No, I am not thirsty.'

Dangling the pendant over the glass, he lowered it to just at and below rim level.

'*Écoutez bien, mes amies. Voilà,* our Bellringer.'

The tone was low but resonant enough and when some of the water was poured out, and then a little more, the tone rose higher and higher until it was bell clear and beautifully resonant.

'Yesterday, madame, when we first met, I asked of Chevreul. You said he was a distant relative.'

'Of my husband's, yes.'

'So it was in keeping with his memory that you should use this stone as a pendulum to induce self-hypnosis since all others round the circle were to have their eyes tightly closed. Questions would be asked. If Cérès was there and could hear you, the bell would be rung.'

This *sûreté* waited. He didn't say a thing. He simply rang it one more time.

'You questioned Jennifer Hamilton and Caroline Lacy at length prior to agreeing to let the latter become a sitter,' said Herr Kohler.

'I did. I was in my cabinet, in that room of rooms which you had the audacity to invade without my permission.'

'First the palm readings,' said Kohler, 'the tarot, the Ouija board and crystal balls, but when the bell rang, it did so from inside that enclosure of yours, you signalling to them that each answer given had been accepted and that you were satisfied.'

'That is correct.'

'But then that pendant was stolen, madame, and you had to know who had taken it,' he countered. 'You needed it. You were desperate.'

'All right, I was. Does that satisfy you?'

'But stolen when, madame?' asked St-Cyr.

'After their fourth visit. It . . . it was always kept on my dressing table with . . . with everything else of mine when not in use.'

'Set down in haste?' he asked, taking out his pipe and tobacco.

'I . . . I was called away.'

'To Herr Weber?' asked Hermann.

'*Oui.* Marguerite came to tell me I had been urgently summoned. Léa and Hortense went with me.'

'And the interconnecting door between your bedroom and the other and its cabinet, was it locked?' asked Herr Kohler.

Ah, damn him, damn him. 'Always but . . . but I may not have done so that one time.'

'It's as the goddess would have informed us, Louis. Even though her maid was still present, and that thing was pinched, Madame still agreed to allow Caroline to become a sitter.'

'I felt it best so as to keep an eye on them.'

'Yet it's a puzzle,' said St-Cyr, gesturing with that pipe of his, 'since the thief from whom it has been recovered stole only items of virtually little use or monetary value.'

Lighting the pipe, he didn't take his gaze from her. 'Mine was the exception,' she said.

'But Jennifer Hamilton didn't know that, madame. Her kleptomania took over, and in the haste to have something of yours, she thought as we first had and you had claimed, that it was some inconsequential thing. But in that exception lies the solution to this whole matter.'

'Caroline wanted to know what had happened to Madame Vernon's husband,' said Kohler, lighting himself a cigarette. 'Jennifer encouraged her because Jennifer had been and still was, very much in love with that one.'

With Marguerite Lefèvre.

'Earlier, madame, you had banished Jennifer Hamilton,' said St-Cyr. 'Though she was very much in love with your maid, and that one no doubt with her, you told Marguerite Lefèvre to end the affair. Things were being stolen, albeit little things but far too many of them. There was rising discontent. You suspected Jennifer and sent her away, but then . . . ah, then, love found a means of returning.'

'Jennifer encouraged Caroline to plead with you and Léa to let her become a sitter,' said Kohler.'

'Marguerite Lefèvre,' asked St-Cyr, 'did you, when asked by your lover and her new partner, allow them in to see Madame's bedroom when she was called away to Herr Weber, and did Madame not soon discover what you had done in her absence?'

There was no answer, only silence.

'And from that point on, madame, since your reputation was fast falling,' said Kohler, 'you realized there could well be some benefit in encouraging Caroline, particularly if that goddess of yours found the answer to what that girl desperately wanted to know.'

'You gave her the L'Heure Bleue presentation phial to cement things,' said St-Cyr.

'Knowing full well that Caroline would show it to Madame Vernon and fan the flames, and that we would soon see through the lie you had told us,' said Kohler, 'because you wanted to draw our attention away from the Hôtel Grand and to the Vittel-Palace and that very woman.'

'If you could prove, through Cérès, that Madame Vernon had killed her husband and we were convinced of it, that would be the crowning touch to a triumphant return,' said St-Cyr.

'Laurence Vernon, inspectors,' said Élizabeth. 'I see that you have rightly dropped the *de*. I was certain she had killed him but knew not of her nor even what she looked like then, having only the present vestige to go on. The *sûreté*—'

'Suspected Irène Vernon but couldn't build an adequate case,' said St-Cyr. 'Such things happen more often than we would like, and she was and still is abundantly aware of her legal rights.'

'Once I got to know Laurence a little in this life, in July 1920, he readily told me of his marriage and that he was worried his family might have got in touch with her.'

'To tell her he had inherited a bundle, Hermann, from the estate of his mother.'

'But the tables soon took it all, didn't they?' asked Herr Kohler.

'He . . . he wanted a loan,' managed Madame Chevreul. 'He said he needed it, that his luck would change.'

'But you refused,' said St-Cyr.

'He became impossible. I left my room and went to the casino's *cercle* to place a few modest wagers of my own.'

'Having asked the management to chuck him out if he followed you,' said Kohler.

'Yes, damn you. Yes!'

'But he persisted. He must have, Louis.'

'Returning again and again to the casino, Hermann.'

'I didn't kill him. She did!'

'Me?' countered Irène Vernon. 'At which casino, please, was I to have found my Laurence, inspectors? Me, in Paris and with hardly a sou to my name? *Bien sûr*, I received just such a letter but could travel nowhere without the cash to do so and did not even know where he was.'

'Irène . . . Irène,' interjected Brother Étienne, 'I must tell them that is not correct. Though much younger and really quite *chic* for one so poor, you were there on the morning after the fire. You wore a light beige beret, a marvellous Hermès kerchief you had picked up somewhere, and a thin brown raincoat, secondhand, I thought at the time, but still very stylish, and you watched from among the gathering as I assisted my brother the abbot when he gave your husband's charred remains the last rites.'

'You fool,' she said. 'Why could you not have held your tongue?'

'Because he's a marvellous gossip, my dear Irène,' said Élizabeth. 'Inspectors, I didn't attend the removal and identification of the body. It had but one arm and Laurence had also lost a huge amount at the tables. Everyone would have known who he was, and I had been seen in his company, so I simply left for Paris on the early morning train. Oh for sure, I suspected what she could well have done, but I had no proof and felt it best to absent myself.'

'Let's ask Cérès, shall we?' said Louis.

'Léa . . . Léa, tell them I'm innocent.'

'With you, was she, in 1920?' asked Herr Kohler. 'Called her in for a little help—is that it, eh?'

'Not at all, Inspector. We didn't meet up again until Besançon in December of 1940.'

'But did Laurence Vernon purchase that pendant for you, madame?' asked Louis.

'When he still had most of his new bankroll?' asked Herr Kohler.

Men! They would now be at her if she wasn't careful. First the one and then the other, each baying for the sheer joy of it. 'He became insufferable and made a terrible scene, begging me to return it to him so that he could cover his bets. He had suffered to save France, he said, was a hero, but had no medals to show for it, just an empty arm.'

'You first loaned him fifty thousand francs,' shouted Irène Vernon. 'Admit that you did or I will swear to it in court!'

'*Garce,* he hated you! Frigid—that is what he said of you.'

'Better that than *une fille des rues,* eh Madame? Inspectors, this impostor killed him. She hit him with an empty champagne bottle and then had a little problem only a fire could solve.'

309

'A champagne bottle?' asked St-Cyr.

'*Oui, peut-être,* but that I wouldn't really know. How could I? Oh for sure, I watched them from the foyer of the Hôtel de l'Ermitage where he was staying. As a couple, they attended the theatre, where séances were held each night, my Laurence even asking the medium to contact the comrades he had lost in battle, that . . . that woman egging him on. Then I found them on the terrace of the Grand and in the shops. That Alexander thing was from Boucheron at 175,000 francs. A pendant and a scheme of their own that was being hatched as they embraced. Bold, I tell you. Having sex in their rooms, his, then hers, and not just during the hours of five to seven before the first serving but afterwards also. *Ah, mon Dieu,* the things the maids told me. The noises she made, the sheets they then had to remove. A wealthy American veteran and a wealthy British girl, unmarried, I tell you. *Oh, là là* what a pullet for my Laurence to pluck, only she had the same thing in mind for him and had had plenty of experience!'

There was silence, but was the outburst over? wondered St-Cyr. 'And years later, Madame Vernon, you found yourself here again but with Caroline Lacy who needed to know the answer to what had happened to him.'

He rang the bell.

'She wouldn't leave it because of that . . . that Jennifer Hamilton,' quavered Irène. 'What was I to have done? Allowed myself to be blamed for something I hadn't done?'

'And on the night of Saturday, 13 February,' said St-Cyr, 'Caroline slammed the door to Room 3–54 in your face.'

'You had gone there to beg that girl to come back to you,' said Herr Kohler.

'They had been fighting—having a raging lovers' quarrel,' said Irène, now in tears. 'My poor Caroline was distraught and coughing terribly. I knew her chest would be bothering her. Always when emotional, the asthma would come on at its fiercest.'

'But she refused to leave—is that it?' asked Hermann.

'Inspectors . . . Inspectors, please, her heart,' said Brother Étienne.

'You found that elevator gate had been opened, madame,' said

Louis. 'You couldn't have known why this had happened but in such a state would have seen how it could well be used.'

'I didn't push that girl. I *didn't,* inspectors.'

'Caroline did leave that room and head back to her own,' said Herr Kohler, 'but as for Jennifer, she stayed put out of fear of encountering you.'

'And Jennifer was the one she wanted to kill, Hermann, but then first Jill Faber and Marni Huntington came up the stairs and went along to their room, and then a half hour or so later, Mary-Lynn and Nora started up those same stairs. They were shouting at each other, the one in tears, the other claiming this whole business was a fraud.'

'Again you waited, Madame Vernon,' said Kohler. 'You hoped Jennifer would hear them and leave that room. The corridor lights were blinking on and off.'

'I didn't wait, as you say, Inspector. I went downstairs to the toilet after the first two had gone to their room. Me, I tried to calm myself.'

'And along that third-storey corridor, Hermann, Caroline stepped out of Room 3–38 with Becky close behind to steady her hand and light one of her cigarettes, even as Mary-Lynn fell.'

'Having been pushed by that one, Inspector,' said Élizabeth Chevreul, pointing at Nora.

'Who had no reason to push her nor to even have accidentally done,' said Louis. 'You see, madame, Nora had stumbled and fallen behind and didn't reach that gate and corridor until afterwards.'

'Then who killed Mary-Lynn?' she asked.

'Perhaps it is that you should ask the goddess.'

'Her gris-gris, Louis. You'd best hand it back to her.'

Again hands were to be joined, eyes closed, but first all items were to be laid out inside the circle: Mary-Lynn's suitcase with the things Jen had stolen and had tried to get rid of when it was taken away; the basket Bamba Duclos had used; and the last meal Jen had eaten: the pound cake, the empty stew pot, pie, and cup of tea; along with everything that had been found in Caroline's pockets.

A single wad of chewing gum was set beside papers of the same,

Becky swallowing tightly, Léa laying a steadying hand on Madame Chevreul's left shoulder, Madame Vernon, flushed and dabbing at her eyes.

Marguerite Lefèvre stared emptily at the things Jen had stolen, until warned by Léa.

'Cérès . . . Cérès, are you there?' asked the medium.

'I am here,' came the distant answer.

The bell was rung.

'Can you reach Mary-Lynn Allan for us?'

'Allan . . . Allan . . . ' began Cérès. 'She was climbing some stairs but says she turned to look back down them through the darkness, for the light had gone off. Nora was yelling at her, she says. Nora was telling her that it was all a fraud and that you, Madame Chevreul, had informants of your own and knew virtually everything that went on in the camp, each person's personal history if needed, all the little things that would make each séance appear real. You had been in that other war as a nurse and knew what its front had been like for those who had fought.'

There was a pause and then, 'Is someone waiting to push her?' asked the medium.

'Yes, oh yes,' said Cérès, 'I didn't know it then, but now.'

'And is that person present in this circle?'

'Yes, oh yes.'

'Who is it, please?'

'She was in tears and didn't want to listen to what her friend was shouting at her,' said Cérès. 'She tells me that she reached her floor in darkness and started towards her room. The lights came on and she blinked to clear her eyes. There was someone, but this person had ducked back out of sight. She went on but was grabbed, shoved—pushed—pitched into space and knew she was falling. "I panicked," she says. "I screamed and tried to grab hold of one of the cables but it tore my face and hands and turned me upside down and I knew I couldn't stop myself. Down . . . down . . . Nora . . . Nora, you were my friend."'

The bell was rung by the medium, who then collapsed, Léa supporting her.

'*Ah, bon,*' said St-Cyr.

The woman was revived—the brush of wet fingers across her brow.

'Madame Monnier,' he asked, 'are you convinced the goddess said "Nora"?'

'*Oui.*'

'Then please have your mistress ask her to contact Herr Weber. Here is the ribbon that was in his sister's hair when that one was tragically killed.'

'Herr Weber, Inspector?' blurted Madame Chevreul.

'Has passed over, but before he did . . . '

'Must I?'

'If you are to prove you still have your powers,' said Louis, 'and that the planets with their asteroids are aligned.'

'Léa . . . '

Again she concentrated on the pendulum and gave the incantation, the ribbon having been stretched out in full view of the sitters and her.

'Ask the goddess to ask him if he hadn't desperately needed something to relay to Berlin that would ensure that Colonel Kessler was recalled,' said Hermann. 'Ask him if the suicide of the girl the colonel had made pregnant hadn't been perfect?'

Cérès's voice was lost, the questions stammered by the medium who could barely find her own.

'Ask him if access to the Vittel-Palace would have presented any problem to the head of security, especially if after curfew and lockup?' continued Herr Kohler. 'That side door's laundry room would probably have been empty, especially at suppertime or after it.'

When most would have been in their rooms or those of their neighbours and friends.

'He could easily have gone down into the cellars, Hermann, and made his way through to that far wing to climb its stairs and wait, then unlock and open that gate when no one would suspect.'

'The former smoking rooms, the location of the poker game, were well to that side of the main entrance,' said Herr Kohler.

'A risk, a gamble, oh for sure, Hermann, but they *did* take that far staircase. Had they not, Room 3–54 was close enough. Nora would most likely have gone into room 3–38 when they reached it while Mary-Lynn, remaining in the corridor, would have continued coming towards where he was hidden.'

'He would first have heard Jill and Marni coming up those stairs, wouldn't have known what the hell to do except wait.'

'That would have put him right on edge, Hermann, but then he *did* hear the other two shouting at each other and could easily have identified them by the names they were using for each other. Parking his chewing gum, he would push the one or both if necessary since it didn't matter to him so long as he could tell Berlin that Colonel Kessler's mistress had taken her own life.'

'Nora, if she'd also been pushed, having simply made the mistake of rushing to her assistance and falling as well, Louis.'

They paused, letting all of that sink in, thought Nora. Again Madame Chevreul looked as if she would faint, Léa now with both hands on the woman's shoulders.

'But Caroline refused to be silent, Hermann. She had seen what had happened.'

'A glimpse if that, Louis, but one she was absolutely certain of, though she couldn't tell any of them and went so far as to even claim she'd been the intended victim.'

'Had also just argued with Jennifer and had, I'm sure, discovered not only that she had never been loved but that Jennifer had used her and had been the one who had been stealing things.'

'A money cowrie was found in one of Caroline's coat pockets,' said Herr Kohler, reaching out to place it in Bamba Duclos's little basket, 'which she had, no doubt, planned to return.'

'A Star of David,' said St-Cyr, 'was found crammed in a pocket—an object, Mesdames Chevreul and Monnier, that you told me Cérès had spoken of last night during the séance you held in the absence of that girl. Something about the Milky Way, I believe.'

Again there was a pause, but this time it grew into a silence so deep, Nora felt she could hear the sitters' collective hearts pounding.

'A meeting place was needed, Louis, and a person to whom Caroline could entrust the note she had hidden in her collar.'

'Unfortunately, *mes amies,* Jennifer knew all about this and went straight to you, her lover, Marguerite Lefèvre,' said Louis, 'to tell you not only what Caroline intended but that she greatly feared the girl would tell the new Kommandant who the thief was.'

'That would, of course, have got straight back to Weber. Léa was all ears when you consulted her, wasn't she, Marguerite?' asked Herr Kohler. 'You went straight to him, didn't you, Madame Monnier?'

'And he, having good reasons of his own to be concerned, suggested the Chalet des Ânes and that he would leave its padlock open since no one would question his having been near it,' said St-Cyr.

'Kessler had been recalled, so Weber could well afford to wait and let them deal with it first, Louis,' said Herr Kohler, 'but only if you, Madame Monnier, swore you'd come straight to him the moment the meeting was over and knew its result.'

'And when Caroline left her room to go to that meeting, Madame Vernon, she had good reason to say to you, "It's not what you think. You'll know soon enough."'

'Marguerite Lefèvre,' said Hermann, 'you were told by your mistress and Léa to wait inside that chalet to convince that girl to say nothing, to just leave it or else. The Americans were conveniently claiming Mary-Lynn's death an accident. Why take it further and bring trouble, why not simply let it rest?'

'You see, *mes amies,*' said Louis, 'no other weapon or evidence of there having been one was found, hence we presume that girl's killer didn't want to physically harm, only to warn, but perhaps Cérès should be asked.'

'You're right, you know,' said Marguerite with a shrug. 'I didn't mean to kill her. It . . . it just happened.'

'Caroline knew you and Jennifer were still madly in love and that she had been lied to,' said Hermann.

'She wouldn't listen. By then she had that yellow star in hand and was thrusting it at me and in tears as proof of Jennifer's stealing. I warned her. She backed away and said she'd been in love with a thief who had never been in love with her but had stolen her heart, and that she was going to tell the new Kommandant not only who had killed Mary-Lynn but who had been stealing things, and then . . . then she would tell everyone else.'

'You snatched up that pitchfork,' said Herr Kohler sadly.

'And then tidied the corpse—an impulse, perhaps—so as to make it look like Jennifer had done it,' said St-Cyr. 'Even though still in love with her, you had to save yourself.'

'Which leaves us with that sprig of beech and coils of bark, Louis.'

Nora knew she would have to tell them. 'All right, I did go there but not until I saw Becky turning away. I had brought those for Angèle, but Étienne had used his *petrolette,* and I guess I . . . I must have dropped them in shock when I found Caroline like that.'

'Which brings us now to another matter,' said St-Cyr. 'Marguerite Lefèvre, did you see Nora head towards that chalet after Becky had turned away?'

'*Oui.*'

'And did you not also see her from your windows, Mesdames Chevreul and Monnier?'

'Since you know we did, so what?' said Léa.

'Hence Nora's worrying that she would be pushed, Hermann, and Madame's warning to us that Jennifer was in grave danger.'

'Madame Vernon having hated that girl, offered answer to their little problem, Louis.'

'You see, Madame Chevreul, you couldn't have Caroline telling anyone that Jennifer had come to your maid for help and that Madame Monnier had then arranged for that meeting place, one that you could both watch even as the brother made a conveniently late arrival. Sergeant Matthieu Senghor, realizing that something was up, wisely ordered Corporal Duclos not to do as he had agreed.'

Again there was an uncomfortable silence.

'A photo had been borrowed by Caroline from Madame Vernon's suitcase,' said Herr Kohler. 'I take it Jennifer imparted that knowledge to you, Marguerite, and where a key to that suitcase was hidden in Room 3–38?'

'Inspectors . . . ' began Élizabeth, only to be interrupted.

'Madame Chevreul, you had to silence Jennifer and put the

blame squarely on Madame Vernon's shoulders,' said Louis. 'You had no other choice.'

'That's why you told us Jennifer was in great danger,' said Kohler.

'And why Marguerite told Jennifer of the telex Herr Weber had received from Berlin this afternoon, Hermann, a telex with details of Nora's background.'

'And why Marguerite then gave Jennifer a little present,' said Kohler.

'Hortense . . . ' began Madame Chevreul.

'Your cook baked this pound cake, madame,' said Louis, using his best *sûreté* voice. 'It was admittedly a last desperate measure, even to making certain that enough seeds would be eaten no matter from which end a first slice was taken, but again, perhaps only a stiff warning was intended since *Datura stramonium* does not often kill.'

'Now, let's not keep that goddess waiting any longer,' said Kohler, 'but have her take us back to the night of 17 July, 1920.'

'Madame Chevreul, you had just gone through a brief two years of marriage,' said St-Cyr.

'And had inherited plenty, Louis.'

'And didn't want nor need to repeat the same performance, had even registered here at the Hôtel Grand under your maiden name.'

'Were free of all such encumbrances,' said Kohler.

'But found yourself wanting a little fun. The theatre, as Madame Vernon has told us, the séances and a little scheme which you had probably no intention of honouring, but then, ah then, Hermann, he wanted the gris-gris he had given her back.'

'He wouldn't listen,' said Élizabeth. 'He said I was just like her.'

'Grasping, like his wife, clinging to your family money?' asked Hermann.

'Madame Vernon hit him, I didn't.'

'Let's ask the goddess,' said Louis. 'We'll have her contact Caroline, since Jennifer was the first to tell us that girl was certain an empty champagne bottle had been used, not a full one which might well have exploded and injured his killer as well.'

'Which was a curious thing for her to have said, Louis. I wonder where Caroline got such an idea?'

Reaching down, he took just such a cork from Bamba Duclos's little basket.

A shrug would be best, thought Irène.

Élizabeth knew it would have to be said, that there was no other way of avoiding things. 'There *was* an empty bottle, inspectors. A Moët et Chandon with its cork still there. It was very late, nearly 0400 hours. Few were about, and yet . . . and yet Laurence wouldn't leave me alone. I headed for the toilets, hoping to discourage him, but he followed. I ran. I passed a side table on which one of the waiters had left a tray and some glasses and that bottle. I pushed the door to that nearest room, then the one to the toilets, and was just able to go back to the first to slip in and gently close its door.'

'There, what did I tell you, inspectors,' said Irène.

'Forgive me, *ma chère* Madame Vernon, but as God is my witness I heard that bottle break,' said Élizabeth. 'I knew Laurence had gone into the toilets first to look for me and then down to the wine cellar of that casino and that you had followed him. You told him what he had done to you. He laughed and told you *exactement* what he thought of you. The bottle was no longer on its tray when I left that room. Brandy, cognac, and liqueurs, *n'est-ce pas*? Lots of those, and all that was needed was a match which you had plenty of.'

'But you didn't come forward after the fire?' asked Louis.

'I couldn't. I was afraid I wouldn't be believed, not with that woman who would simply have accused me, as she has.'

'You loaned him money he couldn't repay,' began Irène. 'He demanded the return of that . . . that thing he had given you. Everyone knew this. They had *all* overheard you.'

'Madame Vernon,' said Louis, 'you will be charged with the murder of your husband and the destruction of the casino. The courts will be lenient—they always are to such. Extenuating circumstances, the loss of the villa you loved, the penury . . . '

'*Garce*,' said Irène bitterly to the woman, 'I did what you had intended.'

Louis rang the bell.

*   *   *

Nora was the last to say good-bye and when she did, she pressed her good-luck penny into Louis's hand. 'I think you'll both need it more than I do. When this war is over you can return it to me. Then I'll know for sure you both survived and won't worry anymore.'

Jennifer's things had already been loaded into the car that would take them to the nearby train station. Colonel Kessler was on his way back to resume command of the camp. He'd have to deal with seeing that everything was settled properly, would no doubt be rather chagrined but glad of his reprieve and grateful that his old friend in Paris had sent them.

'Keep your chin up,' said Herr Kohler, as she hugged him dearly.

Louis shook her by the hand, the two of them lightly embracing, the girl giving him a peck on each cheek and a *'Merci, mes amis,* for all you've done.'

They would return Jennifer's things to her flat in Paris and would inform Thérèse, her maid, of what had happened, but what would they really find when there? she wondered. A fortune's worth of art and antiques?

It took two days for them to reach Paris and that flat, and then another four until the postcard arrived.

'Are well.' Blank, blank. *'Have found employment.'* Blank, blank. *'In wholesale-retail trade.'* Blank, blank.

The *marché noir*—Nora knew that's what they meant. Paris, like everywhere else only more so, had a roaring black market. Gangsters fought to control it; so, too, did the German Army and others of the Occupier but the Résistance was also involved, as were lots and lots of others and just about every citizen.

'Thérèse sends her love.' Blank, blank. *'And tells us.'* Blank, blank. *'It was only a dream.'*

Jen had never had anything much of value in that flat but had lived with the lie of it to hide what could well have been a big failure to her family's business. Having been so worried that this would eventually come out, she had started stealing little things and, once started, had found she couldn't resist the impulse.

*   *   *

Vittel's internment camp, its *Internierungslager,* was one of those all-but-overlooked episodes of WWII. At the time in which *Bellringer* is set, the British and American internees were still not getting along, but they soon did, and quite well. The camp was appropriately liberated by the US Third Army on 4 August, 1944.

Acknowledgments

All of the novels in the St-Cyr/Kohler series incorporate a few words and brief passages of French and German. Dr. Dennis Essar of Brock University very kindly assisted with the French, as did the artist Pierrette Laroche, while Professor Schutz, of Germanic and Slavic Studies at Brock, helped with the German. Should there be any errors, however, they are my own, and for these I apologize.

copyright © 2012 by J. Robert Janes

ISBN: 978-1-4532-7112-4

Published in 2012 by MysteriousPress.com/Open Road Integrated Media
180 Varick Street
New York, NY 10014
www.openroadmedia.com

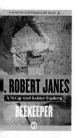

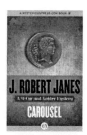
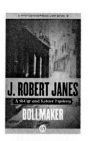
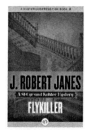
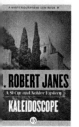
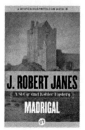
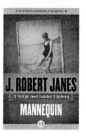
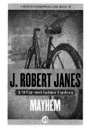
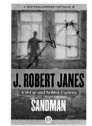

OPEN ROAD
INTEGRATED MEDIA

Open Road Integrated Media is a digital publisher and multimedia content company. Open Road creates connections between authors and their audiences by marketing its ebooks through a new proprietary online platform, which uses premium video content and social media.

CPSIA information can be obtained at www.ICGtesting.com
Printed in the USA
BVOW081107210912

301069BV00002B/3/P